THE GARDEN OF THE STONE

Cariad flexed her fingers, and placed her hands flat on Baldric's chest. She felt his heartbeat, a rapid faint percussion. The silk of his robe was cool against her palms, which felt sensitive and oddly hot, as if she had lowered them too close to flame.

She closed her eyes, narrowing her mind to a pinpoint of concentration, banishing the world around her until there was nothing in it but herself and Baldric, her outstretched arms and the steady rhythm of his blood. Gathering her Gift, she sent it out like a lancet, piercing the barrier of cloth and skin, slipping past the network of bone, probing deep into flesh and muscle until she found his pulsing heart. It was like laying a hand against the edge of a turning wheel. His body resisted, even as it yielded to the pressure she brought to bear. His heart slowed, and his blood with it.

Other Eos Books by
Victoria Strauss

THE ARM OF THE STONE

VICTORIA STRAUSS

THE GARDEN OF THE STONE

AVON · EOS

AVON BOOKS, INC.
1350 Avenue of the Americas
New York, New York 10019

Copyright © 1999 by Victoria Strauss
Cover art by Rowena Morrill
Inside cover author photo by On Location Studios
Published by arrangement with the author
Library of Congress Catalog Card Number: 99-94995
ISBN: 0-380-79752-6
www.avonbooks.com/eos

First Avon Eos Printing: November 1999

AVON EOS TRADEMARK REG. U.S. PAT. OFF. AND IN OTHER COUNTRIES, MARCA REGISTRADA, HECHO EN U.S.A.

Printed in the U.S.A.

WCD 10 9 8 7 6 5 4 3 2 1

Glossary

THE ORDER OF GUARDIANS

Founded after the Splitting of the worlds, to protect the Stone and promulgate the Limits. The Order is ruled by the Prior, and divided into five Suborders. The Suborders are governed by a Staff-Holder, answerable to the Prior, and a Council of Six, answerable to the Staff-Holder.

Speakers—the only Guardians capable of communicating with the Stone. They care for the Stone and the Garden of the Stone, and oversee pilgrimages. Speakers are the most elite and powerful of all Guardians. For most of the history of the Order, the Prior has been drawn from their ranks.

Journeyers—the Guardians charged with teaching the Limits and overseeing their administration within the world. They are responsible for running the Guardian schools, governing the Guardian dioceses and parishes, conducting Novice Examinations, regulating trade guilds and apprenticeships, and providing counsel to governments. Often they become rulers themselves.

Searchers—the Guardians responsible for the Order's learning and scholarship. They maintain the Guardians' Library, and oversee the education of Novices.

Soldiers—the Guardians responsible for defense of the Order. In the Order's early days, they conducted the military campaigns necessary to bring the rule of Limits to the world; now their duties consist of maintaining a ready force and dealing with occasional uprisings by rebels and heretics.

The Arm of the Stone—the Guardians responsible for enforcing the Limits. Their task is to arrest, investigate, and punish those who Violate. They are the most intelligent, powerful, and ruthless of all Guardians. They are nicknamed "Roundheads" for their short-cropped hair.

THE TWO POWERS

Handpower—the manipulation of the world and nature through the use of tools (and by extension, all technology and science).

Mindpower (also known as Gift)—the manipulation of the world and nature by the power of the mind. Mindpower is classified into five categories:

Mindspeech—includes nearspeech, farspeech, and, very rarely, heartsensing (the ability to read others' emotions).

Prescience—includes true foreseeing, and also recollection, the faculty of looking into the past.

Divination—includes neardivining (the sensing of an object's properties by touch), fardivining (the apprehension of events occurring at a distance), and, rarely, sensitivity (the ability to perceive the connections between people and events).

Making—includes some combination of creative, uncreative, or transformative abilities.

Transportation—includes pure transportation (the ability to move people and objects from place to place), and projection (the ability to throw force).

Most Gifts tend to concentrate within a single area of competence, though all reasonably Gifted people can be taught a range of basic skills, including nearspeech, the moving of small objects, the creation of barriers, and the maintenance of uncomplicated illusions such as invisibility.

The Hollow Mountain

One

**ARIAD FLATTENED** herself against the rough wall of the tenement building beside her.

The tenement was a haphazard structure of baked-clay brick, leprous where the outer shell of stucco had peeled away. Each of its four floors was a little wider than the one below, so that it leaned above the street, its top gables only an arm's reach from those of the building opposite. The whole of this sector of the city was crammed with such buildings, like a mouth with too many teeth, all of them constructed in a similar style and overlaid by a larger uniformity of dirt, poverty, and decay. The streets too were similar, snaking and uneven and only two manlengths wide, as were the small squares that broke the streets' mazelike pattern, the fountains where the residents lined up to get water, the communal privies and public pillories and licensed drinking houses. Ashan-istar was a planned city: every part of it had been made to be exactly what it was. These mean streets at its base were a deliberate slum, a holding area for the poorest of the poor.

Silently Cariad edged forward, enough to get a clear view down the narrow alleyway that ran between the tenement building and the one beyond it. The alley was not lit, as the main streets were, but the man she was following carried a globe of mindlight, held before him on his outstretched palm, and its spectral glow picked him out against the surrounding darkness. He was moving more slowly now, his confident progress hampered by the uneven footing and the need to avoid the garbage strewn everywhere about. She and her companions had been shadowing him for nearly an hour, the time it had taken him to walk from the Guardian Orderhouse to the shabby building from which he had just emerged. The route he had used earlier had not included this alley. It was a stroke of luck that he had ducked down it now, for there could not be a more ideal location for an ambush.

Behind her, Laran and Shabishara waited. She sensed their readiness; from Shabishara there was also a pulse of fear, like a hidden current beneath a smooth expanse of water, and from Laran, an edgy exhilaration that matched her own. Cariad loved these risky missions: their immediacy, their urgent swiftness, the way they reduced the cloudy complexities of life to a single clear imperative. She relished the changes they worked in her: the catlike sharpness of her senses, the icy clarity of her focus, the certain knowledge of her own power and control. She was aware of the physical signals of danger, like light running underneath her skin, but unlike Shabishara, she was not afraid. She knew, as she had always known, that she could not be harmed.

<I'm going to do it now,> she thought to Laran. <Stay where you are till I tell you.>

She paused for a moment to balance herself. Then, in one fluid movement, she stepped into the mouth of the alley, aimed her quarter-sized crossbow at the man's shadowed back, and fired. The effect was immediate. The man crumpled bonelessly to the ground. His mindlight winked out, plunging the alley into darkness.

<He's down,> Cariad thought.

They started forward, cautiously, Gifts alert. The dart Cariad had fired was treated with a power-deadening drug, developed by the illegal apothecary network she and the others were employed to protect. An earlier version of the drug had proved effective on ordinary members of the Order of Guardians, but this was a new formula, and the man they had brought down was Arm of the Stone. There was a possibility, small but real, that it might not work.

The alley held the day's heat like a furnace. The stench of rot and sewage, which laid a dense miasma over the whole of this portion of the city, was so intense that Cariad could taste it at the back of her throat. Because they did not wish to risk being seen, the companions used no illumination; they were almost blind as they picked their way forward, ankle-deep in mud and garbage. The Roundhead lay on his side amid the filth, his black robe invisible against the ground, his face and hands pale blotches on the shadows. He was conscious. Through the guard she habitually maintained to mute the intensity of her heartsensing Gift, Cariad felt his rage, his frantic effort to comprehend what had befallen him.

<I sense no Gift.> She reached out to Laran. <Do you?>

<Nothing.> She felt his fierce exultation—the joy of the chase, the thrill of capture. <We did it, Cariad. We took a Roundhead.>

Understanding passed between them. Over the course of their careers the two of them had done and dared a great deal; there were few frontiers they had not crossed. This Roundhead had been one.

Stooping, Cariad ran her gloved hand up the Roundhead's back, searching for the dart. She found it at the base of his neck, exactly as she had aimed it. Not bothering to be gentle, she yanked it out. The Roundhead could not restrain a hiss of pain. It was the only reaction he was able to make. The drug was a paralytic as well as a deadening agent: he could breathe and speak, but no more.

Cariad disarmed her quarterbow, which for safety's sake she had primed with a second dart before entering the alley. She replaced both darts in her belt-pouch, slipped the bow into the leather wallet that hung at her side, and rose to her feet.

<Let's go.>

Laran and Shabishara hauled the Roundhead up between them like a sack of grain. They waited while Cariad summoned, through her making Gift, a binding of invisibility. Moving back to the mouth of the alley, they turned left onto the avenue along which they had come. Around them the city slept, the riot of its daytime activity briefly suspended by the hours of darkness and the need for rest; only drunks and criminals were abroad. Cariad and the others slipped by unseen. Yet though a corporeal object could be hidden from the eye, it still displaced air, still set weight against the ground. A breath of wind followed in the companions' wake, a trail of shadow, a whisper of sound as faint as falling leaves. Those they passed registered presence even as their eyes denied it, a sensation as indefinite and uneasy as a dream.

The street sloped steeply downward, leading toward the docks, broad structures built across the marshes on wooden pilings to give access to the river. The marshes were flooded for most of the year, but the heat of summer transformed them into a vast expanse of sticky mud, rank with the sewage that flowed down from the heights and strewn with an endless variety of garbage—broken barrels, shattered furniture, rusted tools, discarded clothing, wrecked boats, spoiled food, dead animals. There were human corpses too, targets of thievery or victims of feuds or inconvenient family members dumped to save funeral costs. Disease bred here, and vermin, rats and blackflies and fat water-snakes. The thick stands of reeds and rushes disguised treacherous mudholes, capable of swallowing a man more quickly than he could draw breath to cry for help. Still, noisome as it was, it was one of the few places in Ashan-istar where the companions could be certain of being neither witnessed nor interrupted in what they were about to do. More important, it would swallow the consequences.

As they neared the docks, the stench of the marshes overtook that of the city, a sulfurous odor of vegetable putrefaction. The slum gave way to the warehouses and merchants' offices and Guildhalls of the commercial district, shuttered and barred for the night. Ahead, the cobbles of the street ran up against the wooden planks of the dock. Cariad ducked beneath the railing, dropping onto the mud. Laran followed. Shabishara gripped the Roundhead under the arms and lowered him over the edge of the dock. When he was safely delivered Shabishara leaped down, and he and Laran took their burden up again.

Cariad had already scouted their route, tying scraps of white cloth to the reeds to mark the way. Away from the overhanging tenements, the moon- and starlight seemed luminously bright; the markers glimmered against the stalks like night-blooming flowers. It was a little cooler here than in the city, and profoundly silent, a heavy hush unbroken even by the sound of insects.

At last, deep within the marsh, they reached the place Cariad had chosen for the Roundhead's interrogation: a small area where some animal or human conflict had shattered the reeds and pressed them down into a kind of mat.

<It's about time.> Shabishara let the Roundhead's legs fall, and wiped his streaming forehead with his sleeve. <The man's as heavy as a bullock.>

<Roundhead living,> Laran responded sourly, lowering the Roundhead's shoulders to the ground.

On her palm Cariad kindled a ball of mindlight. Its pallid radiance washed across the tangled wall of reeds, the mucky ground, and the Roundhead, helpless on his back. Cariad had been observing him for many days; she was already familiar with the wide proud face, the close-cropped fair hair, the fleshy features, the small light-colored eyes. Close up, he seemed older than he had at a distance, though the Roundhead custom of holding off the processes of physical aging made it difficult to tell how old he really was. Like all Roundheads he wore not Guardian gray but a fine robe of black brocade, with belt and boots of Roundhead red, and gemstone jewelry about his neck and fingers and wrists. With typical arrogance, he had not bothered to remove it for his journey into a place where people would kill for a pair of leather boots, let alone a golden neckchain.

Cariad set the mindlight on the air above his chest. The companions took their places: Laran kneeling on the Roundhead's left, Cariad on his right, Shabishara standing at his feet. Laran, an experienced interrogator, would ask the questions. Cariad, with her heartsensing ability, would monitor the Roundhead's reactions. Shabishara would stand watch.

"Do you know who we are?" Laran asked the Roundhead, using voicespeech because of the man's deadened power.

A series of expressions passed across the Roundhead's face. With his Gift in stasis, the protections with which Guardians customarily bounded their minds was gone, and his feelings were as clear as an unGifted man's. He was in pain from the dart wound, outraged and humiliated and, beneath it all, profoundly shocked. He was Arm of the Stone: most privileged and powerful of all Guardians, defenders of orthodoxy and enforcers of the Limits, their word law and their judgment final. Before this moment the prospect of finding himself in such a plight would have seemed as likely as the moon falling from the sky. Yet through this inner turmoil his Roundhead training, his Roundhead experience, his Roundhead pride cut like a knife. The Arm of the Stone encountered no situation it could not control. Even paralyzed and helpless, he did not doubt his ability to turn the tables on his attackers.

"I can guess," he replied, in a rasping whisper. "What have you done to me?"

"The dart my colleague shot you with carried a power-deadening drug."

Cariad could feel the man's surprise—not that such a thing existed, but that people like herself had access to it. "You will die for this," he rasped. "And you will suffer before you do. No one lays hands upon the Reddened. No one."

From Shabishara came a sharp intake of breath. Laran leaned forward, pulling the cloak away from the Roundhead's left shoulder. Fastened to his robe was a circular brooch, its red enamel surface divided by a jagged black lightning bolt.

<Well.> Laran looked at Cariad. In the wan mindlight his blue eyes were washed to a watery gray. <It seems our friend is more important than we thought.>

<You were in charge of intelligence for this mission, Cariad.> Above his mask Shabishara's eyes were stretched, the whites visible all around the dark irises. <How could you not know this man was Red?>

<The Reddened don't normally travel in secrecy,> Cariad replied. <Nothing my Orderhouse contact told me indicated he was anything but a traditional Roundhead.>

<He's right about one thing.> Shabishara was projecting too hard; Cariad winced a little with the force of it. <We're as good as dead. They won't rest until they've avenged him.>

<How can they avenge what they don't know?> Laran's mindvoice was reasonable <His body will probably never be found.>

<But if it is—>

<If it is, there'll be nothing to show how he died or at whose hand. That's why we agreed to kill him Cariad's way.>

<Kill him now, then,> Shabishara thought. <Kill him and let's get out of here.>

<I'm not going to waste all this effort on a simple assassination, Shara. We brought him here to question him, and that's what I'm going to do.>

<But, Laran, he's Red!> Shabishara took a step toward Laran. What Cariad sensed from him went beyond simple fear. <Reds know things other Roundheads don't. They do things other Roundheads don't. What if he breaks the power of the drug while you're questioning him? What if the three of us can't hold him?>

<Enough, Shara.> Laran's thoughts cut cleanly through the other man's. <The Reddened may be worse than other Roundheads, but they're not superhuman. Right now he's no threat to us. Go back to your place, and let me get on with it.>

There was a pause. With visible effort Shabishara stepped back. But Cariad could still feel the press of his fear, too large, somehow, to fit the situation.

The Roundhead had been following this interchange, his small, attentive eyes flashing from face to face. Even if his Gift had been unbound he would not have been able to perceive what was being conveyed, for the kind of mindspeech Cariad and the others used was Guardian-proof. But Roundheads, because of the mastery they must have of mindprobing, were uniquely skilled and powerful near-speakers, and he could recognize mind-communication even from outside.

"Your companion seems distressed," he said, directing

his words toward Laran but focusing his gaze on Shabishara. "Perhaps he's thinking about how the Reddened deal with those who try to oppose them."

Shabishara stared back, transfixed. "Be quiet, Roundhead," said Laran sharply. "My colleague's thoughts are none of your business."

"Whatever you've planned, you cannot succeed. It would be better for you if you gave up now. Surrender into my hands, and I give you my word I'll request a quick death for you, no torture before or after the probe. That's no idle promise. I am vowed to Jolyon, Second to the Staff-Holder of the Arm of the Stone."

The name rocked Cariad back on her heels. Laran's eyes flicked toward her. He was a sensitive, a diviner capable of sensing not just the properties of objects, but the forces that connected them. But this was more than just his Gift at work. He knew her, knew her story and the place Jolyon held in it.

"No more talk," he said to the Roundhead. He was a skilled projectionist—there was only a fraction of his power in the words, but it was enough to silence the man. Cariad sensed his rage as he struggled to strike back, forgetting for a moment that the channels of his Gift were closed to him. The screen of his Roundhead confidence slipped aside; for an instant she glimpsed the true depth of the ugliness in him, heaped across his soul like the garbage in the alley where he had fallen.

"I'm going to place a compulsion on you now," Laran said. "It'll be easier for you if you don't resist."

The Roundhead's anger surged again, and behind it something more: contempt.

<He thinks you aren't strong enough to go inside his mind,> Cariad thought to Laran. <Or that you fear him too much.>

Laran smiled, just a little. It was true he did not want to enter this man's mind. It was he who had decided, over the objections of both Cariad and Shabishara, that the interrogation would be conducted orally. But Cariad knew that it was not fear, or weakness, that lay behind his aversion. He had been an interrogator for a long time, and had grown weary of exposing the inside of himself to the foulness of others' minds. With the drug and the compulsion, he could extract as much as a scan could—more slowly, but more cleanly, and at a distance.

Cariad sensed the focusing of his Gift, as he gathered and shaped the net of coercion in which the Roundhead would be bound. He released it, using his full strength. The air trembled with the force of it. The Roundhead's eyes flew wide, and then fell closed.

<You hit him too hard.> Cariad leaned over him, her fingers searching for his pulse. The signs of life were there: he was only unconscious.

<I warned him not to resist.>

The Roundhead's eyes opened again. The quality of his regard had changed. He recognized now the strength that held him.

"What's your name?" Laran asked.

The man struggled not to answer. But even a Roundhead's will could not stand against Laran's compulsion. "Baldric," he said at last, through his teeth.

"Why were you in the slums tonight?"

Again he clenched his teeth, but the words came anyway. "Visiting . . . a business . . . associate."

"A business associate?" The man from whose house Baldric had come was a maker and seller of poisons. The city guard, an ubiquitous presence in other neighborhoods, paid little attention to the slums; criminal enterprises thrived there, little pockets of prosperity amid the squalor. "What sort of business?"

"I am . . . an executor."

"Ah." Cariad felt Laran's disgust. Executors were Reds who specialized in the dealing of death, from the accomplishment of individual executions and assassinations to the organization of mass purifications. Every group of Reddened orthodoxers included at least one. "The Roundheads you're traveling with. They're Reddened also?"

"We are all . . . Red."

The Roundheads had arrived in Ashan-istar a little over a week ago, twelve of them, including Baldric. To all appearances they were a pair of traditional Investigation Teams, called in to pursue a charge of Limit-Violation. They brought with them their own clerical staff and servants; within the Orderhouse, they never left the suite of rooms and offices they had been given, and communicated with no one except the Orderhouse's Abbot. Each day at dawn, half of them left the Orderhouse, passing out of Ashan-istar into the arid regions to the east and often not returning until after dark. The rest stayed in the Orderhouse, pursuing their business behind closed doors. So perfect was their secrecy that Cariad's Orderhouse contact was unable to discover anything at all about what they were doing.

The leaders of the apothecary network Cariad and the others were employed to protect feared they had somehow been betrayed, and the Roundheads had been called in as part of an effort to unmask them. The network was guardian not only of its own discoveries but of the work of a dozen other networks that had been destroyed or absorbed into it; if it were lost, the painfully gained knowledge of centuries would vanish, perhaps never to come again. All activity was suspended. Cariad and Laran, experienced in tracking, undertook to discover where the Roundheads went each day; but they cloaked themselves in bindings of invisibility, and employed disattention wardings so powerful that even Laran could not follow their power-signatures for more than a short way beyond the city. Baldric, who sometimes broke from the others to go about his own business, took no such precautions. But his movements shed no light on the purpose the Roundheads followed in such extreme secrecy.

A week passed. The six operatives who formed the network's guard met to discuss the situation. It was decided that Laran and Cariad and Shabishara would follow, trap, and question Baldric, whose penchant for lone nighttime ventures made him a good target.

It was a risky plan. Laran and Cariad had captured Guardians in the past, but neither had ever set themselves against the Arm of the Stone. Once taken, Baldric could not be left alive: a memory-kill could not be trusted to hold against a Roundhead's powerful, interrogation-trained Gift. But in the operatives' collective judgment, the risk was outweighed by the need to know. And they were not without

advantages. Laran and Cariad, and to a lesser extent Shabishara, were themselves highly Gifted. The marshes would
provide protection during the interrogation, and absorb the
evidence after it. And they had the newly perfected drug—
which, coincidentally, needed to be field-tested.

"Why are you travelling in secret?" Laran said to Baldric.

"We have been . . . charged . . . with a secret . . . mission."

"What kind of mission?"

"There are . . . difficulties," Baldric grated. "With the
world's . . . bindings. We have been ordered . . . to document them."

"Difficulties," Laran repeated. The resistance movement
of which he and Cariad and Shabishara were a part boasted
an extensive intelligence network; the problems Baldric re-
ferred to were well known to the companions. "Describe
them."

"On the Guardian Roads . . . the stones . . . crumble."
Cariad could feel, through the pain of the compulsion, Baldric's revulsion at being made to speak of such things to
those who were not Arm of the Stone. "Along the Fortress
Passage . . . the weather guarantees . . . no longer exclude
. . . the snow. In the Orderhouses . . . the mindlight . . . is
dimming . . . and the warmth-bindings . . . have grown un-
reliable."

"Can't these problems be repaired?"

"We do . . . repair them. But of late . . . the pace of failure . . . has accelerated. It is feared . . . that if we do not take
permanent action . . . we may . . . become unable . . . to address them at all."

"And so you've been told to document them."

"To build . . . a precise . . . catalogue. It has never . . .
been done before."

"Who gave you this charge?"

"The charge . . . of documentation . . . came from the
Prior."

"From the Prior?" All Laran's professionalism could not
keep the amazement from his voice. "The Prior charged the
Reddened with a mission?"

"He charged . . . the Arm of the Stone." Baldric's teeth

snapped as he spoke, as if he were trying to bite each word in half. "The Arm's Staff-Holder . . . charged the Second. The Second . . . charged the Reddened."

"I see. And was it also Jolyon who ordered you to keep your study secret?"

"That order . . . is the Prior's. He does not wish to allow . . . the Journeyers outside the Fortress . . . to know the extent . . . of the difficulties. Only he . . . and the Councils of Six . . . know what we are doing."

"What bindings have you come to study in Ashan-istar?"

"The bindings . . . of the Orderhouse."

"And outside it?"

"There is . . . a Guardian Road."

"Ah, but you don't go to the Road. You go out the east gate, into the desert. What bindings lie there?"

"We have been charged . . . to survey everything . . . even the lands . . . where there are no bindings . . . to see if perhaps . . . the difficulties lie . . . in some natural force . . . beyond the bindings . . . themselves."

Drugged and helpless as he was, Baldric's will was still prodigious. <He's dodging,> Cariad thought to Laran. <Telling one truth to avoid another.>

Laran nodded slightly to show he had understood. Cariad felt the shifting as he focused his concentration, tightening the web of coercion he had woven around Baldric's mind.

"I'll ask you again," he said. "Why do you go into the desert?"

Baldric's eyes bulged. The muscles in his neck stood out like ropes. "We . . . have business . . . in the desert."

"Obviously. What kind of business?"

Baldric opened his mouth and shouted, a long cry of pain and rage, shocking in the quiet of the night. He could not stop himself from turning it into words. "The business . . . of our charge!"

"Describe it," Laran said relentlessly. "Describe to me, exactly and precisely, what you go to the desert to do."

Again Baldric shouted, trying to blur the words the compulsion urged him to speak. It was a dreadful sound, like a man being tortured in some unspeakable way; it went on and on as if it would never end.

<Curse it, Laran.> Shabishara shifted from foot to foot. <Can't you shut him up?>

<Let him yell. No one will hear. And if they do, who will care?>

The shout became a groan, then a sigh, as Baldric ran out of breath. Panting, he stared up at Laran. All his arrogance, all his calculation, had vanished. His face was the face of a man who sees, in full and dreadful detail, the shape of his own defeat.

"There is a Gate." He had ceased to fight. The words came without resistance now. "That's where we go."

"A Gate?" Cariad felt Laran's sudden excitement. The twelve Gates that opened from this world onto the world beyond were among the Guardians' most closely-held secrets. Only the Prior, the Councils of Six, the Gates' Roundhead keepers, and the Roundhead world-crossers knew their exact locations. "Where? Describe it precisely."

"It's in a cave in the cliffs due east of the city. Halfway down there is an overhang shaped like the head of a bird. The cave of the Gate is just below it."

<Shara?> thought Laran.

<I know where he means.> Shabishara had spent many years in Ashan-istar and knew its environs like a native. <I had no idea there was a cave there, though. It must be illusion-bound.>

"So." Laran turned back to Baldric. "You're here to document the power difficulties. Those of you who go outside the city document the difficulties with the Gate. Those of you who remain in the city document the difficulties with the bindings of the Orderhouse. Is that an accurate summary?"

Baldric closed his eyes. Cariad could feel his exhaustion. He looked, now, much closer to what she suspected was his true age. "Yes."

"Is there anything else? Any other problem you've come to investigate? Any Violators you're seeking? Any handpower networks you've heard rumors of?"

"Nothing . . . like that."

Baldric's face did not change, but Cariad felt the struggle

behind the words. <He's trying to dodge again,> she thought to Laran.

"Like what, then?" Laran leaned over Baldric. "What else, besides your task of documentation, have you been sent here to do?"

Baldric's teeth clenched. But his will was weaker now, and he gave in almost at once. "We have a second charge."

"Describe it."

"To devise solutions to the power difficulties." Baldric's eyes opened. The bleakness in them was indescribable. Even in defeat, he had contrived to hold something back—a tiny victory, now gone. "Not just better repairs—solutions. We are not to return until we have done so."

"Does this charge come from the Prior also?"

"No. From the Second."

"By way of the Council? Or from the Second alone?"

"From the Second alone. Not even the Staff-Holder knows."

"And what does Jolyon intend to do with these solutions, if you discover them?"

Baldric's eyes fell closed again. "The Second does not share his purposes with those who follow him."

<He's telling the truth, Laran,> Cariad thought.

Laran nodded. "All right, then. Is there anything else you've been told, or any other charges, that are relevant to your presence here? Is there anything you've held back from me? If so, I order you to reveal it now."

"No." Baldric's voice was a whisper. "I have told you everything. There's nothing else."

<It's the truth,> Cariad thought again.

<Cariad, is there anything you want me to ask him?> Cariad shook her head. <Shara?>

<No. Let's kill him and get out of here.>

<Yes. Hold him, Shara, just in case.>

Shabishara's Gift flashed out like a fist. Baldric gasped with the impact of it. Cariad felt the loosening as Laran unwove the net of compulsion he had created.

<He's ready, Cariad.>

Cariad breathed deeply. She flexed her fingers, and placed her hands flat on Baldric's chest. She felt his heartbeat, a rapid faint percussion. She was aware of a heat in her palms, as if she had lowered them too close to flame.

She closed her eyes and narrowed her mind to a pinpoint of concentration, banishing the world around her until there was nothing in it but herself and Baldric, her outstretched arms and the steady rhythm of his blood. Gathering her Gift, she sent it downward like a lancet, piercing the barrier of cloth and skin, slipping past the network of bone, probing deep into flesh and muscle until she touched his heart. It was like laying a hand against the edge of a turning wheel. His body resisted, even as it yielded to the pressure she brought to bear. His heart slowed, and his blood with it. His breathing deepened. He could not struggle: the power of the drug and of his kidnappers bound him fully. But he could rage, and despair. He could grasp at his life as it drifted from him, like a light receding across dark water. Heartsenser that she was, Cariad felt these things— but dimly, muffled by her thick guard and by the skill of long experience, which had taught her how to set aside the messages her Gift tried to bring her.

In the instant before his heart stopped, she opened her eyes. She had learned not to look at those she killed, just as she had learned not to listen to the supplication of their feelings. But this man belonged to Jolyon. She wanted to see his face as he died, to watch as the spark of his life went out. His eyes locked to hers. With the last of his strength he sent his hatred out against her. It was the most concentrated emotion she had ever felt, stripped and purified by the imminence of death. It struck her like a blow, piercing to the heart of her guarded Gift. Her careful disconnection vanished. Fire seemed to ignite across her body, to erupt inside her mind. Fire, borne on the tide of her killing will, passed through the medium of her hands and into Baldric's flesh. Pain burst within him, illuminating the pathway of every nerve, turning his bones to flame. In that instant, Cariad and the fire were the same. Her body sang with the power of it. She held it, allowing it to peak, an impossible pitch of light and agony. Then, deliberately, she released her grip and let it fall away. His life went with it, like the last drops of water slipping down a drain.

For a moment she sat motionless. Her hands still rested on Baldric's chest—cool now, no fire in them. His sightless gaze was still fixed to hers.

<Cariad?> It was Laran, his mindvoice hesitant.

<It's done.> Cariad was exhausted, a fatigue so deep the very air seemed heavy. Laran helped her to her feet. He held on to her, trying to turn her so that he could look into her face, but she pulled away.

They stripped Baldric of his heavy robe, his jewels, his Reddened insignia, his shirt and breeches and boots and fine linen undergarments, and piled these things beside him on the reeds. With the making portion of her Gift, Cariad reached through the solidity of outward form toward the smallest components of matter's construction, and broke the internal bonds that existed on that level. An instant, and Baldric's possessions were gone. It would have been convenient to do the same with Baldric; but flesh-and-blood creatures resisted discorporation. Cariad knew from experience that the result would be a messy heap of everted flesh, which, in the unlikely event that it was found, would provoke much more question than an unclothed and anonymous corpse.

Shabishara cloaked himself in invisibility and departed. Cariad and Laran waited a little, then followed. Cariad looked back as she went, for she wanted to fix forever in her memory the sight of Baldric, sprawled and naked on the reeds. Within a few days, birds and other carrion creatures would render him unrecognizable. Within a month, he would be a heap of bones. Once the rains of autumn brought the river back across the marshes, even those would vanish.

She was aware, through her fatigue, of a sense of fitness: that Jolyon's henchman should be brought so low, and by her hand.

T_{wo}

T WAS still night, but the texture of the darkness had thinned. As usual just before dawn, a breeze had risen to stir the torrid air, carrying with it a little of the cleanness of the desert. The streets were just beginning to fill: carousers staggering homeward, clerks unlocking offices, men with handcarts arriving at the warehouses in hope of a day's work, vendors opening stalls, women lining up for the day's water ration. Cariad and Laran, clad in invisibility, slipped unnoticed between these early risers.

The streets climbed steadily upward, following the slope of the hill on which Ashan-istar was built. The city ascended in sectors, set one above the next like a stack of crates, their succession mirroring the ladder of rank and class that governed here more rigidly than even the despotic City Council. To move from one sector to another required the presentation of identity papers at the checkpoints that marked the divisions between the neighborhoods. Cariad and Laran had forged documents, his listing him as an itinerant carpenter, hers identifying her as his wife. But even if they had been travelling openly they would not have needed to use them, for their destination lay within the commercial district, a long low warehouse in an area entirely given over to such structures.

The warehouse, owned by a member of the apothecary network who was a legitimate dealer in spices, was entirely unremarkable. No one would have suspected the immense basement that opened out beneath it, accessed by hidden

19

entrances and escape routes both in the warehouse itself and the tenements nearby. It was here that the apothecary network carried out its secret business of experimentation and research, and manufactured illegal drugs and remedies.

A thousand years ago, in service to its fear and hatred of the power of the hands, the Order of Guardians had created the Books of Limits: twenty thick volumes of rules and regulations defining the form and setting the boundaries of every tool, trade, and science known to humankind. For ten centuries, the Limits had held technology at the same unchanging level. But the lure of tools was strong, and even the vigilance of the Suborder of Journeyers and the punishments of the Arm of the Stone were not enough to stifle it. Violators were common, individuals whose curiosity or defiance pushed them beyond the rigid confines the Limits set on thought and practice. Occasionally Violators banded together into networks, placing themselves at greater risk of discovery through more intense activity, but through greater numbers better able to protect themselves. The networks were always, eventually, discovered and destroyed. Yet inevitably something was left behind—a memory, a spark, a lone member of the group who eluded capture. As often as the networks were eliminated, they sprang up again.

With the rise to power of the Roundhead faction known as the Reddened, such experimentation became vastly more difficult. For the Reddened, the Arm's traditional mandate of enforcement—the investigation of Violation and the judgment of those who were found guilty—was not enough. Violation should not simply be punished, it should be prevented from ever occurring at all—a goal the Reddened believed was achievable only through the most savage prophylactic application of the Limits. Out of the Arm custom of arriving unannounced to test a community's Limit-compliance, the Reddened created a holocaust. Bands of Reddened orthodoxers roamed the world, descending at will on towns and parishes, turning barns and dwellings inside out, mindprobing every resident, interrogating even the local Journeyers.

The Reddened interpretation of the Limits was narrow in the extreme. They admitted the validity of nothing beyond the original Twenty Volumes, rejecting what they regarded as the liberalizing influence of nearly a thousand years of Guardian interpretation and scholarship. In their view there was no difference between intentional Violation and the small, universal adaptations to which the Journeyers of the world had for centuries turned a blind eye. No longer could a farmer employ a tool, designated by the Limits for a specific use, for a different but related purpose. No longer could a householder make some small alteration, dictated by material or expediency, in the prescribed construction of a cow stall or a privy. Tolerance of such things was also a crime, and, equally, ignorance of them. Family members, friends, and business associates were executed along with the Violators to whom they were connected. For the first time in living memory, Journeyer administrators were put to torture for the lapses of their parishioners, and Journeyer teachers were sentenced to flogging for the inadequacies of the curriculum in the Guardian schools, where the people of the world were taught to live by the Limits.

As the ultimate flouters of the law, the networks were the Reddened's particular target. Had it not been for Cariad's foster-mother Goldwine, leader of one of the two resistances to Guardian rule, the Reddened might have succeeded in their attempt to wipe such activity from the face of the earth. Through the complicated criminal underworld that flourished in spite of Guardian efforts to eradicate it, an offer of protection was extended. Goldwine, who had once trained as a Guardian, had developed an alternative power-canon, a way not merely of standing against Guardian strength, but of defeating Guardian barriers and defenses. Her operatives, skilled in these methods, would enclose the network within a concealing binding tailored to its needs and activities. They would maintain the binding, monitor Guardian presence in the area, and provide the network with relevant intelligence. In payment, Goldwine asked only for access to the networks' discoveries.

Since then, the networks had prospered. Now, fifteen years later, there were more networks in simultaneous existence than ever before.

Still invisible, Cariad and Laran entered the warehouse

through a side door. There was no one to see it open: this early, the warehouse was empty except for the night watchman on duty in a cubicle at the warehouse's center. The air inside was dim and cool, and so thick with spice-dust that those who worked here went masked. Cariad and Laran proceeded toward an area at the back, given over to the storage of things no longer used: old equipment, broken crates, ripped bags, a mule-cart with a cracked axle. Here a false wall had been built across the warehouse's rear. An irregularity in the stone, when pressed, caused a stack of boxes to swing aside, exposing a hidden door. The door gave onto a landing, from which a flight of stairs plunged downward into darkness.

They shed their invisibility, and Cariad summoned mindlight. By this pale illumination they descended, to another landing and a second door. Beyond lay a vast and shadowy space: the workshop of the network. Most activity had been suspended on the Roundheads' arrival in Ashan-istar, and so the room was empty. Even so, the labor continued. Cariad and Laran passed a long table on which liquid bubbled through a twisted forest of glass tubing, and another where powders had been set out to dry—hundreds of identical pottery dishes, each filled with a different substance. They passed the herbary, where plant essences were extracted and reduced, and the confabulary, where formulas were blended. They passed the library, which held a sample of every herb and mineral known to apothecarial science, and the desks of the planners, who assessed completed work and generated new ideas. They passed the glassblowers' furnace, the potters' wheels, the blacksmith's forge. Last they passed the drossing furnace, where the network pursued the transformation of base metals into gold. The furnace was a cylinder of volcanic stone, with a huge bellows apparatus kept in constant action through a motion-binding provided by the network's Gifted guards. A white-hot fire burned at its heart, fed by a steady drip of the thick black substance that bubbled up here and there all across the desert.

Beyond the drossing furnace lay the living quarters, where the guards and the bulk of the network's membership were housed: a warrenlike expanse of small rooms and meager common areas, dimly-lit and low-ceilinged and malodorous. The workshop was vented into the warehouse above, where its smells were lost amid the overpowering reek of spices, but still the basement air was foul. The odors permeated everything, and the smoke from the various forges and furnaces skimmed the walls and floors with greasy soot that came off on fabric and sank deep into the creases of skin. Of the many unpleasantnesses of this posting, Cariad found the pollution generated by the workshop the most difficult to bear. She had a catlike love of cleanliness, and suffered when she was dirty or could not wash her clothes.

The door to the living quarters was low: Cariad, who was tall, had to stoop to pass through it. The cramped spaces received her like a box, enfolding her in the heavy certainty of ordinary routine. In the lamplit hallway they encountered the day detail, heading for the workshop and the outside world; the space was so narrow that they had to press against the walls to pass.

They reached the room they shared. Cariad had been posted to the network for three years, and for much of that time she and Laran had been lovers. Most heartsensers avoided physical relationships, but from early childhood Goldwine had drilled Cariad in techniques of personal guard designed to shield her vulnerable Gift, and so she had never had the difficulty with shared sensation that caused others of her Talent to choose a life of celibacy. Even so, Goldwine had strongly urged celibacy on her foster-daughter. When Cariad decided, in the way of the young women of the resistance, to take a lover, Goldwine had been both furious and fearful.

"Haven't I told you what a danger the love of the body is for heartsensers?" she had said, out of a face as white and set as marble. "The love of the body can trap you into the love of the heart. A heartsenser who loves like that loses her ability to close her Gift against her lover. Haven't I told you, over and over, what a terrible thing it is to be defenseless against another's feeling?"

"I can't defend myself against your feelings, Goldwine. I've never been able to."

"That's different. You're my daughter. I'll never cast you aside. I'll never abandon you. Think of your mother, Cariad. Remember how she suffered. I beg you, don't take this risk."

"Goldwine, I swear to you that what happened to my mother will never happen to me. I will never feel heart love for any man. Please trust me to judge my own strength."

But Goldwine did not. It was one of the only serious disagreements they had ever had.

Inside the room, Laran spat into his palm the poison capsule resistance members were required to carry beneath their tongues when on active duty, and placed it in its keeping box. He fell full-length on the bed, his arm flung across his eyes, his long blond hair straggling across the pillow. He suffered from postmission letdown even more acutely than Cariad did. Through the filter of her guard she sensed his exhaustion, the ashy emptiness that was the opposing face of the intense exhilaration of the chase.

Cariad did not need to rid herself of a poison capsule. Since childhood, she had lived under the promise of a prophecy that made it impossible that she should ever use it; in the whole of her operative career it had not once left its box. She stripped off her clothing and hung it to dry on the line strung across the room's back wall. She felt sweat evaporating: almost the only advantage of the living quarters, situated as they were below ground, was that they were cool. Putting on the shift she used for sleeping, she sat on the bed and took the pins from her hair, releasing it from the coil that confined it during working hours. Thick and heavy, straight as a carpenter's rule and black as midnight, it fell past her waist. It would have been easier to wear it short, as many of the female operatives did, but in a life driven by expedience and bounded by practicality, her hair was the single vanity Cariad allowed herself.

She pulled it forward over her shoulder and began to comb it. It was dirty, like the rest of her, and wet with sweat. The longing for water gripped her—for a deep pool in which to soak away the grime, or failing that, a basin and a sponge. But in summer, when the shrinking river became too polluted to drink, water came from Ashan-istar's wells alone, and was strictly rationed. For the network's guards there was even less, for all were required to yield a quarter of their portion to the network for use in the workshop.

<We did well.> Laran's thought slid into the silence between them, a silence neither had broken since leaving the marsh.

<More than well.>

<The Gate . . . that secret charge. What do you suppose Jolyon intends to do with the information, if he gets it?>

The name, as always, caught at Cariad's breath. <Perhaps he thinks the challenge to his succession will be overturned if he presents the Prior with the solution to the power difficulties.>

<Or maybe he wants greater leverage. Over the Prior himself, for instance.>

Cariad could not stop herself from shuddering.

<Although I wouldn't lay odds that they'll actually solve these problems. This has been going on for close to thirty years. They haven't even made a systematic survey until now.>

<Don't underestimate the Reddened, Laran.>

<I don't. Believe me.>

<Laran . . . > She hesitated. <What was wrong with Shabishara tonight? He wasn't himself. I felt it from the moment we set out.>

<Shara's all right. He's a professional.>

<I know that.> She had never met Shabishara before this posting, but he and Laran had worked together in other settings, and, as much as people who might not see each other for years at a time could be, were friends. <He was terrified of Baldric. Really terrified. It's not what I would have expected.>

<His family was killed by a band of Reddened orthodoxers when he was a child.> Behind her, she felt Laran sitting up. <It was his turn to drive the family's goats to pasture, so he wasn't there when they came. When he got back to his village, it was gone. All the buildings had been put to fire, and the ground had been poisoned so the survivors couldn't rebuild.>

<That's a terrible thing. But it was a long time ago. The fear I felt was closer than that.>

<After they finished with the village they turned their attention to the area around it. They found him in the hills where he had hidden. He was only a child; he tried to be brave. They found him amusing. They kept him for a time, like a pet. He won't talk about it. But you can imagine what must have happened.>

<Yes. Yes, I see.>

Again he moved, away from her this time, toward the edge of the bed. She heard the sound of his boots hitting the floor. Like her, he maintained a heavy mindguard, a screen to protect his unusual Gift from the flux of the outside world that affected him so keenly. But Cariad knew him well, and could read him as accurately as those who were less carefully defended. She knew what was coming.

<Cariad.>

She did not pause in her combing. <Yes?>

<What happened tonight?>

<What do you mean?>

<You know what I mean. What went on there, at the end?>

<I've never killed a Roundhead before.> The comb made a soft swishing sound as it ran through her hair. <He resisted. I had to push. It was difficult for him, but only briefly.>

She felt the air move, and then he was beside her. He grasped her hand to still it, and turned her face so she was looking into his eyes. <Don't try to fool a sensitive, Cariad, especially one who knows you as well as I do. I've seen you kill three men, and not once have I seen you cause pain, much less take pleasure in it. Why was tonight different? Tell me.>

The echo of compulsion was in his thought. Cariad felt a burst of anger. <I'm not your subject. Don't turn your professional skills on me.>

<I'm sorry.> He drew back. <But I can't help wanting to know. You're an assassin, Cariad, but you're not a killer. That's not a difference everyone can appreciate. I wouldn't want it to change.>

Cariad looked down at her hands, at the fall of her black hair. She had not set out to become an assassin. But her power of making, which allowed her to shift the very substance of her flesh, gave her the ability to be anything or anyone, to elude the most watchful guards and gain entrance into the most closely defended places. Early in her training this skill had been earmarked for the accomplishment of particularly subtle and secret missions. Under the tutelage of Goldwine's martial arts master, she proved to have a knack for a thing most Gifted found extremely difficult. Almost any person with power could send nearspeech; those who were stronger could delve unbidden into a mind and steal the secrets hidden there. But it was much harder to reach inside a human body. The flashing network of the nerves, the racing courses of the blood, somehow resisted the ways of mental power. Though killing force could be hurled from outside, the ability to kill from within was very rare.

Cariad, as it happened, possessed this ability in abundance. She knew instinctively how to bypass the stubborn defenses of skin and bone, how to hold focus against the scattering distraction of breath and pulse, how to touch the heart itself and slow it into stillness. It was not something she desired or enjoyed; it was simply something she could do. The martial arts master, a man who had seen long and violent service among the gangs of the black market, told her he had never had a better pupil.

"Most people have to struggle to find balance in this profession," he said. "Fear what you do, and you'll hold yourself too far away from it and become indifferent. Relish what you do, and you'll draw too close, and begin to crave it. Either one can get you killed. But you—you have natural balance. That's as uncommon as the ability itself."

Over the twelve years of her career Cariad had accomplished perhaps two dozen assassinations, Guardians and unGifted alike. She had killed before she left the mountains—members of the resistance who, ill or aged or injured, had consented to be relieved of life—but it was something else to bring death to a man or woman who had not agreed to it. It was a while before she perfected the combination of barriers and determination that shut her victims' rage from her heartsenser's perception, before she learned not to see the supplication in their eyes, before the act became familiar enough that the enormity of taking an unwilling life ceased to press upon her mind. She carried their faces with her, the face of every man or woman she had ever killed, as a soldier might carry the memory of those met in battle. For it was a battle she was engaged in, a battle she believed in with the whole of her being, on whose goals her eyes were always turned. And in a battle there were deaths; there was no other way.

What had happened tonight—strange, unlike anything she had experienced before—was an aberration, an anomaly. Given all her years of careful balance, what else could it be? She did not want to think about it, much less discuss it. But as she looked into Laran's blue eyes, she understood that silence was not an option. Experienced interrogator that he was, he would not leave her alone until she answered him.

<You're right, Laran. It was different tonight. I don't know why. I had no intention of hurting him. I just . . . he just . . . >

<Was it to do with Jolyon? Because he was Jolyon's man?>

<Maybe.> She turned away from his too-perceptive gaze, fixing her eyes on her hands, clasped in her lap. <You know I don't look at them. But for some reason I looked at him, and when I did I saw such hatred in his eyes. . . . Something in me answered it. That's where the pain came from. I didn't will it, Laran. It just happened.>

<But the pleasure.> Laran's mindvoice was very gentle. <Where did that come from?>

Cariad shook her head. <I don't know. It was just an instant . . . I can hardly remember it now.> She closed her eyes. <This wasn't something I wanted, Laran. It frightens me. I wish it had never happened. I never want it to happen again.>

He took her in his arms. He smelled powerfully of dirty clothing, of days upon days of unwashed sweat. <Perhaps

you've been doing this too long, Cariad. Perhaps it's time for you to stop.>

<Stop? Don't be absurd. What would I do if I stopped?>

<You're an experienced operative, a superlative maker. You could return to headquarters and become a trainer.>

<I'd be a terrible trainer. I'd go mad with boredom.>

<Not a permanent retirement, then. Just a hiatus.>

She felt his love for her, warm and clinging like the mud of the marshes. Once, theirs had been a purely physical union, born of rivalry and a shared taste for danger, a joining of two people who desired and respected each other but had no interest in commitment. Neither had expected the friendship that grew between them. While this had not changed Cariad's feelings, it had changed Laran's. She could often sense it in him, like a wall waiting to close her in. It was not the first of her liaisons to take such a turn. Sometimes when she was tired or dispirited, as she was now, she found in herself a desire to skip the declarations, the speeches and the recriminations, and simply leave.

<It's been a long night, Laran.> She pushed out of his arms, sliding away from him along the bed. <I'm exhausted. Can we talk about this some other time?>

For a moment he watched her, his interrogator's eyes moving over her face. Then he nodded. <All right. Another time.>

He rolled onto the far side of the bed, still fully clothed. Cariad braided her hair, and put the sleep cover over the oil lamp that was the room's only illumination. She lay down beside Laran. After a moment he turned over and pulled her close.

She lay stiffly against him, staring up at the low ceiling. She was weary, the peculiar hollow fatigue that always followed a mission, and yet her mind would not be still. She thought of Baldric's capture, his interrogation, his strange death. Was Laran right? Did Jolyon lie at the root of that? She could not deny that the night's events had called up memories in her. Since leaving the marshes she had felt the pull of them. Now, wakeful in the dimness, she surrendered, allowing herself to slip backward, to her childhood, to the phrases of the Tale.

The Tale was darkness. The Tale was the hush and cold of a mountain night. The Tale was the flickering of firelight on rocky walls, the weight and musty smell of leather coverings. The Tale was Goldwine—her quiet voice, the circle of her arms, the sheltering safety of her love. Of course the Tale was much more than just these things. But once Cariad became an adult and there was no longer anyone to tell the Tale aloud, to call its phrases back to mind was to be overwhelmed by these memories, to journey back with all her senses to the caves and caverns of her childhood, where she first learned who she was.

"Long ago," the Tale began, "when the worlds were one. . . ."

The Tale told of Cariad's heritage, of the ancient line of which she had been born and of which she was—almost—the last. It told of her ancestors' centuries-long guardianship of the Stone, the strange omniscient entity that was the most sacred, the most wondrous, the most powerful object in all the world. It told of the warrior Percival, who came amid the chaos of the Split—that terrible time of conflict between the powers of mind and hand that eventually tore the world in two—to steal the Stone. It told of Percival's flight into the new world, of the great black Fortress he built to hold the Stone, of the Order of Guardians he founded on the Stone's authority. It told of the survival of a single child of Cariad's line, guarded by the nurse who was the first to speak the words that became the Tale. It told of the Tale's thousand-year passage down the generations, and of the prophecy the story carried with it: of the One Who Comes, a child born with the Gift that, with its overthrow, had vanished from the line. Gift enough to revenge the ancient wrong, and regain the Stone.

To the child Cariad, this was mysterious, thrilling, powerful. Yet it was the power of legend rather than of life. It was the second part of the Tale she waited for, the part that spoke to her heart as well as her understanding.

"One day, a boy was born of the line. His name was—"

"Bron."

"Yes, my heart." Goldwine's breath puffed out in little

clouds as she spoke. In the mountain caves it was always winter, a cold so deep that fire could barely temper it. "Your father. Like the rest of his family your father had no Gift. Or so he thought until he was twelve years old, when something happened to prove him wrong."

"His brother Serle was arrested for Violation of the Limits."

Goldwine nodded. "You must remember, Cariad, that the Limits and the crime of Violating them are falsehoods, born of the Guardians' ignorance and prejudice. Handpower isn't inferior to mindpower, as they believe. Nor is its practice dangerous to mindpower, or corrupt, or sinful. The powers are different, in focus and in form, but in value and utility they are the same, and we need both, equally, to shape the world to our use. In ancient times, this is how it was. But a thousand years ago, certain adepts of handpower made the Guardians' mistake, and came to believe their power was superior. They tried to replace the ways of mind, to put tools and technology in place of Gift. But mindpower is part of us, rooted in our souls, just as handpower is. We can't destroy something so essential—we can only divide it from our understanding, drive it deep within us to a place where we can no longer see it. Though the handpower adepts tried to kill mindpower, all they managed to do was to push it . . . elsewhere. To this day, no one understands the why or how of it. All we know is that the struggle tore the world in two.

"In the new world—our world, where all the rejected mindpower took refuge—the balance could have been restored. But the Guardians didn't see this. Because the rise of handpower had paralleled mindpower's eclipse, because the adepts of technology had tried to destroy the Gifted, they concluded that the powers of mind and hand were deadly enemies, and it was the lust for technology that had ripped the world apart. And so they made the Limits, to hold handpower in check—in the name of Gift, they claimed, in the name of the Stone, but really in service to their own ignorance. The world they've shaped is as unbalanced, in its way, as the world the handpower adepts made, on the other side of the Split. Perhaps it's worse. In

the world of handpower, anyone can use the tools and machines that exist there. But in our world, the Guardians
hoard all mindpower for themselves, and withhold its benefit from the people they rule.

"For a long time no one saw this—or if they did, they
were quickly silenced. But times have changed, Cariad.
Across the world those of us who see the truth are gathering. With every year that passes, with every action we
undertake, the balance tips a little more, in preparation for
the final blow. When that day comes, the Order of Guardians will vanish from the face of the earth. The Limits will
become dust. The world will regain the full scope of the
powers that are its birthright. And we will know again the
lost harmony of the ancient earth."

This was not the Tale, but Goldwine's cause—the labor
to which, from the age of fourteen, she had dedicated her
life. For Cariad, far from the schemes and attacks and
guerrilla actions of the resistance, the struggle Goldwine
described held the same distant quality as the Tale's beginning. Yet her heartsenser's Gift perceived the passion in
her foster-mother's words, a devotion more binding than
any other in Goldwine's life. Long before she grasped the
meaning of the struggle to which she had been born, and
pledged herself to it in adult understanding, Cariad had accepted it as her own—for Goldwine, whom she loved most
in all the world.

"Perhaps Serle saw things the way we do. Perhaps that's
why he turned his hand to the forging of a tool forbidden
by the Limits. He was betrayed, and arrested by the Arm
of the Stone. They found him guilty of Violation, and sentenced him to be lashed and imprisoned. His family was
required to watch his punishment. It was the sight of Serle's
agony that unleashed your father's hidden Gift. Through
his power he stopped time, and set his brother free."

"How did he stop time, Goldwine?"

"I don't know, my heart. I only know he did. Your father's Gift is very great—the greatest human Gift, perhaps,
that has ever existed. The Roundheads didn't understand
what he had done, or realize that it was he who'd done it.
They put the village under watch. When a plague came,

they sealed the village so no one could leave. The people blamed your father's family for their suffering. They decided to get revenge. Only your father survived.

"Beside the graves of his family, amid the ashes of his home, your father swore an oath. He vowed to devote his life to the overthrow of the Order of Guardians, to destroy all their works and take the Stone away from them. Not because it was prophesied—though by this time he knew he was the avenger of the Tale, the One whose coming his family had awaited for a thousand years—but for himself. His family was dead, and he wanted retribution."

"So he became a Guardian."

"Yes. We can fight the Guardians from the outside, for we are many. But he was only one, and the only way he could reach his enemy was to go among them. Eventually, he was recruited to the Arm of the Stone.

"Now, Serle had survived his escape, and found refuge. Your father found this out. He requested transfer to the Orderhouse closest to the place where his brother was. He and Serle were reunited. Your father discovered that Serle had continued his exploration of handpower. At first your father tried to change his brother's mind. Over the years of his training, he had come to accept the Guardians' untrue vision of the nature of handpower, and he feared for Serle's safety and the safety of Serle's family. But in the end it was Serle who changed your father, and brought him to share his own rejection of the Limits. Your father established a secret workroom in the Orderhouse basements, where he experimented with forbidden tools. He converted many Roundheads to his cause.

"Things might have continued this way for years. But your father had an enemy."

"Jolyon," Cariad said. The name traveled out into the dark, filling her mouth with the bitter taste of loathing.

"One day, when he had become powerful enough within the Arm of the Stone to command such a thing, Jolyon summoned a heartsenser, and sent her to the Orderhouse where your father was, to search for the secrets he believed your father hid."

"That was my mother."

"Yes. Your mother was a heartsenser and a scrivener, but she was also a spy. By the time she reached your father's Orderhouse, he had discovered who she was. Now, your mother and your father were enemies. She believed he was a Violator. He knew she was an agent sent to trap him. Even so, they were powerfully drawn together. In the end, they couldn't fight their need for each other."

"And that's where I came from."

"Yes." Goldwine always shifted a little when she said this, as if she were not entirely comfortable with the thought of Cariad's origin. "Your mother loved your father, not just with her body, but in the heartsenser's way, with all her soul and without defense. But she never let go of her Guardian beliefs, or faltered in her intent to carry out the mission Jolyon had given her. One night, she followed your father to his hidden workroom. He found her. He knew she meant to carry to Jolyon everything she had seen. There seemed to be only one solution."

"He had to kill her."

"So he thought."

"But he couldn't do it. Because he loved her as much as she loved him."

Goldwine never replied to this. From the time she first heard the Tale, Cariad understood that Goldwine admired her father, was in awe of what he had done. Yet her memory of him carried an odd ambivalence. She spoke of Serle, whom she had never known, with greater warmth.

"Because he couldn't bring himself to kill her, he tried to take her memory. But your mother was as Gifted, in her way, as he was. She had a place deep inside her mind where she could hide herself. She pretended to be mind-dead so your father wouldn't suspect he had failed. Secretly, she summoned the Arm of the Stone. They captured your father and imprisoned him in the Fortress, in a cell shaped to the patterns of his power so that even he could not break free.

"Your mother bore witness against your father. But, as Jolyon intended, her success was her downfall. Jolyon hated your mother, you see, just as he hated your father, because he tried to break her when she was a Novice and she wouldn't allow it. He knew that once she took the secrets of a Violator into her mind, she herself would be judged corrupt. And so it was." Cariad could feel Goldwine's bitter anger. "The Guardians branded her and took her Gift away. They threw her outside the walls of the Fortress to freeze to death."

"But you'd seen it happen through your Gift. So you knew to rescue her."

"Yes. But it was your father who saved her life, and yours too, my heart. He and she were cast out of the Fortress together. She was powerless, but your father still had his Gift—it was too stong for the Guardians to take, or even to touch. He put warmth back into her body, and kept her safe till I came to take her."

"Tell me about my father, Goldwine." This portion of the Tale was the only first-hand account of her father Cariad had. From the time she was very small she had sought to draw it out as much as possible. "What did he look like?"

"He was tall. He had black hair and black eyes and white skin."

"Was he handsome?"

"More than handsome. He had a way of speaking that made you want to listen to him. When he looked you in the eyes it was hard to look away. And his Gift . . . his Gift filled him like a light."

"Am I like him?"

"Very like, my heart."

"Tell me what my father said when you met him."

"He asked me who I was, and where I would take your mother. We spoke a little about my cause. Then he asked me for a favor. He wanted you to have the Tale. But he didn't have much nearspeech, and so he asked me to reach inside his mind and take it."

"And you did."

"Yes, I did."

"He gave it to you because of me."

"Yes, my heart. He wanted to leave you a gift, and that was all he had."

From earliest childhood, Cariad had understood what this meant. Her father had loved her.

"What happened then?"

"Your father asked me what my Gift showed for your mother. I told him what I knew—that she would live long enough to bear you, and for a while afterward. Then he asked what my Gift showed for you. I told him that you'd be like him, in your determination and your will, and like your mother, in your strength and steadfastness. I told him you'd share my cause."

"Was he glad? To know I'd be like him?"

"I couldn't tell, my heart. It was only when he spoke of your mother that he showed feeling. The rest of the time he was like stone—a face like white marble, with eyes as dark as the night sky."

"Then what happened?"

"I told him what my Gift showed for him. He didn't ask me to—he said he'd already chosen his path, and didn't need prophecy. But I'd seen that I would speak his future to him."

"And so you did."

"Yes. I did." Goldwine's prescient Gift stirred below these words, powerful and strange. "Then I took your mother and brought her to headquarters. Eventually you were born. You thrived, my heart, from the beginning." Goldwine tightened her embrace, turning her cheek against Cariad's hair. "But your mother . . . Your mother suffered terribly for your father's absence, as heartsensers do when they lose those they love. And her Gift was gone. It had brought her great pain—I think in a way she was glad to be free of it. But losing it was like losing her sight, or the use of her limbs. She didn't know how to live like that. I did everything I could for her, but it wasn't enough. You were just four years old when she died."

These were lacerating memories. Goldwine and Cariad's mother had known each other only briefly, as Novices in the Guardians' Fortress; Goldwine, unable to submit either to the grinding misery of the Novitiate or the unquestioning obedience the Guardians demanded, had defected after just over a year, leaving Cariad's mother alone to follow the path they had planned to walk together. More than two decades passed before they met again. But Goldwine had loved Cariad's mother deeply, a love that survived the years

of their separation, and strengthened in the short time they
spent together before Cariad's mother died.

"After I left your father, he used his Gift to cast the
whole of the Fortress into sleep. He freed the Stone from
its Room, and destroyed the binding that for a thousand
years had held unchanging spring inside the Garden of the
Stone. He shattered the walls of the Fortress, against which
no human force had ever stood, and laid a binding of
warmth across the killing fields outside. Then he took the
Stone and left our world.

"When the Guardians woke inside their desecrated Fortress, they were thrown into a chaos such as they had never
known in all the centuries of their rule. The Arm of the
Stone was charged with the Stone's recovery. Parties were
sent to the far corners of this earth to look for your father,
and eventually, when it was clear he was no longer here,
into the handpower world as well."

"But they couldn't find him."

"No. Nor the Stone. They're still looking. Each year, a
party of Roundheads crosses into the other world in search
of him. But he remains hidden."

"And the Guardians have never told the world the Stone
is gone."

"How could they? It would be the end of their authority,
to admit that they had lost it. They reset the weather bindings in the Garden of the Stone, and rebuilt the Room.
Pilgrims are taken to stand before it as if the Stone were
still inside. Every morning, the Journeyer teachers in the
Guardian schools lead their pupils in the Prayer to the
Stone, as if the Stone were still there to listen. But such a
secret can't be kept. From the first, there were rumors. We
help to spread them. It's one of the ways we fight."

"And Jolyon? What happened to him?"

"Jolyon became powerful. For his help in your father's
capture, he was elevated to the Roundhead Council of Six.
Later he was elevated again, to Staff-Holder's Second. He
and his following, called the Reddened, rule the Arm of
the Stone now. There are moderates, Roundheads who
speak out against Red atrocity, but not enough to stem the
tide of blood. The Reddened are a curse, Cariad, such as

our world has never seen. Even the Arm of the Stone has always bound itself to certain limits. But the Reddened have no limits. They don't even mindprobe as ordinary Round-heads do—they destroy the minds they look into, and leave their victims witless. It's Jolyon's will they follow with these barbarities. It's his vision they serve. Through them, he closes his hand around all our necks."

The cold seemed to have deepened. Images unfolded before Cariad's inner eye: the coals of funeral pyres, the ruins of villages, bloody footprints on poisoned earth. These were things never encompassed by her child's vision, for Gold-wine kept her far from even the reports of such happenings. Yet she possessed an instinctive understanding of them, a thing as unchildlike as the intent that went with them: that one day, when she was old enough and skilled enough, she would confront the man who was her father's enemy, the man who had driven her father out of this world and away from her, and kill him. She had vowed it, an oath like the one her father had made. Each time she heard the Tale she made the vow anew. And each time, like a seal on her promise, she felt a burning in her palms, as if some incorporeal fire had been kindled there.

"There's just one thing left to tell, my heart. By now, most Guardians believe your father is dead, or, if he's still alive, that his Gift has been destroyed by the handpower influences of the other world. There are many who believe the Stone has also been destroyed."

"But those things aren't true."

"No. I don't know how your father has survived, or where he is, or what he's been doing all these years. All I know is that he's alive and powerful, and that he still holds the Stone. And I know that one day . . ."

"One day he will come back."

"Yes. When the Staff breaks . . . when the Garden falls again to winter . . . then he will return to this world, to com-plete the task he began when he took the Stone, and bring the Guardians down forever. And on that day, in the Garden of the Stone, you and he will stand face-to-face."

The words were dense with prescience. There was a darkness to them also, as of things unseen or unsaid; but the darkness was all Goldwine's. For Cariad the prophecy held only wonder. She was aware that it did not belong only to her: Goldwine had made it, equally, for the resistance, so that they might know the end they fought for. But only she would share the moment of its fulfillment. Only she would meet her father face-to-face. She knew him only through his story, a man entirely made of words; yet the fierce yearning she felt for him was a thing she had never felt for any flesh-and-blood person, not even Goldwine. It had always seemed to her that, wherever he was, he must feel the same. Had not Goldwine told him his future, so that he knew, as she did, what was to come? Had he not left the Tale for her—not just the Tale of his ancestry, but his own personal story, so that she might know not just who she was, but who he had been?

Now, lying in the dimness, Laran's heat against her skin and the soft sound of his breathing in her ears, the impatience of the prophecy gripped her as strongly as it had in childhood, when the dimness had been born of mountains and other arms had held her. Over the years, her understandings had shifted. She had learned to recognize the first part of the Tale as myth, with its narrow goal of familial vengeance and its glorified view of her forbears, who in their desire to hold and possess the Stone were surely little different from the Guardians who had taken it from them. She had learned to loathe the Guardians for the present wrong they did, to desire their overthrow not for the sake of an ancient damage inflicted on her ancestors, but for the oppression visited upon an entire world. But the power of the prophecy, of the destiny it held out to her—that had never changed. She was conscious of herself, always, moving toward it. What would happen when she reached it she could not guess; she knew only that, like the world itself, she would be changed, so profoundly and so finally that it was impossible to think beyond it.

Her hatred of Jolyon had endured also. She had long since set her childish vow aside. As she grew older, and began to grasp the realities of the world, she understood that, though personal vengeance was only the smallest of the justifications for killing such a man, it was unlikely that

she would ever get close enough to try. Still, the memory
of the dream remained, far more powerful than ordinary
childhood fantasies. It returned to her, sometimes, in sleep.
When she woke, her hands burned, as they had when she
listened to Goldwine tell the Tale, and imagined how it
would feel to close her fingers around Jolyon's throat. . . .

As they had tonight, just before she placed her palms on
Baldric's chest.

She felt cold, suddenly, with the strangeness of that. Until this moment, she had not made the connection. Laran's
question returned: *Was it because he was Jolyon's man?*
She thought of the fire that had risen up in her, the white-
hot incandescence that had blazed along all her nerves and
turned everything inside her to flame. She had lied to Laran:
she could recall it clearly. She could recall the pain; she
could recall the exhilaration of causing it. She could recall
the pleasure of letting go, of scattering the final remnants
of a life like grains of sand. It was like looking into someone else's mind. She hardly recognized herself in what she
saw. She was aware that her palms had grown hot again,
as if the killing fire had never completely gone out—

No, she told herself, firmly. The memory was strong, and
its strangeness also, but still it was as she had first thought:
an aberration, born perhaps of Baldric's connection with
Jolyon, but meaningful in no other way. Certainly, never
to be repeated. The next time she placed her hands upon
the chest of a man or woman marked for death, she would
feel no fire. There would be no pain. The balance of her
profession, of her inward self, would make it so.

She turned, burrowing against Laran's chest, seeking the
oblivion of physical sensation. Laran stirred, waking, responding. The rhythm of his blood enclosed her, a fierce
song of life, to drown out the last lingering whisper of
death.

Three

ARAN AND Cariad and Shabishara's report—abridged to exclude the information about the Gate and the Reddened's secret second charge, neither of which the apothecary network needed to know—was received with relief. Work in the basement headquarters resumed. To the smoke and smell of the drossing furnace were added the stinks of herbal confabulations, the fumes of sulfur, and the vapors of a hundred noxious chemicals.

The day after the mission Laran went out to leave a full report for Goldwine at the drop point used by the resistance's couriers, and to meet with Hasin, the leader of the local resistance cell. The network-protection group, which operated independently, was not required either to clear its actions with the cell or to report to them, but Hasin needed to know what had taken place, in case Baldric's disappearance produced a hue and cry. But it did not. Cariad's Orderhouse contact reported no conclaves, no search parties, no arrests, no unusual activity at all. The Roundheads' journeys to the desert never paused. It was for all the world as if nothing had happened. Baldric had had a habit of breaking with the group; could it be that he had disappeared before without explanation?

A week after the mission, a communication arrived, delivered to one of the outside members of the network, who worked legitimately as an apothecary. To all appearances it was an order for medicines, but it bore in its upper corner the black triangle that indicated a message for one of the network's guards. Laran, the group's diviner, extracted the meaning that another diviner, far away in Goldwine's mountain headquarters, had imprinted beneath the written words. The message was for Cariad. Her posting with the network had been rescinded. An operative had been dispatched to replace her. She was not to wait until he arrived, but was to return at once to the mountains, where she would receive new orders.

<Headquarters?> Laran asked. <Why headquarters?>

<I don't know.> The journey to the mountains—home not just to Goldwine's headquarters, but to the Guardians' Fortress—was long and arduous; operatives like Cariad, once they left, were rarely summoned back. Throughout her career Cariad had received her missions and postings by dispatch, shifted around the world like a chesspiece at the behest of written words. Her assassination contracts and other confidential assignments, which often involved complex instructions and subterfuges, were an exception; these she was given face-to-face, usually by one of the leaders of Goldwine's many resistance cells. <Whatever it is, it must be very sensitive.>

<Or risky.> He frowned. <I wish this had gotten here sooner. I would have let you carry the information Baldric gave us, instead of trusting it to a dispatch.>

Little preparation was required, since Cariad planned to travel solo and would use her Gift to bypass the various borders and checkpoints along the way. She departed two days later, carrying with her only a roll of blankets, a purse of coins, and her knife in a scabbard strapped to her leg under her traveling dress. Anything else she needed could be conjured up as circumstance required.

Laran walked with her through the exit tunnel that led from the warehouse into the basement of a nearby tenement. The air of the basement was thick with the stench of mold and sewage; the only light came from the door to the street, half-open at the top of a flight of stairs. In this noisome atmosphere they embraced. Cariad could feel, even through Laran's heavy mindguard, the acuteness of his anticipation of loss.

<Take care of yourself.> He stood looking down at her, his face somber. <Don't take any unnecessary risks.>

<You don't need to tell me that.>

<I'll miss you. You know that, don't you?>

<Yes.> She reached out and touched his cheek, suddenly regretful of the impatience she had felt with him lately. <This is a good thing, Laran. I need a change—you said it yourself.>

<Yes, I did, didn't I.> He shook his head. <I'm afraid for you, Cariad. What you go to do . . . it's very dangerous. I can sense it, even from so far away.>

His fear did not move her. Things had not been easy between them since the night of Baldric's death. When they were together she felt him brooding; he studied her when he thought she was not aware of it, as if she were a map he could not quite read. For her part, she felt only eagerness to be gone. She had long ago tired of this posting and its discomforts. There was nothing she would regret leaving, neither the squalid city nor the torrid climate nor her routine-to-the-point-of-dullness duties. And not Laran. Especially not Laran.

<There's no point in anticipating things before they happen, Laran. If there's danger, there's danger. I'll deal with it then.>

<Cariad . . . >

Something was building in him. It was coming, the thing he had never said, the thing she had willed him never to say; she could feel it, rushing toward her on the tide of his rising emotion. She stiffened, as if in anticipation of a blow. But his thought was not what she expected.

<Do you ever wonder what our lives might have been like, if we weren't what we are?>

<What do you mean?>

<If there hadn't been battles to fight. If there wasn't a cause to serve. If we could just . . . live, the way other people do.>

She looked at him. How could she answer such a question? <We're not other people, Laran. This is the only life we have.>

He shook his head again. She could feel the weariness

in him, a sad exhaustion like a child's yearning for sleep. He had seen too much and done too much, memories that had settled like a shroud of ash over the landscape of his belief. She had sensed this in him before, but he had never let her see it so clearly. He was letting her see it now only because he knew they would never stand this close again. He was a sensitive: if she knew things were finished between them, so did he.

"Good-bye, Cariad." He spoke aloud.

"Good-bye, Laran."

Turning, he reentered the tunnel. The door slid closed behind him, so cunningly fitted that even in bright light, it would not be visible.

Cariad left the slums. She crossed the summer-shrunken river on a ferry that moved by means of a rope strung between the banks. She stood with her face turned to the opposite shore, the wind soft against her skin, feeling Ashan-istar drop behind her like a discarded garment. Ahead, the fields that ran along the river's far side were green with irrigated crops. Raised above them on a bed of crushed stone, the Guardian Road unreeled like a ribbon all the way to the flat horizon. She fixed her eyes on the place where it vanished, tumbling over the rim of the world. Already, in her mind, she was traveling.

Cariad's destination lay nearly a thousand miles due north: a vast pilgrim camp in the foothills of the Fortress mountains, the staging-point for anyone who sought entrance to Goldwine's headquarters. Under the best of circumstances, it was a two-month journey. Power-assisted modes of travel could cut the time to almost nothing, but Cariad did not have the Gift for these, and so she went by ordinary human means. For the initial leg of the trip, she had managed to book passage on a merchants' train, which took her as far as the nearest border. Thereafter, she improvised, begging rides where she could, walking where she could not, changing her appearance periodically for caution's sake.

Though she went cross-country from time to time to shorten the distance, for the most part she followed Guardian Roads. The Roads had been built during the early centuries of the Guardians' dominion, to link together the Orderhouses of the world; they lay across the lands like a vast circulatory system, wrapped with ancient bindings to keep their stones in pristine condition, hold away wild animals, and mitigate extremes of weather. Inns and hostelries and eating places stood shoulder to shoulder alongside; for Guardians there were luxurious post-houses, built in massive Guardian style, separated from other structures by a wide empty area like a quarantine. Every hundred miles or so a Guardian checkpoint blocked the Road, manned by shaven-headed members of the Suborder of Soldiers. All travelers, Guardians and unGifted alike, were required to halt here and submit identity papers and travel permits.

Forty years ago there had been no checkpoints. Their presence was a direct result of Goldwine's guerrilla operations—the disruption of the Novice Examinations, the theft of Guardian tithes, the ambushing of parties of Journeyers, the kidnap of Novice candidates, the raiding of Journeyer Orderhouses to free those imprisoned for Violation or other crimes. Goldwine's was not the first group to resist Guardian rule, but it was the first to be composed almost entirely of Gifted, who were not only capable of combating the Guardians on their own level, but possessed a crucial advantage in the form of their alternate power-canon. The Guardians still owned the earth, but Goldwine had forced them to defend their ownership, as they had never needed to do since they first consolidated their rule. It gave Cariad pleasure to see this. Slipping past the checkpoints, clad in resistance-style invisibility, she took a fierce, secret pride in how greatly she and those like her had changed the world.

In the waning twilight of the final day of the ninth week of her journey, she crested a rise and saw the pilgrim camp spread out below: a shadowy sprawl of buildings on evening-blue snow, glittering with torches and fires like some earth-bound constellation. The camp had been built to accommodate the pilgrims who set out for the Fortress every year, in hope of standing before the Stone and offering to its ineffable omniscience a single question. The Stone was no longer there to answer, of course. But though Goldwine and others had worked steadily over the years to disseminate this information, children were taught in the Guardian schools to understand the Stone as the primal source of all Giftedness, and the continued existence of Gift within the world stood in manifest contradiction to the truth the resistances tried to convey. The flow of pilgrims continued—diminished from previous centuries, perhaps, but still thousands strong. The Suborder of Speakers, once the only Guardians capable of joining their Gifts to the tides of the Stone's power, played a charade for them, pretending to submit the pilgrims' questions, providing fictitious replies. In turn, the pilgrims bore witness to an experience they believed was real.

The camp was the size of a small town. At any given time there might be six or seven thousand pilgrims in residence, together with several hundred vendors, tradesmen, and hangers-on, and a permanent staff of Soldiers quartered in the small stone keep that rose beyond the camp's perimeter. Pilgrims often remained for a month or more, recovering from the first stage of their journey and building strength for the second, which would take them deep into the mountains. Much of the camp was given over to dormitories for them, kept warm by means of bindings, providing bedding and a single hot meal a day free of charge.

Just beyond the camp's entrance lay a commercial district, where it was possible to purchase the greater comfort of inn accommodations, hot baths and massages, food and clothing, charms and amulets, travel supplies and mules, medical care and spiritual guidance, liquor and prostitutes and hallucinatory drugs. All but the poorest travelers brought at least some cash with them, hoarding it as they starved and froze along the Guardian Roads so that they might purchase supplies for the mountains, or blessings for safe return, or, for those with more wealth, a brief interval of luxury. The time spent in the camp was a time free of the punishing vows pilgrims took to mark the first stage of their journey, and those who could made the most of it.

Cariad jostled her way through the crowded streets of the

commercial district. She had paused outside the camp to create for herself a pilgrim's overgarment of rough undyed wool, and to shift her flesh to simulate the penitential wounds pilgrims cut into their cheeks and foreheads. The air was thick with the smells of food and animals and people, underscored by the unmistakable presence of latrines. It was full night now, but torches on the vendors' booths and at the entrances to inns and eating-houses threw the darkness back.

Among the dormitories, the dark returned. Cariad used the pale radiance in the sky ahead for guidance. Soon, light began to sift between the buildings, a cloudy luminance that stretched her shadow out behind her. She could hear no sound, but she was aware of a rising pressure against her heartsenser's awareness, the psychic equivalent of the roar of many voices.

She emerged at last on the edge of a vast area, roughly circular and enclosed in wardings to block snowfall. The foggy illumination came from six globes of mindlight, set at equidistant intervals high above the circle's perimeter. Here the Soldiers who maintained the camp had established a small shrine to the Stone, a black granite plinth upon which rested a smooth white dome: a representation of the Room of the Stone. Pilgrims filled the space, packed like insects on snowless earth which glacial temperatures and centuries of traffic had rendered harder than granite. They congregated to seek guidance for the journey ahead: prophetic dreams and visionary trances, inspired understandings that they believed came from the Stone itself, which they hoped would lead them safe through the treacherous mountains.

Except to Guardians, the Fortress's exact location was unknown. Those who wished to reach it must find their own way, a test of purity and spiritual resolve required of all who would stand before the Stone. Successful pilgrims swore an oath that they would never speak of their experience or write it down. This did not stop unscrupulous merchants from hawking false maps and useless guiding charms; and in nearly every city, with the right contacts and enough cash, it was possible to find returned pilgrims engaged in the risky business of selling their knowledge. There were also guides, descendants of returnees who had silently committed a route to memory—a sidestepping of the law the Guardians tolerated only because without it, too few Novice candidates would survive to reach the Fortress. But only a minority of travelers could afford their fees. For most, the journey's second stage was little more than a random wandering amid the hostile terrain, until they met with some mishap or their supplies ran out. The pilgrims did not believe this, of course. They imagined that the thousands who did not return chose to stay on in the Fortress, in a sort of earthly paradise created by the Stone itself, or else, more mystically, that they became part of the continuum of the Stone's contemplation, individual sparks of being remerging with the source of all existence.

Silence lay across the pilgrim-packed circle, the snowbound hush of boreal places. But for Cariad, the air was as clamorous as a battlefield. A roiling flood of faith and desire poured forth from every person here, a storm of feeling that battered at her guard and threatened to overwhelm her senses. Never in her life had she encountered such a concentrated uniformity of emotion. It seemed huger than the gathered crowd, as if the centuries of hope and prayer had somehow imprinted themselves upon this place, and it was not just the longing of those who knelt here that she felt, but of all who had preceded them. Something twisted inside her. As much as she hated the Guardians for anything, she hated them for this: for their perpetuation of this murderous fiction, for the men and women they allowed to die believing the Stone still watched the world.

She stepped forward—or rather down, for the trampled snow rose several handspans above the bare ground of the circle—and began to thread her way through the assembled bodies. At the shrine, among the pilgrims' heaped offerings—coins, jewelry, food, amulets, small effigies in pilgrim garb with the pilgrim's symbol on their chests, emblematic of a successful journey—she left the signal of return: a rawhide strap tooled in the pattern Goldwine's personal guard wore upon their weapons belts.

With relief Cariad left the circle behind. Returning to the

commercial district, she purchased a skewer of meat and a mug of hot wine, and sat on a bench to eat. Snow had begun to fall, tiny flakes that hissed as the torches caught them. When she was finished, she made her way to the camp's perimeter and, gathering invisibility about herself, stepped into the darkness. She moved lightly atop the thigh-deep snow, reaching out with her making power so that the drifts would bear her weight and take no footprints. Among the dense stands of pines that rose on the hills above the entrance to the camp, at the lightning-cracked stump of a fallen pine, she halted. Here, at some point during the night, Goldwine's people would find her.

She shed her invisibility, and the pilgrim guise along with it. She hoisted herself onto the stump, crossing her legs beneath her, adjusting her heartbeat and circulation so she would not freeze to death while she waited. The camp spread out below, veiled in falling snow. As the hour grew late the torches were extinguished, and the streets dropped out of sight. Only the mindlight remained, a gathering of occluded moons. Beneath them, the circle was still packed with pilgrims.

Goldwine's operatives arrived in the deep reaches of the night, emerging from invisibility with hallucinatory suddenness. There were six of them, bundled so heavily in furs and leathers it was impossible to tell whether they were male or female.

<Who waits?> One, standing a little ahead of the others, addressed Cariad—by his mindvoice, a man. He used the nearspeech of Goldwine's people, a first test of identity.

<A traveler,> Cariad responded, beginning the prescribed interchange that was the second test.

<Where do you travel?>

<To the heart of the mountain.>

<What lies inside the mountain?>

<An abyss.>

<What flows within the abyss?>

<A river of ice.>

<Where does the river end?>

<At the center of the world.>

<Good.> The exchange was finished. <Are you Cariad?>

\<Yes.\>

\<I'm Sogren. Photien and I will be your guides.\>

Turning, he signaled the others. Four of them moved away, winking out of sight as they did so. Sogren and the remaining guard flanked Cariad, and linked their arms in hers. There was a pause; she felt the gathering of their Gifts. They stepped forward, and the world vanished in a blur of speed.

This was farwalking, a power-assisted mode of travel that allowed the practitioner to span miles with a single step. Cariad had experienced it only a few times in her life; she found it discomforting and faintly nauseating. Though she kept her eyes closed, she could not shut out the sense of objects rushing toward her at enormous velocity, nor conquer her conviction that impact was imminent. They split the air as they passed through it; the sound it made as it slammed closed behind them was similar to thunder, but deeper and more substantial, like giants' feet upon the ground.

A measureless period later they reemerged into ordinary space. It was twilight. A vicious wind screamed in Cariad's ears, slapping her face with icy hands. She and her guides stood on a wide rocky ledge. The ledge terminated upon a wall of rock, whose blankness was in part an illusion. Powerful bindings held this place, laid to hide the cave that opened here, the entrance to Goldwine's headquarters.

Sogren and Photien, who still held her arms, pressed her forward. She was entirely familiar with the illusion, but she could not help stiffening as they approached the apparently solid rock. She had forgotten how it felt to pass through— no sense of impact, only a soft yielding, like clouds or cobwebs. The wind dropped away, and the light with it, so abruptly that it was like going blind. Almost at once illumination returned: a rising glow of mindlight on Sogren's palm. They stood in a rocky corridor, about twice the height of a man and perhaps four armspans wide, with a sloping, gravel-littered floor. The air was still and deeply cold—the bone-clenching, rock-deep cold of the mountain's interior, a vivid sense-memory of Cariad's childhood. The walls and ceiling glittered in the pallid mindlight, rimed in frost.

Once again Sogren and Photien urged her into motion.
She felt the brush of power as they breached the barrier
that lay just beyond the passage's entrance. It was keyed
to the Gift-signature of Goldwine's people; others, attempting to cross, would be blocked. The isolation of Goldwine's
headquarters was its best defense, and in the early years no
other guarantee of safety had been necessary. But over the
last two decades the Soldiers' search for Goldwine had acquired urgency, and more precautions had been put in
place.

The corridor rounded a curve. A little distance away a
tumbled fall of rock appeared to close it off. This was unfamiliar: twelve years ago, when Cariad had left, the way
had been open. Again Cariad sensed the focusing of her
companions' minds. The fall of rock quivered like a water-
borne reflection, and disappeared. Beyond, the corridor
sloped downward for perhaps another twenty paces, ter-
minating on a metal railing. Past the railing lay darkness.

Cariad and her companions moved forward. At the railing, hardly aware that she was doing so, she pulled the
others to a halt. Before her lay a vastness of vacant space:
the abyss of the identification litany. It was more than a
mile wide and of a depth that had never been measured. Its
walls formed a circle so nearly perfect it seemed it must
have been hollowed out by a deliberate hand. But it was
not humans who had eviscerated the mountain; the fire at
the earth's core had made this place, rising up an inconceivable time ago and leaving the abyss behind when it
sank back to rest. On the far wall an immense accretion of
ice took up nearly half the chasm's width—the litany's
river, a vertical glacier that had intruded centuries ago
through the eruption-fractured peak. It gleamed faintly in
the spectral mindlight that pushed the darkness back a little
way. Boulders and slabs of rock lay entombed within its
milky strata, a record of the giant pressures of its passage.
At its heart it was suffused with color, milky shades of blue
and green that seemed the very hue of cold.

Cariad stood transfixed. For twelve years she had carried
this place inside her mind, like a possession carefully
packed for a long journey. It had accompanied her through

all her different missions and postings, one of the few constants of an existence always in flux. Yet coming now upon the reality of what she had held so long in memory, she found she was not prepared for what she saw. Somehow, in the process or perhaps the repetition of remembering, she had made it less than it was—duller and simpler, and far, far smaller. The immensity of it overwhelmed her now. She clutched the railing, as she had as a very small child; her mind launched itself into emptiness, and for a moment she felt what it would be like to fall.

Her companions' hands recalled her to herself. She allowed them to guide her away from the railing, onto the suspended walkway that opened to the left, curving to follow the contours of the abyss. The thrusting lava had riddled the walls with tubes and galleries; in these, augmented by both mindpower and engineering, were the workrooms and storehouses and assembly halls and meeting chambers and living areas of Goldwine's resistance. Balconies, landings, walkways and stairways clung like cobwebs to the angles of the abyss's sides, power-bound for safety, strung with mindlight like luminous pearls. There were many more of them, it seemed to Cariad, than there had been when she left.

Sogren led the way to the long flight of stairs that gave access to all the walkways. He did not step off on the second level, as Cariad expected, but continued to descend, past the third level and a fourth Cariad did not remember, all the way to the stairs' ending point, a wide landing cantilevered out above the dizzy drop below. Two guards stood just inside the entrance of the passage that opened here. They wore leather breast- and backplates, and their weapons belts were tooled with the distinctive design of Goldwine's personal guard.

<This is Cariad.> Sogren stood aside so the guards could see her. They scrutinized her; Cariad had the impression that they were comparing her to some image they had been shown.

Sogren turned to her. His hood overhung his face, shadowing the small portion of it that was not covered by his mask.

<These are the Commander's personal quarters. You'll be brought something to eat. If you need anything, the guards will get it for you.>

<Thank you.>

He nodded and turned away. Followed by Photien, he began the ascent to the upper levels. For a moment Cariad watched them climb, bulky in their heavy leathers. It occurred to her that she did not know whether Photien was a man or a woman.

She entered the corridor, slipping past the impassive guards. Torches burned in brackets, casting a clear yellow light. The air was warm—not the fluctuating and irregular warmth of a fire, but an even, sourceless heat that enfolded her like a soft garment. Had Goldwine so much power to spare these days that she could maintain heat-bindings? The passage itself looked power-created: its surfaces were smooth, its dimensions symmetrical and its edges squared like masonry. Opening off it was a series of rooms, with mindlight at the ceilings and on the walls—not the caves Cariad recalled from her childhood but real chambers, sculpted as precisely as the passage itself. There was a reception room or anteroom, with tapestry hangings; there were two workrooms furnished with desks and document cases; there was a conference room, with tables and chairs shaped from the living rock; there were several small bed-chambers, simply furnished, and one larger dormitory-style room. Amazingly, there was also a privy, with stalls and seats, and a bathing chamber, where steaming water trickled steadily from a metal pipe into a large pool hollowed into the floor.

Cariad could not resist. She pulled off her boots, her soiled clothing. She soaped her skin and hair, scrubbing savagely at the dirt of more than two months' travel, sluicing clean with a bucket dipped from the pool. The floor of the chamber was cleverly graded and cut with channels, so that the water drained immediately away—though where it went, with the weight of solid rock below, she could not guess.

She stepped into the pool, gasping at the heat against her chapped and abraded flesh, lowering herself slowly until she lay full-length, her hair spreading out around her. When she left Ashan-istar she had been eager to quit the muggy climate, but in the past weeks of northern journeying, she had been so constantly and profoundly cold it had sometimes seemed as if, like the abyss, she harbored her own inner glacier. Now, chin-deep in steaming water, she felt the ice unlock at last.

A long time later she rose from the pool and dried herself on one of the lengths of linen she found folded into a niche in the wall. A woolen overrobe lay across the back of the chamber's single chair. She wrapped herself in it and went out again into the corridor. Someone had been here while she was bathing: a tray had been left before the bathing room's entrance, with covered dishes containing meat, vegetables, and hunks of bread. She was surprised at the variety. When she was a child, all there had been to eat was a kind of mush, nutritious but tasteless, conjured up out of the raw materials of reality by Goldwine's small core of makers.

She ate, and then, deeply weary but too restless for sleep, wandered barefoot about Goldwine's living quarters. The empty, brightly-lit rooms had an artificial air, as if they had been created for display. She had not expected so much change. She had thought things would be much as they were twelve years ago, when Goldwine still lived in the two-chamber cavern Cariad had grown up in, when there were only three levels of walkways, when life was caves and furs and fires on open hearths, and there was no power to spare for anything more than the barest necessities of life. This place, with its smooth edges, its comfort, its warmth, seemed entirely alien.

She lay down at last in one of the bedrooms, wrapping herself in the fur covering that lay across the bed. This at least was familiar: its weight, its musty smell. She closed her eyes, slipping back through time to the nights of her childhood, when Goldwine's love had defined the world, and the mountains had been all there were. As she fell toward sleep, she thought she felt Goldwine's touch—the warmth of her fingers, the brush of her lips. She reached out, murmuring. Her hands were taken, the coverings tightened around her. She drifted into darkness.

When she woke, Goldwine was sitting beside her on the bed. Goldwine's hand rested on the pillow next to Cariad's cheek; her gaze was fixed, grave and steady, on Cariad's face.

Cariad threw off the covering and sat up, flinging her arms around her foster-mother's neck. Goldwine gripped her in return, a pressure as fierce as her own. Among those she commanded, Goldwine was known as a skilled and fearless leader, a brilliant tactician and a masterly campaigner. Yet she was also regarded as unbending, humorless, and harsh. Only Cariad knew the well of love that hid behind her stern exterior. It underlay her earliest recollections; the whole of her childhood shimmered with its light.

"Goldwine," she said. "Oh, Goldwine."

After a time they sat away from each other. Cariad dried her wet cheeks with her hands; Goldwine did the same, laughing a little, a sound that was half a sob.

"Let me look at you," she said. It was their habit to use voicespeech with one another, a remnant of Cariad's early childhood. They spoke the language of Goldwine's own childhood; she preferred it to the common tongue used throughout her headquarters, which was also the language the Guardians spoke. "How thin you are!"

Goldwine herself looked just the same. The broad stern face, the stocky figure, even the hair, cut to her chin like a boy's and showing not a thread of gray despite her sixty-three years, were just as Cariad recalled from the last time they had seen each other, four years ago, in a safehouse halfway between Cariad's current posting and the city where Goldwine had come to carry out some secret purpose. Since Cariad had left the mountains, these brief, sporadic contacts were all they had: six meetings in twelve years, less than ten days of real time in total.

"It's just the journey," she said. "I'll fatten up again. Oh, Goldwine, it's so good to see you. How long have you been here?"

"A few hours. Since you fell asleep."

"You've been sitting here all this time? Why didn't you wake me?"

"You needed the rest." Goldwine reached out to brush back a strand of Cariad's still-damp hair. "I see you found the bathing pool."

"Yes. It's wonderful. Everything seems so . . . comfortable, Goldwine. I had no idea things had changed so much."

"What you see in my quarters is only the smallest part of it. Sometimes I think we've come further in the past ten years than we did in the previous forty. There are more than three thousand of us in the mountains, and in the world—" She pulled herself to a halt, smiling. The skin creased around her eyes, large and lustrous and brown as cinnamon. "But you don't want to hear about that right now. You must be ravenous. I've brought you some clothes. When you're ready you can join me in the small workchamber. I want to introduce you to my staff, and then we can have a meal."

She leaned forward and pressed her cheek to Cariad's. She smelled of oil and metal, an odor Cariad associated with weapons training. Getting to her feet with her usual decisiveness, she left the room. Cariad rose also. She ran her fingers through her tangled hair, plaiting it down her back and knotting the ends to hold the braid. She put on the clothing Goldwine had left: underlinen, breeches and a pleated tunic of some soft blue fabric, a leather belt, laced boots. All of it was as fine and finished as anything in the outside world.

In the small workroom Goldwine sat at a desk, engrossed in papers. She set her work aside as Cariad entered, and, taking her hand, led her briskly through the formerly empty rooms, which now seemed thronged with people. She presented her personal guard—four of them, in addition to the two on duty at the entrance to the passage—her secretary Kaylin, her scriveners Alanis and Joachim, her chronicler Mariano, and her bodyservant Ren. Of all these people Cariad knew only her assistant, Rafer, who had been with Goldwine for longer than Cariad had been alive, and was one of her most trusted followers. Rafer had often cared for Cariad when she was a child and Goldwine was away on campaign; he greeted her with a warm embrace. Unlike Goldwine, the years had not treated him kindly. His hair, which had been mostly red when Cariad left the mountains, was now completely white, and his sharp blue eyes were webbed round with wrinkles.

Presentations accomplished, Goldwine whisked Cariad back to the workroom, where a meal had been laid out upon a table. Goldwine ate sparingly, consuming no more than in the old days, when small portions had been necessity rather than choice, though she seemed to take pleasure in Cariad's appetite.

"Go on, eat it all," she urged. "We have gardens now, and cattle herds, and don't go hungry anymore. But that doesn't mean anything should be wasted."

At last, when Cariad was satisfied, Goldwine poured two cups of ale and leaned back in her chair.

"Tell me about yourself," she said. "I want to hear everything that's happened since I last saw you."

Obediently, Cariad began to speak. Goldwine already knew much of what she described; Cariad had long been aware that her foster-mother required her supervisors to forward regular and detailed reports of her activities. It was an oversight that might have seemed onerous, even accompanied as it was by stern prohibitions in regard to special treatment and exemption from dangerous duty, but Cariad had never objected to Goldwine's attention. It formed a kind of bridge across the gulf of years and distance that divided them, a way to remain, if not close, at least connected. Even so, each time they met they played the same ritual—as if Goldwine did not watch, as if Cariad were not aware of her attention.

Cariad finished by describing her long journey north. "I kept my eye out for problems along the Guardian Roads, in line with what Laran and Shabishara and I found out about the recent increase in binding-deterioration. I did see quite a bit. There were stones shifted out of true, and plants growing up between the cracks, especially at the edges of the Roads. And in one place a flood must have broken through—there was all kinds of mud and debris, which the Soldiers were cleaning up. It didn't seem nearly so bad when I was traveling to Ashan-istar three years ago."

Goldwine nodded. "That fits with what I've been hearing from other sources."

"What do you think is going on?"

"We're not really sure. The bindings have been failing since your father took the Stone, but in the past couple of years there's been a noticeable acceleration. Maybe the Guardians' internal disunity has reached some kind of threshhold. Or maybe the decrease in their numbers has finally had an impact on their ability to repair what goes wrong. Whatever it is, the lapses are starting to become visible. They can't let it get much worse, or the unGifted will start to notice."

"That would be good for us."

"Yes. I'm not surprised that the Guardians have mounted an organized effort like the one that Roundhead described to you. Of course, in their place, I'd have done it a lot sooner."

"It's probably taken them this long to swallow their pride enough to admit there's a serious problem."

"Just as it took them three decades to admit my existence?" Goldwine smiled, a little grimly. "You may be right."

"Jolyon's involvement in all of this concerns me, Goldwine. That second charge he gave his people . . . Laran and I think he means to use whatever they discover to coerce the Prior to set aside the challenge to his succession as Staff-Holder."

"Oh, he's moved beyond that struggle."

"What do you mean?"

"You know the Prior's fallen ill."

Cariad nodded. "Word came just before I left."

"He isn't expected to recover. There'll be a Ceremony of Recreation soon. And Jolyon intends to participate."

"What? But that's impossible! How can he participate if he isn't Staff-Holder?"

"He's persuaded the present Roundhead Staff-Holder to give him proxy."

"*Proxy?* For the *Recreation?* But . . . surely such a thing won't be allowed. Surely the other Suborders will move to stop it."

Goldwine shook her head. "This is no ordinary Recreation, Cariad. A controversy has arisen over the Prioral succession. Siringar, the Journeyer Staff-Holder, is one of the strongest in memory, and favored to succeed. In all of Guardian history, only two Priors have ever come from outside the Suborder of Speakers. And Siringar is quite liberal for a Guardian. The Speakers oppose him because they know very well that the Stone's absence makes them redundant, and they fear what might happen to them under the rule of a non-Speaker. The Soldiers and Searchers and the Arm of the Stone oppose him because of his liberal views. Some of the more aggressive Reds have declared that if he recreates the Staff of Office they'll move to secede from the Order. All this upheaval is very convenient for Jolyon, not just because it makes it easier for him to maneuver, but because there will be a lot of Guardians who'll find the prospect of a reactionary Roundhead preferable to that of a liberal Journeyer. Some may move to block his inclusion in the Ceremony. But many more will support it."

Cariad looked at her foster-mother, horrified. "Could he succeed? In recreating the Staff of Office?"

"It's possible. He's greatly Gifted, and powerfully motivated."

"But then . . . he must be stopped! Something must be done!"

"There's nothing to be done, Cariad. The pieces are already arranged upon the board. The play has already started. All we can do is watch and wait."

"But that's . . . that's . . ." For a moment Cariad could not speak. "How can you be so calm, Goldwine? If he becomes Prior . . . it's unthinkable!"

"It would be a terrible thing," Goldwine acknowledged.

"You can't just mean to stand by and watch it happen! If there's a chance, if there's even a possibility you could stop it—"

"Enough, Cariad," said Goldwine sharply. "The decision has already been made. Besides," she went on a little more gently, "I think I hear more than the operative in you speaking."

Cariad breathed deeply, and turned her face away. She heard Goldwine sigh.

"Sometimes, Cariad, I find it possible to wish I'd never told you the Tale. I know it was what your father wanted. But I don't think he meant his story to . . . shape you as it has. I certainly don't think he meant you to carry his enmity as if it were your own."

"It *is* mine." Cariad kept her eyes averted. "I was born of it."

"Jolyon was your mother's enemy too." There was sadness in Goldwine's voice. "But that's never been as important to you, has it?"

It was true. Cariad barely remembered her mother: a pale face with eyes that were most often closed, a fall of golden hair, a pair of hands whose touch was as light as snowflakes, the sound of shallow breathing. A woman who was familiar but not known, surrounded always by the slightly fearful aura of sickness. It was Goldwine who had raised Cariad, who had taught and comforted and fed and punished her. It was Goldwine she thought of as her mother, not the wraithlike woman who had borne her. Yet even as a tiny child she had recognized the strength of Goldwine's desire for her to love her mother, a desire born of Goldwine's own sad and painful affection; and for Goldwine's sake, and her father's, she had tried to comply. But how could she love a woman she knew only across a gulf of illness, a woman so fragile she spoke always in a whisper and could hardly bear to be touched? How could she love the woman who had delivered her father, her powerful, heroic father, into the hands of his enemy?

"Cariad. There's something I need to talk to you about."

Cariad turned to meet her foster-mother's eyes. She was aware that Goldwine's mood had shifted, though she could read only the edges of the change. Goldwine guarded herself heavily when they were together, for she was aware that Cariad, who could screen herself so well against others' emotions, was defenseless against Goldwine's.

"This mission you and Laran and Shabishara undertook

before you left Ashan-istar. There's a reason I confine my attacks to Journeyers and Soldiers. They're the workers of the Guardian anthill. The loss of a few doesn't mean much to the whole. But the Arm of the Stone is different. Each member is counted individually. Every loss is measured. The Arm doesn't pursue us, for they are content to leave military actions to the Soldiers. But that could change, and it's an action like yours that could change it. If we can bring down the Arm of the Stone, what can't we do? The fact that he was Red only makes it worse."

Cariad shook her head. "Even the Reddened aren't capable of knowing what isn't there to be known. We kept ourselves invisible. My way of killing leaves no mark. Even if the body was found—" She paused. "*Was* it found, Goldwine? Is that what you're saying?"

"No. The body wasn't found."

"Well, then. There's nothing to threaten us. By now even his bones are gone."

"That's not the point, Cariad." Goldwine's gaze rested, level-browed, on Cariad's face. They were not mother and daughter now, but commander and operative, a transition of roles Goldwine seemed to accomplish without effort, but which had always been more difficult for Cariad. "It's the principle of the thing. Given the situation, I have a hard time understanding how you could justify such a risky action."

"The Roundheads' presence in the city was a mystery." Cariad could not keep her voice from rising in surprise. "No one had any idea what they were there to do. The network's leaders feared they had been betrayed."

"As, it turned out, they had not."

"There was no way to know that without doing what we did."

"But it was a reasonable inference. Half of them were going into the desert. Half of them were staying in the Orderhouse. None of them were out scouring the city. Close attention was obviously necessary, but action? I don't think so."

Cariad shook her head. "With all due respect, Goldwine, you weren't there. In our judgment, based on the facts available to us, the network had every cause to be fearful, and the need to know outweighed the risk. Not only that—the situation was a perfect opportunity to field-test the drug. That drug could be very important to us, Goldwine. It gives us capacities we've never had before. You said it earlier—if we can bring down a Roundhead, what can't we do?"

"I would like to hear your professional voice in that, Cariad. But I'm not sure I do."

"What do you mean?"

"You know what I mean." Goldwine's eyes were like agate. "To what degree was your decision to act influenced by your personal interest in pitting yourself against a member of the Arm of the Stone?"

The injustice of this rendered Cariad momentarily speechless. When she had lived in the mountains, she and Goldwine clashed from time to time on personal issues; once she became an operative, Goldwine sometimes questioned or overruled her recommendations for action. But as with everything else between them, the separation between the roles of mother and commander, daughter and operative, was absolute. Never before had Goldwine questioned Cariad's field judgment on anything but strictly professional grounds.

"You know better than that," she said, not quite steadily. "I won't deny that the thought of taking a Roundhead was exciting to me. To Laran as well. But I would never let my personal desires rule my professional judgment. In all the time I've been working for you, I have never done such a thing. This action was the decision of the group, the considered and unanimous opinion of all six of us."

"But whose was the initial suggestion?" Goldwine's gaze did not waver. "I know you, Cariad. This isn't the first time I've had to chide you for taking risk too lightly."

"I'm one of your best agents." Anger was rising now. "Taking risks is what you employ me to do. For twelve years you've trusted me to balance that with what's best for our cause, and I've never once disappointed you. What we did was entirely within the scope of our mandate of protection. What's more, it tested and proved a new weapon. And it obtained valuable information into the bar-

gain. We exercised every care, and covered our tracks beyond any possibility of discovery or inference. This was a
successful mission. You should be thanking me, not questioning me."

"It's not the mission's success I'm taking issue with, Cariad."

"Well, then, maybe it's not *my* professional judgment
that's the problem here. All of this—" She made a wide
gesture, encompassing the food, the furnishings, the
smooth-finished walls. "It's very comfortable. Too comfortable, maybe. Perhaps you've become so comfortable
here that you've forgotten what it really takes to change
the world!"

"What do you know about change?" Answering anger
cut deep furrows on either side of Goldwine's mouth. "You
want the short way, the quick solution—just like your father, who thought he could transform the world through a
single act. Well, the Stone may be gone, but the Order of
Guardians is still here. And I'm the one who's been left to
fight them, to make the way and smooth the path so that
he can come back and finish it. And when it's all over, will
people remember those of us who struggled through the
decades to weaken the Guardians' power so that a single
stroke could bring them down, or the one who struck the
final blow?" Her voice was bitter. "There *is* no short way
to change, Cariad. Change is a struggle, a long journey on
a terrible road. It must be traveled slowly, one footstep at
a time. My pace may not be fast enough for you, but this
is my journey. And we'll make it as I say, until it is complete."

They stared at each other. Goldwine's face was pale. It
was not anger Cariad felt from her now, but something
darker, turning behind her powerful guard. For a moment
there was silence.

"Oh, Cariad." Goldwine passed her hand across her eyes.
She seemed, suddenly, very weary. "Perhaps I'm wrong.
Perhaps it *was* professional judgment that led you to this
action. It's just that I know your impatience, your self-will.
You treat danger as if it were a hill you could climb, as if
the worst that could happen to you would be to slide to the

bottom and be forced to start over again. I know you think you're incapable of failure. I know you don't believe you can ever be hurt, because long ago I prophesied that you and your father would stand face-to-face, and you think you must be safe until that day. But the prophecy doesn't protect you as you think it does. No prophecy can do that."

The dark emotion had intensified—dread? Reluctance? Cariad still could not properly read it. But what lay behind it—that she could read, a clear dark resonance like the sound of a distant bell, the signature of Goldwine's Gift. Cariad knew power and the ways of it. She had lived all her life among the Gifted, and begun mindskill training as soon as she could speak. Yet Goldwine's Gift was strange to her. When it took Goldwine fully, her familiar aspect seemed to slip aside like a parchment mask, revealing something else beneath, huge and cold and far less comprehensible.

"Goldwine." The silent room seemed to swallow up the words. "What have you seen?"

"Nothing." Goldwine shook her head, strongly. "This has nothing to do with my Gift. You're my daughter. I don't have to see the future to fear for you."

It was not the truth. But Cariad recognized the iron core of her foster-mother's will, and knew that Goldwine would tell her nothing more.

Goldwine got to her feet. The brief weariness was gone. She wore again the shield of her usual manner: calm, contained, a little stern.

"That's enough now," she said. "No more arguments. No more rebukes. We have a little time together. Let's spend it well."

She held out her arms. Cariad rose, and went into them. Goldwine's love enfolded her, powerful, unconditional, the only emotion she had never felt the need to guard. Yet that sense of knowledge, of things seen and not revealed, lingered. Goldwine did not often share the insights of her Gift. The prophecy contained within the Tale was one of the few she had ever spoken publicly. But now, though she had not admitted it, she had made another. And Cariad knew, with an instinct as certain as the floor beneath her feet, that it was this that had drawn her back to the mountains, as much as the new orders she would receive.

Four

 **ARIAD ASKED,** but Goldwine refused to reveal the nature of the orders she was to receive.

"I'd prefer not to talk about it informally, Cariad. There's to be a conclave; you'll be told officially then."

"When will that be?"

"As soon as the others arrive."

"What others?"

"Malinides, and whomever he brings with him."

"*Malinides?* Since when have you worked with Zosterians?"

"In this one matter, we've been working together for quite a while. You'll find out in due time, Cariad."

Sensing the finality of this, Cariad did not ask again. She spent some time, however, puzzling over what might have led Goldwine and the leader of the Zosterian resistance to work together. Though the two groups pursued a common goal, they were profoundly divided by ideology. Goldwine's wholesale abandonment of the Limits, her embrace of unfettered technological experimentation, was anathema to the Zosterians—who, though they repudiated the indifferent cruelty of the Guardian system and acknowledged the misery of a populace condemned by technological restriction to backbreaking manual labor and rudimentary medical care, still believed, as the Guardians did, that handpower was a corrupting influence that threatened all the ways of mind. They followed their own, gentler version of the Limits, linking them to a new set of rules known as the Obligations, by which those who had power were made morally responsible for sharing their abilities with those who did not.

It was no accident that Zosterian beliefs carried the imprint of Guardianhood. Most Zosterians had once been Guardians. Cariad's father had founded the movement, during his long Guardian masquerade, at a point when he still believed the Limits necessary, but was determined to foster more enlightened administration of them through internal reform. At its height, the movement claimed thousands of adherents, many of them Arm of the Stone. After Cariad's father was captured, Zosterianism was declared a heresy, and in the savage purges that followed, most Zosterians were killed. A few hundreds escaped, disguising themselves as unGifted or surviving precariously in isolated wildernesses until Malinides, a former Primary of a Roundhead Investigation Team, undertook to seek out these scattered remnants and unite them into the present-day Zosterian underground.

The Zosterians were less a fighting resistance than a converting one. They sought to weaken the Guardians through attrition: receiving defectors, diverting candidates for the Novice Examinations, subverting Journeyers and Soldiers whose faith had been eroded by the savage orthodoxy of the Reddened and the loss of the Stone. Novices and Apprentices pursued their training in the belief that the Stone still rested safe in its Garden; they were told the truth only on Investment. It was a world-shaking thing to discover, after ten years of study and preparation, that the focus of all that endeavor had long ago vanished from the world, and the guardianship from which the Order took its name was no longer of the Stone, but only of the secret of its absence. Some defected at once; others stayed until experience or time tipped them over the edge into unbelief. When they did, the Zosterians were waiting.

At first, Cariad did little more than sleep and eat, seeking to regain the strength lost to her long journey. After a few days she felt vigorous enough to venture out in search of exercise. She found the weapons practice and athletic sessions little changed from her training days, though they had been moved to new spaces and the classes were now much larger. Many of the masters she had known were still active, but there were also many she did not recognize; and though there were a few familiar faces among the trainees, they were people she had known twelve years ago as children. Of the companions of her youth, only a handful remained at headquarters; nearly all of them, like her, had chosen to go out into the world.

The vast majority of those she encountered, therefore, were strangers. Yet everywhere she went, people knew her. She was Goldwine's foster-daughter, of course; but she was also the daughter of the man who had shattered the Fortress walls and freed the Stone, the man who would one day bring the war against the Guardians to a glorious end. It invested her with a certain legendary glamour. Growing up, she had learned to take this in stride, just as she had learned, later, to cope with the fear her assassin skills produced, and the aversion sometimes sparked by others' knowledge of the heartsensing portion of her Gift. But she had been three years with the apothecary network, among people who had long come to accept her, and it was strange to hear again the whispers, to feel the fascination and the curiosity that her passage through the caverns produced. She was never less than deeply conscious of who she was and where she came from, of the long line of her heritage and the promise of her predestined future. But now she seemed, a little, to see herself through others' eyes: her father's avatar, proof and promise in her own flesh of his coming victory.

She spent considerable time exploring. The familiar core of caves and caverns had been embellished by scores of new work and living areas, many of them artificially created. Yet that was only the smallest part of the change. Twelve years ago the complex had housed perhaps a thousand people. Life was not as harsh as it had been in Cariad's early childhood, but it was still difficult, with little in the way of amenities. Power was used almost exclusively for defense and training, and by the group's core of makers, who must create out of the raw material of reality everything necessary for survival, from food to fuel to the metal ore used for weapons manufacture. Now, however, the population had tripled, and comfort was no longer the exception but the rule. Warmth filled every space; bedcoverings were not furs but woven fabrics; everyone wore garments made of cloth. There was mindlight and mindfire, and an abundance of power-sourced automations: motion-sensitive torches, self-opening doors, self-regulating cookfires.

Astonishing as this was, in its indication of an enormous surplus of the power that during Cariad's childhood had been just sufficient for survival, there was something more astonishing still. In selected areas of the complex the technological innovations of the networks had been joined with mindpower to form hybrid devices unlike anything Cariad had seen. There was the furnace chamber where mindfire turned ice hacked from the glacier into boiling water, which was then forced through a network of metal pipes to heat the air of the caverns where the sheep and cattle herds were quartered. There were the long low areas where gardens, planted in mind-made earth and illuminated by miniature mind-made suns, were warmed by the same piping and watered by an ingenious irrigation system that was itself fed by mindfire-melted ice. There were the looms, run by belts and wheels and levers kept in action by motion-bindings, upon which power-bound thread was woven into fabric impermeable to water or knife-thrusts. There were the weapons—experimental bows like the quarterbow Cariad had used for Baldric; daggers and swords and arrow-points of network developed alloys, power-forged so that they would always keep their razor edges; cylindrical devices mounted on carriages, which used explosive powder to launch missiles that burst on impact, delivering sleep- or confusion-bindings.

"It's wonderful, isn't it?" said Goldwine when Cariad expressed her amazement. "When I offered the networks protection all those years ago, all I thought I'd gain was tools and devices. It never occurred to me they might incorporate mindpower into their work. But it's a natural development, don't you think? Perhaps it would have been like this in the old world, if the true balance between the powers had been maintained. I believe it will help us, in the new world, to make sure the balance isn't lost again."

"It's not just the machines, Goldwine. The warmth . . .

the automations . . . How can you spare the power for so many nonessential bindings?"

"The new technology has freed our makers of many of the duties they used to perform, especially food production. But the real reason is that there are finally enough of us. Up to a certain level of collective making power, it's very difficult to maintain permanent bindings. Once you get past that level, it isn't difficult at all—provided you have the united will. Until now, that's something only the Guardians have known. Before us, there was never another group of Gifted that gathered in sufficient strength to discover it."

"I had no idea. That there were so many, I mean."

"Three thousand here. Another three outside, in the world." Goldwine smiled. "It's been quite a while since our only increase came from within, or from the flotsam and jetsam of the Fortress. People seek us out now, Gifted who once wouldn't have questioned their obligation to become Guardians, unGifted whom the Reddened have taught to hate the Limits more fiercely than a thousand years of Guardian oppression ever could. We've had to increase the screening bands to keep up with the flow of new recruits."

Change came to everything. It was to change that Cariad's life was dedicated. Still, something within her found it deeply difficult to accept the changes here. At night her mind recreated the world she had known as a child: the dark rock and glassy ice, the rough caverns and arching galleries, the echoes and the silences, the deep pure cold. She had not dreamed this way in years, not since the wretched months after she first left the mountains, when it had seemed to her that she had lost something so essential that even the cause she served so eagerly could not make her whole. Now, as then, there was an instant on waking when it seemed to her that it was the light and warmth and smooth squared angles that were the dream, and the shadowed world inside her that was the truth.

Malinides arrived a week later, accompanied by a single lieutenant. He went at once to his quarters and did not emerge until the conclave, which had been called for the following day.

He was present when Cariad and Goldwine and Rafer entered the conference room in Goldwine's personal quarters, seated at one end of the stone table with his lieutenant beside him. They were dressed alike in long pleated robes with leather belts. Their heads were shorn in the Roundhead manner. All Zosterians wore their hair this way, not out of any lingering loyalty to the Arm of the Stone, but in order to separate themselves from Cariad's father, a Roundhead who had grown his own hair long as a visible symbol of his political difference. Present-day Zosterians believed that Cariad's father had betrayed the movement by the actions that led to his arrest, and the world by his actions subsequent to it. One of Malinides' first official actions had been to repudiate the movement's founder.

There were two others present: Hasenfal, Goldwine's second in command, an experienced soldier who had been coordinator of the network protection effort when Cariad left the mountains, and Estrellara, Goldwine's long-time director of intelligence. They sat stiffly, several chairs away from the two Zosterians. Cariad could feel the suspicion that filled the air, the sense of people forced to go against the grain.

Goldwine strode down the room. The Zosterians rose as she approached.

"Welcome," Goldwine said. Voicespeech would be used for this meeting; like Guardians, Zosterians could not duplicate the unconventional power-channels Goldwine used. "I'm sorry I couldn't be there to greet you when you first arrived."

"Your staff attended adequately to our needs." Malinides spoke with the cold precision of the high-level Roundhead he once had been. He was a spare man, with a pale lined face and light eyes set deeply beneath bushy brows. He looked to be in his middle sixties, but was probably much older. He wore close-fitting leather gloves, with cuffs extending up under the loose sleeves of his robe, to hide the marks of the torture he had suffered during the Zosterian purges. "May I present my assistant, Sebastiao."

Sebastiao, slender and olive-skinned, inclined his head. Goldwine gestured toward Cariad.

"My daughter, Cariad."

Malinides' eyes flicked across Cariad's face. His feeling told her that he knew who she was. She endured his gaze, trying to control her own antipathy. She had never met a Zosterian she could tolerate. Despite their more lenient ideology, they were Guardians at heart, with the same vision of a world that must be regulated and a populace that must be controlled, and the same absolute belief in their right to enforce those standards in service of a greater good.

"You spoke to me some time ago of her qualifications." Malinides said to Goldwine, as if Cariad were not there. "Perhaps you would do me the favor of reviewing them again."

"Cariad has been an active operative for twelve years." No one would have guessed, from the neutrality of Goldwine's manner, how much she disliked this man. Rafer, at her side, was equally impassive, but Cariad could feel his sharp mistrust. "She began her career as part of a raiding force specializing in the appropriation and redistribution of Guardian tithes. After two years she was transferred to a screening band. She remained there for three years before being promoted to network protection duty, where she has served ever since. In addition, she is frequently called upon to perform confidential short-term missions."

"Confidential missions." Malinides' emotions, only a little muted by his personal guard, were volatile, shifting in a kaleidoscopic succession almost too swift to grasp. Uppermost among them, right now, was distaste—for the mountains, for the need that brought him to them, for the company in which he found himself. "Perhaps you would be more specific."

"Cariad has served as a courier and a spy. She has obtained and planted documents. She's an extraction specialist who has brought many people to safety, including operatives held in Orderhouse prisons. In addition, she has accomplished twenty-five assassinations, through methods that mimic natural causes."

"And her Gift?"

"Let me answer that, Goldwine." Cariad placed a hand on her foster-mother's arm. "I have multiple Gifts, sir. I'm a mindspeaker, skilled in both Guardian and resistance methods. I possess the full range of making power—creative, transformative, and uncreative—which I can use with equal ease in Guardian ways or in our own. And I'm a heartsenser."

"True multiple Gifts are rare." Once again his eyes swept her face, and she felt the heat of his inadequately suppressed anger and resentment. It was not surprising: whatever her qualifications, to him she could never be anything but the daughter of a traitor. "If it's true, you are indeed a paragon of power."

It was not worth a response.

"Very well. I suppose I must be satisfied."

Goldwine led the way up the table to places opposite Hasenfal and Estrellara. She indicated that Cariad should sit on her right. Rafer took the chair on the left. For the first time Cariad saw that he had brought no note tablet. What was about to be discussed must be sensitive indeed.

"To understand the importance of what we're asking you to do, Cariad, you must understand the history behind it." Goldwine turned a little sideways in her chair, so that she could look directly into Cariad's eyes. Her expression was formal, unreadable: the face of the commander. Cariad could feel nothing from her. "The year before you left the mountains a young man came to us, a defector from the Fortress, a Fourth-Year Apprentice of the Arm of the Stone. His name was Konstant. You remember him."

It was not a question. For a brief time, he and Cariad had been lovers. An image rose inside Cariad's mind: a handsome young man with coppery skin and black hair, superlatively Gifted and highly intelligent, but also bitter and moody, prone to black depressions, shadowed always by the darkness of some inner torment. Goldwine's operatives, who patrolled the area around the Fortress in search of castouts and runaways, had found him at the outer limit of their territory, farther than any other escapee had managed to go.

"Yes. I remember him."

"He remained with us for five years before leaving to join the Zosterians. Three years ago he was asked to serve as agent for a plan the Zosterian Council had been working on for some time: to infiltrate the Arm of the Stone."

Cariad felt her mind rock a little.

"But there was a difficulty. The plan's goal was the Fortress. Zosterians have no contacts inside the Fortress, no way to get information in or out. We, however, do."

When Goldwine had been a Novice, always under punishment for her refusal to conform, she had found solace among the servants of the Novice Wing, many of whom were sympathetic to the Novices' suffering. Years later, secretly, she returned to seek out the servants she had known. Through them, she established the nucleus of an in-Fortress intelligence network. Fortress workers were bred to servitude as others were to race and culture, but they were often cruelly treated, and a vein of bitterness ran among them, which could sometimes be turned to resistance. Goldwine's recruiters, disguised as servants, were stationed in nearly every part of the Fortress now, each responsible for a closed cell of intelligencers, whose loyalty was assured through inhibitions implanted at the time of initial contact. None of these operatives had ever been discovered. The care and skill of the recruiters made sure of this; but so did the complacency of the Guardians. They did not question the loyalty of their indoctrinated, unGifted servants, or the impregnability of the Fortress. Ten centuries of unbroken, unchallenged rule had made it so.

"And so they came to us, at Konstant's urging." The words were heavy with a sense of things unsaid. It must have infuriated the Zosterians to ask for help; that they had been willing to do it was an indication of how urgently committed to the plan they were. "Obviously it was an extremely risky undertaking. Even given the benefits of the information it might yield, I probably wouldn't have considered it if Konstant hadn't been involved. But I knew him, his skills and his dedication. He was pledged to this mission heart and soul. He was also capable of impersonating a Roundhead, in the most important sense—he knew how to mindprobe."

"With only a little over four years of Arm training?"

"You know what worm-baiting is."

Cariad nodded. The training of Arm Apprentices to the investigation, interrogation, mindprobing, and torture that were the Roundheads' stock in trade was entirely academic. Even Invested members of the Arm were not allowed to mindprobe unsupervised until the two-year internship that followed their graduation was completed. Sometimes, unwilling to wait, eager Apprentices kidnapped servants or Apprentices from other Suborders, and subjected them to mock interrogations, complete with probes. The custom was known as worm-baiting. Officially it was illegal, since mindprobes could do damage even in the hands of experienced practitioners. Unofficially, it was widely tolerated, for many Roundhead teachers considered it a valuable hands-on adjunct to the Apprentices' theoretical studies.

"For much of his Apprenticeship, Konstant was a member of a particularly active baiting group. Apparently he had an aptitude for the things they did. More than an aptitude, really—a kind of genius. At any rate, he was a skilled mindprober by the time he left the Fortress."

Cariad had not known this. Konstant, deeply reticent about his time as an Apprentice, had told her next to nothing about it.

"My staff and I discussed it and agreed to cooperate." Across from Goldwine, Hasenfal shifted in his chair. Cariad could feel that he, at least, had not been happy with the collaboration. "Specifically, to allow Konstant access to our in-Fortress intelligence network, and to retrain him in our ways of defense so that he could bypass Guardian defenses. When he was ready, we sent him back to the Zosterians. They targeted a Roundhead Investigation Team that was returning to the Fortress on sabbatical. One of the Team members was removed, and Konstant took his place."

"How did he do that? I don't recall that he had the making power for a long-term semblance."

"He doesn't. It wouldn't have made sense to risk that kind of subterfuge among Roundheads anyway. The Keep of the Arm of the Stone is full of illusion-strippers, and our methods have never been tried against them. No, Konstant's disguise was entirely physical."

"Physical? How?"

"My makers have perfected a way of permanently re-forming skin and bone." Malinides spoke, coldly, from the end of the table. "They apply power entirely from outside, according to an established template, so they don't encounter the body-resistance that hampers internal efforts. As long as the subject and the target have the same basic contours and coloring, we can duplicate features very precisely."

There was something repugnant to the idea of this, the irrevocable twisting of living flesh into an alien shape. Cariad could alter her own body by means of her Gift, but these were transient disguises, easily set aside.

"Konstant reached the Fortress without incident." Goldwine resumed the narrative. "As is customary, Team members were separated and reassigned. Konstant was put on administrative duty in the office of the Investigation-Master. The plan was for him to wait six months and then request permanent Fortress placement, but the Investigation-Master was so pleased with him that he requested this himself. Over the next year Konstant maintained his position. He met regularly with his servant contact, and passed on an enormous amount of information. But then events took a different turn."

"Konstant was caught."

"No. Konstant joined the Reddened."

"He joined the *Reddened?*"

"He didn't inform his contact, so we had no idea. We did notice that the intelligence he was giving us had changed. He told his contact his duties for the Investigation-Master had been shifted, that he had begun dealing with administration rather than outside investigations and the activities of the orthodoxers. We believed him, but the contact became suspicious. He took it on himself to investigate. Eventually he found out what had really happened."

"Why would Konstant do such a thing?"

"Actually, he had orders to do it." Goldwine's face was expressionless. "Secret orders, from Malinides. When the contact confronted him, he admitted it."

Anger had sprung to life on the quiet air—Hasenfal's, Rafer's, Estrellara's. At the end of the table, Malinides sat as if carved from stone, his eyes turned on some empty point in space.

"As you can imagine, my people were distressed. There were some—" Goldwine's eyes flicked toward Hasenfal "—who felt we should recall Konstant immediately, and withdraw all further cooperation. But I thought it best to leave things as they were. Konstant's impersonation of a Red was obviously successful, and it seemed to me there might be a lot to gain by allowing him to follow it as far as he could. As it happens, he followed it very far indeed. He became Jolyon's companion."

"Jolyon's *companion*?" Cariad was jolted. "How did he manage that?"

Goldwine shook her head. "All we know is what he told the contact: that he had successfully performed a service Jolyon particularly desired. Six months went by. Everything seemed to be going well. Then, three weeks ago, Konstant vanished."

"Vanished? As in dead?"

"As in defected." It was Hasenfal. The corded scar that bisected his left cheek writhed as he spoke. "The real danger of this mission was never discovery, but reconversion. I've said so all along."

"No." Malinides' voice was glacial. "Konstant would not reconvert. I know this as I know myself."

"Your assurances are meaningless." Hasenfal leaned forward. His face had reddened around his scar. "You've already proved that good faith is only so many words to you. I wouldn't trust you to tell me there was ice inside the abyss. I certainly don't trust you to judge the honesty of a man who willingly conspired with you to deceive us. A man who was once—"

"Hasenfal. Enough." The words held the full force of Goldwine's command. "We have not come here to quarrel."

For a moment it seemed that Hasenfal would not obey. But at last, slowly, he sat back in his chair.

"As it happens," Goldwine said, "I think Malinides is right. But whether or not we agree on Konstant's faithfulness, it's clear that we must find out what's happened to him."

Cariad understood now what was coming. It made her feel as if all the air had left the room.

"That is the task we're giving you, Cariad. You are to enter the Keep of the Arm of the Stone and track Konstant down. If he's been imprisoned, you're to free him. If he's dead, you're to discover how and why, and what he revealed before he died. If he has defected, you're to kill him."

Cariad heard a roaring in her head. The Fortress, she thought. The Arm of the Stone.

"If he's been imprisoned, there are four places he might be." Estrellara spoke for the first time. She was a forbidding woman, big-boned and strong, with creased skin and gray hair pulled tightly back from a frowning face. Her sternness was not, like Goldwine's, a shield for a softer self, but the most basic quality of her being. Cariad remembered her from childhood as one of the few people she had truly feared. "First, the Arm's own holding cells. Second, the prison annex. Third, the cells below the Great Amphitheater, where those who are to be subjected to power-removal or a branding ceremony are held. And fourth, the private cells attached to some of the larger apartments in the Keep."

Cariad struggled for focus. She was aware of Goldwine's regard, clear and much too perceptive. She met Estrellara's hard gaze instead.

"How will I get into the Fortress?"

"The information patrol will deliver you. You may have to stay for several weeks, so it'll be safest for you to take a servant identity. It'll give you legitimate reason to be in the Keep, and allow you to work closely with Konstant's contact. He's a very effective intelligencer, and he knows the underground tunnels extremely well. They'll be your safest way of getting about. There aren't many Guardians down there, other than a few Soldier patrols, and they give access to every part of the Fortress."

"What kind of servant identity?"

"A real one. There's a certain amount of mixing and shifting in the other servant societies—if we were placing you among the Speaker servants, you could say you were from the Journeyer community and had been transferred.

But the Arm community is entirely closed. The only way you can get into it is to take the place of an existing individual. We left it up to the contact to choose. He'll have her there when you arrive. The patrol will bring her back here, and we'll hold her until you're finished and she can be returned. Be warned, though. There are many defenses in the Keep. Konstant survived them, but he wasn't wearing a semblanced disguise. Take very great care when you go into the private Roundhead areas."

Cariad nodded. "This contact. Can I trust him?"

"You can trust him absolutely. He's one of the best we have. Resourceful and dedicated, and for an unGifted, highly intelligent." The words held approval, but no warmth. Estrellara was good at what she did in part because she was not often distracted by emotion. "His name is Orrin."

"Orrin," Cariad repeated. "When will I leave?"

"Three days from now."

"I can leave tomorrow if you want me to."

"No. I have briefings planned, and the patrol has its own schedule. Three days is soon enough."

"Is it possible for me to see a likeness of Konstant's altered face?"

Malinides nodded toward his silent lieutenant. Sebastiao shifted forward in his chair, bending his eyes on his hands, which he held cupped before him. A globe of light appeared above his palms, slowly acquiring form, shaping the head and shoulders of a man. Sebastiao lifted his hands in a tossing motion; the lambent image launched itself into the air and flew toward Cariad, halting a little distance away, revolving slowly to display itself from all angles. Cariad regarded the cropped hair, the blunt unpleasing features, the coarse skin, the heavy neck and jowls. This was a man a good deal older than the thirty-two or thirty-three she knew Konstant to be. She would not have believed a living face could change so much.

She looked at Sebastiao. "Thank you. I've seen enough."

His eyes flickered. The image winked out like a pinched candle. Still silent, he sat back in his chair.

"Is this meeting over?" Malinides addressed Goldwine.

"Cariad?"

"I have no more questions."

"Then yes. The meeting is over."

Malinides rose to his feet, followed by Sebastiao. "I would like your people to take us out of here this afternoon, if that is possible."

"It is. Though you're welcome to stay a day or two," Goldwine said mildly. "It's an arduous journey, even at power-speed."

"I would not willingly remain another hour in this place." Malinides' thin lips twisted, as if he had tasted something foul. "The abominations I have seen here . . . the things of mind unnaturally grafted to the works of hands . . . surely even the corrupt experiments that hurled the ancient world into the horrors of the Split were not as bad as these. Come, Sebastiao."

Sebastiao rose. The two men moved toward the door. It opened smoothly at their approach, revealing the torchlit corridor beyond and the still forms of Goldwine's guards. At the threshold, Malinides turned. His deepset eyes, almost hidden beneath their bushy brows, rested for a moment on Goldwine and then shifted past her, to fasten on Cariad's face.

"You. Assassin." He sounded as if he were biting off pieces of ice. "You are perhaps the last person in the world I would have chosen to represent my cause. But necessity has taken choice away from me. If you find it difficult to serve Zosterian interests, remember that your people, as much as mine, are threatened here. I charge you to carry out the mission you have been given to the utmost of your strength and ability. And I pray . . ." He paused. The coldness in his face was extraordinary. ". . . I pray that you prove more faithful than your father was."

Cariad felt blood flower in her cheeks. "Hope that I prove *as* faithful as my father, sir," she said softly. "Then you will be assured of my success."

Again his lips twisted. Even from here she could feel his chill disgust. He turned, Sebastiao behind him, and left the room.

For a moment there was silence.

<By ice and snow, what a hypocrite that man is.> Hasenfal's mindvoice was tight. <He was eager enough to put his ideology aside when he thought you could be of benefit to him.>

<He never wanted to work with us.> Goldwine had closed her eyes. Her fingers were pressed against her temples, as if they pained her. <He was prepared to let the plan go first. He only yielded because it was the united will of his Council.>

<Why did you let him come here, Commander? We didn't need him for this.>

<He faces as much danger as we do, Hasenfal. The plan is his as well. We owed him the chance to participate.>

<After he betrayed our trust? It's because of him that we're in this position!>

<A lack of honor in others shouldn't preclude honor in ourselves.>

<This bewilders me, Commander.> Hasenfal had risen to his feet. <It has from the start. I've never understood why you agreed to collaborate with Zosterians, or why you believed a former Roundhead could be trusted. Or why you remained loyal to the plan even when it became obvious Malinides had tricked us.>

<This is an old conversation, Hasenfal.>

<I could understand it better if I knew this came from something you've seen.> Hasenfal's scarred face was urgent. <It almost seems it must be. Why else would you summon Cariad more than two months before any of us knew she was needed?>

<It's not my obligation to justify my actions through the workings of my Gift.> Goldwine opened her eyes, fixing him with an agate gaze. <I have never done so. I will not do so now.>

Hasenfal did not back down. <Then let me begin to prepare for attack. Since you believe we haven't been betrayed, let me believe we have been. Then we'll be prepared for whatever comes.>

<I agree, Commander,> Estrellara glanced at Cariad. <We can't know that Cariad will be successful. Or even that she will survive.>

There was a pause. Goldwine's face was like stone.

<Very well,> she thought at last. <Make it so. Now go, both of you. You too, Cariad. I'll talk with you later.>

Cariad got to her feet, trying not to betray her eagerness to be gone. At the threshold, she paused and looked back. Goldwine's fingers were pressed to her temples again, and her eyes were closed. Rafer had risen from his place at her side; his hand rested on her shoulder.

Cariad turned and went out into the corridor. Behind her, the door fell softly closed.

Cariad stood before a mirror made of beaten metal. She had bathed; her hair lay wet down her back, smooth with combing. Torches in wall-holders made the room a study in light and shadow. The air was warm, and very quiet.

She set the comb aside and leaned forward to study her reflection. It was a game she had played since childhood, an attempt to extract from her own features an idea of her father's face. But to look at herself—at the long black eyes and level brows, the strong nose and wide mouth, the pale skin and night-dark hair—was never to see more than her own reflection. All her life she had been told she was her father's image, but the only face she ever saw when she looked into the mirror was hers.

She turned away and went to sit on her bed. She was calm. She had not been, when exiting the conference room. Unable to stay still, she had roamed the walkways and corridors and rooms of the complex for hours, moving at random, blind to everything except what she saw within. A door had burst open inside her mind today, a door she had willed closed many years ago. What she saw behind it was not the dust and cobwebs of an abandoned childhood dream but the banked brilliance of an ambition that had needed only a breath to explode once more into flame. It was a little shocking to find it still so alive within her; yet the shock was born of recognition, not surprise. It seemed she had always known she would one day be given the chance to pursue, with the skill and focus of adulthood, the paramount desire of her youth. As if it had always been this she prepared for in the ever more dangerous and complex missions she took on. As if her rejection of her childish vow had always been a sham, a stopgap, a self-deception.

She would go to the Fortress. She would accomplish the mission she had been given. And she would accomplish another: she would kill Jolyon.

She was too honest to try to justify her intent by telling herself that this was Goldwine's unspoken expectation. That this perfect conjunction of timing, circumstance, and necessity could be construed in no other way; that there could be no other reason why, on the eve of the most important Recreation Ceremony the world had ever seen, Goldwine would send into the Fortress the most skilled of all her assassins. Cariad knew very well that Goldwine proceeded forthrightly, not obliquely. If she truly wanted Cariad to kill Jolyon, she would direct her to do so, even over the opposition of her advisors.

The intent was Cariad's alone. She was well aware that in pursuing it she would be disobeying Goldwine, even if Goldwine did not actually forbid it. And yet she could not do otherwise. There was a clarity to this, a rightness, that went beyond all possibility of objection. The chance had been given her. If she did not take it, it might never come again.

Goldwine's face rose up before her, drawn and weary, as it had been when Cariad left the conference room. She thought of the whisper of dread, the thread of prophecy she had sensed beneath her foster-mother's words just after her return. Was it this Goldwine had seen? Did some injury or danger wait for her in the Fortress, born of her intent—or perhaps simply of the mission she had been given? Or might there be a wider focus—some larger outcome, some more encompassing catastrophe? But Cariad knew herself, knew her strength and her skills. More than that, she knew the prophecy, which assured she must come safely out of whatever peril she went into. If the danger were for her, she would face and overcome it. If the danger were for others, or for the resistance as a whole, she would face that too, and do what she could.

She lay back on the bed, her arm raised behind her head. Konstant, she thought. She had been just eighteen when he joined Goldwine's army, and he had been twenty. Almost from the beginning Goldwine had taken an interest in him, and so he and she were often thrown together. He became infatuated with her, and a few weeks after his induction they became lovers.

At first Cariad was pleased with the relationship. Konstant was beautiful and intelligent and awesomely Talented, with a Gift of mindspeech so finely tuned that he could catch a thought directed to him even from outside the mountain. But he was the most restless person she had ever known, and the darkest, brimming with painful memories and filled with torturous self-loathing. He refused to say anything about his years as an Arm Apprentice; about his defection, he would admit only that he had discovered the Guardians' great lie and knew the Stone was gone. Because of this reticence, as well as the distance he had gone within the Arm before leaving it, he was widely mistrusted, despite the fact that the mindscans of Goldwine's reclaimers confirmed the authenticity of his conversion. There were many who would gladly have returned him to the snowfields where he had been found.

Cariad had not mistrusted him. She had felt the core-deep truth of his horror of what he had escaped, and the real, if hesitant, power of his commitment to Goldwine's cause. But she found his bitter spirit a burden, and it quickly became clear that he expected far more of her than she was willing to give. Using the excuse of her impending departure, she broke things off between them. As she expected, he took it badly. She left three months later. She had heard nothing of him since, until today.

Might Hasenfal be right? Might Konstant have defected? He had hated the Fortress and embraced the resistance. . . . And yet five years later he had left Goldwine for the Zosterians, who were in many ways indistinguishable from Guardians. Might his time among the Reddened have brought him full circle?

The light and shadow of the torches swept the ceiling, an oddly soothing visual play. Cariad was not aware of falling asleep until she started awake to the feeling of a hand on her knee.

"Goldwine," she said.

"I'm sorry to wake you."

"It's all right." Cariad pulled herself upright, shaking back her hair. "You look exhausted, Goldwine. You should be sleeping."

Goldwine made an impatient gesture. "Sleep will wait. Work won't. Are you clear about this mission, Cariad?"

As always, Cariad could read little from behind her foster-mother's heavy guard. She took a breath. Deeply as she desired to follow her private intent, her conscience would not allow her to leave without giving Goldwine the chance to forbid it—if indeed she had seen it, if indeed it were something she wanted to forbid.

"Goldwine . . . I sense that your Gift is driving this mission. I felt it just after I returned. And even if I hadn't, it's as Hasenfal said—why else would you summon me so long before you knew I'd be needed? I know you've seen more than you're saying, and that what you've seen is . . . dangerous, or fearful. I suspect it has to do with me. With . . . with what I'm going to do in the Fortress." She stopped. Now that she had come to it, she found she could not bring herself to speak directly. If Goldwine did forbid her, she would obey; but she hoped, desperately, that it would not be so. "I wondered . . . I wondered if perhaps you had something you wanted to tell me."

There was a silence. Goldwine had turned away as Cariad spoke, and was staring at the torches on the wall opposite.

"Do you know why I've never made more than one prophecy for you?" she asked at last. "Why I've never told you about your future, except for that one thing?"

"Because you don't want to influence my actions."

Goldwine nodded. Shadow moved across her face. "If I tell a person what may lie ahead for her, how can I know she'll behave as she would have if she'd never known what was coming? And if she behaves differently, how can I know that her choices won't change the thing I've seen? The future is mutable, Cariad—you know that. Until a thing happens, there's only possibility. The only reason I gave you even that one prophecy was that giving it to you was part of the vision. And the resistance needed it as well, to know what they fight for."

She paused. Her eyes were still fixed on the torches, though Cariad did not think she saw them. Her hands, blunt and practical, scarred with a lifetime of work and weapon use, pleated and repleated the hem of her loose jacket. Cariad waited, knowing more was coming.

"I withhold knowledge from others so that their choices won't be influenced," Goldwine said softly. "But I don't have that luxury for myself. There are always two levels on which I act—the one on which I do what the circumstances require, and the one on which I know the consequences of what I do. Would I act the same way if I didn't know what would come of it? Maybe. But maybe not. The line between seeing the future and shaping it is very thin, Cariad. That's what's most terrible about a Gift like mine. Not just knowing what will come, not just seeing the lines of possibility leading to a certain goal, but knowing that I can reach in at any point, like someone touching a finger to a reflection in a pool of water, and change them. Sometimes, I admit, I've yielded to temptation. But not this time. This time I don't have a choice." She shook her head. "The answer to your question is no. I have nothing to tell you."

Cariad breathed deeply. Whether this meant Goldwine accepted her intent, or that Goldwine's Gift, capriciously, had not revealed it, she did not know. She knew only that she had given Goldwine the chance to speak, and Goldwine had not done so.

"I'll carry out the mission faithfully, Goldwine. If he can be found, I'll find him."

Goldwine nodded. "Konstant is a good man. Malinides is right in that at least."

"You already know what's happened to him, don't you?"

Goldwine hesitated. "I hope I know. But it isn't the way of my Gift to show me everything, or to come to me when I need it. I've seen the possibility. But not the fulfillment."

"And you need me to confirm it. I understand, Goldwine."

"Oh, Cariad. If I could, I wouldn't let you go. I'd keep

you here, or post you back among the networks. Anything but send you into that black-walled prison."

It was there again, the darkness, the dread, the thread of Gift, turning behind Goldwine's barriers. Cariad reached out and took her foster-mother's hands.

"Goldwine. I'm not afraid."

"I know." Goldwine's fingers tightened on Cariad's. Her face was haggard; she looked, right now, every one of her sixty-three years. "Sometimes I wish you were."

"I'll come back safe. I know you think I rely too much on the prophecy, but you can't deny it guarantees at least that."

Goldwine did not reply. Leaning forward, she took Cariad in her arms. She held her, a long embrace, the skin of her cheek warm against Cariad's own. The darkness was still there, and something more familiar: a weary, burdened sadness, the feeling of a woman who had always known much more than she wished to. Since earliest childhood Cariad had recognized this part of Goldwine's soul, though few who knew her in her guise as resolute and tireless leader would have guessed its existence.

At last Goldwine sat back. "I'll go now. You need to sleep."

"You should sleep yourself, Goldwine."

"I will." She reached out and touched Cariad's cheek. "I love you, Cariad. I love you as much as any natural mother ever loved her natural daughter. You know that, don't you?"

"Of course, Goldwine. I love you, too."

Goldwine pushed herself slowly to her feet. For a moment she stood motionless, looking down at Cariad. Her face was set now, closed, stern: the face of the commander.

"I've seen many things through my Gift, Cariad," she said. "Some of them have never come to be. Nearly all the rest have been shifted in some way, twisted by the process of realization. Only one thing has never altered: your father's return. No matter what happens, that is fixed, immutable. But there's nothing else in all the world that can't be changed. Remember that, Cariad, when you are in the Fortress."

For a moment their gazes held. Then Goldwine turned away. She moved softly to the door and through it, closing it behind her.

For a time Cariad sat against the headboard of her bed, staring at the torches and thinking—about risk, about danger, about Goldwine's Gift, about the possibilities that waited for her in the Keep. At last she rose and put on her nightshift. Lightly she set her unmaking power against the torches, and in the darkness got into bed. Falling toward unconsciousness—all thought suspended, all denial gone— she felt the touch of flame, licking up out of some dark place within her. For a moment it ran like light along the pathways of her nerves. There was a pulse, her own perhaps, slowing . . . and then the fire sank back into the depths, and she crossed the threshold into sleep.

The
Crossing

Five

**ND SO** my decision is rendered. When the time comes, it will be the Second and not myself who enters the Great Amphitheater to participate in the Ceremony of Recreation."

The Staff-Holder's words gave way to a shocked silence. The assembled men—seven seated about the central table, more than three times that number ranged around the edges of the room—were motionless, as still as the figures in the embroidered tapestries that muffled the walls.

The council room of the Arm of the Stone had seven sides, a visual reflection of its function as the gathering place of the Suborder's leadership. It was perhaps twice as high as it was wide, made that way to accommodate the pale core of mindfire that boiled upon the air just below the ceiling, generating neither sound nor heat but only light, a cold intense radiance that banished contrast and edged every object in jet-black shadow. The folds of the tapestries held a darkness as profound as the openings of mines. The space beneath the council table was inkier than the night sky. The robes of the assembled Roundheads were like poured pitch. Everything that was not black was red: the embroidery of the hangings, the mortar between the stones of wall and floor, the painted wood of the chairs in which the Council sat, even the table around which they were gathered, a massive septagon of red marble veined with creamy white, which reminded Konstant of nothing so much as a slab of butchered meat.

91

He stood against the wall behind Jolyon's chair, closely flanked by the others who made up Jolyon's contingent of companions: Baffrid, Saranero, and Ruen. These three were permanent; he, the fourth, was temporary, chosen to answer a need other than protection.

To his right and left, the companions of the Staff-Holder and the other members of the Council of Six waited statuelike at their masters' backs. Thirty years ago, no Councilor would have dreamed of employing a retinue of bodyguards. It was Jolyon who had begun the practice, not long after he was first elevated to the Council, claiming that even in the Keep, surrounded by the strongest defenses the Arm of the Stone could create, he was not safe from his enemies. One by one, the other Councilors followed suit. Now the practice was as entrenched as the tradition of obeisance to the staff of office, which had begun Council meetings since the Arm's inception eight centuries before. Only the Apprentice-Master, Marhalt, refused to adopt the custom. Even in these troubled times, when the divisions within the Council made the companions less a matter of political posturing than of practical necessity, the space behind his chair remained empty.

Like the others, Konstant wore a Roundhead's black robe and red belt, with the red-and-black lightning-bolt insignia of the Reddened pinned to his left shoulder and Jolyon's violet-colored teardrop emblem to his right. His hands, like theirs, were held empty before him in the ritual posture of good faith—a gesture that meant very little, in this place of power-fueled intrigue and treachery, but was required even so. He had not moved a muscle for the past two hours, and would remain motionless for at least an hour more. The restlessness that gripped him whenever he stood this way flickered agonizingly along his limbs, and there was a heavy aching in the small of his back. The disguise he wore required his body to carry nearly fifty pounds of extra flesh; though it had been almost two years, his bones reminded him at every opportunity that this was not the way he was made to be.

"This is an unprecedented decision." Ciadh, the Council's Treasurer, broke the hush. The chamber was laced with power-baffles, so that those who gathered here might meet as equals; they had the effect of baffling sound as well, and Ciadh's soft voice was barely audible. "I'm not aware that anything like it has been done before."

"You are mistaken, Treasurer." Those who knew put the Staff-Holder's age at more than a century and a half. As a matter of course, Roundheads did their utmost to stave off the ravages of aging, but even they could not resist forever: the Staff-Holder's hair was white, his skin lined and loose, his once-powerful body bent by an inflammation of the spine too entrenched for even his self-healing abilities to keep at bay. He leaned heavily on his staff of office, a shaft of onyx capped by an immense faceted garnet. "The original charter of the Order of Guardians gives the Staff-Holders full authority to designate their Seconds as proxies for ceremonial duty. There is not a Staff-Holder in history who has not taken advantage of this."

"With the greatest respect, Staff-Holder, participation in the Recreation is hardly a ceremonial duty." Ciadh was a slight man, with an unstable glance and a nervous habit of twisting his Guardian medal on its thick gold chain. His financial acumen, which had made the Arm of the Stone the largest single landowner in the world, was undisputed, but it was no secret that he was more comfortable inside the Fortress than he had ever been in the field, and the more militant members of the Council held him in some contempt. "It seems to me that the Council's advice should have been sought before this decision was made. It's a dangerous time to break with tradition. The issues that have occupied us over the past few years—"

"Why mince words?" interrupted the Limit-Master, Jehan-Moro. "Everyone here recognizes this for what it is— a transparent attempt to sidestep the Council's challenge to succession."

"Succession is not at issue here," the Staff-Holder replied coldly. "My decision relates solely to a disposition of duty within the Council—which, as you well know, does not require either the advice or agreement of Council members."

"Do you think we're fools?" Jehan-Moro addressed the

Staff-Holder, but his eyes were fixed on Jolyon, hidden from Konstant's view by the high-backed chair. "Do you really expect us to believe this is only a matter of standing in?"

"I have already explained the situation." The support of the staff of office was no longer enough; with his free hand, the Staff-Holder reached out to grip the jet-and-garnet-encrusted finial of his chair. "The state of my health makes it impossible for me to participate in the Ceremony. For the Arm of the Stone to be unrepresented, at this first Re-creation since our separation from the Journeyer Suborder, is unthinkable. I have no choice but to designate a proxy."

"Sophistry." Jehan-Moro possessed a rich orator's voice; even the power-flattened air could not rob it of its resonance. "To send the Second into the Great Amphitheater before the entire assembly of Guardians, vested with a Staff-Holder's authority and charged with a Staff-Holder's duty, is tantamount to an unofficial declaration of leadership. If he completes the Ceremony, in the eyes of the Order he'll be as good as confirmed. This is a coup d'etat, dressed up as a procedural issue."

Sometimes, standing hour after hour in the companion's rigid pose, his mind swimming with the boredom of the Councilors' ongoing conflict, it seemed to Konstant that these were not different meetings he attended, but an endless continuance of the same occasion, like an evil dream from which he could not wake. Each Councilor owned a particular role, and the interaction between them was as unvarying as the mindfire that writhed above their heads. Jehan-Moro was the voice of liberal opposition. Monserrat, the Investigation-Master, was opposition's nemesis, with Rimmon, the Castellan, for his echo. Ciadh, when he could, played peacemaker. Jolyon and Marhalt stood apart—Jolyon because he was so often the subject of the Council's debates, Marhalt because he did not spend words where they did no good. The discord between these two, however, was palpable: it set an invisible stamp of unease across every meeting and formed the subtext of nearly every discussion.

"Perhaps that's a little strong, Jehan." Ciadh's tone was

conciliatory. "It's possible this proxy will go some way toward strengthening the Second's claim, but our challenge will still stand, and until it's resolved no confirmation can take place. It's the break with tradition that concerns me. This isn't an Investment, or an accession, or a bestowing of honor. It's the *Recreation*, the rarest and most sacred ceremony of our Order. If a Staff-Holder can voluntarily surrender participation to a proxy, what's to stop future members of the Council from attempting to compel it? If this duty can be relinquished out of necessity, what's to stop future Staff-Holders from rejecting others out of mere disinclination?" His eyes slid toward Jolyon, silent in his chair. "It seems a very dangerous precedent to set. This is a troubled time for the Arm, for our Order as a whole. To alter traditional practice at such a moment is to tempt chaos."

"Traditional practice was altered when we demanded Suborder status twenty-five years ago," said Rimmon. He was a square-jawed, thick-necked, bearded man, his sandy brows habitually drawn in a scowl. Though not as fanatical as his ally Monserrat, he was a strong supporter of the Reddened; the favor he gave them in matters of provisioning had occasioned some of the Council's more acrimonious disputes. "You didn't object then."

"That was an entirely different situation. There were valid reasons for the Arm not to be independent at the beginning, when the Order was still consolidating its rule within the world and methods of oversight had less precedent to guide them. But Zoster's writings clearly indicate that his ultimate goal was separation from the Journeyer Suborder."

"Yes, yes. We don't need a lecture on our Founder." Rimmon shifted irritably in his chair. "The point is that you've no objection to pitching out tradition when it suits you."

"As in some cases it does very well." Monserrat was dark and vulpine, with deepset eyes that gleamed like the water at the bottom of a well. Councilors were required to renounce their faction affiliations before taking office, but like so many regulations within the Arm of the Stone this meant little, and Monserrat was Red in all but name. "As in your challenge against the Second."

"There's precedent for our challenge." A flush had risen in Ciadh's thin cheeks. "You know the history as well as I do."

"Precedent for the challenge, but not for the form of it." Monserrat leaned forward in his chair. From his vantage point at Jolyon's back Konstant could only see the Investigation-Master in profile, but he had spent a year in Monserrat's service and was intimately familiar with the venom of his gaze. "Not once in Guardian history has any of the Councils appealed a challenge of succession to the Prior. For three years we've been waiting for a decision. In the meantime our discord has spread beyond these walls, forcing all the Arm to take sides. Chaos is already among us, Ciadh. You and your cohorts have put it there."

"Yes, we have done that." Ciadh sat pressed against the back of his chair, as if Monserrat's regard were a physical force that held him there. The chain of his medal was twisted all the way around his fist. "And a bitter thing it was."

"It isn't the disagreement of this Council that's set our Suborder at odds," Jehan-Moro said angrily to Monserrat. "It's the excesses of the Reddened, and well you know it."

"The Reddened pursue orthodoxy." Monserrat turned his shining gaze on the Limit-Master. "The preservation of orthodoxy is the charge of the Arm."

"Is the Arm's charge the levying of mass executions? The razing of villages? The torture of Journeyers?"

"Please." Monserrat held up his hands. "We've already heard this speech."

" 'Where orthodoxy is at stake, no method is unthinkable,' " said Rimmon. "Zoster's words."

" 'Investigation is the master, judgment and punishment only servants.' " Jehan-Moro turned on him. " 'Beware that time and practice do not embolden the servants to steal the master's place.' Zoster's words also."

" 'In enforcement as in medicine, the greater danger of cautery is not to burn too much, but too little.' "

" 'Obedience takes many forms, and of all these forms

the least reliable is that which springs from fear—' "

"Enough!" The Staff-Holder's voice cut through Jehan-Moro's. "Divided we may be, but we are still a Council. Let us behave as one!"

Silence fell. Konstant still could not see Jolyon's face, yet he knew precisely how Jolyon must look: the still features, the distant gaze, fixed not upon the other Councilors but on some indeterminate point of space. There was a quality of otherworldliness to Jolyon; in repose he often looked as if he were dreaming, transported through the power of his imagination to some luminous place only he could see. But this was illusion. Jolyon was never less than fully, furiously present: marking every moment, cataloging every conversation, incising upon his prodigious memory every slight, every disagreement, every ill-considered word.

"Perhaps the decision need not be made now." Once again it was Ciadh, the conciliator, who broke the silence. "The Prior is gravely ill, it's true. But he's been ill before, and has recovered. Perhaps he'll rally this time also."

"No," Monserrat said. "This sickness is not like the others. Even the Speakers admit it."

"The Prior's death is a certainty," said Rimmon. "I applaud the Staff-Holder's foresight in making ready for it. I declare myself in full agreement with his designation of the Second as proxy for the Ceremony of Recreation. If it serves to resolve the issue of succession, so much the better. I'm sick to death of this dispute."

"I declare myself in agreement also," said Monserrat, "although it makes no difference whether we agree or not, since the Staff-Holder's decision in this matter is not contingent upon the approval of the Council. He has presented it to us as a courtesy, and allowed our comments as a courtesy also—more courtesy, I might add, than has been shown by some of us."

"Are you the Staff-Holder's proxy too, then, Monserrat?" asked Jehan-Moro acidly. "Or are you trying on the role of Second—to which, no doubt, you expect Jolyon to appoint you once the Ceremony is done?"

Monserrat's head snapped round like a snake's. But what he might have said was never heard. The Staff-Holder brought his staff down upon the floor with a force that seemed enough to crack the stone. The staffs of the office, created by the Staff-Holders as part of their accession ceremonies, were imbued with the spirits and Gifts of the men who held them. Even in the baffled room that power could be felt, shaking the air like a distant explosion.

"Be silent!" the Staff-Holder cried, his pain and fatigue briefly banished by rage. "I have adjured you once; I will not adjure you again. I will not have such conflict in my chamber!"

Jehan-Moro rose to his feet. He was a slender man, with patrician features and dark skin, across which the harsh mindfire cast a peculiar purplish sheen. He was closely allied with Marhalt, whose pupil he had been; it was he and Marhalt, together with Ciadh, who had formally challenged Jolyon's right to take the place of the current Staff-Holder, deadlocking the Council three to three and making it impossible for Jolyon to accede by legal means.

"I will not be silent." His orator's voice pierced the pall of quiet the power-baffles laid across the room. "How can I be silent when I see our Order bleeding to death before my eyes? All across the world, the great bindings that are a tangible symbol of our authority are unraveling. Every year, more Journeyers and Soldiers abandon their vows, and fewer Gifted children stand for the Novice Examinations. And while we starve, the resistance groups grow fat—stealing the Gifts that should come to us, giving refuge to those who abandon us. It's no coincidence that there is more Violation now than ever before in the history of our Order. If things continue along this path, it will not be long before we lose the ability to fulfill even the diminished purpose our Order serves in the absence of That Which Was Most Precious to Us. And what will happen then? What will become of our world, and of the sacred mindpower we are sworn to protect?"

He leaned forward, placing his palms flat upon the blood-red surface of the council table. His shadow spread beneath him like an inkblot. "It would be easy to say—as some do—that it is the loss we sustained thirty years ago that has brought us to this pass. That our Order has become a hollow shell around an empty Garden, and it is this that drives us from our vows and weakens our will to hold our bindings. But I believe that it is our discord that shapes our present troubles. And what is the source of that discord? The Reddened, and the abominations they visit on the world in the name of orthodoxy. Who can deny that Journeyer teachers abandon their vows rather than face Reddened discipline? Who can deny that Journeyer administrators hang themselves rather than face Reddened audits? Who can deny that Soldiers fall on their swords rather than assist in Reddened punishments? And who can deny that in every Suborder, not just our own, Councilor stands against Councilor and Ordermen fight each other in the hallways in support or opposition to the Reddened?

"This man stands behind it all." He lifted his arm and pointed at Jolyon—a posed, melodramatic gesture that nevertheless carried a powerful burden of accusation. "This man, whose will the Reddened follow as they scorch the earth with their poisonous orthodoxy. This man, who even now maintains his ties to the Reddened leadership, in defiance of the ancient tradition that requires Councilors to renounce their partisan affiliations. Make no mistake. If this man becomes Staff-Holder, the Reddened take office with him. By the mindfire above our heads, I swear that while I live, it will not come to pass."

"Jehan-Moro." Marhalt's voice, light and calm, cut cleanly through the turgid flow of the Limit-Master's oratory. "Enough."

Konstant saw struggle in Jehan-Moro's face. Jehan-Moro was famously his own master, as arrogant in his way as Monserrat; he bowed to no one but the Prior and, by necessity, the Staff-Holder. Marhalt, however, commanded him. He dropped his pointing arm and reseated himself in his chair.

Marhalt stood. The Apprentice-Master was a living legend, so celebrated for the precedents he had set, the Violators he had caught, the handpower networks he had uncovered, that his name was famous even outside the secretive ranks of the Arm of the Stone. His influence now was not what it had been years ago. It was he who had fostered the man who would later steal the Stone, choosing him to be an Arm Apprentice, serving as his Mentor over the course of his education, protecting him in his subsequent controversial career. Marhalt was not alone in his failure to see the traitor's evil; but he had been closer to the traitor than anyone else, and though even Jolyon had never dared question his probity, it was a connection could not help but tarnish him. Still he commanded a following, Roundheads like Jehan-Moro, who remained defiantly moderate in the face of Red fanaticism. And his fame endured—as myth endures, and the deeds of heroes. In eclipse, he owned a freedom not available to many in the full sun of favor. The empty wall at his back was more than just a political statement: he was, quite simply, untouchable.

He was a gaunt man, his cropped hair white, his shoulders stooped. His skin had not creased with age, but thinned and tightened, so that through his living face the skull could be clearly seen. Just as he held aloof from the ostentatious luxury in which other Roundheads of his station lived, he had rejected the Roundhead addiction to youth; it was said that it was only Jolyon's accession to the Council that had caused him, reluctantly, to adopt the age-retarding techniques his colleagues used. Yet for all the frailty of his appearance, he was a man of immense personal power. It could be heard in his quietest word, perceived in his smallest gesture. When, as now, he spoke, it was as if all the light in the room turned his way.

"This decision will not have the result you intend." He addressed the Staff-Holder. "I understand what's truly being done here. I give notice now: I will not allow it."

"You overstep yourself, Apprentice-Master." Anger had briefly rallied the Staff-Holder, but it had also drained him. The arm that held the staff of office was visibly trembling. "You have no power to allow or disallow any decision of mine."

"It is not your decision I mean." In the deep silence, Marhalt turned to Jolyon. "I make you a promise. You shall not have the thing you seek. Upon the Stone I swear it."

The air in the room seemed to tremble. To protect the knowledge of the Stone's vanishment, strong inhibitions of secrecy were set on Guardians at their Investments. The Stone's loss was rarely alluded to aloud, and then only by means of euphemism. To invoke it as Marhalt had just done was a fearsome vow, far more binding than such an oath would have been in the days when the Stone still rested safe in its Garden.

Jolyon rose to his feet. He was a slight man, barely a head taller than the high back of his chair. Yet, like Marhalt, he conveyed a powerful sense of presence. Konstant had found it startling, when he first walked behind Jolyon as companion, to realize how small he actually was.

"Your threats mean nothing to me," he said. "The decision has already been made."

"No path is certain," Marhalt replied, "until it is fully traveled."

They faced each other. Under ordinary light Marhalt's eyes were an unusual shade of topaz, but beneath the white-hot mindfire, they blazed like molten gold. There was a unique intensity to his regard; even a man as vicious as Monserrat could not hold it without flinching. Jolyon did not flinch. He was, arguably, the most powerful man in the Arm of the Stone, not just in the temporal sense but in Gift as well. But of all people in the world, Marhalt was the only one, perhaps, he feared. It was Jolyon, at last, who broke the gaze, turning his face aside. Konstant saw him in profile, pale as the veins in the marble table, his mouth tight with rage.

Marhalt turned and moved toward the door. Jehan-Moro followed, his companions surging forward to surround him, two in front and two behind. After a hesitation Ciadh rose also, his three companions at his side. The door swung open, revealing the red-draped hall beyond; the Councilors passed through it, and were gone.

Silence fell. The Staff-Holder, the remaining Councilors, the impassive companions, formed a motionless tableau. Only the mindfire moved, following the mindless pattern of its dance; and the staff of office, shaking in the Staff-Holder's exhausted grip.

"Assist him."

Jolyon's tone was commanding yet careless, like the snap

of fingers. Two of the Staff-Holder's five companions moved forward, grasping the old man by the arms and maneuvering him gently into his chair. He fell heavily on the seat, closing his eyes and leaning his head against the jeweled back. His face was deathly pale.

"That went badly," said Rimmon.

"I disagree," said Monserrat. "We knew how they were likely to react. Anyway, it makes no difference. The thing is accomplished now, and there's nothing they can do about it—other than orate, of course, which to my mind is quite as bad as anything else."

"They could break the Council."

"No," said Jolyon. He had seated himself again. "They won't do that."

"How can you be sure?" Rimmon's brows were knotted in more than his usual scowl. "It's the obvious solution. It's the only thing that could bar the Suborder from participating in the ceremony. By the Founder, Marhalt practically promised to do it. 'Jolyon shall not have what he seeks,' he said. What else could he mean?"

"Not that, Rimmon." Jolyon's voice was chilly, precise. "A Council unmade can only be remade by the Prior's decree. At the moment, for all intents and purposes, there is no Prior. If the Council is dissolved now, it won't be reconstituted until after the Ceremony. Marhalt had the sympathy of this Prior, but the next one . . ." A pause. Konstant could see, clear in his mind's eye, the curving smile that accompanied it. "Who knows? He'd have no guarantee of finding himself on the Council at all. No. He's as wedded to power as any of us, for all his famous asceticism. He won't willingly sacrifice his authority, even in hatred of me."

"He intends something, Jolyon. He swore it on That Which Was Most Precious to Us."

"He can swear all he likes. The Stone is no longer here to listen to his oaths." Beside Jolyon, Monserrat turned his face away, and Rimmon shifted uneasily in his chair. These were hardened veterans of interrogation and torture, of mindkills and executions. Yet neither one of them would have been capable of invoking the Stone as casually as

Jolyon had just done. "Don't tell me you fear that old man."

"Fear him?" Rimmon said. "No. But I don't dismiss him, either. He's not the power he was, but he's still a force to be reckoned with."

"Let me worry about Marhalt." Konstant could hear the closure in Jolyon's voice. Evidently Rimmon heard it, too. Silence fell once more—a death of sound, a weight upon the ears.

Of all the men who had been in this room, there were only seven who were privy to the real purpose behind what had just occurred: Jolyon because the purpose was his, Monserrat and Rimmon because they were his allies, Baffrid and Saranero and Ruen because they knew all their master's business. And Konstant, because he had stolen the knowledge from their minds. Even so, before this meeting Konstant would not have thought it possible that the other Councilors could fail to perceive the implications of the Staff-Holder's action. Over the tedious hours of the meeting he had waited for someone, anyone, to speak them. But, except perhaps for Marhalt with his promise at the end, even Jehan-Moro had not seemed to look beyond Jolyon's long struggle for succession within the Arm of the Stone.

It was known that the Staff-Holder, prior to this assignment of proxy, had intended to bind himself by the long-standing tradition that decreed the Arm's participation in the Recreation be purely ceremonial—a restriction that, like the Arm's subjugation to the Suborder of Journeyers, reflected the first Guardians' belief that enforcement should be paramount within the world, but never within the Order itself. Yet who, knowing Jolyon, could imagine that he would limit himself in this way? Who could fail to understand that, once inside the Amphitheater, he would use all his strength and all his guile to remake the Staff of Order himself? Did the other Councilors truly fail to see this? Did they see it and not believe it? Or did they fear it too much, perhaps, to utter it aloud?

Konstant felt urgency rise in him, a goad to motion more painful than the restlessness of his aching limbs. The Prior was dying. Time was dwindling. When would he receive what he waited for?

"Are we finished here?" Jolyon asked.

"Yes," said Monserrat. Rimmon nodded.

Jolyon addressed the Staff-Holder's companions. "You may remove him."

The elaborate chair was also a litter. Four of the companions lifted it. The fifth took the staff of office, easing it gently from the Staff-Holder's fingers. He did not stir. They left the chamber, the fifth companion walking at the rear, the staff cradled reverently in his arms.

Monserrat and Rimmon got to their feet. Their companions swept forward to surround them. Jolyon rose as well; Konstant and his fellows positioned themselves around the Second in a diamond shape, with Konstant bringing up the rear. In procession, the Councilors left the room. As he stepped into the hall, Konstant felt the bite of the powerful illusion-stripper webbed across the doorway, keyed to destroy any semblance or visual deception that might attempt to pass it—another of the many safeguards that protected this room and what went on inside it. It was one of the few occasions when he found it possible to contemplate the disguise he wore—the excess of flesh, the painful distortion of his features—with anything other than loathing.

Still, he had reason to be thankful. He had suffered in the Fortress. He had seen others do terrible things, and had done them himself. Yet he had recovered a thing he thought had drifted forever beyond his reach: belief. Belief was what made it possible to endure. Belief was what made it possible to wait.

Six

THE ROUNDHEAD Council moved along the walkway that bound the Speaker Wing to the Keep of the Arm of the Stone. The walkway, power-made of a glassy milk-white material that resembled nothing in nature, was raised high above ground level and wrapped in weather-bindings to keep it clear of ice and snow. Its edges were set with ribbons of mindlight, glowing silver now against the descending evening. The little clusters of black-robed Councilors and their companions maintained a steady pace, strung out at precisely regular intervals, like a necklace of jet beads. They proceeded in order of precedence: the Staff-Holder first in his carrying-chair, followed by Jolyon, then Monserrat, then Rimmon, then Jehan-Moro, then Cidha. Marhalt, a lone dark figure, brought up the rear.

Konstant moved at Jolyon's back. Just ahead and to his left and right, Saranero and Ruen maintained side-guard, while Baffrid, in the lead, walked point. All were tall, burly men: at the center of the diamond-shape they made, Jolyon floated like a jewel in a box, dwarfed by the container that protected him. The walkway's bindings did not mitigate the biting cold, but it was welcome after the heat of the ante-chamber in which Konstant and the others had spent most of the day, waiting while the Councils of Six assembled inside the dying Prior's bedchamber, in accordance with the tradition that required the leadership of all the Suborders to bear witness to the last breath of their ruler. But death, which had seemed certain that morning, did not arrive. Just before the sixteenth bell the Councils emerged, their faces grim. It was weeks since the Prior had slipped into this final illness—too sick to govern, yet ruler until the moment of his death. Even the Suborder of Searchers, the Order's unworldly corps of scholars and teachers, was beginning to become impatient.

Ahead, the Keep gleamed against the deepening darkness, a precisely angled cube of pure white stone, as if the snow had been gathered up and shaped to form a dwelling. Its windows blazed with illumination—the warm glow of candles, the pale refulgence of mindlight. Red flags fluttered from its ebony sills and from the inky crenellations of its roof. Though it seemed as fixed and permanent as the Fortress's ancient walls, in fact the Keep was less than thirty years old. The Arm had built it soon after its separation from the Journeyer Suborder, as a headquarters more fitting to its new status than the portion of the Journeyer Wing it had occupied since its founding. The architecture of the Suborder Wings—a hollow square enclosing the Garden of the Stone—meant that the Keep could not be incorporated into the original design. Rather than annex itself like some poor relation, the Arm had chosen to emphasize its separation. A quarter mile divided the Keep from the Wings of the other Suborders. The walkway, its far end linked to the Speaker Wing by a gated entrance of the Arm's design, was the only access.

The Keep's great doors swung open to receive the Council. Beyond lay the entrance lobby, a huge room with walls swathed in scarlet tapestries and dozens of chandeliers pendant from the ceiling, each enclosed in a bubble of ruby-colored glass. The light they cast was both murky and inflamed, like the dreams of fever; the shadows here were not black but deep maroon. At the chamber's midpoint an enormous sphere of blood-dark garnet hung halfway between floor and ceiling, riding the air as gently as an illusion. A dark radiance shuddered at its heart. Whether this was a reflection of the chandeliers, or some property of the jewel itself, Konstant had never been able to tell.

The Council passed through the lobby, the little groups maintaining their measured separation, and began to mount the black marble staircase that rose at its far end. The upper levels of the Keep—the second, with its offices and work-rooms and refectories, and the third, where the living quarters were—were closed to all but Roundheads. Outsiders were received on the first level, in rooms and offices kept exclusively for that purpose. Because those who entered here must not be allowed to forget where they were and who received them, the spaces were equipped and deco-rated almost entirely in shades of red: tawny carnelians and fiery rubies, smoky maroons and pulsing vermilions, violent carmines and incandescent cerises, corals as translucent as a sunset sky and crimsons as angry as contusions. What was not red was black, like the Roundheads' robes, or with-out hue, ivory and cream and alabaster. It was a color scheme so oppressive that even members of the Arm found it difficult to endure. On the upper levels it was not con-sidered necessary to maintain such ubiquity of red.

On the third floor the procession broke, and each group took its own way along the snaking corridors. In contrast to the richness of the floors below, the third was entirely func-tional, the unadorned stone-block passages illuminated by globes of mindlight and lined with plain red-painted doors. This unpretentious appearance was deceptive. Behind the modest entrances, lavish suites and opulent apartments were filled to overflowing with the personal possessions of the Arm of the Stone, the largest accumulation of private wealth in the world. Not even Ciadh, the Treasurer, knew the sum of the riches gathered here, the reckoning of nearly ten centuries of property seizures and asset forfeitures, con-ciliatory gifts and special tributes, official confiscations and unauthorized appropriations and outright theft.

As Second, Jolyon was entitled to one of the most ex-travagant of the third-floor apartments. Its red door, distin-guishable as his only by the coded symbols above it, had no handle, lock, or latch, and could be opened only by means of a handshaped piece of metal bound to the touch of those authorized to come and go.

Baffrid, in the lead, set his palm in the proper place. The door swung open. Crossing the threshold, Konstant felt the shock of power. Three bindings were webbed across the entrance: an illusion-stripper similar to the one that guarded the Council chamber, a metal-warding set to detect the presence of iron, and an identity-fixer that nullified the warding for the heavily armed companions and Jolyon himself. Jolyon's suite was crowded with such precautions, barriers and guards and screens and traps designed to eliminate semblances, detect surreptitious uses of power, and immobilize would-be attackers.

In the reception chamber—resplendently furnished and carpeted, with fountains of mindlight cascading down the walls—the companions broke their close diamond-shape.

"Stay here," Jolyon told them. Roundheads in general had a dread of mental incursion, but the Reddened, who harvested minds like ripe fruit, had a particular horror of it. Among themselves they used only voicespeech. "I may need you later on."

Konstant and the others nodded. They would wait now— perhaps for an hour, perhaps for much longer, until Jolyon either called them or set them free. A companion voluntarily accepted the task of preserving the life and safety of the man to whom he vowed himself, accompanying his charge wherever he went, watching for danger at his back and measuring risk ahead of him. Yet the mere fact of the companions' presence eliminated most peril. During the six months he had spent with Jolyon, Konstant had neutralized no threats, foiled no attacks. The major part of his duty was waiting—with Jolyon or for him, during meetings and ceremonies and celebrations, through minutes and hours, nights and days. This, one of the least distasteful aspects of his masquerade, had proved one of the most difficult. In his room at night Konstant paced, often for hours, expending between wall and wall the need for motion he could not indulge during the day.

"Talesin."

Jolyon spoke Konstant's false name, indicating by a gesture that Konstant should follow. He led the way through the reception chamber and into the hallway beyond, splendidly appointed with hangings and carpets and lamps. Doors on either side gave onto the luxurious rooms of the companions and the small private refectory where they took their meals. At the hallway's end was the entrance to Jolyon's personal suite. The barrier that blocked it was faintly visible against the wood of the door, an oily rippling like the dance of heat on flat rocks. It was designed to plunge a barb of power into the minds of all who passed, in search of barriers or guards that might conceal treacherous intent.

Konstant carried such guards. The first time he had come here, to swear the oath of fealty Jolyon required of all his companions, he had not been certain he would pass the barrier. Goldwine's power-techniques had been extensively tested on ordinary Guardian makings, but they had rarely been set against those of the Arm of the Stone. He could still remember the fear he had felt as the barrier bit into his mind; it had been all he could do not to break the poison capsule he carried beneath his tongue. But he passed undiscovered. This barrier, though Roundhead-made, was keyed as much as any other to the patterns of Guardian Gifts. Konstant's defenses, made as Goldwine had taught him, followed different patterns, and were invisible to it.

The door swung open at Jolyon's approach. The office beyond was huge and low. A pair of standing candelabra at its far end provided a feathery and uncertain light. Amid the shadows, the mass of Jolyon's possessions bulked from wall to wall, like the wrack of some strange treasure-storm: paintings, sculptures, tapestries, furniture, porcelain, jeweled plate, intricately-woven rugs, open chests spilling rainbows of filmy fabric, closed chests whose contents could only be guessed at. These beautiful things were thrown haphazardly together, stacked and piled without system or care. Dust blurred every surface, quenching the light of gems and tarnishing the gleam of metal. The air was stale, redolent of mold and dryrot, with fleeting undernotes of cedar and sandalwood, of incense stored too long and perfume left to go rancid.

There were many stories about the ways in which Jolyon had amassed this careless wealth: tales of annexation and execution, of huge forfeitures and desperate gifts of supplication. No one knew which or how many were true. It was the same with much of Jolyon's history. It was variously said that he was a pampered scion of one of the most ancient of the mindpower lineages, or a child of the gutters who had been put to prostitution when he was six years old; that he had been the lowest-ranked of his Apprentice class, or one of the most stellar; that from boyhood he had been fanatically celibate, or that during his time in the field he had routinely raped his interrogation subjects, man and woman, young and old; that he mindprobed for sport, or for sexual pleasure; that he could hear what others thought about him; that he was capable of drawing others' Gifts into himself, and punishing them through their own power. Jolyon made no attempt to counter the rumors, even revolting as some of them were. In fact, it would not have surprised Konstant to learn that he was the source of many of them: they served him as effectively as his guards and barriers did, a wall of cautionary wisdom that kept others at a distance, and invested his every word and action with fearful significance.

A wide mahogany desk occupied a small clear space at the back of the room. Jolyon seated himself behind it. There was no other chair: Konstant stood, waiting. He was aware, without thinking of it, of the swiftness of his heartbeat, the tension in his muscles. He had entered these gloomy chambers many times over the past months, but it never became easier to stand before the Second, the sole focus of the raging mind behind that dreaming face. He was often tempted to reach out his Gift and prepare himself for whatever it was Jolyon wanted; but though he regularly penetrated the minds around him, though he was capable of a dozen different levels of incursion, from the lightest thought-skimming to a focused search, he did not dare try such methods on the Second. Another of the rumors held that Jolyon, phenomenally Gifted, was so sensitive to mental incursion he could detect even the intent.

As if in answer to a call, the door to the bedchamber swung open, revealing another crowded tenebrous space. Out of the shadows slipped a shadowy man, hardly taller than a child, with the tan skin, inky hair, and tilted eyes of the far eastern kingdoms. Jolyon glanced at him, and flicked his fingers toward the bedchamber, a gesture that caused his many jeweled rings to flash with color. The little man turned and merged once more with the darkness.

He was Jolyon's bodyservant, and something more, though how much more, and what the more consisted of, no one really knew. Some said he was Jolyon's paramour, others that he was the Second's personal assassin. There were those who swore he was a revenant, a corpse raised and kept animate by its master's will—a theory not so far-fetched among the Reddened, where no other servant could offer such a perfect degree of trust. Except for Council meetings, and ceremonial occasions like the one today, he accompanied Jolyon everywhere, standing at the Second's back during banquets and gatherings and audiences, sitting on a stool at Jolyon's knee while Jolyon worked in his official office on the second floor. No one knew his name, or even if he had one. He was not part of the regular Fortress servant corps, but an outsider Jolyon had brought with him when he returned from field duty to take up his administrative career. Jolyon himself had trained him. It was said that the Second had gone several steps beyond the usual conditioning, making the little man incapable not merely of speaking about his master's business, but about anything at all. Certainly no one had ever heard him say a word.

The servant reappeared, carrying a small leather bag, which he brought over to the desk and laid by Jolyon's hand. He positioned himself behind his master's chair, arms folded and legs slightly apart. His black eyes rested unblinking on Konstant's face.

"I have a task for you," Jolyon said.

"I'm at your disposal, Second."

"It must be carried out immediately. Whatever commitments you have, from this moment they do not exist. Is that clear?"

A companion was not a servant, who owed duty to his master, but a man of rank and privilege who voluntarily offered allegiance to another. Yet the cold command in Jolyon's voice barely acknowledged that. The Second used this tone toward everyone who was not his equal, even Baffrid, who had been vowed to him for close to twenty years. With his peers he used a slightly wider variety of expression: derision, contempt, anger, or, for those who were closest, a kind of chilly familiarity. Konstant had never encountered a person so entirely concentrated within a single range of feeling. Even Monserrat, unpleasant as he was, was capable of flashes of humor, moments of consideration. Such impulses were utterly foreign to Jolyon. He did not reject or suppress them; they simply were not there.

"I'm ready at once, Second," Konstant said.

Jolyon turned and pulled an oilcloth folder out of the document case behind him. Placing it on the desk, he began to leaf through it. His nails were savagely bitten, ringed with raw flesh and dried blood; he often left red marks on the things he handled, a signature as personal as his name.

"I've been looking into your background."

Konstant realized that this was his personnel file. Pressure bloomed inside his chest: the dread of discovery that never entirely left him. Perhaps the task Jolyon wanted of him would not take him outside this room. Self-execution was one of the Second's preferred ways of dealing with problems of loyalty.

"Your dossier indicates that you have crossing experience."

Like physicians monitoring the progress of a disease, the Arm of the Stone regularly sent exploratory expeditions into the handpower world. Talesin, the man whose identity Konstant had stolen, had participated in two of these cross-world missions. Konstant took a deep, silent breath, trying to slow the sudden pounding of his heart.

"Yes, Second. I have."

"Each time you remained for just over three weeks. It says here that you suffered few ill-effects, and that for each trip you needed less than a week of recovery time."

"I have strong shielding ability, Second. Better than most."

"On both occasions you traveled with companions."

"Yes, Second. The standard party of six."

"What if you were ordered to go alone?"

Konstant felt heat rise up from the soles of his feet to the crown of his head. He was grateful, as he found he sometimes unwillingly must be, for the side-effects of the bone-shifting changes Malinides had worked on him: the diminished mobility of the heavy features, the coarsened skin that could no longer gain or lose color.

"I don't believe that would present any difficulty, Second."

Jolyon picked up the sheets he had been examining. He tapped them on the surface of the desk to align them, then returned them to the folder, tying up the laces that held it closed. He folded his bitten hands on top of it and fixed his gaze on Konstant's face.

"You know that two crossings are the official maximum permitted to any Guardian."

"That rule exists to protect those who are weaker, Second. I am stronger. A third crossing would pose no more threat to me than the two before."

"You'd be deprived of the additional barrier-strength offered by companions. That would substantially increase the risk."

"The assistance of companions isn't necessary for me. The second time I crossed, I made several unaccompanied excursions. I found maintaining a solo barrier much easier than meshing my power with others', and attempting to make up for their deficiencies."

Jolyon studied him. The candles, fluttering in a breeze that could not be felt, brushed light and shadow across his face: the pale eyes with their heavy, curved lids, the arching brows, the finely sculpted nose, the straight and serious mouth. Jolyon was seventy if he was a day, but in appearance he did not seem a minute over twenty-five. Like all Roundheads he held fast to youth, manipulating his body through his Gift to keep his skin unlined and perfect, his teeth white and even, his fox-colored hair untouched by gray. He moved with the ease of a young man; his voice too was curiously youthful, sour as an adolescent's, a strange contrast to the graceful tranquillity his face reflected in repose.

"From time to time," he said, "I send men on cross-world missions. Alone. These aren't official missions. They concern the business of the Arm, but I'm the only one who knows of them. If you go, you will be obliged to keep that secret."

"I'll swear by any oath you wish, Second." Unlike those who had gone before him, Konstant was aware that Jolyon was talking about something more permanent than discretion. His cross-world agents did not survive their debriefings.

"You know that since the Stone was stolen from the Fortress by the traitor and apostate called Selwyn Forester, the assembled Councils of the five Suborders have regularly sent Roundhead search parties into the other world. You know that all these expeditions have failed, and that no trace of either the Stone or the traitor has ever been found."

Konstant had never encountered anyone outside Goldwine's resistance who spoke of the Stone with the casual ease Jolyon employed—as if it were not a sacred object or an aching void of loss, but merely an artifact, like the chair he sat in. "Of course, Second."

"What you don't know is that for the past thirty years I've been searching also, in my own way, and with my own men. That is the task I wish you to undertake."

Konstant, who had long ago decided how he would react to this revelation when it was offered to him, shifted his unresponsive features toward an expression of amazement. "A *second* search?"

"Yes." Jolyon regarded him, as if assessing his sincerity. "When the Stone vanished, I suspected at once where Selwyn must have taken it. I knew him, you see. I knew the blasphemy that filled him to the core of his evil being, I knew how little he cared for the precious powers we guard for this world's use. When he vanished, I knew that in his rottenness he must have sought the handpower world. Corruption to corruption—it makes perfect sense. But the Councils couldn't accept it. They couldn't believe that even a Violator like Selwyn Forester would take the Stone into that world, knowing it might be destroyed by the forces there. They were sure he was still here, hiding in some wilderness.

"I didn't wait for them to see their mistake. I began to send my own men through the Gates. I went on sending them even after the Councils recognized their error and began to search as they should have from the beginning. I did not—do not—trust the Councils' resolve. By the time they looked to the other world, many of them had concluded that it was already too late, that the traitor was dead and the Stone with him. Over the years this belief has infected all of them. There's not one Councilor, today, who thinks the Stone will be found intact. There are even some who say the search should be abandoned, that it would be better to leave the Stone in the grave of that evil world than to bring it back to this one as a lifeless hunk of rock."

He leaned forward in his chair. His heavy lids had lifted as he spoke. His eyes were gooseberry-green, with pinpoint pupils like black seeds, the whites overlaid by a tracery of veins.

"I do not agree. Whether or not the Stone is dead, Selwyn Forester still lives. I know that beyond the shadow of a doubt—my men have brought me confirmation of it. His survival is an abomination, a mockery of everything the Order of Guardians stands for. The Councils have lost heart for the search. It's little more than a formality for them now. But my search is a true search, with true tools and true goals." His voice had dropped. "And it will succeed. I will find him, or I will find his bones."

In the simmering silence Konstant found that he was sweating, as if the temperature in the room had risen. He knew the story behind the story he had just been told; he had heard it from the daughter of the man who was the target of Jolyon's obsessive search. He was aware that it was personal hatred that drove the Second, as much as, or perhaps more than, the honor of the Guardians and the loss of the Stone. But no one who did not know this would have heard it in the cold precision of Jolyon's words, or read it in the porcelain stillness of his features.

Jolyon reached out and took up the leather bag his servant had brought. He loosened the laces and turned what was inside onto the surface of his desk: a small globe of smoky glass, enclosing a bright sifting of gold flakes and attached by a glass loop to a silver chain.

"I give all my agents a tracking device like this one," he

said. "It's based on the devices Investigators use to retrieve fugitive Violators. Conventional trackers use only things of the body, hair or fingernail parings or bits of skin, but this one holds something much more powerful—shavings of gold from Selwyn's Guardian medallion. When the Stone was still in this world, its power was used to bind a Guardian's medallion to him at Investment, to his heart and to his spirit. Just as someone who loses an arm will feel bone and tissue that is no longer there, this gold yearns for the man who once wore it. In the other world, it will sense his presence and try to be united with him. If you focus your Gift on that yearning, it'll tell you how to go."

He lifted the talisman, turning it to the waxy candle flames. Light played across the glass, and shimmered on the imprisoned gold. Jolyon's face was the face of a sleeper, of a man dreaming a long, slow dream, immune to change or the passage of time.

"This is yours now." He raised his green eyes to Konstant's. "Come and take it."

Konstant stepped forward, stretching out his hand. Jolyon set the talisman on Konstant's palm, grasping Konstant's hand in both of his own and closing Konstant's fingers around the glass. His grip was dry and very cold. Without warning it tightened; he pulled Konstant violently forward, bowing him across the desk.

"Swear an oath to me." His face was inches from Konstant's own. His lips had drawn back from his teeth. "Swear that you will give yourself body and soul to the quest I've given you. Swear that you will hold nothing back from me when you return. Swear that you will not speak your knowledge to any living soul but me. Swear it on the thing you hate most in all the world."

His eyes were fully open now. His gaze boiled. For an instant Konstant saw, as Jolyon meant him to, what moved behind it: the blood, the hatred, the appetite.

"I swear as you command," he whispered. "I swear on what I hate most in all the world."

A moment passed, another. Jolyon's hot gaze held Konstant fixed, like a weight to a plumb line. He was afraid now, afraid as he had never been in all the weary time he

served this man. Jolyon's Gift opened out around him, a
black abyss into which he might plunge forever. His own
Gift burned in response, hot and high, responding to the
hungry pull of that darkness. In that instant he believed all
the stories he had heard about Jolyon's ability to summon
to himself the power of others, and more, to make them
want to yield to him, for with every nerve in his body he
felt the desire to reach out, to let go, to meet the Second's
Gift with the whole of his own . . . corruption to corruption,
as Jolyon had said . . .

Jolyon unbound his grip, of hand and eye, a release so
sudden that for an instant it seemed to Konstant he was
falling. He forced himself to straighten and move back. The
skin of his face felt tight, as if it had been burned. There
was a pain in his palm, clasped hard around the talisman.
He was aware, suddenly, of Jolyon's servant, whose black
gaze had not wavered since the interview began.

A white cloth lay to one side of the desk. Jolyon took it
up, rubbing it between his hands, as if to clean them.

"The talisman is bound to you now," he said. "Look at
it."

Konstant opened his hand. The glass, which had been
cloudy, was now as clear as water. There was a large red
mark in the center of his palm.

"Through your link with it, you'll be better able to sense
its link to him. Put it around your neck."

Konstant obeyed.

"Now," Jolyon said. "To logistics. You'll leave tomorrow. I've arranged an escort for you, men who have
crossing experience and can assist the Gatekeeper if there's
any difficulty. I've also prepared a map to show you how
and where the ones before you have gone." He gestured
toward the front of his desk, where a folded square of
parchment lay. "Add to it as you travel, to show your progress. Use farwalking to get to the point where the last agent
left off; after that, human means are best. The talisman is
certain, but you are going into an alien world, where any
use of your Gift means a struggle against the currents of
handpower, and you'll need all your resources to hear what
it tells you. You'll remain for two weeks—no more, no

less. At dawn on the day of your return the Gate will be opened for you once every hour, until darkness falls. If you haven't come through by then, we'll know you never will. Is this clear?"

"Yes, Second."

"One more thing." He was still cleaning his hands, passing the cloth over and over across his palms and through his fingers. "If by some chance you find the traitor, you might be tempted to try your strength against him. Resist. The handpower world has certainly made him Giftless, but there's no reason to think it's taken his intelligence. Even crippled, he's far cleverer than you. If you were to find him, only to lose him again . . . well. Let me just say that I would be displeased."

"I understand, Second."

Jolyon had finished with the cloth. He tossed it over his shoulder. His servant snatched it from the air, stowing it in the breast of his tunic and lapsing immediately back into stillness.

"Do you have anything to ask before you leave?"

"No, Second."

"Then we're finished here."

Konstant did not bow: Roundheads made obeisance to no one but the Prior and their own Staff-Holder. He stepped forward to take the parchment from Jolyon's desk and turned to go. He felt Jolyon's eyes on his back, and the servant's, a double gaze that somehow conveyed a single force. The doors swung open. He passed through them, feeling the barrier stab harmlessly into his mind.

Moving down the hallway, he had the sensation, as he always did when exiting Jolyon's rooms, of waking from a dream. Or of passing back into the known world, from which, for the moments he spent in Jolyon's presence, he had been entirely removed.

Konstant did not join the other companions, but went directly to his rooms. Baffrid, Saranero, and Ruen would not miss him. In the mistrustful world of the Reddened they were allies; they had accepted him among them because he was Jolyon's choice, but they had not opened the closed circle of their personal association to him, for they knew as well as he did why he had been chosen and that he would soon be gone. Konstant was grateful for this. They were experienced Reds, these three, seething with fundamentalist fervor, their minds burning with the hideous images of their years as orthodoxers. Every moment spent in their presence reminded him of how near he had come to living such a life.

The sitting room of Konstant's suite was draped with hangings and strewn with carpets, furnished with chairs and tables and paintings that were each the highest example of the craftsman's art. Many were Talesin's own possessions, transferred from the personal store all Roundheads maintained in the Fortress; more were Jolyon's, the overflow of his congested rooms, on temporary loan to the men who shared his quarters. Globes of mindlight hung at the ceiling's four corners, their silvery radiance augmented by the wrist-thick candles set in holders on the tables. Beyond the half-open door lay a bedroom, smaller than the sitting room but just as richly furnished, centered by a great curtained bed. Its vast width was wasted on Konstant, who was required by his Roundhead disguise to forswear women and had no taste for men.

The rooms were empty: he had been promised a personal servant but had never been given one. In the bedchamber he removed the talisman from around his neck. He took off his jewelry—the ear-hoops, the neck-chains, the Guardian medallion, the emerald bracelet that had been Jolyon's gift to him—and placed it all in Talesin's jewel-case. As he closed the case he thought, as he sometimes did, of the man whose identity he had stolen. He did not know what the Zosterians had done with Talesin after Konstant acquired the contents of his mind and took his place; he assumed Talesin must be dead. Talesin had been as arrogant and intolerant as any Roundhead, but he had not been particularly vicious, nor had he supported the Reddened's agenda of fundamentalist reform. He would never have made of himself what Konstant, in his name, had become.

Konstant shed his heavy brocade robe, his black silk shirt and woolen breeches, and put on a sleeping shift and a belted wrapper. Taking the talisman, he returned to the sitting room, averting his eyes from the tall pier-glass by the door. He looked at his own reflection only by accident, or out of necessity. His mind retained, indelibly, the sense-memory of his true appearance, and it never became less shocking to see the coarse shape into which his own fine features had been twisted.

In the sitting room, he held Jolyon's talisman to the light, turning it in his fingers so that the flakes of gold fluttered and fell inside their tiny prison. The little object was solid against his skin; but he had waited for this moment for so long, imagined it so often, that it seemed the talisman might have been shaped by the power of his desire, and if he blinked or turned away it would vanish. He felt the throbbing in his palm, where the red mark of Jolyon's binding had begun to blister: that, at least, was undeniably real.

Tomorrow, he thought. Tomorrow I will be gone from here.

He set the talisman gently on a table. The glass was not quite a perfect sphere; it wobbled for a moment before subsiding into stillness. Turning away, he began to pace, back and forth across the room. Normally an hour of this was enough to tire him, so that he could roll into his lonely bed and sleep for a little while. But tonight his craving would not be satisfied, and he moved from wall to wall like someone cursed by a malign compulsion of perpetual motion.

He had not always been so restless. As a boy it had not been difficult for him to stand still, to hold back, to wait. But since the winter night when he left the Fortress and his Roundhead Apprenticeship behind, immobility had become a torment for him, as if the understandings that cut short his Guardian career had also severed whatever it was within him that tethered him to quiet.

He had truly wanted death that night. The snow received him like a longed-for embrace, the profoundest cold he had ever known, cold enough to quench even the superheated fires of his Gift. He waited until he felt them dying before he himself let go, and spiraled down into darkness. His awakening, in a dim rocky place he did not recognize, was the single worst moment of his life. The strangers who tended him had to tie him to his bed to prevent him from going out again into the snow.

Over the days that followed they cared for him, salving and bandaging his cold-ravaged limbs, feeding him through a tube when he refused to eat. He had no idea who they were, these hard-faced men and women, nor why they were so determined he should live. They did not explain; instead, they talked to him about his flight into the night. It was not truly death he had been seeking, they told him, but liberation. Here, with them, he could be free.

He had no interest in what they said. When they told him the Stone was gone he laughed, for he already knew. When they claimed that they had been Apprentices, he turned away in disbelief. But they persisted, invoking details of the Fortress and its ways no outsider could possess, and at last, reluctantly, he began to listen. Like him, they said, they had succumbed to disillusion. Like him, they had gone out onto the snow in search of death. Like him, they had been saved and brought to this dark place—where, with the help of their rescuers, they found their way back to belief, a new set of convictions founded, paradoxically, on the understandings that had killed the old. If he wished, he too could make this journey. If he let them, they would show him how.

He was aware that they used mindtouch, reaching inside his head to increase the impact of their words. He could have prevented this if he had wanted to. He could have seized their Gifts with his own and shown them what it was really like to tamper with the structures of a mind. But he did not. In the phrases of their faith, he could not help but hear the echoes of truths he himself had seen. From his own painful understanding of the corruption of the system of which he had been a part, to his captors' intense vision of the need for its overthrow, was not after all such a large step. Slowly, in the darkness of his despair, a small flame of hope began to burn. He began to see the possibility of an allegiance different from any he had ever imagined. He began to see that he might, as they promised, remake himself; and, in the reconstruction, leave his past behind.

He learned later that everyone brought in by Goldwine's

rescue patrols underwent a similar experience, a process of deindoctrination Goldwine and her people called reclaiming. Those who came through it were invited, after a series of mindscans to confirm the validity of their conversion, to join Goldwine's cave-bound army. Those who did not, or who refused the offer, were memory-killed and returned to the snows.

Eight months after his rescue, Konstant became a full-fledged member of the resistance. He embarked upon an intensive course of training in the exacting techniques of power Goldwine had developed. Eventually, because of the subtlety and strength of his Gift of mindspeech, he was made a reclaimer himself. In his best moments, he felt reborn. He had a place again, a purpose. When he looked inside his mind he was able to find belief—not as easy or unquestioned as it had been in his Guardian days, but more precious, because he had won it for himself. In his worst moments he felt like a fraud, someone who had pulled a new and glittering garment over the same filthy rags he had always worn. Throwing away his Apprentice medal and adopting a new philosophy had not, after all, made him a different person, any more than teaching his Gift to flow in new channels and turning it to different uses could change its nature.

The fear of discovery haunted him. It had not been difficult to mask his deepest secrets from Goldwine's reclaimers, for Goldwine's mindscans were kinder than the Guardians' mindprobes, and much easier for someone skilled in the ways of mindcontact to outwit. Yet he knew that his Roundhead experience, as well as his reticence about it, caused him to be widely mistrusted. How long would it be before someone guessed the truth that lay at the center of his beautiful disguise? Worse, he was restless. The spaces inside the hollow mountain were by no stretch of the imagination claustrophobic, yet frequently he felt confined, as if there were not enough air to breathe. The work he did, slow and painstaking and precise, made him feel as if he had been ordered to build a haystack by laying down individual pieces of straw. Nor was he completely comfortable with the nature of it. It was a clean use of his power, perhaps the cleanest he had ever experienced. Yet it required him to go very deep into the minds of his subjects, and he was no longer at ease with such incursion.

He often thought that Goldwine, who from the beginning had taken an interest in him, and with whom he had voluntarily shared some of his personal history, understood a good part of his discomfort. But she would not, in spite of his entreaties, send him out into the world. After five years he could no longer fight the urge to flight. He half-expected her to refuse his request for severance, but she let him go without protest.

"Usually I kill the memory of those who leave me," she told him. "But I won't do that to you. The time will come when you'll need your knowledge of me. When that moment comes, Konstant, don't hesitate to use it. A lot depends on it."

Goldwine rarely shared the insights of her Gift. There was no one, except perhaps her foster-daughter Cariad, who knew exactly what or how much she saw. But Konstant habitually skimmed the thoughts of those around him, and what he perceived now told him that his future, or some part of it, was known. He could still recall the dread that seized him. He left swiftly, before he was tempted to dip more deeply into her mind.

Among the Zosterians, to whom he attached himself once he reached the world, he was put to work as a debriefer, the Zosterian equivalent of Goldwine's reclaimers. He traveled widely, working with the defectors and supplicants gathered by the Zosterian convert strike forces. It seemed, initially, more congenial than the work he had done for Goldwine. The travel fed his need for motion, and because so much of the Zosterian core leadership had once been Arm of the Stone, his Roundhead background was not mistrusted. It was rare, also, that he was required to go very far into the minds of those he debriefed. Unlike Goldwine's converts, Zosterian recruits did not need to be persuaded to adopt an alternate belief system, but only to shift the beliefs they held into a slightly different shape.

But he had not anticipated how strange it would be to live again among people who were guided by Limits, even

Limits vastly relaxed and humanized by the Zosterian principles of responsibility and compassion. In this return to
the structures of his youth he discovered, belatedly, how
fully he had left them behind. Six months into his new
service, he understood with painful clarity that he had made
a mistake. Pride would not allow him to return to Goldwine, and he could not face the thought of going out purposeless into the world; so he remained with the Zosterians,
where at least he could continue to work toward the Guardians' downfall. But his restlessness worsened, and the feeling of imposture, the sense that the good things he did were
only a flimsy mask for his inner ugliness. More and more,
when he looked inside himself, it was difficult to find belief—not just in the goals of the resistance, but in anything
at all.

Five years after leaving Goldwine, he was approached
by a representative of the Zosterian Council, and asked to
volunteer for a dangerous undercover mission focused on
the Fortress. He agreed. Even when he learned that the
mission's target was the Reddened, and realized that Malinides—a man of great, if chilly, perception—had guessed
a good part of the truth about his past, he did not step away.
He had had enough of debriefing. He wanted change, a
chance to feel that what he was doing was worthwhile.
And, though he hardly dared admit it to himself, he wanted
hope. Hope that this task would be the one he sought, the
one that would remake him. Hope that in this journey back
to what he had fled ten years ago, he might find what so
far had eluded all his efforts: a chance to atone.

He had been instructed to proceed with the second stage
of his mission six months after arriving in the Fortress. But
it took him nearly a year to find the courage to follow
Malinides' secret order and become Red. This hard-won
status proved something of an anticlimax. Other than the
insignia he now wore, and required attendance at various
informational and propaganda meetings, his situation was
unchanged. He still spent his days in the office of the
Investigation-Master, receiving and classifying reports of
Violations and Investigations and tracking the movements
of Reddened orthodoxers; he still met with his servant con-

tact, Orrin, to pass on the information he gained; he was still far removed from the corridors of Reddened power, and in particular from the ultimate goal of his mission: Jolyon himself. He was aware that a request for transfer to the Second's office might be favorably received, for he had performed well at his dreadful initiation ceremony. But bureaucratic wheels ground slowly. It might be a year or more before such a request was processed and granted. The thought of remaining stationary for that long was intolerable. A more direct approach was required.

Opportunity presented itself in the form of an apostate Red named Rijalba. Rijalba, a former Primary of a band of orthodoxers and once a protégé of Jolyon himself, had publicly recanted his Red allegiance and aligned himself with the moderate Roundheads who spearheaded the opposition to Jolyon's accession. As a mark of favor, Jolyon had given Rijalba a pair of valuable gold-and-emerald bracelets. Several weeks after Rijalba's defection, he sent an envoy to demand them back. Rijalba refused, and wore the bracelets to a banquet the next evening, a deadly insult to the man whose will he had once sworn a blood-oath to follow. Jolyon could do nothing openly, for Rijalba had wisely claimed Marhalt's protection and had been officially received by the Prior. But it was known among the Reddened that Jolyon had set a bounty on Rijalba's head, and that the man who could kill the apostate would gain not just wealth but favor.

The following night Konstant wrapped himself in resistance-style invisibility, and shaped the whole of his Gift to Goldwine's ways of power. He walked past Rijalba's watchful guards, through the iron-wardings intended to block hostile entrance, through the barrier created to exclude all Gifts but Rijalba's—which, keyed to the currents of Guardian power, read Konstant as unGifted—and into Rijalba's unlocked bedroom. From his shoulder he took a cloak-brooch made of gold and sank its long pin into Rijalba's heart. The mind he had destroyed as the price of his Red initiation had cost him torments of guilt, but this killing affected him not at all. Apostate or not, Rijalba was an evil man, who by his arrogance had written his own death sen-

tence. He deserved exactly what he got. Konstant unclasped
the bracelets from Rijalba's wrists and returned the way he
had come.

Early the following morning he placed one of the bracelets in a silver box, attached a note identifying it as a gift
for the Second, and delivered the box to Jolyon's secretary.
He returned that afternoon, carrying the remaining bracelet.
By that time the news of Rijalba's death had spread
throughout the Keep. Konstant was ushered immediately
before Jolyon's First Deputy. Silently, he placed the second
bracelet on the Deputy's desk. The man picked it up, turning it over in his hands for a moment before speaking.

"Are you responsible for this?"

"I am."

"Can you prove it?"

"The man I took them from has a pinhole in his heart."

The Deputy gave him a long look. "Very well. You'll
hear from us."

Konstant returned to his ordinary duties. Seven days
passed—enough time for Jolyon's staff to look into his
background and research his false identity. On the eighth
day he received a notice of transfer, reassigning him to
Jolyon's staff, and an inventory of the goods and currency
that had been transferred to his Fortress store. There was
also a folder of land-deeds, each one annotated so that it
seemed to be a bequest or a favor-gift. He, or rather Talesin,
was now an extremely wealthy man.

For a week he received instruction in the cipher the Second used for his internal documents, then was set to work
in the Internal Violations Division, supervising the large
cadre of staff who maintained the Fortress' personnel files,
a traditional responsibility of Jolyon's position. The work
was hateful, even duller than his duties for Monserrat had
been; it brought him little closer to Jolyon, who rarely entered his official office and when he did was closeted in his
own rooms. But at last, three months after his transfer, a
cloth-wrapped package appeared on Konstant's desk, together with a roll of parchment sealed with Jolyon's violet
seal. The parchment was a summons to Jolyon's apartments, where Konstant would receive a formal invitation to

begin a term as one of the Second's companions. The package contained the silver box he had presented to Jolyon's secretary. Inside, nested in a bed of green velvet that exactly matched the grassy color of the stones, was one of the bracelets he had taken.

The bracelet was a surprise. The commission was not.

Konstant broke the pattern of his pacing. Returning to the table, he picked up the talisman and balanced it on his palm, watching as the fluttering gold settled back to stillness. How had Jolyon contrived to obtain this gold? Even now that the power of the Stone could not be used to cement the connection, the intimate bond established between a Guardian and his medallion at Investment meant that it absorbed and reflected the essence of his spirit. The ruined medallions of condemned Ordermen were buried deep within the earth, banished from the world of light and air so that their corruption could not taint it. The medallion belonging to the thief of the Stone would have been considered especially dangerous. If it was ever discovered that Jolyon had it in his possession, he would face expulsion, Second or not. More than anything Konstant had learned over the past few months, this act revealed the power of Jolyon's hatred, a passion so towering that it was willing to destroy itself to achieve fulfillment.

Konstant had known of Jolyon's hatred long before this night, and of the cross-world missions it drove. His ability to slip invisibly in and out of others' thoughts had served him well over his time in the Keep, but nowhere better than in Jolyon's office, where the public face of business was no more than a veil across the vast well of Jolyon's secret actions and agendas. From Jolyon's Third Deputy, Konstant learned of the long list of assassinations the Second had accomplished, and the even longer list of those yet to be carried out. From the Second Deputy he learned of Jolyon's efforts to find and hoard solutions to the power failures endemic throughout the world. From the First Deputy he learned of Jolyon's intent to participate in the Ceremony of Recreation and remake the Staff of Order himself. And from Jolyon's secretary—a Journeyer power-conditioned to secrecy, the only man Jolyon trusted with the full catalog of his ambition—he learned of the cross-world missions.

The missions were a revelation, not just for what they told him about Jolyon, but for what they revealed about his transfer to Jolyon's service. Jolyon sent two and sometimes three men through the Gates every year. He was always on the lookout for new agents, Roundheads with experience of world-crossing who were accomplished enough to reasonably elevate to companionship yet obscure enough so that their sudden disappearance would not produce an outcry. By chance, Talesin was exactly such a man.

Or not by chance. In the instant of discovery, the memory of Goldwine's face possessed Konstant's mind, and he heard again the words she had said to him before he left her. When he went before the Zosterian Council to describe the resources she could bring to this mission, he had believed himself to be completing the prophecy she had made for him. But what if that had not been the end of her vision but only the beginning? What if it were not the mission she wanted to ensure but his journey to the heart of the Reddened? What if she had seen, long before this moment, that Jolyon would send him out in search of the thief of the Stone—a man whose return she herself had foretold?

Bron. That was the thief's true name. Konstant had learned it from his daughter, Cariad, from whom he had also learned of Goldwine's vision of Bron alive and powerful in the other world, and of her prophecy of Bron's return, with the Stone, to destroy the Guardians forever. Cariad told these stories with extraordinary conviction, as if describing people and places she herself had known. And yet the images invoked by this vivid telling had seemed as distant to Konstant as the Split itself. He had not grown up with the promise of Bron's return. It was neither part of a personal mythology, as it was for Cariad, nor an icon of belief, as it was for the rest of Goldwine's resistance. And so, though he accepted the truth of the prophecy, he had never given serious thought as to how Bron would come back, or when.

But now these questions possessed him. Bron had wounded the Guardians when he took the Stone; over the thirty years since his departure, Goldwine's guerrillas and the Guardians' own internal strife had broken them down even more. Today the Prior lay dying, and Jolyon stood poised to steal the Order's leadership. If ever there were a moment for destruction, it was now. Yet, exiled in the other world, how was Bron to know the time had come?

In the question lay the answer. From the instant he learned of Jolyon's cross-world missions, Konstant knew that this was what he had really been sent here to do: to take Jolyon's quest and make it his own, to find Bron and summon him back. He was fully aware of the difficulties of this understanding—of the challenge of a task more than a hundred others had undertaken and failed to complete, of the ambiguity of a prophecy whose maker intervened to ensure its fulfillment. Yet the understanding itself was absolute, an intersection of timing, circumstance, and prescience too powerful to question.

Since then Konstant had waited—through the tedious months in Jolyon's office, through his weary service to the Second, through all the days that had not given him what he waited for. Now the waiting was over. The subterfuge, the ugly service, the unbearable tedium were all behind him. Of all the nights he had spent in this place, only one remained.

Konstant put the talisman down and resumed his steady pacing. The air was warm and silent; the candles dipped and shivered, and the mindlight pulsed faintly at the corners of the room.

It had seemed terrible to him, once, to think his future known. Yet he had come to take comfort in prophecy's iron grip. For years he had looked at himself and seen only chaos and failure—but Goldwine had been looking also, and she had seen this. It was a powerful knowledge, a light that fell across the circling futility of his life and illuminated it with meaning. It was not only the conversion Goldwine's reclaimers had worked in him that had been rekindled by what he had discovered in Jolyon's offices. Again and again since his flight from the Fortress he had struggled to redeem himself—through reclaiming, through debriefing, through the Zosterians' risky mission. None of it had been enough. But this, an act as vast and significant as the Split itself—surely this would be enough. Surely this would transform him as he longed to be transformed.

It was close to dawn before he felt the muscle exhaustion that let him know it would be possible to rest. He crossed the sitting room, extinguishing the candles as he went, and fell upon his bed. Sleep approached, a black tide to swallow up his teeming thoughts. There was a moment of fear, for the dreams that waited there, and then nothing.

Seven

N THE middle of the following night Konstant left the Fortress with an escort of two Roundheads. They had been present when he rose and had shadowed him all day long, so he was not able to leave a message for Orrin at the drop point they had established. Goldwine would surely know where he had gone. It would have had to be a false message in any case; not knowing how much Goldwine might have told her staff about what she had sent him here to do, Konstant had never passed on to Orrin the intelligence of Jolyon's cross-world missions, or the real significance of his companion commission.

He and his escort traveled out of the mountains by way of the Fortress Passage, a broad thoroughfare reserved for Guardians, invited visitors to the Fortress, and tradesmen. He was aware, from his duties in the Keep, of the accelerating deterioration of the Guardians' bindings, but even so he was surprised by what he saw. When he had come this way two years ago, there had been some curbing stones out of place, a few glazings of ice, and ongoing evidence of the slow, decades-long shrinkage of the weather-bindings at the Passage's margins, where post-houses, once fully shielded, stood half in and half out of snow. But now the snow had advanced all the way to the edges of the Passage, and sometimes beyond, piling drifts across the surface of the road itself.

Konstant carried a document identifying him as Jolyon's envoy, and so his party was not delayed by lengthy halts at the checkpoints the Soldiers maintained even along the

Fortress Passage, to guard against the harassment of Goldwine's fighters. Farwalking was not allowed on the Passage, and so he and his companions traveled by human means, which for Roundheads meant luxurious enclosed carriages drawn by power-bred mules.

Like himself, Konstant's traveling companions wore the violet teardrop of Jolyon's personal service. He had thought he knew the whole of Jolyon's enormous staff of companions, assistants, enforcers, and administrators, but he had never seen these two men before. When, a day into their journey, he judged it safe to skim their thoughts, he discovered why: they were part of Jolyon's force of extra-Fortress executors. They were charged to watch Konstant, and to strike him down if he showed the slightest sign of hesitation before the Gate. If he managed to return, they had orders bring him captive to the Fortress—where, once Jolyon had picked his mind clean, they would cut his throat and throw him into the midden pit beyond the Fortress walls.

Even if he had not known them to be his executioners, Konstant would have been very careful with these men. Outside the Fortress the Reddened's fierce ideology joined them in a seamless single will, but inside, in the corridors of power, their pride and violence divided them into a hundred different cliques and factions, a complex web of enmities and alliances that shifted as the tides did. A large part of surviving among them depended on the ability to track these changes—to know, on meeting others, exactly where they stood in the ebb and flow of influence, and consequently exactly how they should be treated. All Roundheads gave great attention to matters of rank and precedence, but the Reddened were obsessed with such things. It could be worth a man's life to know what form of address to use, whom he should defer to when choosing seating at a formal banquet, whom he should be careful not to precede through a door.

Such understandings were situational as well as hierarchical. In the Keep, Konstant's employment as Jolyon's companion placed him in the upper levels of Reddened rank, but in the outside world his assassin-companions had performed many more services for Jolyon than he. In the present context, therefore, they outranked him. They would not expect him to be deferent—he was a Roundhead, after all—but they would expect him to take the backward-facing seat in the carriage, to allow them to alight first, not to eat or drink before they did. All these courtesies he duly manifested, and as a result the journey went smoothly. Brushing their minds from time to time, he found them watchful but not hostile.

They reached the end of the Fortress Passage a little over two weeks after setting out. Here they abandoned their mule-cart, and took to farwalking, heading north. Two days brought them to a vast and gloomy pine forest. Near evening of the third day, they reached the cluster of natural features that marked the presence of the Gatekeeper's lodge: a jutting boulder in this place where there were no rocks, a grouping of fallen trunks, a huge pine split as if by lightning. The lodge itself was concealed behind a semblance of trees and empty ground, and additionally bound by a repulsion to encourage passers-by to avoid the area. Even here, Konstant could see the effects of deterioration. The semblance, while still thoroughly concealing what lay behind it, was not quite the seamless, natural illusion it presumably once had been. There was a flatness to the perspective, a vague artificiality to the trunks and the spaces between them, like a portion of a painting repaired by a slightly less talented artist.

Konstant's companions sent out the mindsignal of arrival, known only to the keepers of the Gates and the Roundheads authorized to use them. A few moments passed. Then the semblance shimmered and parted, like a curtain drawing back, revealing a large clearing centered by a stone building of typical blocky Guardian design. Konstant and the others passed into the clearing. The semblance reconstituted itself at their backs, exactly the same from within as it had been from outside.

Konstant greeted the Gatekeeper, a fleshy gray-haired man whose yellowing eyes spoke of many years' over-indulgence in drink, and presented him with Jolyon's authorization of passage, a document heavy with the seals of the Second's office and marked all around its margins with the tearshape of his personal insignia. Touching the keeper's thoughts, Konstant saw that he had no idea why Jolyon so often sent lone agents through this isolated northern Gate, and was well-paid to pretend he was not curious.

The keeper invited them to take a meal with him and spend the night in the lodge. Though not Red himself, he was clearly glad of company. The Arm maintained the Gates in impenetrable secrecy; he and his two Journeyer assistants and four Soldier guards held irrevocable lifetime sinecures, and until their retirement from active duty were as captive to the clearing as their tongueless, power-tethered servants. Konstant spent the evening giving the keeper news of the Fortress and the world, while his executioner-companions sat by in disdainful silence.

The following morning the keeper led Konstant and his escorts into the woods. He brought both his Journeyers with him—just in case, he said, for though he was still able to open the Gate alone, he could not always hold it without assistance.

"But this Gate remains reliable, unlike some of the others," he told Konstant. "If you do exactly as I say, you won't have to worry about getting lost."

He brought the group to a halt in a spot indistinguishable, to Konstant's eyes, from any other. Here was the same snow-covered ground, the same tall pines bristling with dead branches. High above, the live foliage began, a dense green-black canopy through which shafts of sunlight stretched like golden wires. Even so it was very dim beneath the trees, an intrinsic twilight that had a weighting effect on the spirit. Konstant, who over the course of the journey had been almost entirely free of either apprehension or impatience, felt the first sharp prick of dread.

The keeper beckoned. He showed Konstant where to stand, nudging him a little forward, a little backward, until he was properly positioned.

"You've passed through before, so you know what to do," he said. "Don't go until you hear me call out. Aim for the center—the edges aren't as stable as they used to be. Passages have been rough lately. There's nothing you can do about that, except to relax your body as much as possible. On no account attempt to use your Gift to ease your landing. The Gate no longer tolerates that. It'll tear you to pieces if you try."

Konstant nodded.

"Fourteen days from now I'll open the Gate for your return, once every hour from dawn until nightfall. If you don't come through in that time, I'll have to assume you never will."

"I understand."

The yellow eyes flicked across his face. "Good luck, then."

The keeper moved away, beckoning his two Journeyers. Konstant glanced behind him: they were ranging themselves at his back, their heads bowed. Further away, his escorts stood watching, ready either to assist if the Gate malfunctioned or to kill him if he hesitated to pass through it. He turned, facing the empty air before him. There was a tightness in his chest. It was beginning.

For a moment nothing seemed to happen. Then, perhaps an arm's-length away, a shimmering appeared, a rapid crystalline flashing like sunlight on gold leaf. The shimmering spread, eating up the air, growing until it was a circle more than three manlengths in diameter. Slowly it began to spin, gathering speed and density, forming itself into a vortex, a cloud of prismatic matter whirling faster than the eye could follow, with a tiny, unimaginably distant point of blackness at its heart. Sparks, bluer than sapphire, spat about its perimeter, and cobalt lightning fissured it from edge to edge. The wind of power breathed from its core, more frigid than any worldly cold, a glaze of ice across Konstant's skin. For a moment his perception split: he looked both with the eyes of Talesin, who had seen this opening twice before, and with his own, which had never beheld such a terrifying wonder.

"Now!"

He heard the keeper's shout. He did not give himself time to think. He leaped, as Talesin had, straight for the dark pinpoint of the vortex's core. Power seized him, the tearing forces of creation and destruction, sucking him into the vacuum between worlds, the *not* outside of space and time. For an instant he felt the wrongness of it, a passage of being where being was never meant to go, a hideous discordance that pierced his flesh and set its imprint on the inside of his bones.

And then he was through, plummeting past chaos and back into existence. He landed on his knees and fell forward into blackness.

When Konstant regained consciousness, his first thought was that the Gate had rejected him. The trees, the dimness, the snow-covered ground were all the same. But he was alone. And he could hear a sound that had not been there before, a kind of distant windy rushing noise; and the air smelled different, the odor of pines undercut by something harsh and strange. These things told him that he was no longer in the world he knew.

He pushed himself to a sitting position, brushing snow from his face and clothing. The memory of crossing was already fading, the incomprehensible nothingness shaping itself to his human understanding, so that now it seemed only that for an instant he had passed through a place very empty, and very cold. His senses were a little stunned, his body a little sore, his knees painful where he had fallen on them, but other than that he did not feel much the worse for wear.

Reaching for his Gift, he found it ready, slightly drained by passage but less so than he might have expected. Carefully, alert for any hint of dissonance, he built a binding of invisibility. For caution's sake, he added a light barrier of protection, to diffuse a little this world's impact on his senses. It did not seem any more difficult to create these defenses than in the other world; he could feel no difference in the way his Gift responded to his command. It was what he had expected. Even so, the confirmation was welcome.

He got to his feet. That morning he had set aside his Roundhead robe, with its long full skirt and hanging sleeves, and put on traveling clothes: leather breeches, a woolen shirt, a thick felt tunic, and a heavy cloak. On his back he carried a roll of blankets and, bound up in roughweave wrappings, the flasks of water and concentrated travel-rations that were supposed to be his only sustenance here, otherworldly food and water being considered too dangerous to eat and drink. His journey, of course, would last much longer than the two weeks Jolyon had given him: at some point he would have to consume the food and water of this place. But he was not concerned. He trusted to Goldwine's belief that the dangers of handpower were a myth, born, like every other evil that afflicted the world of his birth, from the Guardians' misperception of the causes of the Split.

He could still hear the rushing noise, louder now that he was standing. It seemed distant, yet even from far away he could tell that it filled the air more fully than any wind or ocean of his world. Curiosity pulled at him; he began to walk, moving between the tall pine trunks. He did not bother to mark the spot where he had woken. Either he would return with Bron, by whatever method Bron chose, or he would not return at all.

It quickly became clear that the crossing had taken more of a toll than he had thought. His body felt abused, stressed at the joints and sore in every muscle. The snow, though less deep here than in his own world, hampered his movements, and it was a struggle to keep up a reasonable walking pace. He knew he should rest, perhaps sleep a while, before continuing. Yet, having started, he was oddly reluctant to stop. It was not far now: the changing quality of the sound he followed, intensifying with each successive footstep, told him so.

Ahead, the forest seemed to come to an end. Light showed through the trees, and motion, though of what he could not tell, for it did not seem to be objects that were moving, but the air itself, concentrated and strangely colored and unbelievably swift. This bafflement of perception, of seeing something without understanding it, did not lessen as he moved forward; in fact, it grew worse. Before the final barrier of trunks he had to halt, unable to continue, immobilized by what lay before him.

A vast corridor had been hacked into the forest. It stretched away on either side as far as his eyes could follow, exactly uniform and perfectly straight. At its center a wide expanse of stone or some other impermeable material had been laid down, as clear of snow, as flat and regular, as any Guardian Road. For it was a road, this thing, and travel was being undertaken along it—but not human travel. It was objects that journeyed here—huge numbers of them, flashing past at such incomprehensible speed that Konstant could grasp little more than the violence of their passage. They clustered together in their flight, so close it seemed impossible they should avoid collision. The sunlight shattered on their planes and angles, daggers of brilliance striking at Konstant's unprotected eyes. The savage storm-wind of their velocity shook his body, so that he had to clutch the tree beside him for support. Their reek was awful, a hot harsh stench that filled his mouth with the taste of metal. But the noise was worst, a vast singing roar that was more than sound, splintering the air and pounding the ground as if to shake the earth to pieces.

In his mind, from Talesin's memories, Konstant understood what he was looking at. But his senses did not understand it. He could neither process it nor shut it out. It entered through his eyes, his nose, his ears, reached up through the soles of his feet and ran along his bones and sank into his gut. It seemed an eternity that he stood there, beyond horror, beyond wonder, beyond any human feeling he could recognize, while the roadway screamed and his mind stretched toward a breaking point.

At last he forced his frozen muscles into motion and turned to stumble back the way he had come. After a time his knees buckled, and he collapsed upon the ground. There were only the trees now, and the air was quiet. But speed and color still rushed before his eyes, and his body shook, as if the force of that wind were still set against him. In his head the sound went on—a howl of alien power, the undiluted essence of another world.

When he had recovered enough to think sensibly, Konstant understood that things would not, after all, be as easy as he had hoped.

Roundhead cross-world expeditions followed strict rules.

On arrival, travelers established a barrier-protected, semblance-hidden camp near the Gate they had passed through. Though they utilized power-sourced transportation to carry them great distances, they never went so far that they could not return by nightfall. Roundheads had been visiting the same places, and watching the same locations, for centuries, charting the ceaseless change that was, for them, one of the most abominable qualities of the other world. They did this not out of curiosity, but in order to maintain a living catalog of the horrors of handpower, a cautionary store of wisdom that, because it was regularly renewed, could never become stale. Each returning expedition compiled a detailed report, with narratives and commentaries and sketches. New travelers prepared themselves by intensive study of these records, so that every traveler would be equally capable of comprehending what he saw, even if he had never before laid eyes upon the other world.

Konstant possessed the whole sum of Talesin's memories, acquired through a mindprobe at the time of the identity switch. And so he owned not only the words and pictures of the travelers' journals, but Talesin's first-hand knowledge of the handpower world. Talesin had looked upon a hundred roads and their swift traffic, upon artificial constructions that duplicated the flight of birds, upon the endless variety of smaller machines with which the people of this world surrounded their lives. He had walked the empty countryside, where habitations were miles between and the signs of handpower were barely visible and he had moved through labyrinthine cities, where keeps of glass and stone rose up to pierce the clouds and the stench of handpower made the air almost unbreathable. Yet, though these images conveyed Talesin's righteous condemnation of what he saw, as sense-memories they were oddly indefinite, with a flatness of form and an absence of color that suggested that Talesin had viewed everything through a veil of gauze.

This was deliberate. The Guardians believed that any Gifted individual who traveled unprotected through the handpower world must be damaged by the alien forces there. Even brief exposure was enough injure a Gift; prolonged contact led to irrevocable power-death. Worse, the seed of weakness born in every human being, the fatal susceptibility to the lure of tools, might cause an unprotected traveler to willingly succumb and embrace his Gift's demise. Roundhead world-crossers maintained heavy barriers against these dangers, barriers that not only blocked handpower's destructive influence but softened the details of what they saw, so that their minds would not be too deeply touched.

Konstant was fully aware of the deficiency of Talesin's memories, limited not only by Talesin's defenses but by narrow Roundhead prejudice. Still, he had assumed the images would be useful as templates or guideposts, and would be enough to prepare him for what he encountered here. As for barriers, he had not thought they would be necessary. There was nothing in handpower to harm a Gift, after all; and he knew his mind to be free of the Guardian horror of technology. Had he not seen technology in action, when he returned to Goldwine for retraining and witnessed the mechanical wonder her workers had made of her hollow mountain? Had he not spoken with her of her hopes for the future marriage of Gift and machine, of the scientific revolution that would sweep the world of his birth once the Guardians were overthrown? Surely, therefore, he would be able to travel without the heavy protections Talesin had used.

But his experience of the great road showed him that he had been wrong. Either the limitation of Talesin's memory was greater than he had realized, or he himself was not as ready as he had thought. Either way, the *difference* here was too profound to confront unshielded. Reluctantly, he understood that he must barrier himself, at least until he learned to better understand this world. Yet he could not bear the thought of muffling himself as the Roundheads did. There must be a compromise—a barrier that would make the alienness tolerable, but would not exclude so much color and detail.

For a day he rested, deep within the forest, in an area he had cleared of snow and enclosed within a concealing binding. He dozed and woke and dozed again, allowing his strained mind to settle and his overtaxed body to recover.

Then, wrapping himself in the strongest barriers he could construct, so that the world around him became as gray and flat as a shadow, he returned to the road and began to experiment, reducing the strength of his protection little by little until he found a point of balance that allowed him to see clearly, but control the dangerous overloading of his senses. Like Talesin, he could now distinguish the symbol-marked surface of the road from the conveyances that moved along it. He could perceive, instead of a chaos of blurred velocity, a swift but orderly succession of boxy hard-edged confabulations, each with one or more human operators enclosed inside. Unlike Talesin, he could also see the jeweled colors, the differing textures, the faces of the riders. He could hear the sounds and smell the smells and feel the wind, and even, as his comfort and familiarity grew, move beyond the final fringe of trees and stand near the roadway itself.

When he was confident that he had mastered the road, he began to explore more widely, hiking through the forest in various directions and testing his barriers on whatever he found. He moved at human speed, for he was not yet willing to try the complex blending of motion and perception required by power-sourced transportation. The forest, which in his world covered the land all the way to the northern sea, was in this world a tiny fraction of that size. Though it was possible to stand among the trees and imagine untracked woodland spreading out for miles, there was no direction in which a few hours of walking did not bring him to a roadway or a cluster of dwellings. Reversing the direction he and his executor-companions had taken through the forest, it took him only half a day to reach open country, where roads and houses and snowy fields spread out as far as the eye could see.

It was an unfamiliar vista, but not truly an alien one. Other than the roads and their traffic, and the improbably sharp and symmetrical lines of the buildings, the signs of technology were not very apparent here. More jarring was sight of the jagged mountain range that marched across the far horizon, its planes and angles pale with snow. It was a view less clear than he was accustomed to, for the air in this world was more opaque than in his own, but even so these were unmistakably the Fortress mountains. Through Talesin's knowledge he was aware that the worlds were physically parallel, but it was still a little dizzying to see the truth of it so clearly.

On the fifth day, he tested himself against a more complex experience, waiting until night fell and then journeying down from the forest's edge to explore a town he had glimpsed a mile or so away. He crossed the fields, coming at last to a road whose edge he followed, trying not to flinch when one of the metal conveyances—armed against the darkness with blinding beams of light—flew past in a roar of heat and stench.

Reaching the town, he wandered for a time through its streets. Despite the hour, they were full of activity and lit almost as bright as day. From his nighttime observation of the countryside, he knew that there was no true darkness in this world. Light was everywhere: sweeping along roads whose traffic did not pause when evening came, scattered across the hills and valleys in such profusion that it seemed the stars had fallen to earth, set high on poles like small suns shining out of phase, formed into blocks and patterns and fixed to the fronts of buildings, blooming inside houses and overflowing into the night through the great planes of glass that covered all the windows of this world—a thing quite as wondrous, to Konstant's mind, as any of the more complicated miracles of technology.

He had wrapped himself in invisibility before he left the shelter of the trees. The townspeople were not aware of him, even as he moved beside them, or paused to look into their faces. It was the first time he had seen them close, the unGifted inhabitants of this world. Talesin's blurred memories carried the sense of something coarse and outlandish, as if the human form as well as the human mind had been distorted by centuries of handpower use. But in spite of their alien dress and guttural speech, the people he saw were recognizably human, engaged in activities that except for their context could have taken place anywhere in his world. Their strangeness, for him, lay in a thing Talesin did not seem to have much noted—their cleanness, their vigor, their strong well-nourished bodies and unpocked faces and perfect teeth. There were no lepers, no crippled beggars, no starving children. Could it be that technology, which had thickened the air of this world and closed up its spaces with noise and metal, had done away with such things?

The outer portions of the town were as strange as he expected, sharp-edged and brilliant, a symphony of alien textures and outlandish forms, but its center was a surprise. There, cobbled streets twisted between timbered house-fronts that would have been at home in the city where he had grown up. Yet the veil of woodsmoke and the stench of sewage that would have fouled the air in his world were absent here. The plaster was clean, the brick fully-pointed. No one used the alleys as garbage tips, or emptied slop pots from upper windows. It seemed less a real place than a peculiar, inexplicable reproduction of one—as clean, as healthy, as supernaturally perfect as the people who inhabited it.

Trudging forestward through the fields, Konstant felt a sense of satisfaction. This night had cemented the confidence that had been growing in him over the past days of exploration. He looked up at the sky. The stars glinted, fewer and less luminous than the stars of his world, yet essentially the same. He could pick out the constellations, in shape and placement exactly where they should be, and the moon, waxing as it had been when he passed through the Gate. Again he wondered at the parallelism of the worlds. Did they exist in entirely separate firmaments, or did the same stars somehow wheel above them both?

The night air moved against his skin, only a little tainted by the harsh odors of technology. The snow crunched beneath his feet. A rush of joy took him, unbidden and strange. For a moment he felt the sweep of vistas, the stretch of distances, a whole new world spreading out beneath his invisible feet. In that instant he was not the lapsed Apprentice or the restless reclaimer or the counterfeit Roundhead or even the servant of prophecy, but only a traveler. Only himself.

The next morning Konstant seated himself on the ground and prepared to cast his Gift outward in search of Bron.

Guardian power was aggressive, flung from the mind like a weapon. It accomplished its aims by seizing matter at its most basic level and manipulating or recasting it into different forms. Goldwine's power, by constrast, relied less on the fabrication of something new than on the subtle shifting of what was already there. Her operatives achieved invisibility not by building a shell of concealment but by adjusting their own substances so that they reflected the world around them, like chameleons altering their colors to fit new environments. Their inner barriers did not raise a protective wall within their minds, but nudged the currents of their thoughts very slightly out of phase, so that thought deflected attention without actually being hidden. There were certain things, of course, that could only be done as Guardians did them—transportation, the more material aspects of making and unmaking, divination. Nor was there any non-Guardian way of creating the kind of physical barrier Konstant needed to shield himself from the world of hand-power. But in most areas of defense, Goldwine had developed a workable, valid canon of alternative power-knowledge. Over the years, it had provided the resistance with one of its most significant advantages.

She had also invented a signature method of nearspeech, an easy, flowing way of sending that in all its forms was utterly dissimilar to the percussive, tightly focused mindspeech of the Guardians. It was not a technique adapted to farspeech, which by necessity must be projective and precise. But those capable of farspeech could employ it in a wide-ranging receptive mode—which, because it ran in channels so different from the Guardians', could detect not just Guardian Gifts, but the small shifts and stirrings in the realm of mindspace that marked their use, even when the Gifts themselves were hidden. Konstant, whose powerful Ability encompassed farspeech as fully as nearspeech, had under Goldwine's tutelage become a virtuoso of this technique. He had used it sometimes during his Zosterian years to track the movements of Reddened orthodoxers, who often wrapped themselves in concealing barriers when closing in on a village or a parish.

It was in this way that he planned to search for Bron.

According to Cariad's telling of the Tale, Bron knew the prophecy and awaited his summons back to the mindpower world. But the impenetrable shields that hid him from the Roundhead search parties hid him from his summoner as well. These barriers required power to maintain themselves, however, and Bron's power was Guardian-trained. It should therefore be possible to use Goldwine's methods to detect, if not Bron's Gift, then the disturbances created by his use of it. Once these traces were found, Konstant could guide himself by the feel of his own Gift against them, like a blind man following the echoes of pebbles tossed against a wall.

He was aware, uncomfortably, that there were flaws in his reasoning. Bron's Gift might be Guardian-trained, but he was not—had never really been—a Guardian. And it was not just his own power that he had managed to conceal for thirty years, but the power of the Stone. What guarantee was there that even Goldwine's techniques would be effective against such a huge concealment? And if they were, what were the chances that Bron would not know he had been discovered and, assuming Konstant to be another Roundhead, take steps to hide himself again? Yet Konstant had faith in the prophecy, in the vision of himself contained in Goldwine's mind. It was he who was fated to find Bron and bring him back. This was the only way he could think to do it; it must, therefore, be the right way.

When he was ready, he dropped his barriers, so that the full range of his Gift would be available to him. Gathering himself, he launched his consciousness outward. In his own world, he had never reached the physical limit of his sensing in this mode: he had sent thoughts half a world away and received them from senders just as distant. On and on he moved through the reaches of mindspace, a nonmaterial realm that, to him, was as concrete as the forests and rivers of the country where he had grown up. In his world it was a beautiful place—luminous with power, coruscating with the constant play of Gift. In this world, it was like a desert, or a city stripped by plague. There was nothing in it, not even the presence of other minds, only a gray and lightless continuum stretching out forever. Konstant knew he moved, knew he searched, yet he felt motionless and blind. His senses strained, his Gift cried out for light; and still there was no power, or any trace of what he looked for: the small shiftings, the subtle stirrings, the nearly invisible concentrations that marked the use of a hidden Gift.

At last he pulled back. He had gone a great distance; it was some time before he returned fully to awareness of his body. He opened his eyes. It had been morning when he began. It was twilight now, so close to full dark that he could barely see his hand before his face. With the effort of extreme exhaustion he rewove his barriers and lay down to sleep.

In the days that followed he tried again and again to discover the signs he sought. He launched his mind in different directions, in different modes, at different speeds and different intensities. He ranged close; he ranged far. He tapped the limits of his skill, the outer boundaries of his strength. Still there was nothing, only the unbroken monochrome of this world's vacant mindspace. Once he saw a light; flying toward it with a rush of weary exultation, he found it to be his own. He had circled the world and come upon himself.

On the fourth day he resurrected Jolyon's talisman from his wallet. He had never imagined he would need this feeble token, but time was slipping past, and he was growing desperate. Talesin, an experienced investigator, had been familiar with the use of such power-tracking devices. Calling on these memories, Konstant bent his will upon the little globe of glass, opening his mind to whatever truth it might yield.

For a time nothing happened. Then, all at once, the flakes of gold fluttered, as if stirred by some small internal wind, and drifted to the right side of the glass, where they settled, quivering. As it was intended to do, the talisman was indicating direction. It was telling him to go north.

North, he thought. For thirty years Jolyon's agents had been going north, through different Gates, from different starting points. He had the map to prove it, crisscrossed with the ways they had taken, the abandoned ones marked in black, the active ones in red. But what good would it do

to go north, if he could not break through Bron's concealment? He might go north forever and never find what he
sought. In sudden rage he flung the talisman away from
him. It arced between the trees, sparking as the light caught
it, and fell into the snow.

For the first time since glimpsing Jolyon's cross-world
missions in the mind of his Arm-trained secretary, Konstant
understood—did not just wonder or fear, but truly understood—that he might have been wrong. That Goldwine
might not, after all, have intended him to come here. That
the apparent congruity of Jolyon's mission and her prophecy might have been nothing more than coincidence. That
the prescient certainty that had seemed to overwhelm his
understanding might have been nothing more than his own,
old desire to remake himself in the image of some new
action, some new mission, in the hope that he might find
in this one what he had not found in all the others.

For a long time Konstant sat staring at the trees, his body
stiff, his eyes wide and blind. Weariness pulled him down
at last onto his blankets and into sleep.

In the middle of the night he woke, or thought he did,
to the feeling of being watched. A great eye seemed to peer
down at him between the pine boughs. For a while the eye
observed him, cool and dispassionate, then it blinked and
was gone. It left behind a stillness that caused Konstant, in
his dream, to recall the place between the worlds. Yet it
was not fearful, this quiet, but anticipatory—the kind of
hush that precedes the arrival of something vast.

At last there came a stirring, a sense of motion. Somewhere, a door was swinging outward onto darkness. Light
streamed from behind it, brighter than the sun: enough light
to fill all the gray vacancies of this world, and more. Konstant reached toward it, traveling the spaces of dream as he
had those of mind; the light did not recede but stayed, waiting for him.

Then the door swung closed again, and the light was
gone. Released, Konstant fell back into himself, into a place
where there were neither light nor dream, but only the
peace of full unconsciousness.

In the morning, when he woke, he knew exactly how to
go.

Downworld

Eight

HE INFORMATION patrol brought Cariad through the night. There were four of them including Cariad, muffled against the cold in layers of woolen clothing and cold-suits, leather outergarments that covered every part of the body but the face. They moved by means of far-walking, high above the earth, where peaks jutted and glaciers cracked and snow lay heaped a hundred feet deep. It took them less than two hours to travel between Goldwine's headquarters and the Fortress, a journey that in real time might require a month or more. About half a mile from the Pilgrims' Pass, they halted. Farwalking left unmistakable echoes in its wake. From here they would go as the unGifted did.

It was achingly cold. A savage blizzard lashed the darkness, filling the night with screaming winds and swirling tides of snow. The patrol, roped together for safety, moved across the drifts on snowshoes, angled like leaning trees against the gale. The storm made them nearly blind, but they did not need sight: the patrol leader owned a homing Talent, a variant of a divination Gift that allowed unerring movement between two known points.

They were bound to invisibility. They needed no greater concealment to travel undetected. In the outside world, Goldwine's unrelenting harassment had forced the Guardians to adopt a variety of physical and power-based defenses, but with the arrogance of nearly a millenium of unchallenged rule, they believed the Fortress to be untouchable. Beyond the Soldier's lodge that guarded the entrance to the Pilgrim's Pass, the Fortress lay blind, its walls bare of guards or lookouts. Goldwine's operatives slipped in and out at will: the rescue patrols, which salvaged discards and runaways, and the information patrols, which arrived weekly to collect intelligence from the resistance's in-Fortress network.

The party passed the lodge. The mindlight that cloaked its walls was a vague luminance within the heavy snow. A few minutes more brought them to the Pilgrim's Pass. The Pass had been power-cut centuries ago to give access to the Fortress; it ran through the peaks for nearly a mile, so narrow that even at noon the sun did not touch its floor. Its depth blunted the rage of wind and snow, but the cold that breathed from its walls was more profound than the storm. It had been winter here since the world began, and the rock hoarded the memory of every year.

Just before its end, the Pass kinked sharply: left, then right, then left again. The party rounded the final corner, and halted before a miracle.

Beyond the Pass lay a broad alpine plain, ringed all around by peaks, like a bowl with broken edges. At the plain's center rose the Fortress, black upon the pristine snow. Even from this distance it was huge, its walls stretching out to devour half the valley. A pair of enormous gates was set at the walls' midpoint; to their left, the perfection of top edge of masonry faltered a little. It was here that Cariad's father, carrying the Stone, had passed out of the Fortress, blowing the walls to rubble for a distance of two miles. The Guardians had repaired the damage, but they could not get the final courses to hold—as if Cariad's father had left some force behind, struggling always to reenact the original vast destruction.

But that was not the miracle. The miracle lay closer, at the Pass's mouth. Behind the party the blizzard raged, and the distant Fortress was cloaked in storm, but a footstep away it was spring. A verdant meadow lapped against the frozen cliffs, a riotous tangle of grass and flowers that spanned the plain from edge to edge and reached nearly to the base of the Fortress's walls. Above the tasseled stalks, fireflies flashed tiny beacons, and moths skimmed like ghosts. Overhead the sky stretched black and clear, strewn with stars like diamond-chips and centered by a pale cabochon moon. It was a surpassingly strange and beautiful sight. The blizzard-battered mind, astonished, insisted it must be illusion. Yet it was real, as real as the storms around it.

Cariad's companions had passed this way many times. They barely paused to look before bending to the bindings of their snowshoes. But Cariad stood transfixed. She had heard about this place all her life—from Goldwine, from others who had been here—but until this moment she had never seen it. This was her father's work. He had made the meadow when he took the Stone, a message of triumph and power for those who had tried to destroy him. Awestruck, Cariad read that message, as clear tonight as it had been when the Guardians first woke to find their Fortress broken and the Stone gone. Heartsenser that she was, she read another truth as well. There was not just power here, but presence. Something of her father remained in what he had created, twined as deeply into its substance as the roots of the plants he had summoned from the ice. Rationally, she knew he had not left it for her. Yet in this moment, it almost seemed he must have.

<Cariad.> It was the patrol leader, her mindvoice sharp. <Hurry up.>

It required an effort of will to turn away. Stooping, Cariad fumbled with straps and buckles, sliding the snowshoes off her feet, attaching them to a loop on the belt of her coldsuit.

A broad graveled path split the meadow in two. At the patrol leader's signal, the party set out upon it. A single footstep divided ice from warmth. Cariad gasped as the mild air entered her lungs. The breeze was like a caress, saturated with the scents of earth and leaves and flowers. Close to, she saw the surreal immaculateness of the meadow's growth: there were no ragged petals or torn stems, no wilting blooms or bursting seedpods, no sign at all of the cycles of change that marked an ordinary meadow. But then, this was not an ordinary meadow. It had not been born of earth and seed, but of memory and desire.

It did not grow as meadows did, but endured as mountains did—a perfected season of the mind, existing always in the breath-brief pause between maturity and disintegration.

Winter's resumption was more gradual than the plunge into spring. There was an area of increasing chill and diminishing verdancy, then a brown margin shimmering with frost, and then the snow, at first like flour dusted across the path, but rapidly deepening. Cariad and the others paused to resume their snowshoes, and then moved on across the rising drifts. The blizzard reconstituted itself as they went; by the time they reached the walls, it was as fierce as the storm they had left behind.

They followed the walls rightward until they reached their edge, an angle as sharp as a knife. They turned, trudging onward until they came to a black opening in the snow. Here stairs led down to a door that gave direct access to the Fortress' basements. There were three of these doors, located at the Fortress' right, left, and rear. Like the walls, they were unguarded. The Guardians did not fear incursion from outside, and trusted the hostile climate and intensive training to keep their servants in.

Again the members of the party removed their snowshoes. In single file they started down the stairs, moving carefully, for the blizzard had heaped the treads with snow. After only a little way the darkness became complete. Cariad, at the rear, followed the tug of the rope, counting as she went: ten stairs, fifteen, twenty, twenty-five. The rope went slack as the man in front of her halted. In the silence, Cariad was aware of her companions' emotions, stronger than at any other time during the journey: their dislike of the Fortress, their eagerness to be finished and on their way.

<Cariad,> came the patrol leader's thought. <Unrope yourself.>

Cariad obeyed. There was a rapping sound: the patrol leader, giving the coded entrance signal. A pause, and then the scraping of bolts. A slash of light materialized on the blackness, widening to become the rectangle of an open door.

The patrol leader led the way into a roughly circular chamber of hewn rock. An arched opening directly opposite gave onto a passageway. A single globe of mindlight provided illumination, its dim radiance bright after the pitchy darkness outside. The room was bare except for a heap of blankets at its center, and beside them, a cloth-wrapped bundle.

The man who had opened the door pushed it closed. He was dressed in a long leather tunic and a pair of leather breeches, both painted with bands of multicolored geometric symbols. A close-fitting hood concealed his hair and the lower part of his face. His eyes were dark in the mindlight, slightly tilted beneath pale winged brows. His gaze flicked across the faces of the patrol and came to rest on Cariad.

"You're the one?"

"Yes."

"I'm Orrin. Come. She's over here."

He led the way to the blankets. Inside them was an unconscious woman.

"I gave her a sleeping draught," Orrin said. "It'll hold for a few more hours."

"What's her name?"

"Margit."

"Did you bring clothes?"

"Just what she has on." For an unGifted, he was guarded. She could feel his tension, but there was also a strong sense of discipline, and his emotions did not overwhelm her perception the way most unGifted feeling did. He gestured toward the bundle. "And a set of leathers."

"Help me undress her. I need to see her body."

Stooping, she began to unwrap the woman's coverings. Margit looked to be in her early twenties, approximately Cariad's height, but a little fatter around the hips and thighs, with long loose blond hair and soft pretty features. She wore a linen nightshift over a heavy dun-colored woolen undergarment. Orrin lifted her while Cariad slipped the clothing off. His touch was gentle; Cariad sensed his familiarity with the emerging flesh. These two had recently slept together.

When Margit was naked Cariad surveyed her carefully, taking in the moles, the blemishes, the small red birthmark on her right hip, pulling her upright to view her back, moving her hair to examine her ears and lifting her lids to see the color of her eyes.

"Is she suitable?" Orrin said as they laid her back among the blankets. "They said you needed someone tall and slim."

"Yes." Cariad's power of making allowed her to project an illusion without regard to physical dimension, but since she must wear the clothing of the person whose place she was taking, practicality dictated that they be more or less of a size. "She'll do very well."

"She's of my clan. She's a sorting-room worker. Did you see her validations?" He turned Margit's right arm, pointing to a spot just below her shoulder, where two small brands in the shape of open eyes had been set into her flesh.

Cariad nodded. Fortress servants were hereditarily un-Gifted, but many servant babies were born of Guardian fathers, and such unions often produced Gifted offspring. All servant children were scanned for power at the age of three, and again at the age of six. If they were confirmed Giftless, they were branded with the symbol of the Suborder they served. If power was detected, they were taken to one of the basement doors and set outside to die. Over the years, Goldwine's patrols had rescued many of these castoffs.

"I'll give you my clothes now," Cariad said to Orrin. "Put everything on her—the coldsuit too."

Rising to her feet, she loosened the laces of the coldsuit, wriggling out of the cumbersome garment like a snake shedding its skin. Her hair swung loose, falling over her shoulders. Other than a small drawstring bag at her neck, concealed by a tiny binding, she had brought nothing with her but what would go back again on Margit's body, not even hairpins. In quick succession she pulled off her wool tunic, her boots and leggings, her shift, shivering in the freezing air. She did not think twice about standing naked before a stranger; the life she led had long ago stripped her of that kind of modesty. The patrol looked on, impassive. Orrin, who had bent a proprietary gaze on Margit's bare flesh, averted his eyes, taking the clothing Cariad handed him with his head turned away. He looked at her just once, when she stooped to take up Margit's undergarment—an intense regard, quickly withdrawn.

Margit's clothes were coarse and not quite clean; Cariad's nose wrinkled with the body-smell that hung on them. Closing her eyes, she began to prepare for transformation. Inside her mind she built a picture of Margit, assembling detail in all three dimensions, turning the image around before her inner eye like a sculptor with a clay model. When she was satisfied, she summoned her making will and set it against her flesh. By preference as well as necessity, she used Goldwine's body-shifting methods. She had never met or heard of anyone as good at this as she was. Almost any reasonably Gifted person could master Goldwine's bindings of invisibility, but it was quite another thing to mold flesh to a specific image, let alone maintain the transformation for any length of time. Cariad had been taught this skill. But her grasp of it was instinctive, a knowledge that sprang from the same place as her understanding of how to stop a human heart.

Some time later, she opened her eyes. She felt her new shape, a constriction across her body like an unfamiliar garment. She lifted her hands: they were the hands of the woman in the cart now, wider than her own, the nails bitten. Faintly, beneath the solidity of alien flesh, she could see the ghost of her own being: her own slender fingers, the shadow of her own black hair. These were sense-memories, born of her true substance, which endured unchanged beneath the transformation. They would linger for a day or two, and then fade.

She became aware of the pressure of someone's attention. She looked up and found that Orrin was staring full at her. His dark eyes, beneath their upswept brows, were wide in the slice of skin that was all she could see of his face. Awe radiated from him, stronger than any emotion he had manifested thus far. Was it just the likeness, or had he watched her transform? She grimaced a little in annoyance; she should have ordered him to look away.

She moved forward—he fell back a step, involuntarily—and bent to set her fingertips to Margit's temples. She dipped into Margit's mind, sifting through her memory for the faces and names and customs she would need to convincingly maintain her disguise. Thought-harvesting was not her forte, but unGifted minds posed little challenge.

She rose to her feet. One of the patrol members carried a bundle strapped to his back; he lowered it now and unwrapped its leather covering, revealing several hollow metal rods with tapered fittings. Quickly he snapped the rods together to make two long poles, which he slipped through casings sewn down the long sides of the covering, making a narrow litter. The leader and the other man lifted Margit and laid her on the litter, binding her to it with straps.

Orrin pulled the outside door open. Carrying their burden, the patrol went out into the darkness. The leader glanced toward Cariad as she passed, nodding once in farewell.

Orrin closed the door and thrust home the bolts. He went to the blankets and began to fold them.

"Put on the leathers." He nodded toward the bundle. "There are Soldiers down here sometimes. If they see us, they'll think we're transporters."

"Transporters?"

"Transporters are haulers. They distribute food and other goods through the tunnels, from the great caverns where everything is grown to all the downworlds."

"I know that. It's all right for transporters to be out this time of night?"

"Transporters travel all hours. We won't be questioned."

Cariad unwrapped the bundle and pulled on the leather tunic and breeches she found inside, stowing the wrapping in the deep pocket at the tunic's front. She was grateful not to have to call up an invisibility-binding; it had required a great deal of power to shift her shape, a thing that tired her as no physical effort could.

Orrin, carrying the blankets, had already vanished through the doorway. Following, she found herself in a wide tunnel, lit by a strip of mindlight at the ceiling. The walls and roof formed a continuous curve down to the flat floor. The surface of the stone was not rough like that of the antechamber, but as slick as polished marble. Before her, the passage ran perfectly straight and without visible end, vanishing into a pinprick of distance; behind her it was the same. The memories she had borrowed from Margit—a knot of other-consciousness within her mind, waiting to be sorted out and examined in detail—held no recognition of what she saw.

Orrin had pulled ahead, walking with the efficient stride of a man used to long marches. Cariad hurried to catch up.

"How far do we have to go?"

"About an hour, at this pace." His tilted eyes slid toward her and away. She could feel his discomfort—with her? With her altered face? "You'd better pull up the hood. Transporters don't wear their hair loose. Turn here."

He indicated the arched entrance of a tunnel that opened at an oblique angle off the one they had been traveling. It was the twin of the first in everything but length: Cariad could see, ahead, the archway of its ending, where another passage crossed it.

They walked in silence. The Margit-semblance was a tension across Cariad's body; maintaining it was like contracting and holding an unfamiliar muscle. She would not sleep tonight for fear of losing concentration, but after a day or so she would adjust and be able to sustain the semblance without difficulty even in unconsciousness. She was aware, now and then, of Orrin's swift glance. Beneath his unease lay something more—anticipation, wariness, as if he had certain expectations and was waiting to see if she would fulfill them.

"Tell me about Konstant," she said at last. If they were going to be walking for an hour, they might as well use the time. "How did you discover he was missing?"

"Konstant? Is that his name?" A flash of feeling. Orrin had not liked Konstant. "I never knew it. I called him by his alias. I'll do the same for you, if that's all right. It's easier to avoid slips that way."

"That's sensible."

"I found out by chance. He had a belt he won in a duel, very elaborate, embroidered in gold thread and garnets. I'm a clothiery supervisor, and the bodyservants bring me their masters' garments for cleaning and mending. A pile of things came in from one of the prominent Reds, and the belt was among them. I knew Tal . . ." He paused. "I knew *Konstant* might have lost it in another duel or a bet, but I hadn't seen him for a while, and so I did some checking. I found out that all his belongings had been redistributed a bit over a week before. That only happens when a Round-head dies, or if he's been imprisoned and condemned to death."

There was nothing in his precise way of speaking to mark him as a servant. The Guardians ran schools for their workers, where they were educated to the Limits like the people of the outside world, and rigorously trained to the attitude and deportment the Guardians' required of those who served them. In the process, they learned to echo the cadences of their masters' speech.

"Which do you think it is?" Cariad asked. "Death or imprisonment?"

"Well, I haven't been able to find any evidence that he's dead. I've talked to the infirmary workers and the mortuary workers here in the Keep, and they say they haven't seen anyone over the past few weeks who matches his description."

"Would servants know, necessarily? What if whoever killed him wanted to keep it secret?"

He looked at her again, a little more directly this time. "We call ourselves downworlders. Or workers. Not servants."

"I'm sorry." Cariad had recognized the word as soon as he said it, from the store of Margit's memories. "I'll remember."

He nodded, his eyes ahead again. "To answer your question, things done secretly make as much of a mess as things done openly. Guardians don't generally clean up after themselves. One way or another, his body would have passed through downworlder hands. But there are places besides the Keep he could have gone, if someone wanted to keep it quiet. I can check on that, if you like."

"If he's imprisoned, where do you think it's most likely he would be held?"

"I know for a fact that the Keep's cells are empty. And

people I trust have told me that no one like him has been brought into either the Amphitheater cells or the prison annex."

They had come to a hublike area formed by the intersection of five passages. Orrin touched her elbow, indicating that she should turn to the left.

"What about private cells?"

"It's possible," he said. "But a lot of time has passed. They don't generally keep prisoners privately for more than a couple of weeks. Either they kill them, or pass them on to the public holding areas."

"Suppose he knew he was in danger of discovery. Might he have tried to get out of the Fortress on his own?"

"It would have been easier to ask me for help. I told him when he arrived that I could hide him if he needed it, where no Guardian could find him. I don't know if he believed me." Again the current of dislike. "So, yes. He might have done something like that. And if they thought he was a defector, they'd declare him dead, which would explain the redistribution."

"What about a mission? Could Jolyon have sent him outside the Fortress on some kind of errand?"

"Then why the redistribution?"

"Perhaps something went wrong. Perhaps he was killed on the way."

"But why would he leave without saying anything? I can see it if he was about to be discovered. He might not have had time. But if it was a mission, surely he would have let me know. We had a drop point. If he couldn't tell me in person, he could have left a message."

"He might have been coming and going by power. He might have thought he'd be back before you noticed he was gone."

"I suppose that's possible."

"Well, if it was a mission, someone on the Second's staff will know what it was. His Deputies, his personal secretary, his companions. Do you know any of these men by sight?"

"Most of them."

"And the Second. Do you know him?"

"Yes." A shudder of feeling ran through him, as if he

had been touched by a cold deeper than that of the passageway. Cariad drew in her breath. For a moment something rose up in her, dark and urgent.

"One more thing. Do you think it's possible Konstant might have defected?"

"No," Orrin said positively. "For one thing, he'd still own his clothes and furniture. For another, I'd be dead." He shook his head. "But it's not just that. I never knew a man who took so many risks. He stole documents off the Investigation-Master's desk. What he couldn't steal he copied. He watched with me in the behindwall passages. He always carried that poison capsule under his tongue, and he was ready to use it. No one walks the edge like that unless he has true faith in what he's doing. And a man with that kind of faith isn't going to defect."

They were admiring words, but Cariad could still feel the acid counterpoint of his dislike. Konstant had evoked a similar reaction in many of the Gifted with whom he worked, in part because of the darkness of his spirit, in part because of his powerful Gift, which by both training and inclination he used in ways distasteful to non-Guardians. But Orrin was unGifted. He had neither ability nor reason to perceive what Cariad herself had often suspected when in Konstant's company, that her thoughts were being surreptitiously sifted and evaluated. Had Konstant treated Orrin contemptuously, or failed to adequately credit his obvious resource and intelligence? Certainly he had underestimated Orrin's ability to ferret out a secret.

She looked at the man beside her. The risks Konstant had taken were great, but no greater than those Orrin faced. She knew, or thought she knew, why Konstant had chosen his course; but why had Orrin? Other downworlds hosted dozens of servant intelligencers—all unaware of one another's identities, run by Goldwine's recruiters in servant disguise—but from Estrellara she had learned that Orrin was the only intelligencer in the Keep, now or ever. The resistance maintained no recruiter in the Keep; that meant he had been approached by someone outside it. What would cause a servant of the Arm—more indoctrinated, more regimented, more cloistered than any other corps of Guardian workers—to turn against his masters? And what had caused the recruiters to believe he would be receptive?

As if in response, he turned his hooded face and met her eyes. They were exactly of a height: she was able to meet his gaze without inclining her head up or down.

"They told me you're a heartsenser as well as a maker."

"Yes."

"Does that mean . . . ?" He paused. "Can you read my thoughts?"

"No." She was often asked this question; even among the Gifted, there was misunderstanding of this rare aspect of her ability. "Heartsensing is a variant of mindspeech, but it's not the same. I can only read your emotions, and only the strongest of those, because I maintain a mindguard. In any case, even if I could read your thoughts, I wouldn't. We're trained from childhood not to intrude that way."

"Even on the unGifted?"

There was considerable bitterness behind that question. "On everyone," she said, intrigued.

He shook his head. She felt it again, the flaring of his distress. "You can't imagine how strange this is. You have her face and body. Yet you're nothing like her. You don't speak as she does, or stand as she does, or move as she does. I see her on top, and a stranger underneath. It's like watching someone possessed by a spirit."

"Actually—actually, Orrin, I need your help with that. I have the feel of her in my mind. But people don't usually have a very accurate idea of their physical selves, and she seems to have a fairly poor view of herself. I'm having a hard time putting my inward sense of her together with the way she should be outwardly."

"Yes. Yes, Margit doesn't think much of herself." A difficult mix of feeling accompanied the words, as if he had cared for Margit and been annoyed by her in equal measure. "She believes she's ugly, though she isn't by any means— you saw that for yourself. And stupid, which she isn't either, though she is . . . naïve, I suppose. Gullible. She was easy to play tricks on, when we were children."

"You're cousins, yes?"

"Yes. All of us in the clan are related, one way or an-

other. The kinship between Margit and me isn't close,
though. There are many degrees of removal between us."

"I sense she's embarrassed about her height."

"Yes. She doesn't stand straight, the way you do. She
stoops a little. Curves her shoulders. And her neck—she
holds it forward, like this—"

"Stop." Cariad halted. She rounded her shoulders and
ducked her head, fitting the feel of it to the feel of Margit
in her mind. "Is this right?"

His eyes moved over her; she could feel him subordinating the uneasiness he felt in looking at her to her request
for objective judgment. Once again she was struck by the
disciplined quality of his emotion, so unlike the confused
fog of feeling that rose from most unGifted minds.

"Bend a little more," he said. "Push your head forward
just a bit. There. That's it."

"And her walk. She . . . shuffles, yes?"

"That's right."

For a little while they continued, Cariad questioning, Orrin prompting. At last, when Cariad was satisfied that she
had fixed Margit's voice and manner in her physical memory, they moved on.

"You made a good choice," she told Orrin. "A shy girl
with limited social activities and few friends. I won't have
to waste a lot of time maintaining this identity."

"Yes. No one pays much attention to Margit."

Again she felt the mix of emotions, coupled now, inter-
estingly, with something like guilt. Guilt at the way he had
used her? At the inequity in their feelings? Did he know
Margit was fathoms deep in love with him?

They were traveling a tunnel that curved gently to the
right, an unchanging angle that despite their swift forward
pace produced an eerie sense of being fixed in place. By
now they had passed through so many intersections and
made so many turns that Cariad had lost all sense of direction. In her premission briefings Estrellara had warned of
the complexity of the tunnel system, but Cariad had not
imagined anything as labyrinthine as this.

"Is it much farther?" she asked.

"Not much."

"How on earth did you carry her all this distance?"

"I didn't. A group of transporters brought her in a cart."

"What?" Cariad stopped walking.

"You don't need to worry." He halted also, turning back to face her. "It's safe."

"We maintain no recruiters among the transporters. None of them serve our intelligence network. I wasn't aware that had changed."

"It hasn't."

"What did you tell them? How did you explain bringing a drugged woman to one of the outside doors?"

"I told them the truth."

"You told them the *truth?*" Cariad could not believe her ears. "You informed a nonallied group of downworlders that I was entering the Fortress?"

"The transporters have no interest in politics and intrigues, upworld or downworld. They think only of the food they haul and the goods they trade, and of living their lives undisturbed. They won't betray you."

She shook her head, angry. "How can I be sure of that? This is a serious lapse, Orrin. You weren't authorized to reveal my presence to anyone except your recruiter—"

"I was authorized to do whatever I needed to do to establish an identity for you, and to assist you in maintaining it." He was angry also, a fierce emotion blazing suddenly into being, swallowing the careful control he had shown till now. "You need my help to do what you have to do here. It'd be best if you acknowledged right from the start that I'm competent not only to advise you, but to make decisions in areas you don't have the understanding to judge. Don't think I don't know about the contempt you Gifted have for people without power. I've known it all my life— first from the Guardians I have to serve, now from you whom I choose to serve. But knowledge is power too. And in this place I am the one with the knowledge. We are equals here, whether you like it or not."

He had moved toward her as he spoke. They were eye to eye now. Cariad bit down on her anger. Yet beneath his hard words she sensed not pride or self-will, but injury. And he was entirely correct in his assessment of her need for his expertise. Estrellara had told her she could trust him; therefore, she would.

"You're right," she said. "I accept your judgment. But from now on, consult me before you make a decision. Fair enough?"

He stared at her. He had expected contempt, reprimand, the full outrage of one with power challenged by one without.

"Fair enough," he said. He turned and began walking again. His anger was gone—overcome, she suspected, by an effort of will similar to her own. She had the feeling, more from instinct than from anything he had released, that he regretted letting go of himself as he had just done.

After only a few more minutes the tunnel lost its curve, and in doing so gained an end: an arch that spanned its width and height, closed by a pair of iron gates. As they approached, Cariad felt the spark of power.

"There's a binding here."

"Yes. On the lock." Orrin stooped to set down the blankets he carried, and then reached through one of the gate's grids and pulled a fat set of iron links through it. They were closed by a padlock. "It's bound to accept its key only from the hand of the Master of the storehouse, who unlocks the gates for transporter deliveries. So even if the key is stolen, the thief can't use it." He reached under his tunic, and drew out a pair of slender pointed rods. Kneeling, he inserted them into the lock, manipulating them delicately. "But there's nothing to tell it what to do when you use something other than a key . . . of course, you don't need this, because you could just walk through these bars, couldn't you? But I can't get past any other way. There."

The lock snapped open. He removed it and pulled the chain free. Cariad looked at him, impressed.

"That's very clever."

His fair brows drew down. Inexplicably, her praise had annoyed him. "Why is it always such an astonishment to you people when someone who isn't Gifted knows something about the ways of power?"

Cariad judged it wiser not to answer. Orrin picked up the blankets again, and pulled one of the gates a little open.

Cariad slipped through. He followed, rethreading the chain through the loops set on either side of the gates' meeting point and closing it with the padlock. Beyond the gates was a lobbylike space, with sacks and crates set against the walls and a variety of debris strewn across the floor. To either side, arched openings let onto darkness.

"This is the warehouse," Orrin said. "Do you recognize it?"

Cariad looked into her mind. For an instant she was Margit, her heart beating so she could scarcely breathe, passing beneath the archway on the right and along cold aisles stacked with boxes and barrels and bins of produce, following a faint candle-glow to a hidden place strewn with blankets and sacking. The image carried with it a tangle of others—fragmentary and intimate, fraught equally with passion and embarrassment. Margit, shy and awkward and fearful of men, had been a virgin before she slept with Orrin.

"Yes," Cariad said.

"Then you know that I've . . . taken up with her. With Margit." Again the mixture of affection and guilt—more guilt this time. "It made it easier . . . to get her where she needed to be tonight. Also, I thought it would be useful. It gives you a reason to be seen with me, and to be out of your bed after hours."

Cariad felt a stab of annoyance. How many of these unasked-for machinations had he undertaken? "That wasn't necessary. I hadn't planned that we should be seen together at all. And I can leave a binding on my bed."

"But I can't," he pointed out. "And if we are to work together it must be after hours, for I can only get free for short periods during the day, and you won't be able to get free at all. As for being seen . . . we don't have watchdog wardings down here, or fardiviners who can extend their awareness through the rooms and hallways. But this is a confined community. No matter how much care we take, if we meet it will be known. I thought it would be best to deal with that ahead of time."

Cariad reminded herself that she had determined to trust his judgment. "Very well. Since you've established this as a meeting place, we'll continue to use it. Can you come tomorrow night?"

"Yes. She and I . . . we used to meet at the twenty-third bell."

"The twenty-third bell it is." Cariad began to pull off the leathers she wore. "Where do these go?"

"I'll take care of them."

Cariad closed her eyes for a moment, reaching for the feel of the woman whose identity she had borrowed. Her shoulders curved; her neck bent. To her own body, this was an artificial, uncomfortable stance, but to the shifted shape she wore, it was natural. She felt the constriction of the semblance ease as she shaped herself to the template of her disguise.

"That's it," Orrin said softly. There was wonder in his voice. "I can't see you anymore. You're her now."

Cariad turned to go, her gait Margit's slightly awkward, toes-inward lope. She felt his eyes as she slipped out of the warehouse area and into the corridor beyond.

The corridor's walls were constructed of light gray stone blocks, and the floor and ceiling were tiled with polished flagstones. Torches in metal holders provided illumination, the stone above them printed black with soot. The air held the even warmth of a heat-binding. All downworlds were built to the same pattern, with a work area for the laundries and weaveries and bakeries and craft shops, an official area for the Guardian school and assembly hall, and this long corridor that linked the two. Doors opened on either side, the entrances to the domiciles of the clans. They were marked above their architraves with the symbols of service: the cooks and food handlers, the clothmakers and dyers, the infirmary and mortuary workers, the fixers and cleaners, the stone- and wood- and metalworkers, and at last, the tailors and launderers.

Entering here, Cariad passed the family quarters, where married couples, children of less than six years, and elders past the age of work were housed in separate apartments. Beyond lay the central common, a broad low-ceilinged area that served the same purpose as a village square. The youth quarters, where children lived once they turned six and began to train for service, opened off this space, as did the apprentice shops where a clan's more specialized skills were taught, the unmarried quarters to which young clan members graduated when they entered service, and the kitchen and refectory that served them all.

Cariad entered the unmarried women's quarters, passing into a close warm darkness lightened somewhat by the glimmer of shaded candles set in wall niches. Wooden beds marched neatly across the floor, each mounded with a sleeping form. She found the bed she knew to be her own, and slipped between the rough linen sheets, drawing the blankets to her chin.

The bed smelled of Margit, the same musty scent that clung to her clothes. The air was uneasy with shadow, with the breathing and sighing and shifting of the other women and with the feeling of their dreams. Cariad knew she should concentrate on maintaining the semblance; she should also pick through the memories she had taken, in preparation for tomorrow. But the dark thing that had risen up in her in the cold passageway would no longer be held back. Somewhere above, Jolyon walked the hallways of the Keep, divided from her not by continents and circumstance, but only by air and stone. Lying on her back, she stared at the ceiling, as if the power of sight alone were enough to bridge the remaining distance.

Nine

ARIAD SAT cross-legged upon a pile of blankets in the cavelike space where Orrin and Margit had conducted their assignations. She had conjured mindlight to guide herself through the darkened storeroom, along shadowy aisles of stored food and drink, past bales of cloth and crates of finished goods and piles of raw materials. When she reached the little hideaway, she found that it was set about with candle stubs and small oil lamps. Extinguishing the glow of power, she awakened flame upon them all, an illumination that was as much shadow as light. In Margit's memory, this was a magic place, cushioned with soft draperies and bathed in golden radiance. To Cariad it was a cramped, uncomfortable burrow, unpleasantly chilly and annoyingly dim.

The twenty-third bell had sounded a little while before, but Orrin had not yet arrived. Waiting, Cariad uncrossed her legs and drew them to her chest, wrapping her arms around her knees to hoard her body warmth. She had let go of Margit's curved and diffident posture as soon as she entered here: she could still feel the relief of being straight again. She wore Margit's nightclothes and a thick woven shawl she had found among Margit's belongings. The wakefulness of the night before, the tedious labor of the day just past, and the heavier-than-usual mindguard she needed to protect herself against the chaotic emotions of the unGifted, had left her drained and weary. She would not sleep this night either—because of her exhaustion the Margit-disguise still required a conscious effort to maintain, and she did not dare close her eyes for fear of slipping back toward her own form.

A servant's day began at the fifth bell. The older unmarried women got up first, slipping out into the common area and bringing back lighted torches, setting them in place while the rest of the women rose, yawning and chatting and complaining according to their various natures. Following Margit's memories and the others' example, Cariad made her bed and folded her nightdress into the chest at its foot, and put on daytime clothing: a linen petticoat, a gray woolen skirt, a white three-quarter-sleeved blouse, and a black laced bodice. A large red eye, twin to the brands on her arm, was embroidered on the left shoulder, and the sigil of the tailoring and laundering clan on the right.

She followed the other women to the necessary rooms, and then to the long, low-ceilinged refectory. Six tables ran its length, set so close there was space for only the narrowest of aisles between. The benches were crowded with downworlders. Vats of porridge simmered on braziers near the entrance; loaves of bread and pitchers of ale were already set out on the tables. The air was hazy with torch smoke, but not as much as one might expect in a closed space, indicating some form of air exchange. Mealtime proctors patrolled the room, carrying slender staffs, which they used to tap the shoulders of those who became too boisterous.

Cariad dished up her breakfast and took her place among the girls who formed Margit's small circle of friends. Memory told her that Margit, always reticent, had become almost completely mute since her involvement with Orrin; she sat quiet as the girls giggled and whispered, responding as necessary with smiles or nods. Under cover of her silence she watched the room, a strange double observation that joined Margit's unquestioning understanding of these surroundings to her own outsider's perspective.

On one level the breakfasting workers were like any group of individuals, talking and interacting in entirely unremarkable ways. On another, they were clearly creatures of a confined world. Unlike other Guardian workers, who were allowed to move around fairly freely, Roundhead servants never left their downworld. None of the people here had ever felt the sun on their faces, a thing that showed in the unweathered smoothness of their skin, and in its translucent, underground pallor. There was also an extraordinary recurrence of physical likeness: everywhere, Cariad saw permutations of Orrin's tilted eyes, shades of Margit's blond hair. This was a single family, its blood concentrated by centuries of inbreeding. The years of training necessary to master a clan's more exacting skills made exogamous marriage impractical, and though the careful keeping of genealogies ensured that marriages satisfied a required degree of ancestral distance, every husband and every wife were kin to one another. Over time the patterns of resemblance had refined themselves so narrowly that it was possible to tell just by looking at a servant's face whether she was a food handler or a cleaner or a seamstress.

When the meal was done Cariad followed the procession out of the clan's quarters and into the central hallway, threading her way through the crowds of workers bound for the upper levels. There were cooks in aprons, meal servers with trays, cleaners with brushes and buckets, tailors with sewing kits, all moving in orderly two-by-two formation toward the staircase that gave access to the world above. Cariad herself continued past the staircase, toward the work area that housed the skilled craft shops that fabricated, maintained, and repaired everything in the Keep, from cutlery to clothing to wall-hangings. The laundries were here as well, with their huge soaking vats and wringing apparatuses and rinsing pools and drying rods. Here, in a large room devoted solely to this purpose, she and fourteen other women spent all day sorting the laundry of the Arm of the Stone.

The sorting room was brightly illuminated by a dozen torches. Rows of waist-high tables, with piles of sacks beneath them, were ranged at its center, and huge hampers for dirty laundry were set along its walls. These held linens only. Roundheads followed the Guardian custom of communal ownership in regard to undergarments and toweling and bedsheets, but their shirts and breeches and robes were their own property. The tailoring and laundering clan included a special cadre of workers who did nothing but maintain these rich garments.

Each woman took an armful from the hampers, carried it to the tables, and examined the items one by one, dispatching them into the sacks according to their labels: Launder Only, Special Cleaning, Mending, Discard. Periodically, male members of the clan came in to dump more laundry into the hampers, or to haul away the filled sacks. Now and then one of the supervisors appeared to make a circuit of the room. In other downworlds, the Castellan and his deputies provided this kind of oversight, but the Arm of the Stone, with its abhorrence of menial tasks, preferred to train servants to such duty.

Cariad had Margit's hands and eyes, and the memory of how she had used them in this task, but theoretical familiarity could not make up for the fact that she had never physically performed such actions: never run her hands over an undertunic to evaluate whether it was worn or frayed or needed mending, never held up a sheet to scan it for stains that needed special treatment. The other women, noticing her slowness, attributed it to an assignation the night before; they teased her, sharp comments that stopped just short of being cruel. Cariad did not reply, but ducked her head and smiled a secret smile. Memory indicated that Margit, a frequent butt of others' jokes, was pleased by this particular teasing; she was proud of her love affair, the only one she had ever had, and enjoyed the others' surprise and envy at her alliance with a desirable man.

The hours of work were long ended. Cariad had eaten, strolled about the common area with Margit's friends, even lain for a while in Margit's bed. Yet the labor of the day was still with her. A parade of sheets passed before her mind's eye, a procession of underlinen. She saw frayed underarm seams, unraveling hems, sweatstains and foodstains and stains whose origins she did not wish to consider. She smelled the mixed stinks of perfume and sweat and bodies too long unwashed—not just in memory but in fact, imprinted upon her hands and arms, lingering in her clothes. The musty odor that had repelled her when she first put on Margit's nightdress was not Margit's uncleanness,

but the uncleanness of countless others, a mark of her service as distinctive as the stained hands of a dyer. Margit
endured these things, day by day, in perfect equanimity—
had endured them since the age of thirteen, would endure
them until the day she grew too old to work. Contemplating
the narrow box of this existence, Cariad's skin crawled in
horror. She had ridden in attack upon bands of Journeyers,
patrolled city streets beneath the eyes of Guardians, entered
Orderhouse dungeons and brought to safety those held inside. She had been exhausted and hungry, bored and fearful, injured and in pain. Yet none of these things had
burdened her spirit as this single day of menial labor had
done.

Outside in the storeroom, there was a sound of footsteps.
The blanket draped across the opening of the little space
moved aside, and Orrin slipped into the light. He folded
himself into the corner opposite, like Cariad drawing his
knees to his chest and wrapping his arms around them.

They had not met since last night: as a supervisor, he did
not eat in the refectory, but took his meals in a separate
dining room in company with other high-ranking workers.
Now, for the first time, she saw his uncovered face with
her own eyes rather than through Margit's memories. The
sharp features, the high wide cheekbones, the translucent
blondness, were recognizably of his clan; but the broad
forehead and pointed chin were very much his own. He had
the look of an intelligent fox, an impression heightened by
the tilted eyes and upswept brows she had observed last
night. It was a face rather different from the idealized image
Margit cherished, less perfect but more interesting. Like all
male downworlders of the Keep, he wore his hair cropped
short in the Roundhead manner. He was not dressed for
sleep, but in his workclothes.

"How did it go today?" he asked.

Cariad shrugged. "I'm slow yet. Fortunately the other
women put it down to my presumed state of lovesickness."

He smiled, revealing white teeth, the incisors a little
longer than the rest. "I told you there aren't any secrets
here."

"Especially not when a person tells the secret to everyone she knows."

"She did that?" Cariad could feel his chagrin. "She promised me she'd keep it to herself."

Cariad did not point out the illogic of this reaction, based on what he had said last night. His ambivalence toward Margit, and the consequences he would reap from the association he had made with her, were not her concern.

"I've been thinking about how to proceed," she said. "From what we talked about last night, it seems to me that Konstant is either dead, or else gone beyond my power to ascertain. Now, I know you've already checked on Roundhead deaths here in the Keep, but you said there were other places a body could go. I'd like you to check those as well. Meanwhile, I'll make a survey of the public cells."

Orrin had been withholding his gaze from her face, as he had last night, staring instead at one of the little oil lamps. Now his eyes jumped to hers. "I've already told you he isn't in the public cells."

"Have you seen them for yourself?"

"No, but I know people who have. Isn't that good enough for you?"

"It has nothing to do with it. As a human being I may believe everything you or others tell me, but as an operative I don't have that luxury. When I report to my superiors, every conclusion I make must be backed by my own personal certainty. Even if you'd looked those cells over with your own eyes, I'd still have to see them for myself."

He glanced away as she spoke. Distantly, through her guard, she could feel him examining the resentful currents of his reaction. At last he nodded. "I understand."

"Can you make me tunnel maps, to guide me to the prison and the Amphitheater?"

He shook his head. "You saw what a labyrinth the tunnels are. I can walk them, but I'm not sure I could draw them. It's better if I go with you."

She hesitated, but only for a moment. "All right. That leaves the private cells. What can you tell me about them?"

"All the Council members have private cells, except for the Apprentice-Master, who doesn't live in the Keep. Probably the Councilors' First Deputies do also, and possibly come of the more influential Reds. That's all I know. Only bodyservants are allowed in the inner corridors of the third floor, and bodyservants can't talk about their masters. I can't even tell you where the apartments are."

"That doesn't matter. If you can identify these people for me, I can track them to their suites."

"I can identify them for you."

"Good. One more thing. I'd like you to find out as much as you can about Konstant's activities in the weeks before his disappearance. If it turns out he isn't in the Fortress, it may give me some idea of where he's gone."

He nodded. "I'll take care of it."

"I think it'd be a good idea to get the identifications out of the way first. Can we start on that tonight?"

"Actually, if you can wait till tomorrow, there's an honorary banquet. The Council will be there, and most of their staff. You can see them all at once."

"Very well. We'll meet at this same time tomorrow, then."

She put her hands against the floor, pushing herself to the half-crouch which was greatest extension of height possible in this cramped place. Abruptly, she was seized by dizziness. She sank back, her head hanging, waiting for it to pass.

"What's the matter?" She sensed his quick move toward her, and its equally quick retraction. "Are you ill?"

"Just tired." She closed her eyes, dry and sore from so many hours of wakefulness, and pushed her fingers against them. Just as the shell of the Margit-disguise was not quite firm, its feel was not quite familiar; she had yet to lose the odd shock of touching flesh whose shape was not her own. "I didn't sleep last night."

"Why not?"

"It takes a little while for the semblance to become automatic. If I sleep before that, I risk losing control and slipping back toward my own form." Again she rubbed her eyes. "It's still not set. I won't be able to sleep tonight either."

"You could sleep here."

"Here?" She raised her head and looked at him. He returned her gaze. At some point—she could not recall exactly when—he had ceased to avert his eyes from her face.

"Why not? There's only me to see you. I can keep watch and wake you at the fourth bell."

She hesitated. She did not like the idea of sleeping under his eye. It was one thing to be witnessed, as she had been the day before, in the process of a willed change, and quite another to be observed in an involuntary loss of control. But she desperately needed rest.

"All right. Thank you."

She folded her shawl into a pillow and lay down on her side. She was so exhausted that just to close her eyes was to begin the slide into darkness. From the widening distance of that descent, she was aware of Orrin nearby; she felt warmth enfold her, and smelled the musty scent of woolen blankets. He was watching her. She knew it even through the drawn curtain of her eyelids, even through the muffling tides of sleep. It occurred to her that she should order him to look away. But she could not rouse herself enough to speak.

The next night—well-rested, the Margit-semblance effortless at last—Cariad made her way to the warehouse area. Orrin was waiting, not in the cubbyhole where they had met last night, but beneath the warehouse doorway. He carried a short ladder.

"What's that for?" she asked.

"You'll see."

They traversed the central passageway. It was empty: a servant's day ended as early as it began, and with the exception of workers needed for late cooking or serving duty, the clans were abed by the twenty-first bell. The guttering torches sent shadow sliding at their heels. The upper regions of the Keep were crowded with bindings and power-automations, but belowground everything but the heat-bindings and the mindfire that burned in the kitchen stoves was manual.

They reached the stairway and began to climb. Wide and steep, it led in three flights to the top of the Keep. Each flight terminated on a landing, with mindlit passageways leading off on either side. The passages, so cramped that there was barely room for two people to pass, snaked for great distances between the outer and inner walls of the Keep, linking the basement world with the work areas of the upper levels, so that servants could travel between the two without ever entering their masters' space.

At the second-floor landing they turned left. At last Orrin halted.

"This is it," he said. He laid his hand on the surface of the inner wall. "The Hall of Six Reds. It's the second largest banquet room in the Keep." Cariad nodded: she had committed the floor plan of the Keep to memory as part of her premission preparation. "There are several places to watch, but this is the best. It's directly opposite the high table."

He set the ladder in place and mounted it. Just below the juncture of wall and ceiling, a strip of metal was set flush with the stone. A loop protruded from its center. He hooked his finger through the loop and tugged. With a soft grating sound the metal came free. Light reached through the opening, and the muted hum of voices was suddenly audible.

"I've always wondered," Cariad said, "why the Arm allowed spy stations to be built into their behindwall passages."

Orrin had set his eyes to the opening; now he tucked the strip of metal into his belt and began to back down the ladder. "All behindwall passages have spy stations. It's traditional."

"Yes, in the rest of the Fortress." No one knew the origin of the spy stations—whether the Guardians had included them in the Fortress's original design, or whether the downworlders, who had done the actual building, had incorporated into the structure of their world the means to keep watch on their masters. "But the Keep is new."

On the floor again, Orrin shrugged. "The private areas of the Keep were built to the Arm's design, but for the behindwall passages and the downworld they used traditional plans. Maybe the plans included the spy stations. Maybe the Arm wanted to reserve the right to spy on itself.

Though I've never seen a Roundhead back here. Not many downworlders use the stations, either."

"No?"

"Curiosity is not a quality the Arm encourages in its workers."

His face had closed. Behind it, she sensed the flow of memory, conveying an impression of limitation, or perhaps discipline. Had he been punished, when he was young, for being curious? Yet in adulthood, he still watched.

"Go up," he said. "I'll describe the Council members."

She mounted the ladder. The spyhole, a little broader than the width of her face and about a half a finger high, afforded a surprisingly complete view of the banquet hall. The ceilings of the passage and the hall were level, but the hall had greater depth, and she found herself gazing down from a considerable height. As its name implied, the hall was six times red, its walls, floor, and ceiling each made of a different stone. It was lit by mindlight, not formed into globes or sheets but fountaining down the walls like cascades of stars, and by masses of candles in standing candelabra—thousands of points of brilliance, caught and multiplied thousands of times by the gleaming plate upon the tables and the rich jewels of the Roundheads. Of all the objects in the hall, only the workers, moving like shadows among the glittering company, did not shine.

"The high table is directly opposite." Orrin's voice rose softly from below. "The entire Council is seated there. The Staff-Holder is at the center. One of his companions is behind him with the staff of office. To his right is the Second . . ."

He went on, identifying each of the Councilors in turn. Cariad only half listened. Her gaze had stopped on Jolyon. She saw the russet hair, the pale skin, the brooding mouth and heavy eyes. He was slight, his head rising only just above the shoulder of the man beside him. His hands lay loosely on either side of his plate, the food on it barely touched. He wore a great weight of jewelry, his wrists and fingers bound with gems, his ears dripping gold, the breast of his robe nearly solid with chains and necklaces. In the brilliant light of the hall he seemed improbably youthful.

A marble stillness overlaid his features, as if he were dreaming with his eyes open.

From the time Cariad could remember, Jolyon had leaned enormously across her life, almost as hugely as her father did. Yet she had never speculated about his physical appearance as she did about her father's, perhaps because even in the full flush of her childhood passion for revenge she had never truly believed she would get close enough to see him. In her mind he had always been what the Tale made him: an idea, a force, vast and faceless as the sky. To see him now, defined by flesh and shaped by bone, was as strange and powerful as anything she had ever experienced, like encountering within the limits of daily reality the prophetic images of a dream.

She became aware that Orrin was tugging at her skirt. "Let me up again," he said. "I'll see if I can find the Deputies."

For a while longer they traded positions, Orrin climbing up to survey the hall, then prompting Cariad where to look. At last he ran out of faces to identify.

"You might as well go," she told him. "I'll stay. I want to begin the tracking tonight."

She felt his resistance, strong and immediate: he did not like being dismissed. But he did not protest. Instead he reached inside his tunic, and held something out to her.

"If you're going into the Keep, you should take this."

Cariad looked at the thing in his hand. It was an irregular lump of metal, dull silver in color, its pitted surface streaked with what looked like soot, as if it had been salvaged from the ashes of a forge. "What is it?"

"Crossing bracelets are made of this metal. It isn't shaped, but it'll get you past the barrier as well as a bracelet would. I know you can get through without it, but it's a good idea to have it even so. There might be alarms set up on the other side."

Cariad took it from him, turning it over in her fingers. The downworlders of the Keep were severely restricted in their ability to move about their masters' space. Barriers blocked all access points between the behindwall corridors and the Keep proper, and the bracelets, issued only to body-servants, cleaners, tailors, and a few others, were the sole means of passage. Margit's memories indicated that the bracelets were objects of power, bound to match the structure of the barrier, but there was no power in the cold thing Cariad held in her hand.

"This isn't bound," she said.

Orrin smiled. "Everyone thinks the bracelets are bound. Actually they're not. It's the metal they're made of that the barrier recognizes."

"Really?" Cariad was surprised.

"Yes. It's logical, if you think about it. The Arm hates menial tasks and wants as little contact as possible with those who perform them. That's why there are so many barriers to keep us out of Roundhead space. That's why the Castellan would rather train people like me to supervise than use his Deputies, the way it's done in other down-worlds. It's the same with the bracelets. If they did bind them, it would mean setting an initial binding, and then checking every year or so to make sure the bindings were working as they should. This way, all they have to do is give us the bracelets and see that we have no access to the metal, so there's no danger of accidental passage. They let us believe the bracelets are bound—a piece of metal is just a piece of metal, but a bound bracelet is something special. The person who wears one will take his duties that much more seriously, and won't be as likely to let someone else borrow it for an hour or two. Of course . . ." he shrugged ". . . I wasn't actually sure I was right about all of this until I found myself on the other side of the barrier."

As in the tunnel two nights before, Cariad was struck with admiration—not just for his cleverness, but for his audacity. For an unGifted worker to try himself against the workings of Roundhead power, based merely on his faith in an idea, required either towering foolishness or astonishing courage. As limited as her acquaintance with him was, she did not suspect Orrin of the former.

"I'm impressed. And not because you're unGifted," she added, remembering his earlier response to a compliment.

"I don't think it would have occurred to me to think of such a thing."

"It's not that impressive." He smiled. This time her praise had pleased him. "I spent a lot of time thinking about this kind of thing when I was younger. I was bound to be right about some of it."

"If you have no access to the metal, where did you get this?"

"From the transporters. I couldn't tell them what kind of metal it was, but going by my theory I could tell them what kind it wasn't. They'd bring me bits and pieces, and I'd try them out."

"I see." She turned the metal over in her fingers once more, and then slipped it into the pocket of her skirt. "Well, thank you. I'll take good care of it."

"The kitchen entrance is just a few hundred yards that way." He pointed down the corridor. "The servers will stay until the last Roundhead is gone, but the cooks will leave earlier."

Cariad nodded.

"Leave the ladder when you go. I'll come back for it later."

"All right."

He looked at her. He had run out of things to say. Once again she could feel his unwillingness to be dismissed. But she met his gaze, silent, and after a moment he yielded, turning and moving off down the passage. He walked well: straight and swift, with a balanced economy of motion. The sense of double observation, which had lessened over the past day, returned: for an instant she saw him not only as herself, to whom he was merely a clever and resourceful stranger, but as Margit, to whom everything about him was achingly familiar and heartstoppingly beautiful.

She climbed the ladder again. She was pleased to be alone. This was how she preferred to work, free of the encumbrance of companionship, constrained only by the necessities of the situation and her own will.

She observed the banquet hall as course followed elaborate course, as speeches were made and toasts were drunk. She inventoried the identifications Orrin had given her, fixing the faces in her memory: the Deputies, the assistants, the companions, the Councilors. At the center of the high table the Staff-Holder sat motionless in his chair, as if he were asleep; directly behind him one of his companions held up the staff of office, its garnet finial flashing in the mindlight. Jolyon sat on the Staff-Holder's right. Next to him was the Investigation-Master, an intense sharp-featured man, deep in conversation with the bearded Castellan, who sat at the table's outer edge. To the Staff-Holder's left was the Limit-Master, slender and dark-skinned and, if his expression were any indication, deeply bored. The Treasurer, beside him, appeared less bored than nervous, his ringed fingers restlessly twisting and untwisting the chain of his Guardian medal. Furthest to the left sat the Apprentice-Master. He was a gaunt, white-haired man, his black robe bare of jewelry other than his Guardian medal. He was the only Councilor who did not have a companion to stand behind him. He seemed isolated in the crowded room, as if enclosed in an atmosphere of his own making.

But always, as many times as she removed it, Cariad's gaze returned to Jolyon. Like Marhalt, the Apprentice-Master, he conveyed an impression of isolation. There was a zone of empty space around him, an invisible margin others did not cross. The workers who set plates or cups before him pulled back even as they reached forward; the Investigation-Master leaned away rather than toward him to address him. At his back his three companions waited, their eyes roving the room. Directly behind his chair stood a small black-haired man, dressed in servant garb, though by his appearance he was not part of the Keep's downworld cadre.

It was well past the second bell when the final course was brought in. Cariad slipped from the ladder and made her way to the access point between the behindwall regions and the interior of the Keep. There she called up a Guardian-style veil of invisibility. It did not offer the assurance of Goldwine's methods, but she did not want to stress the Margit-semblance by shifting her flesh still further.

The barrier, meant for the unGifted, was entirely physical. It yielded easily to Orrin's lump of metal. Orienting herself to the map inside her head, Cariad set out for the banquet hall. Like everyone in the world, she had heard tales of the Arm's wealth, but what she saw as she passed through the Keep—the rich fabrics and rare woods, the exquisite paintings and sculptures and frescoes and bas-reliefs, the parade of marble and alabaster and semiprecious stone—was so astonishing in its opulent abundance that after a little while it did not seem quite real.

Reaching the banquet hall, she stationed herself opposite the doors, a pair of ebony portals with the Arm's eye-symbol inlaid in red at their midpoint. After a little while the eye cracked at its center and the doors swung outward, turning on their hinges until they rested flat against the wall. A torrent of Roundheads poured into the hall, an agitation of rich black robes and crimson belts and scarlet boots, liberally highlighted with gold. The Council emerged last, a stately procession arranged in order of precedence. Marhalt brought up the rear, a lone black figure, like a punctuation mark at the end of a complicated sentence.

Cariad fell in at Marhalt's back. At the dusky staircase that joined floor to floor Marhalt turned, moving downward. The Apprentice-Master was ascetic for a Roundhead; he had never claimed the luxurious Keep apartments to which his rank entitled him, but remained in the Apprentice College, in the same modest suite he had always occupied. The other Councilors began to climb. At the stairway's top the procession broke, each Councilor taking his own direction. Cariad followed behind Jolyon. His companions surrounded him, one in front and two at his back. His servant walked at his side. The companions were tall, powerfully-built men whose broad figures all but hid their diminutive charge from sight. Swiftly, they threaded the labyrinth of passages, a maze of turns and angles that Cariad committed to memory as she went. Now and then, as they rounded a corner or passed an intersection, they moved apart, and she caught a glimpse of Jolyon, slender in his black robe, his russet head bent as if in contemplation. Even from behind he shone with gold: the necklaces he wore were draped across his shoulders to hang equally fore and back.

Entranced by these flashes of vision, Cariad forgot herself and drew too close. One of the companions wheeled about, his hard face alert. Cariad froze. The companion's eyes swept the corridor—once, twice, a third time. At last he turned away, lengthening his stride to catch up with the others. Cariad followed, at a greater distance this time.

Jolyon and his attendants halted at last before one of the red doors. The lead companion set his hand against the wood. There was a pause, and then the door swung open. The group moved through it, and was gone.

Slowly, carefully, Cariad approached the door, all her senses alert for barriers and wardings. A handshaped piece of metal was set into the wood—matched, no doubt, to the hands of Jolyon and his retinue. There was no other visible means of entry. Close to, she could feel that at least two barriers lay across the entranceway. From her experience in other settings, she guessed that one of them was an illusion-stripper.

She gazed at the blank red surface of the door, wishing, for perhaps the first time in her life, for a power she did not possess: fardivining, which would have made it possible for her to look through the wooden planks, through the stone around them, through all the walls of Jolyon's private spaces and into his most protected inner sanctums. She thought of him, of his russet hair and marble face, of his surprising slightness: a man of words abruptly reduced to flesh, a great thing suddenly made small. Small enough to kill.

Something moved in her. She shuddered. Her palms seemed to burn. She moved her hand upward to a point just below her collarbones, pressing her fingers against the drawstring bag hidden there. She was cold, cold as the river of ice at the heart of Goldwine's mountain. Yet inside her there was fire.

A long time later, she stole away.

Ten

N THE night of her arrival, listening as Orrin described the redistribution of Konstant's belongings, Cariad understood with the gut instinct of her profession that Konstant was dead. But instinct, no matter how tested by experience, was not fact. And so she proceeded with as much care as she would have taken for someone she knew to be living.

Each night she met with Orrin in the chilly warehouse and heard his reports on the tasks she had given him. As a supervisor, his movements were not monitored; so long as the work he was responsible for was completed, he could go about the Keep more or less as he wished. Cariad was aware that at least some of his information came from the transporters, but for the most part he did not detail his sources, and she did not ask. Eventually she would have to verify whatever he had told her, but for now she was content to trust him. She did use her Gift to monitor him as he spoke, alert for any elision or uncertainty, but there was none, only the solid feel of thorough work. Even knowing as little of him as she did, she had not expected otherwise.

The meeting over, she made her way to the third floor of the Keep, where, cloaked in invisibility, she waylaid and overpowered Roundhead bodyservants, who went about their masters' business regardless of the time of night. Binding them to unconsciousness, she scanned their minds, searching for the locations and occupancy of private cells, and anything else that might be of interest.

Later, she descended to the second floor, where she spent

186

an hour or two in Jolyon's office suite. If Konstant had been sent on an official mission, there would surely be some record of it there. She had been ready, the first time she approached the offices, for a variety of ingenious defenses; but there was only a lock, easily turned by only a moderate application of making power. Inside, she discovered an equal lack of power-sourced precautions. Once she began her search, she realized why. Although the office's public papers—the official reports, the minutes of certain meetings, the personnel files—were clear enough, Jolyon's staff maintained most of their documents in a complicated cipher. By the end of the first night, Cariad knew she would find nothing to help her. Even so, she continued the search, unwilling to declare defeat until she had made a full examination. She copied down examples of cipher on scraps of parchment, to be passed to Orrin to give to the information patrol. It would provide Goldwine's codebreakers with something to puzzle over.

By the close of her sixth night in the Fortress, her bodyservant scans had disposed of any possibility that Konstant was being held privately on the third floor, and her fruitless search of Jolyon's offices was complete. On the seventh night she gave Orrin the cipher samples and a verbal message for the information patrol, outlining what she had discovered so far and her suspicions as to the outcome of the mission. He left to deliver it, and she returned to the third floor, where she roved about the passages, ending up at last, as she often did, before the door she knew to be Jolyon's. She stood outside it for a time, watching. The bodyservant of one of the companions emerged, but she did not follow; she had already pursued and scanned him, as well as two of his fellows. From their minds she had learned the exact night of Konstant's disappearance, as well as the fact that he had never been held in Jolyon's private cells. That was all. The servants knew no more, not even whether Konstant had departed alive.

It remained now only to canvass the public holding areas. Accordingly, on the eighth night she and Orrin set out, bound for the prison annex. They wore Orrin's transporter leathers, not for camouflage but for warmth in the frigid tunnels, since Cariad, for caution's sake, had wrapped a veil of invisibility about them both.

Aboveground, the annex lay only half an hour distant, but through the tunnels the journey was much longer. Every destination in the Fortress, Orrin explained to Cariad, could be reached by a variety of routes, although no one knew why there were so many, or why the tunnels turned and shifted and bifurcated instead of traveling directly from point to point. Only at the Fortress's outer edges, where the doors opened onto the outside world, did they run straight: four passages that traced the exact shape of the walls, enclosing the inner tunnels like the sides of a box.

Orrin proceeded swiftly, making turns and threading intersections with easy certainty. He knew where he was not simply within the tunnel system, but in relation to the Fortress above. He narrated their progress as they went, moving diagonally from the Keep at the Fortress's left rear to the Soldier Wing at its right midpoint: the walkway that joined the Keep to the Speaker Wing, the Speaker Wing itself, the Garden of the Stone—Cariad thought of her father, whose feet had once rested on the ground above her head—the Soldier Wing, and at last the prison annex, extending from the rear of the Soldier Wing like a long black arm. The air beneath the Wings was sharp with the scent of sulfur: the Great Cess, Orrin explained, a vast pit punched deep into the mountain to accommodate the drainings of the Suborders' basement cesspits. The Great Cess was located almost exactly below the Garden: ten centuries of waste swimming beneath the most sacred of all the world's sacred places.

As she did when she worked alone, Cariad abandoned her Margitisms, moving with her own straight-shouldered gait, matching Orrin's quick pace with her own long stride, speaking in her own clear voice. They talked as they went, at first about procedure, then to pass the time. Orrin was intensely curious about the outside world. From his behindwall eavesdropping he had gained a surprisingly substantial knowledge of people and politics, but he had no notion of geography and only the vaguest idea of culture. Cariad found herself telling him about her travels and postings, the places she had lived and the sights she had seen. Orrin hung on her words with the breathless fascination of a child. She did not need her heartsensing ability to read the longing in him. In this, as in so many other things, he was unlike his fellow downworlders—who, placidly contented with their lives of service, showed little interest in the world beyond the Fortress.

It did not seem to distress Orrin to be wrapped in Cariad's power. Nor did he appear to have any conceptual difficulty with the fact that, although their visibility to one another did not change, they were hidden from other eyes. In her experience of the unGifted, such easy acceptance was unusual. Even the members of the networks, dependent as they were on the Gifted operatives who guarded them, found it distressing to view the exercise of power at close range, a superstitious fear Cariad understood in theory but whose irrationality, in practice, only irritated her. But the downworlders of the Fortress were born and bred with power, and interacted with it all their working lives. Cleaners and tailors crossed barriers without a thought, and passed daily through doors that opened of their own accord and into rooms that lit in response to entry. Downworld children climbed up to dip their hands into the mindlight that ran in strips along the ceilings of the behindwall corridors, painting each other's faces with their glowing fingers or writing graffiti on the walls. Downworld cooks pirated the mindfire of the stoves and ovens, using long-handled ladles to scoop it up like butter and drop it into metal boxes with grilled tops, which those in private apartments used to heat water for tea or for washing.

And yet in this also Orrin was not quite like his fellows. He was not just comfortable with power: he *knew* power, with a depth and confidence a Gifted person might have envied—though, since he himself was not Gifted, it could only be an outlaw knowledge. The lockpicking and the crossing metal were only the beginning of the trespasses he had undertaken. He had deduced which of the Keep's watchdog bindings were keyed solely to the detection of Gifts, so that an unGifted person could move past them as if he were invisible. He had discovered that most barriers, when touched, focused their power upon the point of impact, leaving a breath-brief gap at their outer edges for an agile person to slip through. He had found that if he crouched close to the floor, torches and candles sensitive to entry would not be triggered. He had learned that doors keyed to open automatically would remain closed if approached at an extreme oblique angle.

All this expertise had been gained at great personal risk, for if his masters ever discovered his unraveling of their secrets, they would surely execute him on the spot. Nor was it of much use to him, unGifted as he was and bound to a life of service. It was clear, however, that the urge to know drove him far more strongly than any sense of self-preservation. Cariad found this fascinating, and oddly admirable. She was not certain, in his place, whether she would have had so much courage.

The prison annex had its own small downworld, servants who cooked prison food and cleaned the cells and made prison-clothes. There was nothing to bar entry, for only Roundheads locked their workers in. The annex itself held no Violators—unGifted Violators were either executed or mindkilled, while Gifted Violators had their Gifts removed, a process that nearly always made them witless. Virtually every other kind of wrongdoer was confined here, however: Guardians who had committed crimes of passion, servants caught in a variety of misdemeanors, Novices and Apprentices in confinement for some infraction of the rules, and criminals from the outside world, bandit chiefs and mass murderers and serial rapists and highwaymen and political dissidents and academics whose writings were deemed subversive.

In addition, there was an asylumlike area for Guardians who had gone mad. It held neardiviners and sensitives, and a few prescients, but in the main the occupants were heartsensers: specialists, like Cariad's mother, in intrigue and espionage whose minds had broken under the stress of their empathic Gifts. This was the heartsenser's curse, the fate Goldwine had held up to Cariad throughout her childhood. Cariad had never really feared it, any more than she feared death. She had been brought up to defend herself with methods the Guardians did not allow their heartsensers—who must remain always receptive—to employ, and had never encountered an individual or mass emotion she could not screen away. Yet now, moving between these weeping or staring or whispering lunatics, she felt a kind of superstitious dread. One day the prophecy would be fulfilled, and she would no longer be safe from death or injury. It might become possible, then, for her to lose herself as these pitiful wrecked people had done. She had always known this, but never so clearly as now.

Cariad and Orrin spent two nights surveying the prison, a nightmare journey through three levels of cells and dungeons and locked dormitories. They saw men and women who paced freely from wall to wall, and others who were bound with metal straps to iron frames, and still others who were chained neck and wrist and ankle with the blue-glowing power-warded manacles used to confine Gifted prisoners. They saw cells where men had clearly been confined for decades, their hair and beards falling below their waists, their bodies skeletal and scabbed with filth. They saw cells that had been bound to heat or cold, and others that contained illusions, for the suffering of those inside. They saw, at the end of a long blind corridor, a cell that had obviously made to isolate a powerful Gifted wrongdoer, for it was entirely hung with pearly power-damping matrices, so thick they completely obscured the black stone of the walls. There was a little grating inset upon the door; peering through it, Cariad saw the cell was empty.

On the tenth night they set out for the Amphitheater, the last of the public holding areas Cariad needed to survey. The Amphitheater was near the front of the Fortress, a walk of nearly three hours from the Keep at the Fortress' back. The Amphitheater had no servant downworld: the tunnel entrance led directly into the holding area. Here there was a gate, locked with a padlock; Orrin reached for his lockpick tools, but Cariad placed her hand on it and snapped it open through her Gift. The Amphitheater's cells, like those in the Keep, were vacant. A detail of Soldiers stood guard, lost in a trance of boredom. Cariad and Orrin stole past, cocooned in their veil of invisibility, peering into the empty spaces. It took them less than half an hour to finish.

They began the journey back. Cariad was conscious of her fatigue, which seemed deeper than it should be, even given the travels of the past few nights. It was the drudgery of the day that made the difference: the hours of unbroken standing, the unpleasantness of passing her hands over others' filth, the monotony of the work. She thought, sometimes, of Margit, who was not conscious of these things, who did not see her life as a prison, but as a wondrous passage alight with possibility of marriage, children, festivals, celebrations. A life lived in snatches, in the narrow margins of the work that was its sole justification, yet valued as if it were whole.

Turning at an intersection, they saw a group of transporters a little way ahead. They had passed such groups before; always they had slipped by unseen. But this time Orrin put his hand on Cariad's arm.

"Let go of the invisibility," he murmured. "I'm going to ask them to give us a lift."

"Are you sure—"

"Don't worry. I know them."

Cariad released the invisibility-binding. Orrin ran to catch up with the transporters, who halted, greeting him with obvious familiarity. There were four of them, three men and one woman. They wore leathers, painted with bright-hued transporter symbols. Their long hair was twisted into braids and decorated with colored cords and beads, and wild beards concealed the faces of the men. Transporter carts were always brilliantly painted; this one was an eye-aching shade of blue, with a yellow railing running around all four sides and decorative designs in green and cherry red.

When Goldwine had begun to establish her in-Fortress intelligence network, the transporters were among the first downworlders she attempted to recruit. With their high mobility and pan-Fortress contact, they seemed ideal agents. But all her efforts ended in failure. The vein of Guardian-focused bitterness, which could often be tapped among other downworlders, did not seem to exist in the transporters. They passed most of their working lives in the isolation of the tunnels, beyond the orbit of Guardian observation, and in the solitude of that environment they had evolved a deep sense of their own difference from the other groups belowground. The Guardians in charge of the Fortress' food production system, whose supervisory efforts were focused principally upon the agricultural workers and their many tools, tolerated the transporters' eccentricities in a way they never would have had the transporters been part of an ordinary downworld, where service was of a more direct and personal nature, and the roles of servant and master were more intimately interdependent. As long as they reliably fulfilled their duties, the transporters were left largely undisturbed to practice their odd customs and to live their nomadic lifestyle within the vast cavern system where the food they distributed was produced.

Orrin turned and beckoned. "Come on," he called. "They can take us most of the way."

The cart was empty except for a pile of roughweave sacks at the front. Cariad clambered up, pulling some of the sacks toward her to make a softer place to sit. Orrin followed. The transporters bent to the long curved traces, and the cart sprang forward, so well-balanced that it scarcely jolted. The transporters settled into a steady jog, swift enough to produce a slight passage wind. They began to sing, a repetitive chanting tune with words too slurred to make out.

"What are they singing?" Cariad said to Orrin.

He cocked his head, listening. "It's a song about a very stupid boy who loved a girl from a different clan. The girl's father didn't want his daughter to marry such a stupid boy, so he decided to set the boy a task he couldn't possibly perform. He told the boy to go out into the tunnels and bring back all four elements: water, earth, wind, and fire. Things that exist naturally in the caverns, you see, but not in the tunnels. The boy was cleverer than the father thought. He found a dagger of ice hanging from a tunnel ceiling, and melted it in a pot. He collected clods of mud that had fallen off transporters' boots, and brought them back in a basket. He filled his lungs with cold tunnel air, and breathed it out over the warm fires in the kitchen cave of the father's clan. By now the father was concerned—he'd never imagined the boy could be so resourceful, and of all the tasks he'd set, only one remained. As it turned out, he needn't have worried. To get fire, the boy ran after a transporter cart, holding a spill of cloth to one of its wheels, which are shod with metal and sometimes throw up sparks as they go. When the spill caught, he put it in his pocket for safekeeping. His clothes caught fire, and he burned to death."

Cariad could not help laughing. "What a gruesome story."

"Most of them are. Feuding brothers who pursue each other through the tunnels. Forbidden lovers who creep outside the Fortress to die on the snows. Vengeful husbands who kill their unfaithful wives and leave their bodies at the entrances to their lovers' downworlds."

"You recognize transporter songs. You greet them in the passages. They bring you information, and bits of metal. How do you come to know them so well?"

"The metal is nothing special. They'll bring anyone anything, as long as there's something to trade for it." He adjusted his position on the cart floor, pulling his hood a little away from his face. He looked weary, his skin blue-white in the unforgiving mindlight, his eyes—which were not brown, as Cariad had first thought, but a deep clear gray— bruised underneath with fatigue. They were harder on him than on her, these long nights of wakefulness; she possessed the body-control to offset at least some of the effects of exhaustion but he had no such resources. "As for the rest, I've been exploring down here since I was eight years old. You can't spend time in the tunnels and not meet transporters. I've run alongside a lot of carts. Helped pull them, too."

"You learned to pick the lock when you were eight?"

He smiled his foxy smile. "Yes."

"Why did you do it?" She looked at him, curious. "Even as a child, you must have known what would happen to you if you were caught."

"What does a child really understand about such things?" He shrugged. "I'm inquisitive, I always have been. When I was in training I used to plague my teachers with questions. What is mindlight? Why are there barriers? If the Guardians can make doors open and torches go on and off automatically, why can't they make laundry wash itself and clean clothes fold themselves onto the shelves?" He grimaced a little, remembering. "I was punished fairly often."

"I can imagine."

"Eventually I learned to stop asking out loud. But I never stopped asking inside my head. It was like a game, a game I could play by myself. I decided that if the people around me wouldn't give me answers, I'd find them on my own. So I began to think about the things that puzzled me. One of the first things I worked out was how it might be possible to get past the lock on the tunnel gates. I spent a little time teaching myself to be a lock-pick, and then one night I went out and tested my skill." He shook his head. "I doubt I'd have had the courage to do it if I hadn't been so young."

"You do it now."

"That's different. I have the habit of it. I'm so used to it that it hardly seems dangerous, though of course I know it is."

Cariad nodded. She was familiar with the way repetition flattened the immediacy of risk. Even ambushing groups of tithe-collecting Journeyers had begun to seem routine after a year or so. It was one of the reasons she had so craved the perilous special missions.

"My first expedition wasn't exactly a success. It only took me about ten minutes to get completely lost. I don't know what would have happened if I hadn't met a group of transporters. I'm sure they were as surprised to see me as I was to see them. The Soldiers sweep through pretty regularly, and workers sometimes use the tunnels to get from one downworld to another, but there aren't generally children down here. They were very kind to me. They gave me something to eat, and made a detour to bring me home."

"Weren't they curious about how you got outside the gate?"

"I'm sure they were. But they didn't ask, and I wouldn't have told them even if they had. It took me a couple of weeks to get up the courage to go out again. I took along a bag of dried beans to mark my way. After that I went out whenever I could."

"And you were never caught?"

"Not by anyone in the Keep. I did run into Soldiers now and then, but I'd stolen tunics from other downworlds, and they thought I was a Speaker child, or a Journeyer. Sometimes they'd leave me alone, sometimes they'd drag me back to whatever downworld they thought I came from. If I was with a transporter group, they'd hide me in their cart. They must have passed the word about me, the transporters, because after a while they all seemed to know who I was. They were good about letting me tag along—they even gave me my own set of leathers. They thought I was very funny with my bag of beans." He smiled. "They called me the Make-Path Boy."

Cariad smiled also. She could see it, somehow, very clearly: a young Orrin, doggedly laying trails through the tunnels as he learned their shape by heart. "How long did it take you not to need the beans?"

"Oh . . . years. You've seen how complicated the tunnel system is. The Guardians have maps, but all I had was my own memory—I didn't dare mark anything down. The transporters helped. I must have been a terrible pest, with my constant questions, but they were very patient with me. The only thing they wouldn't do was bring me to the caverns. I thought at the time that it was the caverns they wanted to keep secret, but really what they didn't want was for me to come there with them. They're very careful about who they let cross over."

"Cross over?"

"Into their world. Into their lives. Transporters go everywhere and see everyone. They have lovers in other downworlds, even husbands and wives. But it's rare for them to bring outsiders into the places where they live. Transporter husbands and wives visit their nontransporter spouses in their own downworlds. If they have children, they're either wholly transporters or wholly downworlders. They agree beforehand which it'll be."

Cariad nodded: it was this insularity that had defeated

Goldwine's recruiting efforts. "So did they let you cross over?"

"Yes. About a year after I began exploring." He shook his head. Cariad sensed the ghost of childhood wonder, alive in him still. "It was like discovering a whole new world. I never imagined a life like theirs. A life not confined between walls of stone. A life without bells, without curfews, without supervisors. A life where children don't grow up in dormitories. I fell in love with their life. I thought it was the life I was really meant to have. I begged them to let me run away and join them."

"But they didn't let you."

"They couldn't let me." Cariad sensed a flare of feeling, as if his mind had just shied away from something hidden. "But they did the next best thing. One of the bands adopted me."

"Adopted you? Really?"

"Yes. I have an adoptive mother and father. And I wear the clan necklace."

He reached inside his leathers, tugging free a thong threaded with a pendant, which he pulled over his head and handed to her. The thong was dark from being worn so long against his skin. The pendant was carved from some rosy, translucent stone, shaped with great skill to the likeness of a beech-leaf.

"This is beautiful."

"Yes. They're fine carvers."

"Isn't it dangerous for you to wear it?"

He shook his head. "If a Roundhead found it on me I could say I got it in trade from another downworld. They wouldn't recognize it."

He held out his hand. She set the necklace in it. He slipped it around his neck again and tucked it out of sight.

For a little while there was silence between them. The walls flowed by like ribbons in the mindlight. Orrin had set his eyes ahead, in the direction of the transporters' forward progress. He sat easily against the side of the cart, his body relaxed, one arm resting atop his drawn-up knee, the other draped over the yellow railing. His face was foxy even in profile, with its pointed nose and winged brows. His expression was calm, but Cariad could feel the pull of his emotion, dark and unsettled, as if what they had just discussed had stirred difficult thoughts. She had the sense, as she often did, that he was attempting to hide himself from her—as if, as much as he had told her, there was more he had held back.

It was a melancholy story, of freedom gained by night and given up by morning. She thought of him, a lonely misfit among his conforming kind, wandering the maze of tunnels, desperate to discover what lay beyond the bounded world he lived in. What must it be like, to have one life and want another? But Orrin had many lives. He was a Keep downworlder, an adopted transporter, a resistance intellingencer, a seeker of knowledge for knowledge's sake— and something beyond all of these, something that bound the various lives and made them one, something still unknown.

"Orrin, how did you come to join the resistance?"

He glanced toward her, a quick flash of his gray eyes. "The recruiter from the Speaker Wing approached me."

"How did she know about you?"

"Your people are down here every week to meet the information patrols. I was seen, coming out of the gates."

"Why did you agree to serve?"

He was silent for so long she thought he might not answer. "Why do you want to know?" he said at last.

She could have told him that because she had once been a resistance recruiter herself, she had acquired a professional interest in the motives of those who joined. She could have pretended to personal curiosity. Instead she answered honestly.

"I want to know why you risk your life to serve a cause that works to benefit a world you've never seen. Why you risk your life to serve people whose goal is the destruction of the only home you've ever known."

He was staring at her now. "Why do other downworlders serve? How different could my reasons be?"

"I don't know why other downworlders serve, Orrin. You're not like other downworlders. In fact you're not like any unGifted I've ever met."

"Oh?" The word held an edgy challenge. "And in what way do I stand above the crowd?"

"I've known unGifted people as resourceful as you, maybe even as courageous. But I've never met an unGifted who knew power the way you do. Or who had so little reverence for it."

"Power is a Gift. But it's also a learned skill, like swordplay or blacksmithing. I have no reverence for the swordsman, whose expertise can be duplicated by anyone with the talent for it. Why should I be in awe of a Guardian, for whom it's just the same?"

"It isn't that simple, Orrin. A Gift is much more than the ways in which it's manifested, just as good swordplay is more than the methodology that guides it. You may know the training that makes the swordsman dangerous, but if you're not trained yourself you can only know it from outside. Don't let your understanding of his technique trick you into thinking you don't have to respect his art."

"I don't. Believe me. I respect power as I respect sickness. As I respect death. As I respect the things that do me harm. I've seen power used to hurt, and I've seen it used to kill. I've seen it used for personal gain, and for petty spite. But I've never seen it used to help or heal, or to serve the common good. The Guardians say the powers of the mind are precious, and that they must be preserved at all cost. But what does that mean to someone like me, who lives outside the benefits power can give, who never feels its touch except as imprisonment or punishment or pain? As far as I'm concerned, mindpower could vanish tomorrow and the world wouldn't be worse off."

Cariad stared at him. She could not quite believe he would say such a thing to her. He met her gaze, unflinching.

"Anyway," he said, "it's not quite true to say I have no reverence for power. I have seen one act of power that awed me. Yours. When you changed your shape."

His tilted eyes held hers. She sensed, suddenly and clearly, the pulse of his sexual attraction. It was a feeling she had noted, on and off, almost from the beginning. Until now she had dismissed it—after all, she wore the shape of the woman he had been sleeping with before she arrived.

But this was different. There was a deliberateness about it, a quality of willed release that was the opposite of the willed seclusion she had felt earlier—as if, knowing what she was, he had chosen to speak to her this way rather than through words. As if his desire were directed not at the shape she wore, but at herself, the real self beneath the illusion—a thing that could not be, for he had known her only for twelve days, and had seen her true face only once.

Over the time they had spent together, she had come not just to respect Orrin, but to like him. It was almost possible, sometimes, to forget he was unGifted. Yet her regard for him had not gone further than that. Now, against her will, she felt a change. Images rose inside her mind: Margit's images, a knowledge of him that did not belong to her, yet was as complete and detailed as if it were her own. Blood suffused her cheeks. She turned away to hide her face. Still she could feel his eyes.

"All right," he said. "If you still want to know why I agreed to serve your cause, I'll tell you."

She nodded.

"When I turned thirteen and graduated to service, it got much harder to slip away at night. I couldn't go out into the tunnels nearly as often as I had before. But I needed to do something. So I began watching at the spy stations during my off hours, and thinking about things like how to get past the behindwall barriers. By the time I was fifteen, I knew a lot about politics and the Arm of the Stone, and had worked out most of what I know about the wards and barriers and automations in the Keep. I was very proud of myself. I'd bypassed all the restrictions meant to keep me in, and knew my masters far better than they knew me. And I'd never been caught, never even been suspected. I was sure no other downworlder had ever accomplished what I had. And then . . ." He paused, like someone hesitating before a dark doorway. "And then one day I saw the truth behind my pride. And everything changed."

Cariad could feel the struggle in him. It was not that he did not wish to speak: he did, an abrupt desire for communication that bore an uncomfortable kinship to the attraction of a few moments ago. But he was having difficulty finding the words. What he was about to say to her he had never told another soul.

"You have to understand how we downworlders are raised, Arm workers most of all. From childhood, from babyhood, we're taught that we are lesser beings because we have no Gifts. We learn that in the great scheme of things, the role of the unGifted is to serve, and the role of the Gifted is to be served. This is the only significance our lives can have. In fulfilling it we fulfill the right and proper order of the world, so that the Gifted can better protect it for us.

"I believed that. Why shouldn't I? It was all I knew. Even when I disobeyed, I still thought that what they'd taught me was the real shape of the world. But where did I fit into that? A boy without a Gift, who'd discovered the flaws in the creations of the Gifted? An unGifted boy who had broken all the boundaries Gifts had made to pen him in? One day I looked at myself, at the things I knew and the things I'd done, and I saw that I was *not* a lesser being. I was *not* inferior. And everything I'd been brought up to believe just . . . fell away."

Something had opened in him, a black pit of bitterness, canceling all his careful control. Reflexively Cariad tightened her guard, unwilling to absorb into her mind the darkness flowing from his. But the power of his feeling tore at her Gift, and though her guard was as heavy as she could make it, he still broke through, with an immediacy that shocked her.

"Do you know what it means to lose belief like that?" His gray eyes were wide; a flush stained his pale skin. "To understand that every instant of your life is false and meaningless and utterly without value? To look at the years in front of you and see a prison—worse than a prison, because a prisoner doesn't have to pretend to be humbly happy with his imprisonment? All my life I'd looked for understanding, and when I finally found it, it was the worst thing that had ever happened to me. I was defiant, yes, but I never dreamed that what I was doing was anything more than adventuring. I had no idea I was destroying something, not until the moment I realized it was gone.

"I didn't know what to do. I thought about taking a knife

and killing myself. I thought about going outside the Fortress and letting the mountains do it for me. I thought about confronting a Roundhead and telling him everything. I wanted one of them, just one, to know I was as good as he was." He laughed, a wrenching sound. "Believe me, I know how stupid that is. I didn't do it, of course. I didn't do anything. I went on breathing. Time passed. I learned to accept that this was all there would ever be for me—to breathe away the minutes of my life until there were no minutes left."

He paused. The storm of feeling had dwindled, the fire in him becoming ash.

"I spent five years like that." His voice was quiet now. "That's a long time to live without belief. But I can see it was a good thing. If your recruiter had approached me sooner, I don't think I'd have accepted. I hated the world I lived in. But I don't think I was ready yet to destroy it."

"What changed your mind?"

He sighed. "My brother Ravenal. When he was sixteen and I was nineteen, he was chosen for the bodyservant corps. My parents . . . my parents and I always had our differences. But Ravenal and I were close. He knew I was going outside. He never wanted to come with me—he wasn't restless, the way I was. But he liked to listen." He pressed his lips together. "You know what they do to bodyservants, don't you?"

Cariad nodded.

"Once a year they're allowed to come back and visit. When Ravenal came, there was a feast. All our kin to the third degree of removal sat together at the table, every one of them thrilled to their fingertips that a relative had been so honored. Ravenal smiled and nodded and hardly said a word. Later on, he and I went walking. I knew about the conditioning. I knew he wouldn't be able to talk about his master. I also knew that after a few years most bodyservants stop coming back. But until that night I never put those things together." His voice was tight; Cariad could feel his pain. "He could tell me that he was warm, or that it was late. He could ask questions about the family. But there was hardly anything else he could say that didn't make him choke and gag. The conditioning . . . the conditioning didn't just make it impossible for him to talk about what he did for his master, but about anything like it. He had almost nothing left to say."

The transporters slowed to make a turn. The cart swayed, and Orrin caught himself with one hand on its side. He had turned his face away again, in the direction of their travel.

"I found a baiting victim once, about a year after I began exploring. They often get dumped in the tunnels, especially when they've been badly damaged. This boy was an Apprentice, a Soldier, I think. His tongue had been torn out. He didn't seem to know it—he made shapes at me with his lips, trying to talk. Looking at Ravenal, all I could think of was that boy. The difference was that Ravenal knew. Before he left he apologized to me. He *apologized*." His voice was savage. "As if it were his fault.

"A few months after that I met your recruiter. I accepted what she offered. I'd lost everything that meant anything to me. I didn't care anymore what happened to the rest. I was finally ready to tear it all down." He turned suddenly to look at her. "I still am. But it's been ten years. It's not personal anymore. You asked me why I'd follow a cause that would destroy the only world I've ever known. Well, the Fortress may be smashed to rubble, and the Guardians defeated, but why shouldn't the world below the ground survive? The bindings in the caverns have lasted a thousand years—why shouldn't they last a thousand more? Why shouldn't we downworlders build a new way of life on the ruins of the one our masters forced on us?"

"But Orrin, you can't possibly know—" Cariad tried to interrupt, but he would not let her.

"You asked me why I'd serve a cause that works to free a world I've never seen. Well, I may not have seen it, but I've been hearing about it since I graduated to service and began to listen at the spy stations. And it seems to me that this place isn't so very different from what's outside. We unGifted are imprisoned, not just here but everywhere, held captive through false understandings of our own value and the value of Gifts. The freedom I fight for is the freedom of people like me to believe they are as human, as worthy of respect and privilege, as any Gifted. That's why I serve your cause, even though it's a Gifted cause, even though I know your people value power as much as the Guardians do, and think just as little of those who don't have it."

"That is not so!" Angry now, Cariad raised her voice to match his. "We speak for all the people of the world, Gifted and UnGifted alike! There are many unGifted among us. The artificers of handpower who work at our headquarters—"

"Ah, yes. Artificers. Craftsmen. Footsoldiers. Even operatives like me. But where are the generals? Where are the commanders? And when your revolution is complete, will the unGifted be allowed to help you shape your new world? Will they have a voice in governing it? Or will they just be ruled, as they always have been, by Gifted masters who claim to know what's best for them?"

Cariad stared at him. Everything in him lay behind these words. The desire, the bitterness, the belief they conveyed were as strong as anything her Gift had ever showed her. Something in her stood in awe before so much passion.

"We'll never rule the world as the Guardians have," she said, quietly. "Whatever happens, that never will."

For a moment he did not speak. "I wish I could believe you. But what am I to think? I know what your recruiter did to my mind. I know what she would have done if I'd refused her offer. I know what she does when she scans me. I risk my life every day for you, and still you don't trust me enough to leave my thoughts alone. Do you treat the Gifted who serve you that way?"

"It's a matter of certainty, Orrin. We can't risk betrayal. By anyone."

"And when will you believe we won't betray you? A decade from now? A century?" He shook his head. He seemed, suddenly, very weary. "I don't even know why I've told you all this. How could you understand? You're Gifted. I'm not. It's as simple as that."

Cariad said nothing. His words held a complex personal bitterness she did not wish to confront, and anyway, she could think of no answer that would satisfy him.

"Well," Orrin said. He had drawn himself back against

the side of the cart again and was sitting with his knees drawn up and his arms clasped around them. "That's my life story. Now you owe me yours. How did you join up?"

"I didn't join. I was born to it."

"Your parents were resistance members?"

"Yes," she said. It was as true as it needed to be. "I was born in the mountains. I began training as soon as I began talking. I became a full operative when I was eighteen. I've been working ever since."

Her life, reduced to four sentences. Beside Orrin's tale of choice and loss, it seemed very small. She had gone daily into danger; if she had never risked her prophecy-guarded life, she had often risked her health and comfort. But she had never had to struggle as he had, either to get understanding or to keep it. She had never been alone as he had, asking questions into a painful void. She had never lost a faith as he had, or worked to build a new one up from nothing. Everything had been provided, held out to her by those who loved her, beliefs and understandings received as easily as a coin from a proffered hand. For reasons she did not entirely understand, she felt shamed by this.

"What was it like, growing up in the mountains?" Orrin asked. "Where did you get food? Do you have growing spaces, the way the Fortress does?"

And so she told him, stories of dim caverns and frost-furred galleries, of rock-deep silences and air as still as ice. It was the home of her childhood she described, not the warm, clean mechanical marvel Goldwine had made of it. Orrin would never see it; it would not matter to him which truth she told, the one that existed or the one she carried in her heart. He watched her as she spoke, over the tops of his knees, his gray eyes steady on her face. She could feel his attention, but of that more intimate feeling he had released earlier there was no trace.

At last, at the turning of the tunnel that led to the Keep, the transporters drew to a halt. Cariad and Orrin climbed off the cart. Orrin called soft words of farewell. The transporters bent to the traces; they vanished down the corridor, their soft singing trailing behind them, like smoke.

As they passed into the Keep's downworld, the bell that

announced the hours rang: four peals. In an hour, the work-day would begin. Cariad felt a heaviness descend on her. For a little while she had been free—had been, as far as it was possible to be while wearing another's form, herself. Now she must take up her disguise again, go back into this dark world, where people slept like moles below the ground and moved like insects between the walls, where outside air never penetrated and every breath was tainted by the stench of dirty laundry. She glanced at Orrin. Did he feel this also, each time he returned? But all she sensed from him was weariness.

"What's next?" he asked.

"I'm not sure. I need time to think."

"Shall we meet tomorrow night?"

"No. I need to sleep, and so do you. The night after."

He nodded. She turned away, bending her neck, drawing in her shoulders, surrendering her body to the prison of Margit's stance. Orrin remained behind, as he always did, watching her as she went. As the dim corridor swallowed her, she thought she felt it again, that gaze that somehow pierced the semblance and touched the hidden self within.

In the shadowed sleeping room she lay on her back, as she had the first night she had come here. But she did not think of Jolyon. She could not deny that her awareness of Orrin as an attractive and clever man had tonight become something more. She thought of the look he had turned on her, of the wish that had gone with it. She felt the echo of that wish now, within herself—clothed, as it had been earlier, in images she did not own.

No, she thought, pushing the images from her mind. She could not afford the distraction. Experience had taught her the unwisdom of personal involvement with men whose status did not match her own, an area in which Orrin fell doubly short. Margit would return soon enough. Once he had her back, he could fulfill his wish with her.

Eleven

**HE FOLLOWING** morning, standing in Margit's place in the laundry room, her hands engaged in work that by now she did almost as automatically as Margit had, Cariad assessed her progress.

The past ten days had disposed of all possibility that Konstant was imprisoned in the Fortress. Nor did it seem that he had died there. Orrin had stolen into the Keep's mortuary, and read the logbook where the names, ranks, details of preparation, and cremation dates of Roundheads who had died were entered. He had taken the tunic of a Speaker servant from the store of disguises he kept hidden in the warehouse, and gone out to speak with the downworlders who worked the midden-pit, a great well of trash yawning half a mile wide outside the Fortress walls. It was the repository not just of garbage, but of all non-Guardian corpses: pilgrims dead of cold, prisoners dead of torture, Novices dead of neglect, Apprentices dead of baiting, servants dead of any cause at all. If Konstant had been killed in secret by someone who wanted to delay discovery of his death, he might well have ended up here. Downworld society had a hierarchy, just as Guardian society did: in his guise as a Speaker servant, Orrin outranked the midden workers, and his right to make such inquiries was not questioned. But Konstant had not passed through their hands either.

And yet the redistribution of Konstant's belongings, as well as Cariad's own gut feeling, argued that he was indeed dead. If had not died in the Fortress, he must have died outside it—but had it been in the course of an attempted escape, or during a planned absence of some kind? Cariad was inclined to believe the latter. Orrin had discovered that two Reds had arrived at the Keep in haste the afternoon before Konstant's disappearance. They were conducted directly to Jolyon's quarters; when they departed, in the small hours of the following night, a third Roundhead was with them. From her foray into the minds of the servants of Jolyon's companions, Cariad knew that Konstant had vanished overnight, closing himself into his rooms earlier than usual, gone the next morning when his breakfast was delivered on a tray. It seemed very likely, therefore, that the third Roundhead had been Konstant.

A mission or a journey of some kind, then, on Jolyon's behalf, undertaken in company with Jolyon's men and resulting somehow in Konstant's death. From the lack of any movement against the resistance, and the continuing absence of any signs of military mobilization, it did not seem likely that Konstant had been discovered and mindprobed, then executed. That left foul play, or simple misadventure. There was only one way to discover which: Cariad must enter the mind of one of Jolyon's staff.

From the moment she arrived in the Fortress, she had known she might have to do this. Because of the risk and complication involved, she had left it as a last resort. She was uniquely strong in every area of making, but only averagely skilled in the manipulation of minds—mindscans, memory-kills, sleep-bindings, compulsions, and the like. Servants, unGifted as they were, presented no challenge; but Guardians, with their trained Talents and well-defended thoughts, were another matter. Also, nearly all of Jolyon's assistants and Deputies were Reddened Roundheads; if she took a Roundhead, the only certain way to make sure he did not remember her would be to kill him, and unless she had no alternative, she did not want to raise Jolyon's suspicions or cause him to guard himself more closely by killing one of his associates. She was not entirely certain, anyway, that she could capture and hold a Roundhead unaided. She had brought with her the means to do this artificially, but that was for a specific purpose, and she was reluctant to use it otherwise.

She decided, therefore, to begin with Jolyon's personal secretary. The Arm of the Stone did not perform its own clerical work, but employed others to do it for them: Jolyon's secretary was a Journeyer, specially trained by the Arm and conditioned to secrecy. It was possible, of course, that he might not enjoy Jolyon's full confidence. The conditioning of the Arm-trained had never been known to fail, but even so Jolyon might not be willing to trust a Journeyer with his most secret business. If that were so, she would have to move on to one of Jolyon's Deputies.

That evening she pretended illness, excusing herself before the evening meal and going directly to the sleeping room. There she placed a semblance on her bed and, binding herself to invisibility, made her way to the behindwall passages.

For the convenience of those they served, the Arm-trained lived not in the Journeyer Wing but in the Keep, in an area of the second floor set aside for their use. Cariad found them at supper. Invisibly she walked between the tables. She had never seen her quarry, for she had visited Jolyon's offices only at night, and the Arm-trained did not attend honorary banquets. Even so, she found him easily, the only man who wore both the triple-chevroned secretary's sash and the violet teardrop of Jolyon's service. He had the pasty skin and loose flesh of a person unused to exercise, and his shoulders were pulled inward in the scrivener's curve. Physically at least, he would be an easy target.

Cariad retreated to the hallway. When the secretary emerged she followed him to his room, ducking through the door just behind him. He felt the wind of her passage and paused, his brows drawn in puzzlement, but then, seeing nothing, closed the door and started for his desk.

Cariad seized him from behind, clamping one arm across his chest and the other around his throat so he could not cry out. With all her force she sank her Gift into his mind. She felt his defenses tearing. He stiffened, and then went limp. She allowed his weight to carry her to the floor, supporting him against her like a lover.

The whole of his mind was open to her now, packed like a document-case with the remembered content of letters, reports, minutes, warrants, certifications, and decrees. Because thoughts were languageless, these memories were free of the cipher that would have rendered the physical documents incomprehensible. Like someone paging through a filing case, Cariad slipped past Jolyon's correspondence and the multitudinous records of his official meetings, past the archives devoted to the in-Fortress discipline for which the Second was traditionally responsible, past the long list of those he had killed and the even longer list of those he planned to eliminate, past the informal notes and secret memorandums and private reports that traced the ever-rising arc of his desire: to be Second, to be Staff-Holder, to be Prior. She need not have worried about Jolyon's confidence in his conditioned assistant. Everything was here, in minute and chilling detail, a staggering record of ambition and intent.

When at last she found what she was looking for, in a part of the secretary's mind that had the feel of things never written down, she could not at first believe it. Her Gift hovered above the incredible information, stunned to immobility. This was not something she would ever have imagined, ever have dreamed. Yet in the instant of discovery, a host of understandings shifted and fell into place, and the shape they formed made perfect sense.

She withdrew from the secretary's mind, burning away the traces of her intrusion as she went. It was easier than she had expected: it was not the strength of the man's Gift, but his prodigious memory, that had gained him his position, and the rigidity of his conditioning meant there were no secret places where memory might have leaked, like water soaking through a coverlet onto the mattress below. She dragged him, still unconscious, to his desk, and heaved him into the chair behind it, arranging him with his head thrown back and his elbows on the chair arms, as if he had leaned back a moment to rest his eyes and fallen into a doze. He would not remember walking to the desk or sitting down, but in her experience people were unlikely to question memory lapses associated with sleep.

She returned to the downworld sleeping room, already darkened for the night. Slipping into Margit's bed, she allowed her invisibility and the semblance that made it seem she had been here all along to dissolve simultaneously, so that anyone watching would see no change. Her body ached with exhaustion, with the accumulated strain of eleven days of drudgery, eleven nights of intense activity and insufficient rest. But her mind, leaping with discovery like a bonfire set alight, would not allow for sleep. The knowledge she had gained tonight went far beyond the goal of the mission she had been given. She understood now why she had really been sent into the Fortress: to discover this very thing. The feel of it was like an opened door.

The following night, just after the twenty-third bell, she made her way to the warehouse. Light reached out along the shadowy aisles, leaking through the loose weave of the cloth that muffled the entrance to Orrin's hideaway. Pulling back the fabric, she ducked inside. Orrin was seated cross-legged against the left wall of crates. He had pushed the lamps and candles together in the center of the little space, so that they made a pool of brilliance in front of him. Cariad crouched down opposite.

"I followed Jolyon's secretary to his room last night," she said, without preamble. "I've found out what happened to Konstant."

Across the candle flames, his eyes widened. "Tell me."

"It was a mission after all. Jolyon sent him into the handpower world, to search for the man who took the Stone."

"The *Second* sent him to do that?" The Guardians had not attempted to hide the loss of the Stone from their servants: every downworlder in the Fortress knew the Stone had been stolen and who had taken it. "I thought the Investigation-Master was in charge of the search parties."

"He is. The official ones. But Jolyon is conducting his own search, in secret. He has been for years."

"Why?"

"Because he doesn't trust the Council. And because he has a personal grudge against this man. Even his Deputies don't know what he's doing. Only his secretary, his companions, and a few of his executors have any idea. And the cross-world agents, of course, but they're killed as soon as they're debriefed. That's why Konstant's things were redistributed. He was still alive at the time, but as far as Jolyon was concerned he was already dead."

"So . . . is he dead?"

"He was supposed to stay two weeks in the other world. On the fourteenth day they held the Gate open for him from dusk till dawn. He never came through."

"So he *is* dead."

"That's what Jolyon and his people think. But I think he's alive."

"Why?"

Cariad took a breath. The night before, she had decided to tell him the truth, or at least a good part of it. She was aware of the risk—she had no idea what he felt about the Stone or the man who had stolen it, and even his radical notions about power and politics might not make it possible for him to accept what she would say. But it seemed to her that he ought to know. It was justice: to him, to the life he lived, to the chances he took.

"I have to go back a bit to answer you. My mother has a very powerful Gift of prescience. When she was still a girl, she saw the timeline that led to the theft of the Stone. She saw the man who would take it. She saw that he'd bring the Stone into the other world. She saw that he'd survive, and the Stone too, undamaged by the differences there. And she saw that one day, a long time later, he would return."

"Return? To our world?"

"Yes. The Guardians teach that mindpower dies in the other world, that there's no Gift strong enough to survive the forces of undiluted handpower. But that's a myth, as much of a myth as the thief's death. He's as powerful as he ever was—the greatest Gift that ever has been or ever will be, greater than the Gift of any Guardian ever born. When he returns, he'll unleash that power on our world. He'll destroy the Guardians, utterly and forever."

Orrin looked at her. She did not need her heartsensing to read his doubt. "You believe that?"

"I do."

"Just on the strength of your mother's prophecies? I've heard that prescients aren't always reliable. That they can see falsely or misread their Gifts."

"My mother's prophecies aren't your ordinary predictions, Orrin. She has a uniquely powerful Gift. In all my life I've never known her to be wrong. Most of the prophecy has already come true, exactly as she foretold. The rest will too."

He shook his head. "Even if you're right—if he does return, and is as powerful as you say—I find it hard to believe that one man could destroy the entire Order of Guardians."

"Not just one man. The man who took the Stone. The man who ripped the Fortress's heart away. The man who made rubble of two miles of Fortress walls."

"Why didn't he do it thirty years ago, then? He had the chance. He had the Stone. Why wait?"

"Thirty years ago the Order was too strong. He took the Stone to weaken the Guardians enough for us to fight them, and we fight them to weaken them still more so that when he returns he'll be able to undo the rest. The Guardians still rule the world, but their hold on it has never been so frail. Everywhere, the resistances oppose them. Violation is epidemic. Their numbers are shrinking. Their bindings are failing. When my . . . when the thief comes back, he'll reach out with his Gift, and the Guardians will vanish from the earth. I swear to you that this will come to pass."

Orrin ran a hand through his cropped hair. She could feel the struggle in him, the imbalance between his perception of her as a person to be trusted, and his instinctive resistance to what she was telling him.

"It's strange, you know," he said. "I always admired him. The thief of the Stone, I mean."

She looked at him, surprised. "Why?"

"When I was a child, the dormitory mothers used to tell the story of how he betrayed the Arm and cast the Fortress into sleep and desecrated the beautiful Garden and took the Stone. I'd speak the curses along with everyone else, but in my heart I always wondered at the courage it took to do such a thing. At the strength he must have had to keep his secret for so long." He stared down into the pool of flame. "I thought perhaps, if he had been born a downworlder, he might have learned to pick locks too."

"It doesn't disturb you that he was a Violator?" Cariad said curiously. "That he took the Stone into the world of handpower?"

Orrin shrugged. "If what your people have told me about handpower is true, then Violation doesn't mean very much, does it? As for the Stone . . ." His eyes flicked up. In each dark iris she could see the reflection of a pointed flame. "The Guardians teach us that it's sacred, and that our world isn't whole without it. But the Stone has been gone all my life, and the world doesn't seem to have changed very much. It seems to me it doesn't much matter where the Stone is."

Cariad looked at him, marveling. "You're an extraordinary man, Orrin."

He smiled without much humor. "For an unGifted, you mean."

"No. For anyone."

He pressed his lips together. Feeling flared in him, and the struggle to repress it, but she could still read his bitterness. "So how does Konstant fit into all of this?"

"My mother's never said exactly how the thief will return, or when. But I believe she knew that Jolyon would give Konstant this mission. I believe she either gave him direct orders to find the thief and summon him back, or knew he'd do it on his own initiative. He knows about the prophecy, you see—we all do. Either way, I think he accepted Jolyon's mission as his own quest. That's why he didn't return when he was supposed to. He's still searching."

Orrin frowned. "He could just as easily be dead, as the Second thinks he is."

"No. This is the prophecy. It has to be. It fits too well to be anything else."

"That's circular logic," he objected. "And even if you're right, the Arm of the Stone has been sending men after the thief for years. Why should Konstant be the one to find him?"

"The resistance uses ways of power different from the Guardians'. Obviously the thief has hidden himself from Guardian power, but maybe our techniques will detect him. The thief knows the prophecy too—maybe he'll recognize Konstant when he arrives. Truthfully, Orrin, I can't tell you exactly how it will happen. I just know it will. I *know* it."

He was silent. The upward angle of the light cast his features into sharp relief. She could still feel his resistance, but it was less strong than before.

"All right," he said. "I'll accept that things are as you say. What now?"

"The information patrol will be here in two nights. I want you to tell them where Konstant is, and what I think he's doing there. Tell them to bring Margit on their next pass, along with a full kit for me, including a quarterbow and darts."

"A quarterbow and darts," he repeated. "You're finished, then. In just over a week you'll be gone."

"Actually . . . I don't plan on leaving with the patrol."

"You don't?" She felt something in him, a compound emotion that seemed to encompass both hope and fear—focused on her, undeniably, but muddied by his efforts to conceal it. "Why not?"

"There's more to the prophecy. I'm part of it. I have to be here when the thief returns."

"Why?"

"I can't tell you." It was the one piece of the truth she could not give him; to do so would be like handing him her soul. "All I can say is that I have a part to play in his return. The night I got here, you told me you could have hidden Konstant. Could you do that for me?"

"You're already disguised." He was frowning. "Why do you need to be hidden?"

"My mission isn't quite finished. There's one more thing I have to do. Once I've done it, it won't be safe for me to stay in the Keep, even disguised."

He stared at her. "What are you going to do?"

"I can't tell you that either. It's for your own protection, Orrin. It's too dangerous for you to know."

He shook his head. "If it's so dangerous for you, it'll be

just as dangerous for those who help you. It'd be one thing if it was just my life. But there are others involved. How can I ask them to take you in without knowing what I'm committing them to?"

"You'll know once it's done. I promise you that. But I can't tell you now."

He was silent. She could feel his mind turning, sorting out the implications of what she had said. She waited. She did not have to ask his help; she was perfectly capable of compelling him through her Gift. But something in her shrank from the idea of that. What he had said about the resistance two nights before had stung her. She did not want to be the one to prove the angry accusations he had made. It felt too much like betrayal. Even if she removed his memory of it, she would still know that she had done it, and feel ashamed.

"All right," he said at last. "I'll hide you. On one condition. That when you leave here, you'll take me with you."

She stared at him, astonished. "You want to leave the Fortress? What about your family, your clan? What about the things you said the other night, about building a new world on the ruins of the old?"

"I don't want a ruined world," he said with passion. "I want the one outside. I've always wanted it. There'll be battles to fight, even once the Guardians are gone. You'll need people. You accept unGifted, you told me so yourself. There's room for me."

"I couldn't guarantee anything, Orrin."

"Why not? You said your mother's the one who sent Konstant here. She must be pretty well up in the hierarchy if she can do that. You must have some influence."

"In matters of the resistance I'm just another operative," Cariad said sharply. "I get no special favor."

"That's my condition. Take it or leave it."

She looked at him with something like wonder. "You know I can compel you, don't you? You know I don't have to ask."

"Yes. But I think that if you wanted to do that, you would have already."

They watched each other. She could feel the effort it cost

him to hold her gaze. He was fairly certain of what he had just said to her, but not completely. Did he also know that she did not have to follow either option, and could survive alone? Yet even as she thought this, she knew she would agree. It was not a large request; he deserved much more, for all he had risked and done. Behind that thought, uncomfortably, lay another: until this moment, she had not realized she would miss him.

"All right," she said. "I'll do what I can."

There was a pause, and then he smiled. Not triumph: relief.

"When will you need to disappear?"

"On the night Margit returns. I'll take care of the thing I mentioned then. It shouldn't take me more than a few hours. You can wait for me at the gate or outside, whatever you choose. Is it far, where you'll take me?"

"Yes. I'll have to arrange a meeting somewhere in the tunnels, otherwise I'll never get back in time."

Cariad nodded. "It's settled, then."

There was nothing more to say. They went their separate ways.

They met again, three days later. Orrin had delivered the message Cariad gave him; in a little less than a week the patrol would return, with Margit.

Cariad moved like a prisoner through the days that followed. There was a defined limit, now, to the time she must endure the hateful routine of Margit's work and wear the unnatural shape of her flesh. Yet the knowledge, rather than easing her loathing of her situation, only removed the veil of habit that had made it bearable. Each seam she ran her hands across, each stain she examined, each hole she poked her fingers through, awoke her more acutely to hatred of this pointless existence. Each time she removed her clothes and saw legs and hips and breasts not her own, she became breathless with the need to be herself again. It was as if the tether of her training, the steady discipline that had carried her through the boredom and unpleasantness and routine of all her other postings, had somehow snapped, a failure of control that was both frightening and, perversely, exhilarating.

Within her mind, some inhibition had also broken. In the days she had spent searching for Konstant, the purpose that lay behind everything she did in the Fortress rose up now and then to the forefront of her consciousness, dark and glittering like the sky at night. It felt like desire, like fear, like a hand closing round her heart; it was so strong sometimes that it stopped her in her tracks. She was always able to push it down again, to subordinate it to the imperatives of her mission. But now that the mission was done, and only time lay between herself and her intent, Jolyon possessed her thoughts. She saw his brooding face in her sleep and in the waking dreams of her hours in the sorting room. The glitter of the gold in which he wrapped himself seemed to flash at the corners of her eyes. The phrases of the Tale turned in her mind, tracing the pattern of treachery she had come here to avenge; the images she had taken from Jolyon's secretary paraded through her thoughts, a revelation of ambition and bloodshed that, more than anything that had gone before, made it clear that what she planned to do was not just desire, but necessity.

Since Baldric's interrogation, she had not often allowed herself to think about how he had died. Now, however, she could not stop remembering, and her palms burned a little, nearly all the time. Sometimes she thought of balance, and, briefly, felt the touch of fear. But this tether too had been severed. She knew, as clearly as she had ever known anything, that she wanted to give Jolyon the death she had given Baldric. To let the killing fires rise again, to open her nerves and muscles to their power. To savor with all her senses the feeling of a life going out. It was the death he deserved. What was balance, beside that?

Goldwine's face rose up before her sometimes, dark with dread. Cariad understood, now, the possibility that her foster mother must have seen. Goldwine's Gift had shown her little of what would follow on the prophecy's fulfillment, but she knew as well as Cariad that it marked the end of the time in which Cariad could not die. And yet Cariad was not afraid. Her father's return, her own intent, rose too hugely in her mind. All her life she had walked the path of prophecy, but on the night she discovered where Konstant had gone, she had tumbled off the path and into a river. She felt it constantly now—the flow of prescience, an irresistible cataract speeding toward an ineluctable conclusion. Her plan for Jolyon was part of that. It was born of the same root, partook of the same reality. The Tale stood behind it, and the centuries of her ancestry, and her father's unknown face. Goldwine might have seen it, or she might not; either way, it was meant to be.

On the night of Margit's return, Cariad left Margit's bed for the last time. Orrin was not in the warehouse when she arrived, and so there were only shadows to witness her journey back to her own flesh. Letting go of the semblance was much easier than creating it had been. The constriction of the false shape slipped away like a falling garment. When Cariad opened her eyes, the body she saw was her own. She held up her hands, gazing at her own long fingers; she pulled over her shoulder the braid of her own black hair. She put her palms to her face, feeling the familiar angles of her own features. No matter how long she remained in another's shape, her body never lost the instinct-memory of its true contours. To touch them now was like waking up, like coming home.

When Orrin saw her he stopped short, taking her for a stranger. But recognition followed almost at once. He came forward, silent. She could feel the question in him, but he did not ask it.

She bound them both to invisibility, and they set out through the tunnels, retracing the way they had taken on the night of her arrival. At each turn or intersection she left a drop of mindlight, to guide her on the way back. They walked without speaking. Cariad was aware that Orrin watched her as they went, furtive sidelong glances that barely turned his head. He radiated emotion, a volatile mix of tension, reluctance, determination. And fear—but not for himself. His fear was all for her. He was struggling, like a man outmatched by a larger opponent, to hold all of this in check: he did not want her to know what, or how much, he felt.

They reached the antechamber. Cariad made them visible again, and they crouched down to wait. The air was frigid; the walls breathed cold as if they were made of ice. Cariad fixed her eyes on the door, watching her breath unfurl in clouds of vapor. Her heart shook her body with every beat. Her clothing was clammy beneath the arms, and there was a painful tightness in her throat. These symptoms were familiar from other missions. From experience, she knew they would soon be gone.

The patrol's coded knock sounded, sharp and sudden. Orrin got up and hauled the bolts aside. The patrol entered, carrying Margit between them, bound deeply into sleep. They set the litter down; Cariad and Orrin lifted Margit off it and laid her gently on the floor. Working quickly, they unlaced her coldsuit and removed the garments she wore beneath it: soft leather boots, woolen tunic and trousers, linen shirt, linen underwear. Rising, Cariad stripped off her nightshift and undersuit and pulled on the clothes they had just taken off, while Orrin redressed Margit in her own garments.

The patrol leader handed Cariad a leather belt, with an attached wallet and a dagger in a scabbard. Cariad untied the laces of the scabbard and pulled the dagger free: the blade was made of one of the power-bound alloys, razor thin and sharp. Inside the wallet was the quarter-bow she had asked for, and six darts. She drew her fingers gently along the quarter-bow's shaft. She had not been fully certain Goldwine would send it.

<How long before she wakes?> she thought toward the patrol leader, buckling the belt around her waist.

<Three hours. Maybe less.>

<You know I'm not coming back.>

The patrol leader nodded.

The men finished dismantling the litter and bundling it up. They wrapped it in the discarded coldsuit, and one helped the other bind it on his back. Orrin moved again to the door and pulled it open. The air of the outside world crept in, only a little colder than the room itself.

<Do you have a message for your mother?> the leader asked, pausing on the threshold.

<Tell her ... > For a long moment Cariad hesitated. <Tell her I love her.>

The leader nodded. She turned, her men behind her, and vanished into the darkness.

Orrin pushed the doors closed and shot the bolts home. The concussion echoed inside Cariad's head. For an instant the world went dark. She blinked, and light returned. But not the same light. In the time it had taken to bar the door, everything had changed. The last barrier was gone. She was free now to act.

"The sleep-binding will hold for three more hours," Cariad told Orrin, who had returned to stoop by Margit's side. "How will you get her to the Keep?"

He looked up. His face seemed even paler than usual. "The same way I brought her. There's a transporter group waiting at the first entrance." He rose, and came toward her. "Will you be riding with us?"

"No."

He nodded. "I'll wait for you. By the gate."

"If I'm not there by the dawn bell, don't stay. Come back the next night. I'll meet you then."

"I thought you said this ... thing you're going to do would only take a few hours."

"I did. But you never know. So if I don't arrive, don't wait."

He looked at her. They were standing face-to-face, the clouds of their cold-condensed breath mingling in the air between them. The conflicted turmoil of his feeling wracked him like a fever; he seemed on the very edge of control. But Cariad barely sensed it. An excitement was rising in her, a wild euphoria. The urge to action filled the whole of her consciousness. Her muscles burned with the labor of keeping still.

He reached out and laid his hand upon her arm. "Be careful."

Cariad laughed. Not at his words: at her exhilaration, at the joyous pulse of her Gift, at her core-deep understanding of her own invulnerability. But he could not know that. His face changed. He stepped back. He stooped again to Margit, and with some effort lifted her up in his arms. He turned, his steps heavy with the weight of his burden, and left the antechamber.

Cariad watched him go. She regretted her reaction. But she was fully shifted into performance-mode now, a state of being that was of, but not engaged with, the world of ordinary human actions and responses. She was aware of her readiness, of her power, of the fine balance of her control. She felt the river of prophecy all around her, so powerful that it seemed to overrule the truth of the unmoving stone beneath her feet.

With her making power she conjured a binding of invisibility—not the Guardian illusion she had used in her time as Margit, but a full resistance-style shifting of the substance of her flesh, so that she became indistinguishable from the world around her. She set out at an easy run, following the tiny mindlight marks she had made, extinguishing them as she passed. She caught up with Orrin and the transporters just beyond the first tunnel turning. Orrin was arranging Margit in the cart. The little group felt her go by, for she was moving fast enough to stir the air. Orrin turned his head, following the wind of her transit with his eyes.

She reached the gate of the Keep's downworld. She laid her hand on the lock and snapped it open. She passed through the warehouse area and into the wide, night-deserted corridor, skimming like a shadow toward the stairway that led to the upper domains. She took the stairs two at a time, all the way to the third floor, and crossed the barrier that shut the servant world away from the inner sanctums of the Keep. She still carried Orrin's lump of metal, heavy in the little bag around her neck: the barrier yielded without protest, depositing her in the featureless, snaking corridors of the Roundhead living area.

Outside Jolyon's chambers, she paused. From her previous forays and her mindscans of his companions' servants, she knew that he employed extensive barriers against intruders. Even the walls were protected, with Gift-wards draped like veils across the stones. All these bindings were keyed to the shape of Guardian Gifts; she knew from experience that her own Gift, trained to entirely different channels, was invisible to Guardian defenses. But these defenses had been made by Roundheads. There were three major hurdles to her intent: this was the first.

She set her body against the wall. The gray blocks, nearly a foot thick, offered a more difficult passage than the door, but they were defended by only a single binding, whereas the door was barred by at least two. Closing her eyes, she summoned up the full force of her making power. Those with making Gifts knew that the solidity of matter was an illusion: at the most basic level of being there were only tiny particles dancing in infinite space. A making Gift could regroup these particles or disperse them—or, if it were very strong, pull them aside to make an opening, and hold the space long enough for a human body to slip through.

The feeling of crossing was like fever: an expanding lightness, a sense of heat, a spinning giddiness. Cariad sensed the wards all around her, like light; but they did not see her. A heartbeat, and it was over. She opened her eyes on the other side of the wall.

She stood in a sumptuous, deserted chamber, strewn with maze-patterned carpets and lit by mindlight flowing ceaselessly down the walls. Silently she traversed it. The door on the other side was not bound, and she passed through it as easily as an expelled breath. Beyond lay a hallway, with more doors opening off each side. These were the suites of the companions. According to the knowledge she had taken from the minds of their servants, at this hour they would be abed.

This was the mission's second hurdle. The servants she could easily bind into sleep, for they were unGifted. But the companions were Roundheads, and she did not think she could make a sleep-binding strong enough to hold them. The only way she could be sure they would not wake and interrupt her was to kill them. She would do it manually, to save time and strength.

She melted through the first door. A rich sitting room lay beyond, the globes of mindlight at its corners dimmed for the night. The air was warm and heavily scented, a heady incense smell with a hint of less pleasant things beneath. The door to the bedchamber stood ajar, a slice of blackness against the figured tapestries that hid the walls. She slipped soundlessly through it, her dagger already drawn. At its tip she had set a pearl of mindlight, to guide her way. The tiny radiance revealed the shadowy mass of the bed, its coverlets thrown back. The bodies of the two men upon it showed slightly darker than the pale sheets. By his bulk, she recognized the closest as the largest of Jolyon's companions, Saranero.

A dense odor of wine and sweat and perfume rose off the bed; Cariad thought fleetingly of the sorting room, and the laundress through whose hands these soiled sheets would pass. Saranero lay on his back. She positioned the luminous tip of the dagger above his heart and then, with the precision of her training, plunged it into his chest, burying it nearly to the hilt. He died at once, without a sound. Bracing a hand against his bare shoulder, she wrenched the dagger free. A little of the mindlight was left behind, a ghostly shimmering at the edges of the welling wound.

She killed the second man as well. She did not recognize him, though by his cropped hair and the rings he had not removed, he was a Roundhead. Reentering the sitting room, she passed through the narrow door that opened onto the tiny chamber of Saranero's bodyservant, and bound him deeply into slumber.

The next companion, Ruen, was alone. He was not drunk like Saranero, but he slept the heavy sleep of a man secure amid impenetrable defenses, and she dispatched him with equal ease. She bound his bodyservant, and then moved on. She found the third suite empty. She had known there was a chance of this, for her servant mindscans had showed her that Baffrid, the third companion, often spent the night elsewhere. It was not what she would have liked, but it would have to do. Baffrid's bodyservant was there, in his little room; she bound him as she had the others and then left the suite.

She halted just before the arched double portals that marked the entrance to Jolyon's private apartments. Beyond them lay unknown territory. She had never been able to catch and scan Jolyon's bodyservant, who went nowhere without his master, and the other servants had never entered Jolyon's rooms.

She pulled the little bag she wore from underneath her tunic and slipped it over her head. Inside were Orrin's lump of metal, her poison capsule, several short cylinders that could be fitted together to make a blowtube, three tiny fletched darts, and a ceramic vial. The vial held a small measure of the power-deadening drug she and Laran and Shabishara had used on Baldric. She had carried it with her to the mountains, along with the formula, intending to give it to Goldwine, but because of her foster-mother's reaction, she had never done so. It was a decision that, in retrospect, seemed almost prescient. This was the key to her intent: the thing that shaped a viable plan out of a feverish dream.

She removed the vial, leaving the blowtube sections and the darts—which she would have had to use if Goldwine had not sent the quarterbow—in place. It held just enough to treat two of the little quarrels. The drug, heavy and viscous, dried quickly to a leathery film, which would re-liquefy when it met the heat of flesh. She primed the bow and tucked the second dart into her belt, where she would be able to reach it easily, but where it would not pierce her clothing. She corked the empty vial and replaced it in the bag, then hung the bag again around her neck. She got to her feet, the bow ready in her hand.

This was the moment. She had wondered how it would feel when it came. She was aware of her readiness, her purpose, her power, the beating of her heart and the rhythm of her breath. But these were only the things she had brought with her. What lay ahead, on the threshold of initiation, was suddenly too huge to see.

She moved forward, slipping through the wood of Jolyon's door. There were barriers here, as there had been outside the apartments, but they too were keyed to Guardian Gifts and could not detect her. She found herself in a dim, low-ceilinged chamber, packed like a warehouse with great piles of goods. Before her, a narrow aisle cut between the towering stacks, running up against an open area in which two standing candelabra diffused a flickering yellow light. At the center of the light was a desk. Behind the desk

was Jolyon, his head bent, reading something spread out
before him. She could not see his face, only his russet hair,
a slice of forehead and a jut of nose, the sooty blackness
of his robe—and, of course, the gleam of gold, heavy on
his shoulders and at his wrists.

For a few breaths the shock of vision held her motionless. She had not expected to find him here: she had thought
he would be in bed.

She began to move, placing each foot with silent care.
The odor of dust was heavy on the air, undercut by faint,
ripe whispers of decay. To her left and right, the mountains
of Jolyon's possessions rose high above her head, massed
together without system or care. She glimpsed the shadowed curves of porcelain, the dim gleam of metal, the dark
planes of framed paintings, the weighty mass of heroic
sculpture, the clotted folds of tapestry, the gossamer drift
of silk, the varied bulk of furniture. The goods at the top
were whole, but those at the bottom had split and splin-
tered, unable to bear the weight above. Beneath these, perhaps, lay the dust of others: disintegration heaped upon
dissolution, a constant subsidence of form into nothingness.

She reached the margin of candlelight. Jolyon read on,
oblivious. He was alone: his servant was nowhere to be
seen. Raising the quarter-bow, she sighted on his shoulder.
She steadied herself, took a breath and held it, and fired.

He clapped his hand to his shoulder. His head snapped
up. For an instant he looked straight into her invisible face.
Then the drug overcame him. He fell heavily forward onto
his desk. She heard the crack as his forehead struck the
wood.

She let go of the discipline that had hidden her. Three
strides took her to the desk. She had primed the quarter-
bow with the second dart immediately on firing the first;
holding it ready, she reached out with her Gift, searching
for power. She felt his astonishment and incomprehension,
the pain of his bruised forehead; but there was no trace of
power.

The third hurdle had been crossed. He belonged to her
now.

Thoroughness, as well as caution, dictated that she go in

search of the servant, and bind him as she had the others. But her hands were burning, and she could not wait. She set the quarter-bow on the desk. Circling round it, she wrenched back Jolyon's chair and took hold of his shoulders, dragging him from where he sat. He felt light and bony, like a bird; it required very little effort to pull him around the desk and lay him on the floor.

She knelt beside him, looking into his face. His skin was pale, as dense and unlined as a youth's. His eyes, large and cloudy-green, blazed into hers. Like Baldric, his shock at what had happened to him eclipsed all other emotions. She could feel his mind struggling for understanding.

"Who are you?" His voice was a dry whisper. "How did you get through? What have you done to me?"

She did not answer. He gasped, struggling against the drug. His shock was becoming rage, a black storm of fury that seemed too large for his slight body to contain. She did not try to shut it out. His helpless passion delighted her.

"Who sent you?" he rasped. "Siringar? Marhalt? Tell me."

"No one sent me," she said softly.

"That's impossible."

She leaned toward him. She could feel the fire rising in her. Her chest was tight; her fingers burned. "Look into my face. Do you know who I am?"

His lips worked. "You are a dead woman," he hissed.

"Look into my face." She was close enough now to count the veins in his eyes. "Tell me who I am. Tell me who my father is."

She felt his incomprehension. For a long moment his eyes moved across her face, measuring her features. And then, suddenly, understanding: she felt its arrival, like a blow. He drew in his breath.

"It can't be," he whispered.

"It is."

"But she died. The heartsenser died."

"She lived. So did I."

"Why should I believe that?"

"You already do. I can feel it."

"So you're a heartsenser too." It was not as much of a

struggle for him to whisper now. She could still feel his outrage and his lingering astonishment, but these unconstrained emotions were yielding to something else, more controlled and more calculating. "You have your father's face."

"So they tell me."

"Your mother—is she still alive?"

"That's not your concern. Nor anything else, now."

"So you've come to kill me."

"Yes," Cariad said simply. The fire had moved up her arms, was closing toward her heart. She longed to touch him. But she did not.

"Why? You say no one sent you, but you must serve someone."

"Does it matter?"

He blinked up at her. "What have you bound me with?"

"Something even a Roundhead can't break."

"So you've done this before."

"I have."

"You must be fearless, then, as your father was. Or perhaps just arrogant, as he also was. It was his arrogance that was his downfall. Perhaps it'll be yours as well."

"Be quiet," she told him. "I'm not interested in your opinions."

"Perhaps I'll keep you alive," he whispered. "After I question you."

She laughed—at his useless Gift, at his incredible Roundhead pride, which made it possible for him to imagine victory even as he stared into the face of his executioner. Death laughed with her, all the deaths she had ever accomplished—a long road of killing whose culmination had always and forever been this moment. The fires clamored for release, a light along every nerve, a searing promise of ecstasy. Still she held back. She did not want merely to kill him. She wanted to incinerate him, to turn him into dust, to reduce him to a stain upon the floor. She wanted to obliterate him in such a burst of light and heat that everything in this room became ash as well.

"May I say one thing before I die?"

She set her hands upon his chest, on the cold ropes of

gold with which he bound himself. She felt the shock of that touch throughout her body.

"Say it."

He drew in his breath. "Look up."

Cariad raised her head. A small man stood a little distance away. Jolyon's bodyservant. How had he gotten here without her sensing him?

Beneath her hands, something had changed. She looked down at Jolyon. He was smiling.

"This isn't good-bye," he said.

She did not have time to draw even half a breath. A black void opened up before her, as if the earth had flown apart and pitched her into the abyss beyond the sky. The killing fires left her, sucked outward, into the darkness . . . and then returned, a bolt of power that slammed her to the floor. Stunned, she struggled for understanding. What had happened? Whose power was this?

Above her appeared the servant's round, almond-eyed face. It filled her vision, blocking the dim ceiling above. He reached out his index finger and set it upon her forehead. She began to fall, into a darkness that went down forever. For an instant she saw Goldwine, her face set and stern as it had been on the night they said farewell. And then there was nothing.

The
Barren
Shore

Twelve

ONSTANT LAY sprawled on his back, his face turned to the sky. It had begun to sleet, a light fall of ice that glittered in the not-quite-darkness, lancing his unprotected face with tiny needle-sticks of cold. He could feel that the temperature was dropping, that the snow beneath him, melted by his body heat, had begun to freeze again. The cycle of his mounting fever, which for more than a day had dragged him back and forth between poles of heat and chill, made it seem that everything inside him had turned to fire, and so the cold was not painful but welcome.

Three weeks had passed since he woke on the forest floor to find the knowledge he had been seeking inside his mind. The sense of presence that filled his sleep vanished with the return of consciousness; he knew, without testing the understanding, that if he extended his Gift he would find the reaches of mindspace as empty as before. But the knowledge remained: a feeling of place, a sense of direction as precise as a map. There were no images associated with the knowledge, or an exact endpoint, but this did not concern him. Bron waited at the finish of the journey. He knew that now, as certainly as he had ever known anything.

Konstant broke camp, inventorying his provisions, rolling up his blankets, hitching his pack onto his back. He hesitated, but at last retrieved Jolyon's talisman. As Jolyon had promised, it was bound to him; its separation had wakened a small, calling voice at the bottom of his consciousness, which he could not quite bring himself to ignore. He

233

could not remember where he had thrown it, but when he closed his eyes and quieted his mind he was able to move directly to it, and set his hand on it without looking.

Based on the parallelism of the worlds and his own knowledge of geography, he had decided on a route: north and slightly east until he reached the sea, where he would cross to the cold lands on the other side, and go north again, almost to the top of the world. He planned to travel by means of farwalking. His transportation ability, while not large, was more than adequate for solo journeys, and he could sustain a pace for a long time without tiring. He was aware that his progress must be cautious, at least until he was used to navigating this world, which was so much more crowded than his own. But he did not expect to have difficulty with the traveling itself. He anticipated no more than a week of travel time.

Almost from the moment he set out, he understood that he had been wrong. As when he had made barriers and woven bindings, he had no trouble summoning up his Gift. But this time it did not respond predictably. Farwalking depended not just on power, but on the practitioner's ability to judge the shape of the world even while moving through it at impossible speeds. Now, slipping into the blurred realms of Gift-enhanced travelspace, Konstant found himself uncertain of the distances he was covering, confused as to the relationship of the geographical features around him, and unable to maintain a clear sense of direction for more than a few moments at a time. This last was especially disconcerting, for his understanding of the compass had been one of his strongest skills as a walker.

He slowed his pace, and then slowed it again. He limited his range, power-traveling only between points he could visually reconnoiter while standing still. This made it possible to move forward without injuring or killing himself, but his progress was dismayingly slow, and the constant stopping and starting was far more tiring than maintaining a steady speed would have been.

He had never experienced such disorientation, not even in his training days, yet there was an oddly familiar feel to it. It came to him, after a little over half a day, that the confusion he had suffered in the powerless void where he farsought Bron had been similar. In that place also his understanding of speed and distance had deserted him, and the unrelenting emptiness had produced the same sense of tipping wildly out of balance. It had not occurred to him that he might encounter such a thing outside of mindspace, but perhaps it should have. It was not just the mindspace of his world that was crowded with power, after all. The potential, display, and maintenance of power were everywhere manifest on the corporeal plane. Just as he had never before extended himself into mindspace and found it empty of the light of Gifts, he had never before reached out through physical space and failed to come up against the workings of others' Talents. It was as if, without those boundaries and signposts, his Gift could measure neither itself nor the world around it.

None of Goldwine's theories had anticipated this. From her assumption that a Gift could not be harmed by the currents of the handpower world, it had seemed to follow that the workings of power within that world would be the same. Nor did anything in Talesin's memories indicate difficulty with Gift-enhanced transportation. But Roundhead traveling parties followed the same routes over and over, century after century, never deviating from the paths mapped by the first explorers. Roundheads did not need to sense the world around them when they farwalked: like blind men in a familiar room, they already knew where to go.

Konstant revised his travel estimate: three weeks, maybe more. He struggled to set aside his impatience at the delay, to bite back his frustration at the frequent halts and the tedious time it took to properly survey the terrain. This was a different reality, he told himself. He was traveling it as no one of his world—other than Bron—had done before. He was moving slowly, but he was moving; the journey would take longer than he had planned, but he would get there. Surely experience would give him back his transportation skill. And if not, he would keep going, on his hands and knees if he had to.

He moved onward, walking by day, camping at night in

wooded or waste areas. And indeed it did seem to become easier: the halts less frequent, the disorientation less numbing. He kept as much as possible to unpopulated places, but the land of this world was crowded with habitations, and he was not able to avoid passing close to towns and cities. In the density and confusion of these regions, his disability intensified, and he was forced for safety's sake to go at foot-pace. Making the best of these intervals, he used them to test himself, pitting his senses and defenses against the people and phenomena he encountered. He could walk by the side of roads now without flinching. He could slip through crowds of people and absorb strange sights and sounds and smells without confusion. The light no longer startled him, and the conformation of buildings and houses no longer seemed so odd.

Out of habit, and also to acquire information about the places he moved through, he eavesdropped on the thoughts of the people he passed. The unGifted minds of this world were as defenseless as those of his, and since thoughts had no language, his ignorance of the tongues they spoke was not a hindrance. But the thoughts he overheard, their context and content, were largely alien, and it was often difficult to make sense of the bits and pieces he gleaned. A mindprobe would perhaps have yielded better results, but he had sworn an oath to himself, and he would not break it, even here.

Spending so much time at ordinary speeds, he began to perceive a thing he might not otherwise have noticed. Technology, clamped like a mask across the familiar contours of the earth, had not after all banished squalor and poverty—as, in the pristine village where he first tested his barriers, he imagined it might have. That village, with its clean streets and fine healthy people, was not the only, or even the most typical, face of this world. He passed through habitations whose construction was alien, but whose meanness and dilapidation was entirely familiar. He encountered people dressed in the skimpy vivid clothing of this world, with machines on their wrists and at their ears and in their hands, whose faces were as degraded and desperate as the faces of the poor in his world. He came upon a huge plain of refuse, metallic and glittering, crawling with machines and patrolled by carrion birds, and understood that this was the price of the towns' and cities' cleanliness. He entered, and then retreated from, a vast region of roads and metal trackways and filthy sprawling buildings, where sky-high chimneystacks belched storms of smoke, and the air was dark and almost too thick to breathe and smelled fouler than anything he had ever known.

That night he found soot in all the creases of his skin, and when he blew his nose to rid himself of the lingering stink, the mucus was black. The lessons of the third year of his Arm Apprenticeship came back to him, the special class in which he and others had studied the Roundhead travelers' reports of their expeditions. What he had seen today was beyond anything described in that class, a monstrosity worthy of the most fevered dream of Guardian orthodoxy. For the first time in many years, he felt a tremor of unease at the thought of a power that could create such things. But this was a world without balance, he reminded himself. In his own world, when Bron had made it new, the powers would coexist in check and in harmony, and neither the extremity of this place nor the oppression of the Guardians' Limits could ever come again.

On the eighth day of his journey he ran out of the food and water he had brought with him. Because he had been careful with it, it had lasted him three days longer than it was meant to. Late that night he slipped invisibly into a darkened house and filled his pack with food he found there, fruit and bread for the most part, since much of what he saw was either unrecognizable or unappetizing. He made camp in a wooded area not far away, and called up mindfire to roast the squirrel he had killed earlier with a power-enhanced stone throw. The meat, tough and gamy, was like any meat, the stolen apples like any apples. The bread was spongy and bland, and the water—which he had acquired from streams or falls along the way, refilling the flasks as he emptied them—tasted of metal. He was aware of a certain amount of apprehension as he ate and drank. He still trusted that there was nothing of handpower that could harm a Gifted person. Yet there was so much here that was not what he expected, and now that it had actually come to consuming the substance of this world, he found himself afraid.

He sat for a time before sleeping, the food settling uneasily inside him, looking up at the sky through the thin screen of branches overhead. The moon, nearly full, shone down from above; the enormous illumination of this world reached up from below, a pale haze laid across the darkness and the stars. He thought of how far he had come, and how far he had yet to go. He thought, with longing, of the world he had left behind.

Out of the quiet of the night, a great wave of loneliness rose up and struck him, so sudden that it took his breath. Not for physical companionship—he had never cared greatly about that—but for power, for the play and spark of other Gifts. He had known before coming here that he was journeying into an empty place, but across the days of his journey, reaching over and over into the void that was the only place power could go in this world, he had learned the true meaning of emptiness. He felt that understanding now, not only with his Gift but with his heart and mind: the terrible isolation of being the only one of his kind in all the world.

He fell ill two days later, a sudden cramping in his gut followed by nausea and a convulsive flux. He staggered on until he came to an abandoned structure, a low brick building with its windows punched out, overgrown with winter-killed vines. The building was filled with the remains of dead machines; he huddled among these rusted hulks, too sick even to use his Gift to ease his suffering, the sky looking down at him through the holes in the roof. The floor was made of stone, and the cold of it ate up through his blankets, so that his body became a rictus of shivering and his jaws ached from the chattering of his teeth.

It was said, by Roundheads, that when the currents of the handpower world began to kill a Gift, the first sign of it was just such illness. He had already been here nearly a week longer than any Roundhead party, and from the start his barriers had been lighter than theirs. Could it be that he was experiencing the beginnings of power-death? The thought produced in him a kind of clutching horror. According to Goldwine's teachings, that could not happen, but now, wracked and wretched, cold down to his bones and surrounded by the stink of his own sickness, he was aware as he had never been that Goldwine's teachings were only theory. She had never visited this world—as the Roundheads, for all their prejudice, for all their barrier-blinkered vision, had.

He forced himself to eat and drink—it might well have been the food that made him ill, but if he did not consume it he would starve. On the eleventh day of his journey, better but not recovered, he moved on.

In the time that followed he never again became as sick as he had been, but his guts would not settle and as often as not he brought up what he ate. His strength, or his Gift, continued to falter. On the fifteenth day he realized that he must choose between his barrier of protection and his binding of invisibility. On the eighteenth day, he realized he must give up either his barrier of protection or his ability to farwalk. To his surprise, the removal of these guards made little difference. The people he passed did not seem to find him particularly remarkable, and the unfiltered reality of the handpower world seemed much like the shielded version he had seen through his defenses. Perhaps he had been here long enough to acclimate, or perhaps it was just that ill-health had dulled his perception.

He had some time ago lost track of exactly where he was. He was able to keep himself heading north, but he had no idea how much distance he had covered, or how much there was left to travel. The whole of his will was focused now on just two things: moving forward, and closing his mind to the desperation that prowled the periphery of his thoughts and every day grew harder to shut out.

On the twentieth day, he woke to a catch in his throat and the beginnings of a fever. As the day moved on the fever mounted, and the catch became a knife, slashing at his chest with every indrawn breath. He attempted to block the progression of the symptoms, but this sort of self-healing, which in his world he had successfully performed, did not seem to be effective here, or else he no longer possessed the strength to accomplish it. By evening, it was clear to him that he could not stop what was happening in his body—and that if it were not stopped, it might kill him. He must get help, even if it meant giving himself into the hands of the people of this world.

He found a road and followed at its edge, hoping it would lead him to a town where there were physicians. But his weakness betrayed him. He stumbled over an unevenness in the ground and fell, rolling into a ditch. For a moment he lay, catching his breath. When he tried to rise, he found he could not.

He had been lying there ever since, as afternoon dwindled to evening, as the sky grew dark and sleet began to fall. Light passed across his vision; he was not sure whether it was the light of vehicles along the road or some illusion of his fever. The cold reached up from the snow he lay on; soon it would begin to work its way inward, taming the fever-heat inside him as, long ago, the mountains had tamed the fires of his Gift, until there was nothing left to quench, and everything in him was gone.

He knew enough about prophecy to know that it was only as fixed as the vessels of its fulfillment. It endured as they did, and if they failed, it could be broken. He had failed. The Prior would die now, and Jolyon would take his place, and Bron would never know that the time for return had come. Yet this understanding, which should have produced in him an agony beyond bearing, seemed not part of him at all, but a kind of light hovering outside and above him, a thing he could apprehend but not truly feel. Perhaps he was too close to death. Or perhaps, in the unarguable imminence of his own ending, it was enough to know that the struggle was over, and all choice had finally been taken from his hands.

To the light of understanding was joined another light. That door had never reopened; that Gift had never again touched his sleep. But Konstant knew, as surely as he knew he was dying, that Bron watched him: had been watching all along the miserable course of his journey, was watching now. In his near-delirium he imagined he could see that gaze, where before he had only sensed it, a cool glow hovering just below the sleet-filled clouds. Unblinking, it rested on him, a power that had revealed itself and now refused all help. Unblinking, he stared back, while the traffic on the roadway swept beams of light across the night, and the cold crept slowly inward toward his heart.

Thirteen

A LONG time later—or perhaps not: Konstant could not really tell—the light seemed move closer, a powerful illumination that made twinkling jewels of the falling sleet, and burned his eyes so that he closed them and struggled to turn his head away. He felt hands on his body, lifting him, laying him on a soft surface in a warm place. He opened his eyes to see whether he was dreaming, but what he saw was so strange that he closed them again.

Travel followed. He woke intermittently to a sense of motion, and once was aware of being carried through the cold of the outside world. He woke again to discover that he had come to rest, in a bed heaped with coverings that were far too heavy. He threw them back; someone drew them up, murmuring in a language he did not understand. He thought he felt power, enclosing him as intimately as his skin, reaching into his body to make right what was wrong; he thought he heard a voice, speaking in his own language, but when he tried to answer his tongue was too thick to form the words. Afterward, he was not able to tell what had been true and what was dream—huge, disjointed fever-dreams, complex and terrifying.

At last he rose from a long dark interval with no dreams at all and found himself properly awake. The fever-fires that had burned in him were gone. His body felt cool and light, as if the whole of him, inside and out, had been scoured clean. He lay on his back in a wide bed, naked underneath the quilts. Around him was a large room, with smooth white walls and a high white ceiling. A covered light burned on a table—the clear powerful illumination of this world, steadier than candles and warmer than mindlight. The air was deeply quiet. He could hear the singing of the silence, a pressure against his ears.

Cautiously he raised himself to a sitting position, propping himself against the drift of pillows in which he had been nested. Besides the bed and the table, the room contained an armchair covered and cushioned in maroon fabric, and a tall cabinet with many drawers. A patterned rug in stormy shades of red and blue covered most of the floor, with dark polished boards visible around its perimeter. There were two doors of a wood that matched the flooring, one half-open and one closed, and a smaller set of double doors. Gem-blue draperies along one wall indicated the presence of windows. Otherwise, the walls were bare, without ornament or decoration. It was a room of considerable austerity. Yet the richness of the fabrics and the intricate beauty of the rug seemed to indicate that it was taste, not want, that made it so.

The room raised many questions, as did his presence here. But one thing was not in doubt. Konstant knew, with absolute certainty, whose house this was. He sensed the truth all around him, filling the room as completely as the air: power, the unmistakable pulse of an awesomely great Gift. After so many days of emptiness, it was relief profounder than he could have imagined to feel that touch again. He was aware of the currents of his own Gift, a faint echo of the vast force that ruled here—not dead or injured as he had feared it might be, but alive and vital. It was like regaining the use of a lost sense, a healing as deep and essential as the one that had occurred inside his body.

A glass tumbler of water stood on the table beside the bed, with a plate of wafers beside it. He was hungry, he realized, and very thirsty. The water was clean and sweet, the wafers brittle and salty. He ate and drank cautiously, pausing often to see what his stomach would do, stopping before he was satisfied.

He pushed the heavy covers back and sat on the bed's edge, waiting a moment for his head to clear before rising to his feet. The air was warm against his bare skin, an enveloping sourceless heat that reminded him of the warmth-bindings of the Keep. It seemed strange to be upright: his head was light and his legs weak, and between them his body seemed to drift, as if it had come unmoored from the rest of him. Looking down at himself, he was shocked to see how his time in this world had pared his flesh, refining from his bulky Talesin disguise a starvation shape he had not worn even when travel for the Zosterians forced him to live rough for weeks at a time.

There was no sign of his clothing, and the room contained no wardrobes or garment chests. Slowly and a little unsteadily, he made his way over to the cabinet, which proved to be empty except for a single drawer containing stockings and what he took to be underclothing. A mirror hung on the wall above. Straightening from his inspection of the drawers, he was arrested by his own reflection. The face before him, which was not his own, was no longer really Talesin's either. It seemed a third man who looked back at him, his cheeks hollowed by starvation, his arms and torso slack with muscle-wasting and marked like a map with the shadow of every bone. Konstant raised his hands to his cheeks: the man in the mirror did the same. Even touch was not enough to produce a sense of connection with the scarecrow image.

He turned away. The short walk from bed to chest had exhausted him. He longed to lie down again and sleep, but urgency was rising in him, a pressing consciousness of wasted time: of the days of his overlong journey, of the unknown period he had lost to sickness. It was not the fervid, restless compulsion that had preceded his passage through the Gate, but a more weary desire, centered mainly on the need for completion. He wanted nothing more than to finish his task and be done.

He needed clothes. Perhaps there was a dressing chamber. He crossed the room, the rug soft under his bare feet, and looked into the space beyond the open door. The shaded light behind him glinted off glossy white tiles and gleaming white fixtures which, after some study, he tentatively identified as bathing facilities. The second door gave onto a hallway, with walls and ceiling as white and plain as those of the chamber he was in. Behind the double doors he found what he was seeking: breeches and shirts and less familiar garments, hanging from a rod in an alcove about as deep as his outstretched arms. He dressed slowly, fumbling with unfamiliar fabrics and closures. The clothes, though loose, were correct in proportion, but the shoes, lined up on the floor beneath the garments, had been made for someone smaller, and he could not get them on.

Barefoot, he left the room. On his right, the hallway terminated in a blank white wall, and on the more distant left, in a door whose wood matched the dark-planked, uncarpeted floor. At wide-spaced intervals along the ceiling, globes of cloudy golden glass depended from brass stalks, diffusing a pale amber light. It was as silent here as it had been in his room—a deep, singing silence, as if he were the only person alive in this place.

He began to walk toward the hallway's far end, trailing one hand along the wall to support himself. Closed doors to his left indicated other rooms. There were no doors to his right, only the unadorned white wall, broken some distance away by a long segmented panel of glistening black. It took him a moment, when he reached it, to recognize this as a window, paned with great sheets of glass and opening onto a night as impenetrable as any he had ever seen. Cold radiated from the window's surface, like the breath of some polar creature, brushing along his skin as he passed it by.

Opposite the window, a wide staircase broke the continuity of the left-hand wall, a sweep of dark wood curving unsupported toward a distant marble floor. Walls and ceiling flew away here, to make a well of open space. The top of the well was set with more panels of shining black. From the well's midpoint, on a long cord that reached nearly halfway to the ground, hung an astonishing confection of light, a gathering of pinpoint radiances like a cloud of stars. Konstant recognized, in the diamondlike clarity of the illumination, the signature of this world, though in its extravagance and beauty it seemed more akin to the mindlight creations he had seen in the Keep.

He braced his hands on the railing. Around him the silence sang. His body trembled with weakness. If he went down, would he have the strength to come up again?

He heard no sound, glimpsed no movement from the corner of his eye. But all at once he knew he was not alone. He turned. The door at the end of the hallway stood open now. Before it waited a tall, slender man, dressed according to the fashion of this world in a high-necked shirt tucked into a pair of narrow breeches. Shirt and breeches both were black, as was his hair, close-cropped like a Roundhead's. His clean-shaven face was ivory-pale. Even from a distance, Konstant could feel the force of his gaze.

Bron.

Weakness forgotten, Konstant started forward. Bron waited, unmoving, like someone atop a mountain watching an approach from far below. A little distance away, Konstant halted. He could have reached out now and touched the other man, yet the calm immobility of Bron's observation made him feel as if he still stood considerably beneath the mountain's peak.

He took a breath. <I have—>

Bron lifted his hand, an unmistakable gesture of prohibition. "I prefer voicespeech," he said aloud, in Guardian-language.

Konstant paused, reorienting himself. "I have a message for you," he said. "A message of great importance."

Uttered aloud, the words seemed flimsy, without weight. For a moment Bron did not reply. Konstant was tall, but Bron was taller: Konstant had to look up, very slightly, to meet his eyes. They were extraordinary eyes, long and dark and very clear, surmounted by level black brows. In their shape, and in the strong aquiline features, Konstant glimpsed the shadow of Cariad, Bron's daughter, whom he had not seen in more than twelve years, but whose face was painfully etched upon his memory.

"Very well," Bron said. "Come in."

He stepped aside, gesturing Konstant into the room beyond the open door. Konstant had noted, from the outside, something odd about the light within; as he crossed the threshold he realized that the illumination was not of this world, but of his own. Mindlight obscured the ceiling, a glowing cloud rippling with currents of greater brilliance. Standing branches of candles were set about the room, their small clear flames shuddering with the air of Konstant's passage, and with Bron's, as he entered behind Konstant and pushed the door closed.

The room was large, a white cube filled mainly with empty space. What furnishing there was displayed the same mixture of richness and austerity Konstant had noted in the room where he had woken. To the left of the entrance a pair of low couches, simple in line and covered in emerald fabric, made an L-shape before a wide hearth tiled in shades of gold and green. A desk in some beautiful golden wood, with a set of matching cabinets beside it, was set at the room's far end. There were no rugs to hide the patterning of the marble floor, a geometric inlay in various hues of cream and gold. The left-hand wall was entirely obscured by shelves, crammed with an astonishing number of books; the right wall was unornamented, save for a large painting enclosed in an elaborate gilded frame. The painting's subject appeared to be light, perhaps a fiery sunset, and water, perhaps a turbulent ocean, though it was so blurred in form and execution that Konstant could not be sure. As for the wall that faced the door, it was not a wall at all but a single sheet of glass, extending in a seamless curve from floor to ceiling. Night, impenetrably black, pressed against it.

"Sit." Bron moved toward the desk. "You must be hungry. I'll have something brought up."

He picked up an instrument that sat on the desk's surface, waiting a moment and then speaking into it words Konstant could not understand. Konstant sank down on one of the couches. The cushions were as yielding as a bed. A fire leaped on the hearth, reaching out fingers of warmth; a cluster of candles burned upon the ledge above. They were welcome, these familiar sources of heat and light, as welcome as the feeling of power had been when he first woke. He put his head back and closed his eyes. Weakness hummed along his limbs, the lingering whisper of his illness.

"I really didn't expect you up for another day or two. You were very sick, you know."

Konstant opened his eyes, pulling himself back from the edge of sleep. Bron had seated himself on the other couch, half-turned, with one leg crossed under him. His arm rested against the couch's back, bent so that his closed fist supported his temple. His dark eyes rested on Konstant's face. In age, Konstant knew, he must be seventy at least, but he looked no more than forty.

"How long was I . . ." Konstant cleared his throat. "How long was I unconscious?"

"Five days. I was able to bring your body into balance, but it's going to be some time before you get your strength back."

"They say . . . the Roundheads say this world makes the Gifted sick before it takes their power."

Bron's lips twisted a little. "In that, as in most things, the Roundheads are mistaken. This world did make you sick, but it was nothing to do with your Gift. There are . . ." He paused, searching. "There are . . . creatures, for lack of a better word, living creatures a thousand times smaller than a mote of dust. They exist everywhere, in our bodies and in the world—all the worlds, not just this one. You take them in with every breath, with everything you eat and drink. You give them out each time you exhale or cough, every time you excrete."

"Creatures?" Konstant said, bemused.

"It's not really a good analogy. But there's no other way to say it in your language. It's not something your people understand, the invisible universe of life that exists beneath the one we can see. You believe that sickness and infection come from foul humors or tainted air or impure blood or spiritual unfitness, but they don't, they come from these . . . creatures. The creatures of your world are different from the creatures of this one. Your body wasn't accustomed to them, and so you got sick. You probably drank out of streams, yes? And ate whatever you came across? I did the same when I first arrived here. I got sick, just as you did."

Konstant was silent. Before his inner eye rose an image of the world—this world, his world—boiling like an anthill with malign invisible life-forms. His mind, battered by illness and experience, moved instinctively to reject it. Yet, with what he had already seen, how much stranger was it to imagine this?

There was a knock at the door. A middle-aged woman entered, tall and strong-boned like a horse, with small light eyes and gray-blond hair pulled tightly back from her face. She set the tray she carried on the cushions beside Konstant. Straightening, she looked at Bron and spoke. Bron replied. She glanced at Konstant, clearly disapproving, and spoke again. This time, Bron's response held a perceptible edge. She shrugged, a gesture eloquent of others' folly, and left the room, closing the door softly behind her.

"She's been taking care of you," Bron said. "She wasn't pleased to see you out of bed."

Konstant thought of the presence he had sensed beside him during his sickness, of the hands that drew the quilts back up when he threw them off. He looked down at the tray. It held a bowl of steaming broth, a plate of bread, and a tumbler of water. He felt his stomach cramp. Best, perhaps, not to eat just yet.

"I'm grateful," he said, transferring his gaze back to Bron. "For this. For my life."

Bron smiled, a lifting of his lips that caused his dark eyes to crease at their outer corners. "You're welcome." The smile vanished. "You're one of hers, aren't you? One of Goldwine's."

"Yes."

Bron nodded, as if in response to some inward confirmation. "I felt you pass through the Gate. I feel all the passages, all the Gifts that come into this world. I knew right away you weren't a Roundhead. I only met her once, but I never forgot the feeling of her power. So." The dark gaze was steady. "This message. You said it was important."

Konstant breathed deeply, in and out. He had composed the words of the summons months ago, engraving them so deeply on his memory that he heard them in his sleep. In imagination he had lived the moment of delivering them a hundred times or more. Yet now the moment had arrived, it seemed scarcely more concrete than the dreams that preceded it.

"When you and Goldwine met on the snows outside the Fortress, she made a prophecy for you. She told you that you would free the Stone. That you would pass through a Gate into the handpower world. And that one day, long after, you would return to our world, with the Stone. The first two things have come to pass. I'm here to tell you that it is time for the third."

For the first time the ivory shell of Bron's composure seemed to crack. A series of emotions chased one another across his face, too swift and volatile to properly read.

"Return?" he said at last. "Why?"

"To bring freedom to our world. To end the rule of Limits. To strike the Order of Guardians down forever."

For a moment there was silence. Then, shockingly, Bron laughed. It was not a laugh of mirth, but of sheer incredulity. "You can't be serious. You crossed through a Gate and struggled through this world and nearly died so you could tell me that?"

Konstant stared at him. "I don't—"

"You're insane." The laughter was gone. "What makes you imagine such a thing could be done? Or, more to the point, that I'd be willing to do it?"

Konstant felt himself spinning, ruinously off balance. Speaking the summons, he had believed himself simply to be formalizing an existing understanding. Bron had revealed himself. He had saved Konstant from almost certain death. He had brought him to this house. Why would he do these things, unless he had already consented to what Konstant had come to ask?

"Because it has been prophesied." Konstant's voice was distant in his own ears. "You know the prophecy as well as I do."

"I most certainly do not. Goldwine did make a prediction for me, when we met that one time, though I never asked her to. But there was nothing in it about . . . return, or about destroying the Limits. Whoever told you this story got their facts wrong."

Anger bloomed at last, tardily, rising up through Konstant's chest and across his neck and altered face. "I don't think so." He met the dark eyes squarely. "It was your daughter Cariad who told me. And Goldwine who told her."

Bron's mouth opened. "My . . ." The word hung on the silent air. He could not seem to bring himself to complete the question. Konstant watched him. There was a grim pleasure in the sight of this formidable man, whom he would wager had not failed to control a situation in all the years since his escape, so suddenly and completely taken aback.

After a moment Bron spoke again.

"Perhaps you'd better tell me the whole story." His face had closed. It was impossible to tell, by looking at him, what he might be thinking. "Everything, from the beginning. Start with yourself. Who are you? How do you come to be carrying this message?"

Again Konstant breathed deeply. The heat of his anger had banished the floating unreality of his weakness. He felt stronger now than since he had awoken. This was a test, he thought. A test of his resolve, or his sincerity, or something else about him. It had to be.

"My name is Konstant. I was an Apprentice of the Arm of the Stone. In my fourth year I defected. Goldwine's patrols found me on the snow. They rescued me and brought me back to her headquarters."

"Why did you defect?"

"After you took the Stone, the Guardians killed every foreigner in the Fortress, and bound every Orderman to silence. They rebuilt the Room of the Stone and reset the weather-bindings in the Garden. When pilgrims come the Speakers play a game of answering, as if the Stone were still there. Novices and Apprentices are kept in ignorance until their Investments, and then bound with inhibitions so they can't speak the truth. Except for Guardians and the resistances, there's no one in the world who knows for certain what happened. Oh, there are rumors—that the Stone was stolen by a renegade Guardian, that it was destroyed in some disaster—but most people don't believe them. I certainly didn't. But there was . . . a situation . . . that made it possible for me to see the truth in the mind of one of my Apprentice masters." It was far less than the whole of what had happened, but it was true enough. "I saw that everything I'd been working toward was built around a lie. And so I ran away. As I said, Goldwine's patrols found me. She gave me sanctuary. I accepted her cause."

"So easily?" Bron had resumed the deliberate pose—one leg beneath him, one arm bent, his temple resting on his closed fist—that he had abandoned to his earlier surprise. "It's a long way from Arm Apprenticeship to a belief like that."

"Not so far, for me," said Konstant, shortly. He saw Bron's eyes flicker: registering his tone, evaluating it. But this, the bitter crux of his defection, the painful why and how of his lost allegiance, was no one's business but his own. "For me, the difficulty was believing that it was possible for anyone to set themselves against the Guardians and succeed."

"And what convinced you?"

"Understanding what Goldwine had accomplished. I had no idea, until her people showed me, how much the Guardians have had to change the way they are within the world because of her. They hide that—they pretend the checkpoints along the Guardian Roads have always been there, that Journeyer traveling parties have always had to go escorted by Soldiers, that it's bandits and not the resistances that seize half the Novice candidates before they ever reach the Fortress. But they know, and we know, the truth. The Guardians still own the world, but Goldwine has forced them to patrol it like a city under siege."

Bron smiled. It was a complex smile, suggesting memory and admiration, and a host of less readable emotions. "She spoke to me a little about what she planned to do, when we met that one time. I thought, sometimes, that it might be as you say. So you were convinced to adopt her cause. What then?"

"I was put in training to her ways of power. She's developed alternate techniques of defense, most of them invisible to Guardians. I had an aptitude, and she took an interest in me. That's how I met your daughter. She told me your story, the story of your ancestors—she called it the Tale. And the prophecy. She told me that as well."

Konstant paused, waiting for the question he was sure would follow. But Bron said nothing. He had shifted his face away and was gazing into the flames that fluttered on the green-and-gold hearth. After a moment Konstant continued.

"I stayed with Goldwine for five years. But her headquarters are in the mountains, and I wanted to be in the world. So I left and joined the Zosterians."

"There are still Zosterians?" Bron turned from his contemplation of the fire, his voice lifting in surprise.

"Yes. They're a resistance now, an underground."

"I knew a Roundhead once who swore to destroy them all."

It was Jolyon Bron meant. Konstant could see no trace of feeling in his still face, or hear it in his voice.

"They nearly were destroyed. But some escaped the purges, and survived in hiding until the present leader sought them out and recreated the movement. That was about fifteen years ago. They still follow most of the principles you laid down. They've written their own Books of Limits—ten of them to the Guardians' twenty, more lenient, and with more room for technological innovation."

"But still Limits."

"Yes."

"Did you convert again, then? Become a Zosterian?"

"No. No, the opposite, in fact. Being back among the Limits showed me how far I'd left them behind. But . . . I didn't want to go back to the mountains, and the Zosterians do serve the cause of Guardian overthrow. So I stayed. Then, about three years ago, I was asked to volunteer for a special mission. To take on the identity of a Roundhead, and infiltrate the Arm of the Stone."

Bron raised his brows. "You have the skills to carry off such a deception?"

"If you mean, do I know how to mindprobe . . ." Konstant glanced away from that steady gaze. "I was an Arm Apprentice long enough to acquire that skill, yes."

"So." There was judgment in the word, cool and absolute. "You were a worm-baiter in your Apprentice days."

"I was." Konstant felt no impulse to explain. Bron did

not know what he was judging, in any case, for the kind of baiting group Konstant had been a part of had not existed in Bron's time. "I accepted the mission. The Zosterians sent me back to Goldwine for retraining. It was a joint undertaking—the two resistances don't see eye to eye, but they both wanted the information the mission could give. I was inserted into an Investigation Team returning to the Fortress on sabbatical."

"How was that done? Not a semblance, surely?"

"No. The Zosterians have worked out a method of physical disguise. Bone-deep. Permanent. This is not my face." He resisted the urge to raise his hands to his altered features. "The insertion was successful. I reached the Fortress, and was put to work in the Investigation-Master's office. I stayed there for a year, and then, as I'd been ordered, presented myself for membership in the Reddened."

"So the Reddened also still exist."

"More than exist. They're the most powerful of all the Roundhead factions now."

"That surprises me. I'd have thought them too extreme for anything but a fringe position."

"Jolyon was made Investigation-Master after you left. He was given responsibility for the Zosterian purges, and he used the Reddened to carry them out. Their success gained them a lot of credibility. They were also one of the few groups that maintained a consistent position in the time just after you took the Stone. The Stone was gone, they said, but the world remained. If the Order had lost one of its charges, it must hold all the more tightly to the other. People must be bound to the Limits more strictly than ever before, and the Arm must cleanse itself of the liberalism that was eating away its moral fiber—proof of which, they said, was that someone like you could become a Roundhead. The Arm must also separate itself from the Journeyers, whose administrative incompetence had allowed the purity of the Limits to become fatally corrupted."

"The Arm of the Stone, a Suborder? That's counter to Zoster's core principles. He recognized the danger of an independent organ of enforcement. That's why he founded the Arm as a branch of the Journeyers."

"Yes, but there's also quite a bit in Zoster's writings about the importance of keeping the Arm's internal governance free of the authority of the Journeyer Council, and the need to hold the enforcement of the Limits apart from their teaching and administration. The Reddened used that to argue that separation had been Zoster's goal all along. They had a lot of support, not just from the reactionaries, but from moderate Roundheads who had never been Zosterian, and were angry at the damage they thought the movement had done to the Arm's prestige and unity."

"And agreed, no doubt, with the Reddened's view that my tenure within the Arm was a sign of some kind of deep moral decay."

Konstant nodded. "Separation and renewal became synonymous. Eventually the Council voted as the Reddened wanted and petitioned the Prior for Suborder status. The Reddened weren't as extreme then as they are now, and the Prior agreed with many of their arguments. Eventually he granted the petition. After that no one dared challenge them."

"In my time there were Roundheads who were determined that the forces of extremism would not prevail." Bron's voice was soft. "Tell me, is Marhalt still Apprentice-Master?"

Konstant nodded. "Though he isn't as powerful as he was."

"Because of his connection with me, I presume."

"Yes. And also because he's one of the few who openly opposes Jolyon and the Reddened. He and the Treasurer and the Limit-Master brought challenge to Jolyon's right of succession after he was made Second. The Council has been deadlocked ever since. The Staff-Holder would like to step down, but he can't until the challenge is resolved."

"So Jolyon is Second now. When did that happen?"

"About three years ago. The previous Second died of a seizure. No one could prove it wasn't natural, though a lot of people suspected it, especially when the Staff-Holder brought in a Red sympathizer to replace Jolyon as Investigation-Master."

"That's a dangerous degree of authority for a man like

Jolyon." Bron's tone was cool. "Even if he never manages to become Staff-Holder. It must make the other Suborders very nervous."

"It made the Zosterian leadership nervous. Part of my mission was to get close enough to Jolyon to assess his defenses. To see if he might be vulnerable to an assassination attempt."

"And did you? Get close to Jolyon?"

"Closer than anyone expected. I became his companion."

Bron blinked. "His companion?"

"It's not what it sounds. A companion is a sworn follower, a Roundhead who agrees to take upon himself the responsibility for a Councilor's life and safety."

"That's not something that anyone thought necessary in my time. Has it become so dangerous to govern within the Arm of the Stone?"

"Jolyon thinks so. Generally companions volunteer themselves, but Jolyon is more particular. He selects his companions, based on specific criteria."

"Which you fulfilled."

"Which my identity did. Jolyon has a need for agents of a certain type. When he finds them, he elevates them to companionship, and observes them for a while. If he judges them satisfactory, he sends them out to undertake a mission for him."

"And what is this mission?"

"To enter this world, and search for you."

For a moment Bron was silent. "That explains something I'd wondered about," he said at last. "Why sometimes the searchers come in groups, and sometimes solo. How long has this been going on?"

"Since you left. It took the Council several years to realize they had to search this world instead of ours. But Jolyon always assumed you'd gone to this one. Even after they began to send parties here, he continued hunting you on his own. He does it in secret. The Council has no idea."

Bron had turned his face to the fire. "It must eat him up to fail," he said, softly. For a moment he sat without moving, his dark eyes narrowed upon the flames. Konstant could sense the currents of his thoughts, turning behind the impenetrable composure of his ivory profile. He was tempted, very tempted, to reach out with his Gift and touch the edges of that flow. But he knew Bron's power, not just through the stories Cariad had told him, but through his direct sense of the Gift that filled this house. Perhaps when he was more recovered . . . but not now.

"So that's how you got here." Bron shifted again to look at him—a motion of his head only, for the rest of him stayed as still as before. "Jolyon sent you."

"No. Jolyon was only the means to get me through the Gate. It was Goldwine who sent me. That's why she agreed to collaborate with the Zosterians. That's why she trained me. So that by becoming Jolyon's messenger, I could be hers."

Bron dropped his hands to the green cushions of the couch. He pushed himself upright. Slowly, lacing his fingers behind his back, he walked over to the green-and-gold hearth, and stood there, a tall dark figure, staring down into the fire.

"And this is truly her message you bring me," he said. "This message of summons and destruction."

"It is."

"Why now?"

Konstant sat forward. The rest had been background, told because Bron required it, but this was the heart of the matter. He felt the power of it, rising in him like the flames Bron gazed upon, no longer the weary impulse to which he had woken but fresh and strong and urgent, as it had been in the Fortress.

"Since you took the Stone, the Order has been crumbling. The works of power they've set upon the world are decaying. Their numbers are dwindling—every week Journeyers and Soldiers abandon their vows, from horror at the excesses of the Reddened or from disillusionment at the absence of the Stone. And now the Prior is dying. Jolyon plans to take his place, and set the Reddened in rulership across the world."

"Jolyon?" Bron turned, resting one elbow on the candle-crowded mantel. "You said he was Second, not Staff-Holder."

"The Staff-Holder is too ill, or says he is, to endure the Ceremony of Recreation. He's given Jolyon his proxy."

"That's highly irregular. Surely the other Suborders won't allow it."

"Two of the Suborders will welcome it. The Journeyer Staff-Holder is the most Gifted of all of them, but he's liberal for a Guardian, and the Soldiers and Speakers can't tolerate the idea that he might be the one to remake the Staff. Jolyon is already allied with the Soldier Staff-Holder, who will back his claim with arms if necessary. The Speakers will support his inclusion also, because they believe his Gift will neutralize the Journeyer's and allow their Staff-Holder to get the advantage."

"They'll be sorely disappointed, then. If this Journeyer is half as powerful as you say he is, Jolyon will still be no match for him."

"But Jolyon's Gift is one of the greatest in the Order."

Bron laughed, briefly. "Then Jolyon is a better illusionist than he was when I knew him."

Konstant shook his head. "What do you mean?"

"When I knew Jolyon there were a few things he was good at. He could mindprobe fairly well. He was an accomplished projectionist—he knew how to focus a force-sending tightly enough to kill a man if it struck him in the head or chest. And he was very, very perceptive about the things people feared or hated. He used these things to make himself seem larger than he was. But the truth is that he never had more than an average Gift—enough to get him into the Arm, certainly, but not enough to challenge a powerful Staff-Holder. From what you say, he's found some way of concealing this, of tricking people into believing a myth about himself. Perhaps he even believes it himself. But the Recreation will expose him for what he really is. After that, he'll never be able to fool anyone again."

Konstant did not know what to say. He could not dispute Bron's personal memories. Yet he himself had felt the hungry tides of Jolyon's power, opening out before him like the end of the world. It had not felt in the least like illusion.

Bron lifted his arm from the mantel and paced back to the couches. He sat down, one leg tucked under him, as he had before. He fixed his dark eyes on Konstant's face.

"Is there anything more? Have you anything else to tell me?"

"I've said everything I came to say." As if the words were a signal, Konstant felt the returning whisper of illness, a soft tremor along all his limbs.

"Then I'm sorry. You've come a long way and suffered a great deal. I recognize your belief in what you've come to tell me. I acknowledge the difficulties you've faced." Bron shook his head. "But I will not answer your summons."

For a moment Konstant was too stunned to speak. "But you must," he said at last, stupidly.

"Why? Leaving aside the question of whether I'm willing to be sucked back into the affairs of a world I left behind thirty years ago, you've said nothing to convince me that intervention is necessary. You've described Goldwine's successes, and the Zosterians'. You've told me of the decay of the Guardians' power and the attrition of their numbers. The path of your world is set. The Order will fall. You don't need me to make it happen."

"You're wrong." Dizziness seized Konstant. The proportions of the room seemed to ebb and shift, as if the air had suddenly become liquid. The emerald color of the cushions stabbed at his eyes; even the big painting seemed more fiery than it had been, as if the setting sun had sunk closer to the horizon. "The path *isn't* set. It may be true, what you say about Jolyon's power; I don't know. But I tell can you this: whether by power or by trickery, he *will* be Prior. I've looked into the minds of his followers. I've seen the scope of his ambition. I know what he's done, and I know what he can do, and I know that he will do even more than that to achieve his goal. And when he does, everything we've talked about today will end. Goldwine, the Zosterians, the changes, the gains—they will all end. Jolyon will make sure of it. He'll burn the world to ashes if he has to. And he'll take pleasure in the destruction. You told me to believe you—now I tell you to believe me. This is what will happen if you don't come back."

"It makes no difference." Bron watched him, unmoving,

unmoved. "Even if I believed everything you've told me, and agreed with you in every detail, I still wouldn't choose to return. I'm finished with your world. I was done with it the moment I left it. I care neither for it, nor for anything in it."

"But this is not a matter of choice. Not for you, not for me, not for any of us. This is foreordained. This is prophecy—"

"No." Bron held up his hand: a gesture of absolute prohibition. "Of all the things you might say to me, that is the one that would least dispose me to do what you want. I despise prophecy. I always have."

Silence fell, echoing in the barren room. Konstant sat, numb. He had dismissed that first refusal from his mind, certain his narrative was a test, certain that, when he reached its end, Bron would give him the consent he had come for. Even now he could not quite believe it was not so, that he had not simply dreamed all this, another delusion born of fever.

"You may remain here until you're fully recovered." Bron had risen to his feet again. "My housekeeper will see you have all you need."

"Why?" Konstant whispered. "Why did you rescue me, if you only meant to refuse?"

"Meant to refuse?" Bron looked down at him. "I didn't mean to do anything—except, perhaps, to save your life. I had no idea why you were in this world, until you opened your mouth and spoke your absurd summons."

Anger roared through Konstant, like the fires of his illness. It propelled him to his feet. It sparked his Gift, flung it outward. He thought, later, that he must have gone a little mad. But in that moment he believed that he had not only the need, but the right to know Bron's mind, to see the whole text of his refusal, to understand why he defied the call of prophecy and made a mockery of the message Konstant had nearly died to bring him.

But he did not manage to touch even the edges of the other man's thoughts. A huge force exploded into being, falling on him like an avalanche. He could not move, could not blink, could not breathe. He felt his ribs buckling under the pressure. A universe of light burst before his eyes. Behind it, he knew, was the face of death.

The force vanished. He fell to the floor, clawing for breath. He heard his own nightmare gasps. The light was still there, prickling all across his vision, closing inward at the edges.

"Don't ever try that again." Konstant rolled his eyes upward. Bron stood over him. His gaze was like black fire. His ivory face was terrible in its blankness. "If you do, I can't promise that you will survive undamaged."

Bron moved away. After a time Konstant felt hands on him. Somehow he was lifted to his feet. It was the woman who had brought the tray, as strong as the horse she resembled. She pulled his arm over her shoulder, supporting him round the waist. She moved, bearing him with her. He had no choice but to go.

Fourteen

OR A time—he was never certain, afterward, how long—Konstant descended once again into a world of nightmare and delirium. He emerged at last, after an interval of darkness he could not measure. For a moment, still not entirely awake, he imagined that his meeting with Bron had been a fever dream, like the others. But then he saw the clothes he had worn, neatly folded across the arm of the maroon chair, and knew it had been real.

He lay among the pillows, staring at the ceiling, despair and self-hatred twisting like knives inside him. The disgust he felt encompassed even this—for how many times in his life had he felt exactly thus, and what good had it ever done him? In his hopelessness he was angry even at Goldwine, for entrusting the burden of prophecy not to a whole man but to a cracked vessel like himself, who had reached his goal not by his strength but by another's, and then had squandered that second chance by delivering the summons in such a way that, unthinkably, it could be refused.

After a while he pulled himself together, and set himself to think about the situation rationally. For the past hour and more he had been turning the heat of recrimination upon himself alone. Yet should it not be Bron he was condemning? Was it not Bron who had refused? Who was he to abandon faith in his ability to complete the task Goldwine had given him, before all paths to that task were closed? He was alive. He was in Bron's house. Perhaps he was not meant to try once, but many times. Perhaps he was not meant to achieve the goal easily, but to struggle. It might be that he would not succeed; it might be that the prophecy would be broken after all. But if that did come to pass, it must not be he who made it so, through his own, old failings of doubt and self-hatred. He had received a charge. He had journeyed here to fulfill it. As long as he was breathing, that was what he must try to do.

It was a familiar exercise, this willed rejection of despair, this deliberate shifting of focus from the darkness inside him to the necessities without. Since his escape from the Fortress he had been sliding, with dreary regularity, between these poles of feeling. Always, at some point, he lost his grip on hope and purpose and spiraled down again; he suspected that one day his resolve would fail him and he would be unable to climb back up into the light. But not today.

The first thing was to recover his physical strength. Accordingly, he remained in bed, sleeping often, eating whatever was given him. Bron's housekeeper brought him meals on a tray, remade his bed, and gave him little medicine pellets to swallow, caring for him with a forceful thoroughness that spoke more of efficiency than compassion.

He could not understand a word she said, nor she him, but he was easily able to dip into her undefended mind to follow her thoughts and to gently project his own meanings so that she believed his words were in her language. The unGifted minds he had encountered on his journey had been difficult to comprehend, full of strange references and alien images, but this woman's thoughts were not like that, perhaps because of her isolation in this lonely house, perhaps because of her narrow temperament—but mostly, Konstant suspected, because Bron had done something to her mind, so that she would not find it strange that the ceiling of his sitting room was covered by a sheet of living light, or that time went by and he never aged a day.

The first things he learned from her were practical: her name, Emme; how to manipulate a small lever set into a panel beside the door to make light spring from the ceiling; how to control the heat in the room by opening or closing the louvers of the gridlike device that ran at the base of one wall; the fact that what he had thought was a peculiar bathing option in the little tiled room in fact served the same purpose as a privy. The moment he discovered this he insisted on getting up to use it. Emme protested—she was a rigid caregiver, and believed he risked a relapse through any exertion greater than sitting up in bed to eat. But he was tired of being tended with bedpans, and in any case it was clear to him that she derived a certain satisfaction from being thwarted. This was the way, she believed, the world treated those who knew the proper ways of doing things. It pleased her to see it proved, even at her own expense.

From Emme, Konstant learned that Bron, a man of immense wealth, had caused the house to be built a little over seven years ago, working from plans he himself had drawn up. He hired her and her husband to staff it just after it was finished. It was a lonely existence. There were no other dwellings upon this rocky coast, and the nearest town was miles away. Food and other supplies had to be ordered in bulk and hauled in along the single road, kept clear of snow and ice at Bron's expense. But Emme did not object, neither did she seem to find it curious that someone should want to live in such isolation. Toward Bron and everything to do with him she exhibited a calm, uncritical acceptance, whether it was the question of how he had acquired his wealth, or what he had done in the years before he built the house, or the signs of power he did not bother to conceal, or Konstant himself, the first person besides Bron and Emme and her husband who had ever slept under this roof. It was clear that she was deeply loyal to Bron, proud both of her service and of the man she served; yet so complacent was her fidelity that Konstant could not help wondering whether, like her blindness to Bron's Gift, it had been artificially instilled.

A few days into his recovery Konstant began to spend part of each day out of bed. At first he simply sat, or paced briefly about the room. Later, when he felt stronger, he descended the graceful sweep of the staircase and wandered through the house. His original clothing, ripped and filthy, had been discarded, but Emme had kept his boots, and so he was able to go comfortably shod. She had kept his belt also, and the wallet attached to it, with Jolyon's talisman inside. This he began to wear around his neck, not out of any desire to keep it by him, but to avoid the annoyance of its small calling voice, which spoke to him whenever he was more than a few rooms distant.

He knew the plan of the house from his examination of Emme's mind: the great foyer, the many sitting rooms, the huge library shelved with books from floor to ceiling, the music room filled not with instruments but with mechanical devices, the high-ceilinged dining room, the vast kitchen walled in gleaming cooking and food-keeping machines, the greenhouse complex where vegetables and flowers grew beneath banks of glowing violet-hued lights.

Even to an eye untutored in the aesthetics of this world, it was clear that the furnishings were very fine. Yet considering the space available to hold them and the wealth of the man who owned them, they were remarkable as much for their scarcity as for their quality. The walls, all painted the same flat white, ran on yard after yard without ornament. Echoing tracts of vacant floor divided chair from couch and door from door. No complex carving or elaborate fabric adorned the furniture; the window- and door-casings were entirely plain. There were some extraordinary features: the starburst chandelier in the stairwell, a similar one in the dining room, the breathtaking panels of gold-striated marble that paved the floor of the foyer, a gleaming bronze sculpture taller than Konstant himself in one of the sitting rooms. Yet such extravagances were few, and obviously carefully chosen. It was the house itself that was the marvel, with its immense rooms and soaring ceilings, its enormous bowed windows and glittering skylights, its perfect angles and precise, harmonious proportions. It was as if its furnishing had been deliberately limited to emphasize this fact.

And yet Konstant found it oppressive, and the more he wandered the huge spaces, the more this perception weighed on him. Each chamber was different, and held different things, but in their empty perfection they were all the same. Nothing ever changed, by so much as an inch of displacement or a fleck of dust. Now and then, pausing in a doorway, he found himself uncertain of whether he had passed this way that day or the day before, or perhaps even the day before that. Silence ruled: the loudest he had ever heard, a roaring hush that overwhelmed him whenever he stopped moving. He felt, sometimes, as if he were the only living being present, or as if the others had been bound into slumber and he was the only soul awake. Or as if he himself were sleeping, dreaming a long repetitive dream.

Often he came upon Emme, dusting the library shelves or mopping the kitchen floor or preparing food for cooking; more rarely, he met her husband Kari, a bearlike man who was responsible for maintenance and spent much of his time in the greenhouses. But he never encountered Bron. Bron was present, Konstant knew, not just from Emme's thoughts but from the power that filled the house as fully as the silence did, a song only another Gifted could hear. The hope of a meeting was the main reason Konstant engaged in his explorations. But it was as if the other man, already voluntarily confined within the house itself, had determined to sequester himself still further while Konstant remained, shutting himself into his workroom and not coming out for even for meals. Had Konstant's use of his Gift been a trespass too terrible to forgive? Or was it simply that Bron had guessed his purpose and was determined to evade it?

Four days into his walking convalescence, Konstant went to the door of Bron's workroom and knocked. For much of his time here he had been too sick to feel restlessness or impatience, but now that he was regaining his strength the old fires were rising again, and he was tired of the waiting game Bron seemed to have decided to play. He had no plan beyond admittance; it would be enough just to reestablish contact, a toehold for his assault upon the walls of Bron's refusal. But the room gave back only silence. He knocked a second time: again there was no reply. Anger shook him, as sudden as an indrawn breath. He raised his fist to knock a third time. But the silence, somehow, held him back. There was a speaking quality to it, a sense of warning. It seemed, suddenly, as clear as a spoken refusal.

At the long window halfway between Bron's room and

his, Konstant paused. It was only just past noon, but the light was already beginning to wane. At this time of year, so close to the top of the world, it was day for little more than an hour in each twenty-four. Through the glass, he could see the rocky promontory upon which the house was set. Constant sea-winds scoured it clean of snow, but ice rimmed the shoreline, great layers and floes of it, stretching far out into the restless ocean. The sun, which had not quite managed to lift itself clear of the horizon, was now in the process of sinking down again.

It was an indescribably bleak prospect. In its context, the house, with its luxurious warmth and comfort, seemed less a marvel than an aberration, a mad folly set down in a place where nature and sense said no such thing should be. Bron was equally hidden no matter where he was; what had possessed him to build a mansion on this barren shore, where even seabirds did not visit and in the deepest part of winter the sun barely rose at all?

Nearly two weeks ago Konstant had forbidden himself the pitfalls of doubt and rededicated himself to the purpose that had brought him here. But now, looking out at the dying day, he felt himself sinking into doubt again, like the weary sun reclaimed by the eager sea. Wandering aimlessly through Bron's great house, it had begun to seem to him that what he saw was not merely the shape of Bron's personal taste, but in some mysterious sense, the man himself. In the bare walls and vacant spaces, the choice furnishings and strange art objects, he read wealth and discrimination, restraint and confidence, strength and absolute self-sufficiency. But he also saw coldness, rigidity, sterility—and will, the kind of implacable resolution that had set a house upon a wasteland, that had rejected one world and turned its back upon another, that had walled itself up within a façade so closed and perfect that he did not wish to consider it too carefully, for fear of what it might tell him about what he could accomplish by remaining here. He could wait: he could wait forever if he had to. But if Bron chose to withhold himself, what good would waiting do?

He stood before the window, watching as day drifted away and night returned, as his altered face took ghostly shape upon the glass. He felt as insubstantial as his image, a shadow-man adrift in a sea of silence, out of sight of any shore. At last he made his way to his room, where he paced, striving through motion to drive away the dark mood that gripped him. He did not pause until Emme's soft knock at the door announced the arrival of his supper.

The next afternoon Emme informed Konstant that Bron had requested his presence in the dining room for the evening meal.

The dining room was a large white chamber at the center of the house. There were no windows, though there were skylights, gleaming black triangles randomly breaking the uniformity of the ceiling. The only furnishing was the table, a massive slab of glass supported by a grid of black metal struts that seemed scarcely strong enough to hold it up, and the twelve chairs around it, stark curved forms of the same metal. A chandelier hung above the table's center, a burst of blue-white light like a star frozen in the moment of its explosion. Two places were set beneath it: white porcelain, silver utensils, crystal goblets. Bron sat facing the door, sipping wine. His dark eyes followed Konstant as he crossed the room.

"Good evening," he said. His tone was neutral, neither warm nor cool.

"Good evening." Konstant seated himself. The metal chair, which he had expected to be hard and unwelcoming, was flexible and surprisingly comfortable. It occurred to him, irrelevantly, to wonder why Bron, who never entertained, needed so many chairs around his table.

"You seem much recovered since I saw you last," Bron said.

"Yes." Konstant was finding it unexpectedly difficult to face this man, to look into his eyes. The memory of the force that had nearly killed him was still strong enough to catch at his breath. "I still tire quickly, though."

Bron smiled, faintly, as if to acknowledge that Konstant, too, was playing a waiting game. "It's not surprising. You were very sick." He set down his goblet. The sound of glass striking glass was musical in the quiet room. "You knocked at my door yesterday."

"Yes," said Konstant, surprised. He had not expected such a direct approach.

"I was occupied. That's why I didn't reply. I bear you no ill will, you know. You acted as your situation dictated. As did I."

"I . . . Yes. Yes, that's so."

"I see no reason why we should avoid one another while you remain here. I thought perhaps we might take the evening meal together from now on."

It was a little bemusing, this sudden reversal of the rigid avoidance of the past days. Konstant had hoped for this, of course, but he had not thought it would occur so easily. "Thank you," he said. "I would enjoy that."

Emme brought in the first course, a pale soup thick with cream. Bron poured Konstant a glass of wine. They consumed their soup, spoons clinking against the porcelain of the bowls, glasses chiming against the surface of the table. Between these small sounds the silence wove a heavy fabric. The light cast by the starry chandelier was cool rather than warm; within it Bron was a study in black-and-white, with his ivory skin and dark eyes and the sleek ebony cap of his hair. As before, he was dressed in black—a heavy knitted tunic this time, its sleeves pushed up above his elbows, and loose trousers of some silky material. All of it was very plain and without ornament; he did not even wear rings. He ate steadily, attentive to his meal, as contained and easy as if he were entirely alone.

Over the second course, he spoke.

"Emme's been taking good care of you, I hope."

Konstant swallowed a mouthful of food. "Very good care. I'm grateful. It's trouble for her, I know."

"Nonsense." Bron waved away Emme's inconvenience with one long-fingered hand. "I'm sure she's glad of the change. Our lives don't have much variety. I hope you haven't suffered too greatly from boredom."

"I've been too ill, really, to do much but eat and sleep."

"Of course. But you're regaining your strength now. You

must feel free to use anything you find here to entertain yourself."

"Thank you." There was an unreal quality to this small talk. Bron did not strike Konstant as the kind of man who made conversation for politeness' sake.

Emme cleared away the plates, and brought a salad. Bron reached out and refilled Konstant's glass.

"Tell me," he said, "Why did you want to become a Guardian?"

Konstant coughed a little on his wine. "It wasn't really a question of wanting," he said when he could speak. "From the time my Gift first manifested, it was what everyone assumed."

"Including you?"

"Especially me. All through my childhood I was told I'd been born to be a Guardian. It never occurred to me to imagine a different future."

"So you were doing what was expected of you."

"I suppose I was." It was not the truth, or not entirely. He had never been a zealot, even in his Roundhead days—a thing that had made it easier, once he grasped the magnitude of the deception at the Order's heart, to accept that the Limits were deception also. But he had been ambitious. He had wanted the wealth and status that being a Guardian, that being a Roundhead, could give him. That desire had been wholly his own.

"Your Gift is mindspeech, yes?"

"Yes."

"Your Gift is powerful." Bron watched him. "I can see why you were chosen for the Arm of the Stone."

"I was groomed for it, actually, from the first day I entered Guardian School. By the time I was nine I'd learned all they could teach me. My last three years were mostly spent coaching the younger students."

Bron smiled—a dark smile this time. "I had a similar experience, though not by virtue of my Gift. I imagine you passed the Novice Examinations without difficulty."

Konstant nodded.

"And then the journey to the Fortress. How did you manage that? Did your parents buy a guide?"

"My mother didn't have that kind of wealth. But she was a woman of business, and she . . . owned . . . something a rich man wanted. In exchange for it, he agreed to sponsor me." In fact his mother had been a courtesan; the thing of value had been his beautiful older sister, born to follow the same profession. Her contract, which under other circumstances Konstant's mother would have sold for a high fee, had been given gratis to the man in question, the price of Konstant's passage. It was something that could still, when he thought about it, make him feel guilty. "I was lucky. We made the journey in less than six months, with no casualties."

"Lucky indeed. And then?"

"And then I endured the Novitiate." It was becoming an effort for Konstant to hold himself to the part he knew he must play. What was the purpose of this excursion into his dead past? "I passed the Apprentice Examinations with honors and was made a Journeyer. After a year I was chosen for the Arm, just as I and my mother and all my teachers expected. You know the rest."

Bron considered him for a moment, not speaking. "You don't like talking about yourself, do you?"

Konstant glanced away from the uncomfortable perception he seemed to see in those dark eyes. "There are subjects I prefer."

"Very well, then. We'll discuss other things. Tell me about the resistance headquarters. I believe you said they were in the Fortress mountains?"

And for the rest of the meal they discussed Goldwine, and the marvels of her hollow mountain. Bron listened as Konstant spoke, questioning and commenting from time to time. It was impossible to tell what he was thinking. Emme moved in and out, removing and replacing plates, pouring cups of a hot bitter drink. Bron laced his with cream and spoonfuls of sweet white crystals; Konstant did the same.

Upstairs in his room, enclosed once more in the house's roaring silence, Konstant replayed the evening in his mind. The sudden reversal of isolation, the personal questions: surely there was a purpose to it though for the life of him he could not think what that might be. But it did not matter.

Contact had been reestablished. Now he could set about his task.

The days passed and the conversations continued. At Bron's prompting, Konstant spoke about the accomplishments of Goldwine's resistance, about the Zosterians and how the principles they followed differed from those Bron had originally laid down. He described the attrition of the Guardians' power, outlined the divisions within the Arm of the Stone, discussed the power struggle precipitated by the Prior's impending death. He spoke, at length, of the Reddened, and the atrocities they carried out in the name of orthodoxy.

He had no objection to these discussions. They allowed him, in a dozen different ways, to paint a picture of a desperate world, which was at least a part of the message he had come to give—though he was careful never to speak with too much passion, or to appear too deeply invested in what he said. It was a slow method of proceeding, and frustratingly ineffectual. It was Bron's sympathy Konstant sought to awaken, his compassion, his sense of moral outrage. For decades, in the mindpower world, Bron had followed a secret agenda, risking his life and the lives of others in the passionate pursuit of change. Surely it was not possible to abandon such dedication so completely as Bron claimed to have done. Surely, even in renunciation, some echo must remain, some spark that might be rekindled to a blaze. But as the nights slipped by, Konstant could not see, in the calm face across the table, any shadow of acknowledgment, or any sign that Bron was moving closer to commitment.

He schooled himself to patience, though urgency struggled like flame within him, and the desire to abandon restraint and shout his need directly into Bron's face was sometimes overpowering. He was aware of time drawing out; at some point, his pretense of convalescence would cease to be a viable excuse for remaining under Bron's roof. He did not allow himself to dwell on this, any more than he allowed himself to dwell on failure, or even on success. His task was simply to persist, word by word and night by night, until an endpoint was reached and persistence became either unnecessary or pointless. He did begin to pace again, however, back and forth between the walls of his room—attempting, as he had during his service to Jolyon, to exhaust his restlessness through physical motion.

And always, underneath it all, there was the question: Why? Why were they talking about these things? Why was Bron, who had stated in no uncertain terms his rejection of the world of mindpower, willing to spend every night in discussion of it? Now and then Bron terminated the conversations with odd abruptness, rising and stalking from the table, or issuing a curt dismissal. At such times he conveyed an impression of anger or disgust—at Konstant for speaking? At himself for listening? Konstant could not tell. Yet in these moments it seemed to him that the mask of Bron's aloofness slipped a little, affording a glimpse of something very different underneath. He could not help but think that, in spite of what Bron had said, in spite perhaps of what he wanted, something in him still turned toward the suffering world of his birth.

But these moments were few and far between. Most often, it seemed to Konstant that Bron's cool, detached curiosity was exactly what it appeared to be. In this light, his interest was merely voyeuristic, like someone sitting at a window and watching a murder take place below. Konstant could not help disliking him for it, more and more with each passing day. To find this feeling in himself was as strange, in its way, as anything he had encountered here. It would not have occurred to him that such mundane categories of human reaction could apply to a man like Bron, who after all was a legend, with a legend's exemption from the ordinary strictures of moral judgment. But then, he had believed that when he found Bron, he would find a liberal, a reformer, a man opposite in every way to the Guardians whose walls he had knocked down. Konstant had never, somehow, much considered the other side of this: that Bron had also, for a substantial portion of his life, been a Roundhead. It was this that Konstant chiefly saw when he looked into Bron's calm, closed face. The aloofness, the arrogance, the impression of great power held in check: all these were

Roundhead qualities. He did not sense the iron core of cruelty, the fanaticism, the relish for pain—though perhaps those things were only better hidden.

In the wide-ranging scope of the conversations, there were three issues that remained unaddressed. The first was Bron himself. He spoke no word of his time in this world, of how he had come by his wealth or what he had been doing across the years of his exile. The second was Cariad. Konstant had thought at first that he might ask about her, but he never did, even in the most general terms. The one time Konstant mentioned her, in connection with Goldwine's protection of the handpower networks, his face became so icy that Konstant took care not to utter her name again.

The third was the Stone. Bron's Gift occupied the spaces of his dwelling as entirely as the air itself; seemingly, there was no other power present. Yet the Stone must be here, for surely Bron would not keep it distant from him. But why would he shield it inside his house, where his own Gift was undisguised? Could it be that the Reddened were right, that the power of the Stone had been lost or damaged? This was a Giftless realm, after all; Konstant himself had suffered in its emptiness, and he did not know what it might mean for the Stone, Gift in its purest form, to extend its awareness into a vacant world. Though he tried, in a dozen different ways, to ask, Bron turned the questions aside—without anger, but with a firmness that brooked no appeal.

One evening a little over a week and a half after the two men had begun to meet, Emme offered Konstant brandy to finish his meal. Konstant refused. By now he was so used to reading Emme's meanings and projecting his own that he was scarcely aware of the fact that they spoke different languages. When Emme had gone, Bron spoke.

"You do that so easily. There was a time when I would have envied you."

Konstant looked at him, surprised. Bron had witnessed such exchanges on many occasions; this was the first time had chosen to comment. "Why?"

"Until the very end of my time in your world, I had no

nearspeech at all. I could force myself to reach inside others' minds, but I couldn't voluntarily let anyone into mine. It was a great handicap for a Roundhead, as you can imagine."

"But basic nearspeech is the simplest of the mindskills." Konstant was astonished. "Even those with the smallest Gifts can master it. And your Gift is greater than any I've ever known."

"A Gift is the servant of the mind that owns it. I had many secrets when I was part of your world. They were strongly barriered, but I was too afraid of discovery to open my mind even a little. When the Prior tried to kill my Gift in punishment for my so-called Violation, all my barriers were broken, and I was freed forever from the need for secrecy. Since then I've been able to nearspeak. But never comfortably. Not like you."

In all the time they had spent together Bron had never said so many words at once about himself. Experimentally, Konstant offered something in return.

"My earliest memories are of thought-reading. I didn't know it was forbidden until I got to Guardian school. After that I taught myself to do it secretly. I skimmed my masters' minds all through school, all through the Novitiate, all through the Apprenticeship. No one ever knew."

Bron raised his brows. "That's no mean feat, especially with Roundheads."

"The trick of it is knowing how deep you can dip. People can often feel it if you touch their guards, but if you stay just above, they have no idea you're there."

"That must require a fine degree of control. And of judgment." Bron smiled a little. "To know whom you should not try it on."

"I never make the same mistake twice." Konstant met Bron's eyes squarely. He had never, in the course of their discussions, come to relish this man's company, but it was some time since he had feared what he might find in Bron's dark gaze. "At least, not in regard to mindskill."

Bron smiled more widely, and let it pass. "It must have been very useful in your resistance career, this thought-skimming."

"Yes. And in the Keep. I doubt I'd have survived without it."

"Mindspeech was survival for me also, oddly enough. When I first got to this world I didn't have the advantage of acquired memories, as you did. All I had was what I'd learned during my Arm Apprenticeship, and my own surmises, based on my experiments with technology and my beliefs about its nature. But it was all theory. It didn't come close to preparing me for what's really here."

"Actually, the acquired memories didn't help me nearly as much as I thought they would. The Roundheads who come here go very thickly barriered. It takes most of the detail out of what they see."

"And prejudice, no doubt, blots out the rest. Well, I didn't have either prejudice or memory to fall back on, and it became clear to me very quickly how little my handpower dabbling was going to help me in understanding this world. The only thing I could think to do was to go into people's minds and borrow their knowledge. It wasn't the option I would have chosen, given the choice, for I dislike such incursions. And it was difficult, for in many ways the minds here are very alien. But human beings are human beings, here or elsewhere. There's always some point of connection."

"Did your Gift work as you expected it to?"

"Not at first. It took me a little time to adjust. I take it you had the same experience."

"Yes." Konstant did not wish to confess the extent of his disability. Here in Bron's house, surrounded by Bron's power, the fires of his Gift burned exactly as he was used to, for they did not have to go out into emptiness, and could take their measure against the blaze of another power.

"I got sick sooner than you did, though," Bron said, "because I didn't bring provisions. It's a good thing Jolyon waited a little before he sent his henchmen after me, because there was a point at which I couldn't have defended myself."

"But you did recover."

"Yes. Like you, I spent some time wondering whether I'd been wrong about this world. But once I began to acquire knowledge, I saw that my Gift was as safe here as it had ever been. Safer, really, because I didn't have the entire Order of Guardians pursuing me. But the Gates did open, and Guardians did come through. Even with the defenses I'd built I thought it best not to stay in one place too long. I've been nearly every place there is to go in this world, seen almost everything there is to see. I never knew your world half so well."

He stopped speaking. Silence flowed in to fill the void his voice had left—the peculiar, roaring hush of the house, stopping up Konstant's ears like water. The table, the chairs, the used plates and crumpled napkins, the brandy bottle and the empty wineglasses, seemed to float upon a sea of quiet. It was strange, almost dreamlike, this abrupt shift from impersonal discussion to personal revelation— like coming suddenly upon a door which had always been locked, whose essential nature it was to be locked, and finding it inexplicably ajar. Konstant did not trust it. Yet within mistrust lay fascination—for what might be waiting in the hidden room beyond?

"It's strange, the parallelism of the worlds." His voice slid smoothly into the hush. "When I came out of the forest after passing through the Gate, and saw the Fortress mountains . . . I knew it would be so, of course. But truly, I don't think anything I encountered here was stranger than that."

"Yes." Bron nodded. "I remember that feeling. It seems to go against the laws of nature, doesn't it? Even two plants grown from the same batch of seeds don't turn out the same. With peeled worlds there are many more variables. And yet all of them are physically identical."

"Peeled worlds? What are those?"

"Peeling is what I call the process of Splitting." His eyes were fixed upon his brandy glass, and the pool of amber liquor within it. "It seems a more accurate description of the process—not a splintering, like a cracked rock, but a sloughing, like an onion skin."

"You said . . . *all* of them."

"Yes. There aren't just two worlds, yours and this one. There are dozens of worlds. Hundreds, perhaps."

"*Hundreds?*" Konstant was disbelieving.

"If a Split could happen once, why not ten times? Twenty? Even more? I don't know exactly how many worlds there are, but I do know there are a lot of them. I've breathed their air. I've set my feet upon their soil."

"There are . . . Gates into these other worlds?"

"No." Bron reached out and placed his hands on either side of his brandy glass, turning it gently back and forth between his palms. "The Gates are the Guardians' creation. There's nothing like them in any of the other worlds I've seen. But there's an entryway, a place where all the worlds touch—not an artificial making, but something natural. It's as if the worlds can't quite let go of one another and hold on at this single point."

"And you've actually been through this entryway?"

"Yes."

"Do the Guardians know of it?"

"They know *of* it, in the sense that they were once able to recognize it as a place of power. But I doubt they ever understood its true nature. I can't fault them for that. I've only found a handful of worlds where people recognize it for what it is."

"But you recognized it."

"Not the first time I saw it. That was in your world, after I . . . well, just before I left. It looks like a flat black circle in the snow—there's nothing in its appearance to indicate what it is. But about a year after I arrived in this world, I came upon an exactly identical circle, in the exactly corresponding location. It seemed to me then that it could only be a Gate, though not like any Gate I'd ever heard of. When I entered it, I didn't find myself in your world, as I expected, but somewhere completely different. I tried again, and wound up someplace different still. Slowly I came to understand that there are many worlds, and that this circle gives access to them all."

"Did you never get lost among all these worlds?"

"I might have, that first time. But I thought I was going into your world, and so I left . . . a marker behind in this one. It guided me back."

"The Stone?"

Bron smiled faintly, and did not answer. "As I grew more

experienced, I realized that each of the worlds has its own particular . . . feel, or essence. If you know what it is, you can hold it in your mind as you enter, and that's where you'll find yourself."

"And all these worlds are different?" It was at once fascinating and repellant, to think that the universe might be so complex. "As different as this world and the world of mindpower?"

"Some are. But most are quite similar, not just to each other but to this one. Human history tends to express itself in certain predictable forms. Even the peeled worlds succumb to that in the end."

"What do you mean?"

Bron was still rolling his brandy glass back and forth between his palms. Beneath the starry chandelier the liquor was the color of topaz; it climbed the sides of the glass and slipped down again, like a small imprisoned ocean.

"There's a dominant direction to the course of human history. The rest is digression. Human beings are volatile and changeable, and digressions occur fairly often—different races, different powers, different lands. Sometimes these digressions are significant and endure for a long time, parallel to the central flow of history. Always in the end they get pushed aside. But occasionally, even though they're too peripheral to survive, they're too important to vanish, as extinct animal species do. In that case they don't die, but peel off—or split, if you prefer. This world often retains the memory of them, in myth and story, but it quickly forgets they were ever real. With the peeled worlds it varies. Sometimes they remember the peeling—sometimes they make a business of remembering, as your world has done. In that case, whatever it was that caused the peeling generally survives. But most of them forget. And when they do, the same thing happens all over again. The dominant flow reasserts itself. The digression is swallowed up again. And the worlds become much like this one."

"But then . . ." Konstant could not quite believe he was hearing this. "But then you're saying that handpower is the natural direction of humankind."

"I'm saying that, given the choice, people choose technology. Think about it. What is Gift but an intrinsic talent, manifest only in a minority of the population, useless even to those who own it without long and rigorous training? And once the training is done, what utility does it offer, except to its possessors and those they choose to benefit? But technology is available to anyone who can obtain it and can be used without the slightest understanding of its underlying principles. And its utility, its direct benefit, is staggering. Its harms are staggering too, but that's rarely clear at the outset."

"But what you're saying is hardly different from what the Guardians preach, that without the Limits handpower will overwhelm the world and bring another Split!"

Bron's eyes flicked upward. "Yes. And that may be the central irony of my life, that the Guardians are right. It *is* the Limits that preserve the powers of the mind. It *is* the Order's rule that guarantees the continuance of mindskill. If the artificial stasis the Guardians have imposed on your world is ever lifted, it will rush toward technology like a river bursting a dam, with all the force of a thousand years of repression. It won't take more than century and a half, or maybe two, for mindpower to vanish, first pushed aside, then scorned or perhaps persecuted, at last forgotten or only half-believed, like the myths about the world's origin. Perhaps there'll be another peeling to accommodate it. Perhaps this time it will simply die. Either way, if you value your Gift, you'd better hope it's the Zosterians who win the battle for your world, not Goldwine."

Konstant had to bite down on his tongue to stop himself from speaking. He wanted to gather up the sum of Goldwine's teachings and hurl them into that implacable ivory face. Balance, he wanted to say, it's balance that's the key, the ancient balance that existed at the dawn of time, the new balance inside Goldwine's hollow mountain. But this was Bron's house. He was at this table only by Bron's sufferance. He could not allow himself to squander this opening, this apparent loosening of Bron's guard, to gratify his own offense. And so he closed his lips upon the words, and schooled his voice to quiet.

"I'm sorry. I don't mean to dispute what you tell me. But I find it very strange."

"I'd be surprised if you didn't." Bron had transferred his gaze back to the brandy glass. He was no longer turning it between his palms; his hands lay idle on the crystal surface of the table, the long fingers loosely laced. "It took me years to come to these understandings. Decades. When I first arrived here I believed, as I'm sure you do, that the ideal world was one in which the two powers existed side-by-side, as equals. I was prepared to spend the whole of my life working toward that goal. I believed in it so strongly, in fact, that I set out to achieve it here."

"Here? But there's no mindpower here."

"Actually, there is. It's deeply hidden, but in some minds the sparks of power do exist."

"Truly? But when I was searching for you in mindspace, I sensed nothing. Only emptiness."

"Yes, because you were probably looking for active power. The power here is dormant. It's not understood or recognized. You have to reach very far into a mind to find it."

Konstant considered this. It was true that he had been searching for the spark of active power. And though he had skimmed the thoughts of those he encountered in this world, their alienness had held him back from dipping too deeply. The only mind he had explored more than superficially was Emme's—and she, he was quite certain, had no power.

"So if this world never completely lost its mindpower—" he knew he should not say it, but he could not stop himself "—what does that mean for your digression theory?"

Bron smiled a small smile at his brandy glass. "It's a good question. The only answer I can give you is that even the things that vanish leave traces behind. The sparks of power in this world are like the footprints of the great reptiles that used to roam the earth. The tracks of something once living, and now gone."

"So the sparks aren't true Gifts?"

"No. But I didn't know that when I first detected them."

"How did you discover it?"

Bron hesitated, and for a moment Konstant thought he would not answer. But then he breathed out—a sound that, from anyone else, Konstant would have labeled a sigh—and began to speak.

"When I first came here, I had certain expectations of what I'd find. I knew this was a world out of balance, even more one-sided than the world the Guardians had made. But I believed that the benefit of unfettered technology would make up for that, in a way mindpower never could. I thought there'd be no disease, no famine, no poverty, no single repressive ideology to force the world into an unnaturally uniform order. And certainly some of that is true. This world is a chessboard of different ideas, different powers, different beliefs. There's comfort and health and longevity, luxuries and advantages undreamed of in your world.

"But that's not the whole picture. Unfettered technology is often poisonous. Some parts of this world have been all but destroyed, and almost every area is at least somewhat affected. There are governments that within their spheres are as repressive as the Guardians ever were. As for health and plenty, it doesn't exist everywhere, and where it does, it's not available to everyone. There are nations in this world where you'd hardly know technology existed. There are nations that are wonders of technology, and hide appalling waste and want and misery at their hearts. I know you must have seen something of this in your traveling. You passed through one of the poisoned places, didn't you?"

"Yes." Konstant thought of the towering chimneys and the air that had turned the inside of his nose black. "Yes, I did."

"But you didn't expect this world to be a kind of physical paradise, the way I did. It was a terrible disillusionment for me to discover that it wasn't so. In your world, I'd staked all my beliefs on the value of handpower, made it my life's work to pursue the development of technology. And now I saw that I had been wrong—or if not wholly wrong, at least substantially mistaken. I began to wonder if this persistence of misery was something basic to the human condition, if human beings are by their nature driven to tyrannize and deprive and suffer, no matter what powers they have access to. Or if, perhaps, these things weren't human failings so much as symptoms of the lack of balance here. And I began to wonder what might happen if balance were returned to this world, if the skills of mind were reawoken. I'd already discovered the sparks of mindpower, so it seemed possible to attempt it.

"I suppose that much of what drove my determination was the desire to have a cause again. I'd spent all my life in pursuit of one cause or another; I had the habit of it, and I found it difficult to imagine living any other way. But I truly did want to build a better world. I knew it might take a century even to begin to see results, and three or four to bring meaningful change. But I had the time—with my Gift, I can preserve my body indefinitely. I knew it would take enormous wealth, but that I could create. I knew it would take patience. That I had most of all. I didn't spend the first part of my life in hiding, and twenty-five years among the Guardians, for nothing."

Was it bitterness that lent his voice such an edge? Konstant shifted in his chair; its metal seemed suddenly far too hard against his back and thighs. He was by now deeply uneasy with this flow of reminiscence, whose purpose he could not begin to guess. For the first time it occurred to him to wonder whether there might be a price for the passage of these secrets.

"I decided on two approaches. The first was education. For the most part this world's memory of mindpower exists only as myth. But there are people who believe in its reality—primitive people, mainly, who've missed the benefits of technology, but also in advanced cultures, sometimes enough to pursue it through scientific study. One of the first things I did was to seek out these experimenters and give them funds for their work. The experiments themselves weren't of much value, but they widened the circle of believers. And belief, it seemed to me then, was half the battle.

"The second thing I did was to set myself to seek out the sparks of mindpower directly. I wanted to test them—

to see how they might be drawn out of dormancy, how technique might be implanted so that they could be used. For close to fourteen years I did this. I can't count the number of places I've visited, the number of approaches I've tried. I've taken different faces, entered dreams, touched minds I bound to sleep, embodied myself as a ghost or a spirit. I've planted suggestions, created false memories, even given direct instruction. Now and then I had a breakthrough . . . someone who could be taught to receive a thought, or make a flame, or move a coin across a table. And I did, several times, find true prescience. Oddly enough, it's the only power in this world that's anything like its equivalent in yours. But even that was too small, too limited, to be awakened into a real Gift.

"I began to realize that what I was trying to do couldn't be done. That what I'd thought were markers, pointing me toward what could be, were really only the scars of what once had been. I went on traveling for a time. I had to know that one more spark, one more attempt, wouldn't give me what I sought. At last I was certain. When I was, I stopped. I built myself this house. I retired to it. Since then I've been thinking. About what I've seen, about what I know, about what I tried to do. About why I failed. About the worlds, and the forces that govern them. I've come to many understandings. I've given you most of them tonight. But they aren't for you."

He lifted his brandy glass and swallowed all the liquor that remained. He set the glass back on the table, its base chiming against the crystal. He raised his eyes and fixed them on Konstant's face. It was like a veil falling. In the distance Konstant seemed to hear a door slam closed. He knew, suddenly, what was coming.

"I hadn't planned to do this tonight," Bron said. "But the conversation led to it, and I suppose it's just as well. It's been clear for a while now that you're fit enough to travel. It's time for you to leave my house. To go back to your world. I want you to take a message with you. Goldwine once did me a service, and it seems to me that I owe her the truth of why I won't return. Tell her what I've said to you. Tell her that I've taken up too many causes in my life and won't take up another. Tell her that what she wants me to do may well destroy your world, and that though I'm done with it, though I care nothing for it, I won't have that on my conscience. And tell her . . ." He leaned forward, his hands flat against the tabletop. His eyes were like obsidian. "Tell her that I do not expect ever to see another messenger of hers. She had no right to send you here, with your stories and your faith. No right to try and coerce me through prophecy. No right even to ask this thing of me."

He pushed back his chair, its legs scraping loudly on the floor, and rose to his feet. Except for his white face he was all black, like an animate shadow.

"So. Is that clear?" And then, sharply, when Konstant did not answer: "Well?"

Konstant struggled for a response. His mind seemed paralyzed; all he could find were disjointed phrases.

"I . . . I need some time. To prepare. For the journey. I had trouble . . . trouble farwalking on the way here. I want to be sure . . . to be sure my Gift has acclimated."

"You can have two days."

"Two days?"

"There's no reason why I shouldn't put you out this very night. Two days is more than you need."

"But that's . . . I need to . . ."

Bron did not move. His expression did not change. But all at once Konstant saw, in the pale face and flat black eyes, the man who had stood over him in the workroom, whose Gift had seized and nearly killed him. His chest constricted at the memory. The protest withered on his tongue.

"Enough," Bron said softly. "No more pretense. I know as well as you do why you've lingered in my house. I know as well as you do why you want to remain. I've been patient with you. Don't test me further."

Their gazes held. Konstant did not dare even to blink. At last Bron glanced away. He circled the table, and was gone.

For a long time, Konstant sat motionless beneath the starburst chandelier. It was over. The words repeated themselves in his mind, but he did not yet believe them. He did not yet believe that hope was gone. He did not yet believe that prophecy had been broken—not by him, through the weakness of his will, but by Bron, through the strength of his.

Fifteen

HEN KONSTANT finally gained his room, he did not sleep. He paced instead, back and forth, his feet bare to mask the sound of his motion. The silence of the house surrounded him, as thick as honey. But it did not oppress him, as on the nights that had gone before. Instead it fed the rage within him, for it spoke to him of the sterile, bitter man who had created it, and of his betrayal, not just of prophecy, but of his Gift and his own legend.

It was exhilarating, this anger, liberating—not just in its strength, but in the unambiguous clarity of its outward focus. This was the anger he had reached for a month ago in the wake of Bron's first refusal, a pure white-hot fury unvitiated by inwardness or recrimination or any sense of personal failure. He regretted only that it had taken him so long to find it. Not until tonight had he grasped the depth of Bron's isolation, the absoluteness of his retreat. Not until tonight had he recognized that Bron the legend, Bron the hoped-for liberator, was really just a bitter, disillusioned man who had lost both faith and the will to get it back, who was sunk so deep in the mire of his own pessimism that he judged it wisdom rather than apathy to refuse the call of prophecy. And yet these things had all been present in that first meeting. They had sat behind Bron's ivory face, looked out of his dark eyes. They had spoken in his chilly response to Konstant's urgent words. They had reached out in the force that had taken Konstant by the throat and nearly killed him.

Bron had ordered him out of his house. He had no choice

but to go—but he would not go empty-handed. If he could not bring the entire prophecy to fulfillment, he could at least pursue a part of it. If he could not lead Bron back to the world of his birth, he could at least try to take the Stone.

It was an intent not so much conceived as revealed, emerging from the waning shock of the evening like a landmark out of a receding fog. He was aware of the hubris of it, the near impossibility of success. All his attempts to discover the signature of the Stone's power had ended in failure. In his explorations he had seen no locked rooms, or sensed any barriers or illusions behind which the Stone might be hidden. What was the likelihood, therefore, that he might actually locate it? But it was no longer a question of success or failure, or even of life or death, though he knew what must happen if Bron discovered him. The task he had come to do had been taken from his hands; he knew now, as certainly as when he lay sick beside the icy road, that his mission was lost and the future he had expended so much hope and pain trying to ensure would not come to pass. And yet he was still here. As long as he was here, he must still try. All that was left to try was to find the Stone.

For the first thirteen years of Konstant's life, the Stone had been to him what it was to all the people of his world: a benign presence that overwatched his days and nights, that heard his prayers and knew him utterly, as it knew everything upon the earth. For his seven years in the Fortress, it had been that and also what it was for Guardians: the fount and sustenance of all human Gifts, the most sacred charge of the world of mindpower, from whose service and protection the Guardians took their name. When he discovered, in a single shattering moment, that the Stone had been absent from the world for the whole of his life and more, that the service to which he was pledged depended upon the perpetuation of an enormous hoax, that the corruptness to which he had given himself had no purpose beyond the cruelty of the men who ordered it, all his belief vanished. He understood that he was alone and always had been. His prayers had gone out into nothingness. The source of his Gift was himself, and nothing more.

Eventually, under the tutelage of Goldwine's people, he found a new belief and learned to see the Stone as they did: a wondrous entity, but not divine; an object of power, but not power's foundation. In the context of the Stone's absence, it was a belief that made far more sense. All Goldwine's followers knew that Bron held the Stone; all knew he would one day bring it back. This was as it should be. The Stone was Gift, and a Gift belonged in a world of Gifted. More than that—and Konstant had always suspected that this was most important—whoever possessed it would also possess its power. It was part of Goldwine's vision of the world to come, the world that rose from the ashes of the overthrow Bron had been meant to accomplish, that this would be she. She would not hold it prisoner, as the Guardians had, but in trust for humankind. When she had learned to harness its vast forces for human benefit, it would be given to the world.

When he joined the Zosterians, Konstant found himself within a different frame of reference. Like the Guardians they had been, the Zosterians held that the Stone was the original source of human power. Unlike the Guardians, however, they had fitted that basic principle to the reality of the Stone's absence. They believed that the passage of time had made Gift a human quality. That was why, though the Stone was gone, Gift endured within the world. Rather than pine for what had been lost, or waste resources searching as the Guardians did, the Zosterians preferred to move forward. They had declared the Stone dead. They employed their own calendar, dated from the year of the Stone's theft, to mark the fact that an era had ended with that loss, and all the time after it was new.

Konstant had been as long with the Zosterians as he had with Goldwine, but their beliefs had never tempted him. Before coming to this world, he had been certain, as Goldwine was, that the Stone still lived. Because he did not believe it divine, however, or essential to any reality he knew, the thought of encountering it had not occupied him to the exclusion of all else, as it would have a Guardian. It had been Bron who filled his thoughts. It had been Bron whose imminence had caused his breath to catch in mingled awe and anticipation. Bron's legend, Bron's significance, was as monumental as the Stone's, yet the Stone was wholly alien, wholly other, while Bron was a living man who could speak and be spoken to. Who could tell what might be heard from such a being, what might be learned?

Konstant knew now how misplaced his expectations had been. Any legend, met face-to-face, must shrink a little, in light of the inevitable distance between the story and its human avatar. But there could not be many cases in which the story and the person to whom it was attached were so at odds. It was a bitter disillusionment, this difference. Over Konstant's time in Bron's house it had steadily mounted, turning beneath his waiting, struggling beneath his refusal to question or to doubt. Now, in this final rejection, it had opened out into something very close to hatred.

Striding back and forth between the walls of his room, silent in the silence, Konstant was aware that the act he planned was not simply a last-ditch effort, a stopgap choice to salvage a ruined mission. It was justice. Whether or not the Stone had survived its time in this world, Bron did not deserve to be its keeper. Or rather, he deserved to be deprived of it—for his failure of will, for his betrayal of prophecy, for the echoing void he had made of his life.

Konstant was aware of his own failings. He knew he was not fit to sit in judgment on any man. Yet there was no one else here to judge, and so he would pass sentence. He would take the Stone out of this house and leave Bron truly solitary. Or he would die in the attempt.

When morning arrived, Konstant descended to take breakfast in the kitchen. Dipping into Emme's thoughts as she served him, he saw the list of supplies Bron had ordered her to assemble for him: clothing, camping gear, money. Her understanding of his departure carried no particular emotion; she was more concerned by the task of properly composing his travel kit. Of such details her life was made.

He returned to his room. There, gathering his power, he shifted himself to resistance-style invisibility and spent the next seven hours searching the house, floor by floor and room by room. He did not expect to find anything. His previous explorations had been comprehensive, and like all the operatives Goldwine trained, he was adept at illusion-spotting. If there had been any kind of binding or concealment, he was certain he would have sensed it. But thoroughness demanded that he check one final time.

As he had anticipated, there was nothing. Just two possibilities remained: Bron's bedchamber and his workroom. The single time Konstant had seen the workroom, he had noted no physical object that might conceal the Stone, or sensed any work of power other than the mindlight. But he had been sick and distracted, and he had not really been looking. Bron was in the workroom now; according to his habit, he would remain there until late that night. Konstant planned to begin, therefore, with the bedchamber.

He spent a little time checking the door for bindings and wardings. There was no reason, really, why there should be any, in a house where the only other inhabitants were unGifted, but he had thought it possible his arrival might have motivated Bron to change that. He found nothing. Returning to his room, he waited until Emme brought his evening meal on a tray—a guarantee, as much as anything could be, of a period in which he would not be disturbed, for he knew she would have delivered Bron's tray first. As the sound of her footsteps receded down the stairs, he shifted himself back to invisibility and stole out into the hall.

At Bron's door, he set his will against the lock. He was not a maker, and could not perform the kinds of creative and transformative acts a true maker could, but like any Gifted person he was capable of a range of basic power-techniques, including the small-scale manipulation of solid objects. Somewhat to his surprise, however, the door was open.

Bron's bedroom was larger than Konstant's and more luxuriously appointed. A large bed centered it, with a dark wood head- and footboard and a cover in shades of gold and amber. There were also chairs and chests and a desk, and a magnificent brown-and-gold carpet that covered the floor from edge to edge. Except for windows shrouded in swaths of amber velvet, the walls were as bare as Konstant's own.

Konstant began to search. He did not know what he was searching for, neither size nor shape nor any other attribute, but he did not think about this, trusting he would recognize anything of significance. He did not think, either, about the traces he might be leaving, despite his greatest care, to tell Bron someone had been here, or about the possibility that Bron might leave his workroom, or about the wards and bindings that must surely guard the Stone, or about what he would do if he actually succeeded in finding it. The whole sum of his awareness was fixed upon the action of his hands, on the rhythm of his breath and the beating of his heart. This was how it had been, sometimes, during his Zosterian service, when he slipped past Soldier checkpoints or dared Journeyer parties upon the open road: a canceling of self granted only by extremest peril, a brief passage into a mode of being where the moment was all that mattered.

Last he searched the alcove where Bron kept his clothing. Here, in the back corner on the floor, he found a wooden box, smooth with age and bound with strips of brass and iron that showed the marks of hand-tooling. It was small—too small, surely, to hold the Stone. Yet, imperfect and irregular as it was, it did not look like a product of this machine-made world. His hands trembled a little as he lifted the wooden lid. When he saw its contents—a scattering of dry soil, a few scraps of rusted iron—disappointment shook him like a blow.

He replaced the box where it had been and closed the alcove door. There was nothing here—nothing, at least, that he could perceive with his physical senses. He moved to the room's center and closed his eyes. Stretching his awareness until it touched the boundaries of all four walls, he tested for noncorporeal signs: the sparking traces of binding, the dull weight of illusion. He extended himself to the utmost limits of his Gift, until his head ached and sparks burst behind his eyes. Still there was nothing.

He left Bron's bedroom and went to his own, remaining there until Emme came back to remove the meal tray, and then returning to the hall, where he sat down against the wall to wait. He was shifted according to Goldwine's methods, which would have prevented any ordinary man of power from sensing him, but Bron was no ordinary man of power. He had felt Konstant's passage through the Gate, and recognized the difference in the way Konstant used his Gift. There was no guarantee that even the resistance's invisibility was proof against that perception. Yet, as in the bedroom, there was a dreamlike lack of urgency to this consciousness of peril. If he were to pose questions about the actions in which he was engaged, there were more pressing ones to ask. What were the odds, for instance, that Bron did not know exactly what Konstant intended, exactly what Konstant had been doing all day and what he planned to do tonight? What were the odds that, wherever the Stone was hidden, it was concealed in such a way that Konstant would be capable of finding it? What were the odds that he would survive long enough to discover which of these mistakes he had made?

Such questions were pointless. He could only do as he was doing.

A long time later, the door to the workroom opened and Bron emerged. He moved unhurriedly down the hall, his face tranquil as it nearly always was, though more weary than Konstant had ever seen it. At the long window he paused, looking out, though the illumination inside and the impenetrable overcast night made it impossible to see anything. From his vantage point, Konstant could see both Bron and his reflection—pale twins, one on a dark ground, one in light.

Reaching out, Bron placed both hands flat against the glass, and stood that way a moment, palm to palm with his reflection. It seemed an apt symbol of the monolithic solitude in which Konstant had found him, to which he would return once Konstant was gone. And yet Konstant had the impression, suddenly, that Bron was not merely solitary but alone, that there was sadness in his unguarded gesture, or perhaps longing. He could not tell why, in this moment of resolve and dread, such a thing should occur to him.

Bron moved away from the window and resumed his interrupted progress. His eyes swept over Konstant, unseeing. He opened his bedroom door and entered, closing it softly behind him.

Konstant waited—first for Bron to discover his incursion and come raging out of his room, then for the radiance visible beneath the door to be extinguished, then for Bron to plausibly fall asleep. Around him the silence sang and sighed, like an ocean in which he might drown. The amber light shed by the golden lamps seemed to throb a little, keeping time with his heartbeat.

At last he rose, his legs cramped and stiff, and made his way to Bron's workroom. He paused, searching. Here also, there were no bindings, no barriers. Here also, the door was unlocked. He pushed it open and passed into the room beyond.

The candles had been extinguished. The fire was a heap of orange coals in the grate. There was only mindlight to see by, a rippling pearly radiance much brighter than moonlight, but with the same coldness, the same exaggeration of shadow, the same leaching of color. Opposite the door, the window-wall looked out into the night, a space so black it seemed the world beyond had been erased.

Konstant began to search. He turned over the cushions of the couches, swept his hands across the fireplace tiles, tipped the books away from the shelves, inventoried the drawers of the desk and the cabinets beside it. Nothing was locked; everything was open to him. Finished with the furniture, he examined the walls, explored the glass of the window, paced the room until he had covered every inch of floor. Done with that, he gathered his Gift and sent his awareness outward in search of binding or illusion.

After a time he opened his eyes. There was nothing. Nothing he could see, nothing he could feel. He was not truly surprised. A sense of charade had been growing in him as the day slid by, an understanding that what he had set himself to do was futile and doomed to failure—as futile and doomed to failure as his own pretense that it was not so. It seemed less astonishing to find himself here, in this moment of defeat, than to remember that ages and hours ago he had imagined he might succeed.

He sank down where he was, in the middle of the floor.

He was aware of the marble inlay, cool and slightly irregular beneath his palms. Above him the mindlight stirred. He felt empty, drained. He knew he should rise and return to his room. But he could not summon up the will, just now, to move.

His eyes, trailing about the room, came to rest on the great painting, hanging in solitary splendor on the stark white wall. He stared at it, at the absurd ornateness of the golden frame, at the blurred image the frame contained. Had it not made him think, before, of a sunset sky above a tossing ocean? Yet now it seemed to him that it was mountains that were pictured here, with forests on their lower slopes and snow at their peaks. And that the sky above them did not hold the setting sun, but the sun rising.

He felt his breath catch. The painting. Could it be?

He found himself on his feet, with no clear memory of having risen. To the eye, the semblance of an artwork was true in every detail—he could see the texture of the canvas, the blending of the pigments, the ridges and whorls of the brushstrokes. Yet, up close, he could also see that what looked from a distance like the indefiniteness of a careless style was really something else. The painting was moving. It was motion so slow, so infinitesimal as to be barely visible, yet unmistakably the image was stirring—the clouds shifting, the mountains reshaping themselves instant by instant, as if eons of geographical time had been compressed into seconds. Konstant realized that he had seen this motion when he was in the room four weeks ago, when he imagined that the sun had moved closer to the tossing sea. But he had put it down to the illusions of fever.

He reached out with his power—delicately, just enough to sense. He did not feel the spark of Gift or the shape of binding, but there was definitely something out of the ordinary: a sense of blockage, yielding like cobweb yet absolute like blindness, a baffle against his Gift. It was so seamlessly woven into the structure of the room that the broad focus he had used before had not picked it up—like a textural irregularity in a piece of cloth, invisible to the eye and only just perceptible to touch.

Was the painting the Stone itself, enclosed in an envelope

of illusion, or was it the doorway to the Stone's hiding place? He stretched out his hand, meaning to lay it against the canvas. But he did not get that far. Inches from the textured surface, something seized him and threw him backward. He felt himself flying through the air, and then nothing at all.

He came back to consciousness not slowly, but all at once. He opened his eyes upon what seemed to be a swirling ocean of milk, fraught with currents of brilliance. It was a moment before he recognized it as mindlight, and realized that he was lying on his back on the floor of Bron's workroom.

He turned his head. Bron knelt nearby, as still as one of his pieces of furniture, his dark eyes trained on Konstant's face. He was not dressed for sleep, but as he had been earlier. Konstant felt no surprise. Perhaps it was the shock of the blow, or the lingering influence of unconsciousness, but it seemed to him that he had already experienced this. He knew, at any rate, how it must end.

"I wasn't sure you'd see the painting," Bron said.

Konstant pushed himself to a sitting position. His limbs felt numb and heavy. "I saw it when I was here before," he said, his voice harsh in the quiet room. "It was an ocean then."

"Even so, not everyone would have noticed the change."

"You knew I would try this." Bron nodded. "You left everything open for me." Bron nodded again. "Why?"

Bron did not answer at once. "To tell you the truth, I'm not completely sure."

"Is it the Stone itself? The painting? Or just a doorway?"

"It's an illusion. A shield, but also to some degree a reflection of the power it conceals. The Stone is behind it."

"The Stone's intact, then? Undamaged?"

Bron smiled a little. "Of course. There's nothing in this world to harm it."

"Why can't I sense it, then?" There was something surreal in this calm progression of question and answer, at the very edge of death. Yet he wanted to know. "How can a human Gift hide it so completely?"

"It isn't hidden. It's as present here as it was in your world. It speaks with a different voice, that's all. A voice you don't know how to hear."

"What do you mean?"

"The Stone's nature is to be conscious. To observe. That's the same in every world—I know, because it has gone with me in my travels. But its awareness is shaped by what it sees, like a mirror giving back the image of what it faces. And so, just as each world is different, the Stone is different in each world."

Konstant shook his head. "I don't understand."

"Your world is a world of Gifts. In your world, therefore, the Stone mirrors Giftedness. But in this world, which is shaped by handpower, it mirrors technology. Because you know it as Gift, that's how you search for it—for the voice of Giftedness, which is your own voice, really, greatly amplified. But in this world the Stone speaks of handpower. And so you're deaf to it."

"But the Stone *is* a Gift."

"No. Gift is human. Gift is inseparable from will and intent, from skill and desire. Such things are irrelevant to the Stone. It simply *is*. It simply *watches*. Its existence and its manifestation are one and the same. Your people understand it as Gift only because you know no other way to think of power. But though Gift is power, power is not necessarily Gift. And that, of course, is another reason why you can't hear it."

"And you? Can you hear it?"

Again Bron smiled. It was a more complex expression this time, invoking memory and understanding and experience, and a strange tenderness. Like, Konstant thought, the smile of a lover. "Oh, yes. I can hear it."

"It shouldn't be here. Whether it's a Gift or not, it's more like human power than anything that exists in this world. I know I don't understand it, yet still I can see it's so. The Stone doesn't belong in this place. No power does, not even yours."

Bron did not answer. His face had smoothed; it was impossible to tell what was going on behind it. Drawn by impulse and desperation, and by the fact that he had nothing left to lose, Konstant reached forward, seeking the currents of Bron's thoughts. But clearly Bron had been prepared for this. It was like running up against a wall. Never had Konstant encountered such a mind-defense: monolithic, utterly impenetrable.

Bron blinked at the contact, like someone registering the brush of insect wings.

"It's time for you to go," he said.

"Go?"

"Yes." He stood. "Come. Your travel kit is ready."

Konstant struggled to get his mind around it. "You aren't going to kill me?"

Bron's brows drew together—not in anger, but in puzzlement. "Why should I kill you?"

"Because of what I've seen." Konstant felt himself becoming dizzy. "Because of what I know."

"I don't need to kill you. I can take your memory."

Konstant got his knees under him, and rose, unsteadily, to his feet. "You'll take my memory and send me out into the world like an imbecile? I'd rather die."

"No, no. I'll take only what's essential for you not to betray me to the Arm of the Stone, should it capture you. The rest I'll leave. Didn't I say you were my messenger? I want you to deliver my message, if you can."

"I can't get back. I didn't mark the Gate I came through. And even if I had, I couldn't open it."

"I'll give you that knowledge also. You are strong enough to manage it."

"And you'll stay here." Konstant's face was on fire. Despair and rage clutched at his chest. "You'll stay here, with the Stone, in the dark and the cold, while my world goes down in blood and fire. And you won't lose a minute's sleep over it, will you? You won't give it another thought."

Bron regarded him, his expression remote. "No," he said. "I won't."

Konstant laughed. It seemed to tear his throat. "I've met some hypocrites in my time, but not one of them comes close to you. You have power like no one in all the history of our world, yet you lock it up in this sterile house and do nothing with it. You had a vision of how things should be, and you weren't able to make it happen, and because you couldn't have the world on your own terms, you turned your back on it and walled yourself away on this barren shore like a corpse inside a tomb. And now I've come to offer you a cause to fill that empty space you call a soul—a cause that has nothing to do with you and what you want, but with a world and what it needs—and what do you do? You refuse. You turn away. I know my life is worthless. But yours is worse, a sinkhole of selfishness, a swamp of self-pity and self-will. And when I think . . . when I think how my world will suffer, while you drift through the centuries of your life without pain, without change—"

His voice broke. Bron had not moved. The ivory-pale planes of his face seemed as hard as porcelain, and as brittle. The pause stretched out, like a thread spun nearly to the breaking point.

"Come," Bron said again.

Hopeless, Konstant went.

The travel kit lay just outside the door of the workroom. Konstant struggled into the heavy outergarment and slipped the straps of the pack onto his shoulders. Silent, Bron preceded Konstant down the curving stairs, and across the marble floor to the front door of the house. There he turned. He reached out his hands. Konstant flinched back.

"Don't touch my mind," he said. "I won't betray you. I swear it."

"Stand still," Bron commanded, unmoved. "Or I will bind you."

His fingers, dry and very warm, closed on Konstant's temples. Konstant stiffened, but there was no pain, no crushing impact, only a tiny jolt, as if a spark had shot from Bron's skin to his. Bron withdrew his hands. Konstant looked inside his mind. He could discover no difference.

"I've given you a route to the Gate you came through originally," Bron told him, "and the understanding of how to open it. The memory loss will be gradual over the next day or two. It's easier on the mind that way." He pulled the door open. "Now go."

Konstant could not move. He knew the battle was lost. But he could not, of his own will, step out into the night.

"Please," he said, hearing the raggedness of his voice. "It doesn't matter what you do to me. But don't abandon my world. You have the power to change everything. How can you stand back and refuse to use it?"

And now Bron, who had left all his rooms open for Konstant's exploration, who had only blinked when Konstant touched his mind, who had listened without emotion as Konstant heaped him with insult, seemed to fly into a rage. His mouth pulled taut; his eyes went flat. He seized Konstant by the shoulders, with hands that felt like iron bands, and thrust him into the dark so violently that he stumbled and fell, sliding down the two steps that led to the door, landing hard on the flagstones at the bottom.

The door fell closed behind him, a solid, final sound.

For a moment he remained where he was, half-lying on his side. He heard the sigh and slap of the ocean, and saw the clouds above his head, a little lighter than the impenetrable blackness below. The pain of his fall echoed in his bones, but he was barely aware of it. He was not dead, and yet he felt as if that closing door had marked the end of his life.

At last he picked himself up. He adjusted the travel-pack on his back, and began to walk, stumbling a little, down the wide path that led from Bron's door to the road that was the only way in or out of this desolate place.

At the road's edge, he paused. He had never seen the house from outside before. It shone against the night, as white without as it was within, its window-walls pouring light into the darkness. Yet still it looked like something hidden, like a polar animal hunched against the arctic winter, its great gleaming eyes blind with sleep.

Fury rose in him, and despair, and a black tearing hatred—of Bron, who had turned his back upon a world, of himself, who had been trusted to bear the weight of prophecy and proved unequal to the task. He unfastened his outergarment. Reaching under his shirt, he pulled out Jolyon's talisman. Though it was bound to him, he had meant to give it back to Bron, for the gold inside had once belonged to him. But somehow he had never done so.

With all his strength, he hurled the talisman toward the

house. He heard the sound as it struck, the small clink of glass on rock. Let it lie here, entombed upon this icy shore like the man it had been meant to find. Once he had gone far enough, he would no longer hear it calling him.

He turned and struck off into the night.

The

Twisted
Staff

HEN CARIAD opened her eyes, she thought she had gone blind. She could see nothing—or rather, all she could see was whiteness, luminous and depthless and entirely without detail. Fear wrenched her upright, her heart pounding, and she realized that after all she was not blind, for she could see her own body, a blanket next to her, a basin a little distance away. It was the room she was in that had produced the illusion, a room without door or window, a room whose walls, ceiling, and floor were made of some lambent pearl-white material so entirely featureless that it was only in relation to the objects it held that it was possible to see it had any dimension at all.

She sat still for a moment, reorienting herself to awareness. There was a heaviness at her neck. Reaching up, she discovered that a metal collar had been placed around her throat. A chain was attached to a loop at the back, trailing down to lie in coils behind her, rising again to vanish into the wall at a point just above her head—waist-height, if she had been standing. She set her fingers against the place below her collarbones where the little bag of darts and drugs had hung: it was gone. Her clothing was gone as well. She was naked beneath a sleeveless shift, and her feet were bare. Even the cord that tied her braid had been removed.

She put her hands up to her face in disbelief, feeling the coldness of her skin, the heavy fall of her unbound hair. Surely she had opened her eyes upon a dream. There was not really a chain at her neck. She was not really confined in a tiny cell with glowing walls. It had not really happened, the thing that hung inside her mind like an appalling nightmare: that she had gone to kill Jolyon, and instead had been captured.

But she could not will away the evidence of her senses—the whiteness of the room that filled her eyes, the weight of metal that dragged at her neck. And she could still see Jolyon's smile, and feel the impact of the power that had slammed into her and made her helpless. And the face that had loomed over her, the face of Jolyon's bodyservant . . . and his finger on her forehead, and the dark void into which she had seemed to fall forever. . . . How could it be? Her midnight forays on the Keep's third floor had not shown her this. In the minds she scanned, Jolyon's servant had appeared as a man a little mysterious for his silence, a little mistrusted for his outsider's status and Jolyon's peculiar dependence on him, but not otherwise remarkable.

Somewhere within her, something terrible struggled for release. She had known, when she set out for Jolyon's rooms, that she might fail. She had even identified the points where failure was most possible: the passage through Jolyon's walls, the killing of his guards, the moment just before she loosed the drugged dart. But she had believed that failure meant retreat, or, if she were unlucky, chase and escape. She had not thought of capture, any more than, in the other missions she undertook, she had thought of death. She knew the prophecy was unreeling toward its endpoint. She understood the imminence of the moment in which its guarantees would cease to overlook her life. Yet that moment had not yet arrived—and in its separation, as much as in its closeness, the promise of her safety had seemed as sure as ever.

She understood what she must do now. She feared to do it, for she suspected what she would discover; but she must know for sure. She closed her eyes and, with an effort of will, turned her concentration inward, summoning the un-making power of her Gift, the power she needed to undo her bonds. But though she called with all her strength, with all the discipline of her training, her Gift did not respond. It was as if a barrier had been thrown around her mind.

She could see her power, deep inside her like a core of fire. But she could not touch it.

She opened her eyes again. She had known it must be so. The cell had told her, with its pearly walls—which she had seen, nights ago, as she and Orrin moved invisibly through the prison annex, and recognized as wards set against the practice of Gifts. For a few moments, in Jolyon's chambers, she had believed he belonged to her. He never had. Now she, absolutely, belonged to him.

She felt a shifting, deep in the darkest recesses of her soul. The world seemed to slip upon its axis, the bright air of the cell to grow dim and unreal. Horror took her, huger than any emotion she had ever known, so enormous it seemed the boundaries of her body had flown away. She pulled her knees up within the loose folds of her shift and bowed her head upon them, rigid against the storm that raged within her. The future unfolded before her inner eye, a cascade of appalling consequence, a dreadful vision from which she could not look away. She saw Goldwine, the resistances, Orrin, the handpower networks, the servant intelligence cells—all the things that would fall or be destroyed as a result of the truths Jolyon would extract from her undefended mind. She saw the campaign of destruction Jolyon would undertake, an orgy of purification that would make the Zosterian purges seem trivial. She saw her father—or rather, the tall, featureless image of him the Tale had given her. His return was certain; Goldwine had sworn it. Yet the deliverance it promised . . . was that certain also? Or might Jolyon, seeing it in her mind, find a way to alter it?

Goldwine's face rose up before her, terrible with prescience. *This* was what she had seen. *This* was what she had dreaded. She had warned Cariad: *There is nothing else in all the world that can't be changed.* But Cariad, blind with intent, had not listened. She saw that intent naked now, bare of the clothing of justification in which she had dressed it, an ugly grafting of adult will and hubris onto an absurd childhood dream. Twenty-five men she had killed deliberately, and many more in battle—all of them deaths accomplished, not one of them a death desired. But she had wanted this one, wanted it so much that she had twisted the world around her to fit its shape, and closed her eyes to the true nature of the risk she took. Now, for her will, not one, but thousands would die. The resistances would die. Orrin would die. Goldwine would die. And she . . . she would die also. Whatever Jolyon chose to do with her, torture her or question her or make her witless by mindprobing her in the Reddened way, one thing was certain: when he was finished, he would kill her.

Her heart felt as if it would burst from her chest. In a distant part of herself, she was aware of the shame of it, that her own death should horrify her so, when there would be so many others. But not once in her prophecy-charmed life had she confronted death as she was confronting it now—not as an abstraction, not as something that happened only to others, but real, inevitable, imminent. She had known she must face this someday; but she had not thought it would be so terrible. She had not thought she would be so afraid—the paralyzing, nightmare fear a child feels, when she first looks beyond the bright circle of what she knows and can control, and perceives the formless darkness that surrounds her.

Cariad did not know how long she huddled there, while understanding and recrimination threatened to shake her mind apart. At last the needs of her body roused her. She got to her feet, the chain dragging out behind her, and used the basin. Then she took the blanket and wrapped herself in it, and sat down against the wall, tugging at the collar until the chain fell forward across her shoulder. She could feel the cell's bindings at her back, a faint crawling vibration, as if a hive of bees were working on the other side.

The intensity of her emotion had died back a little. The understandings remained, bleak and undeniable, but around them the world was settling again into its accustomed shape. She might indeed have fatally shifted the shape of the future. Yet, if nothing was certain now, then equally, anything was possible. Orrin would alert his recruiter once he realized she had vanished; perhaps a rescue attempt would be made. The Guardians would have to remove her from the cell to probe her; perhaps there would be a chance for escape then. Or maybe Jolyon would come to see her here. The bindings would block his Gift as they did hers, and though she was chained her physical skills were intact.

In her heart, she knew it was vanishingly unlikely that any of these possibilities would come to pass—or, if they did, that they would be enough to save her. In her heart, she knew how she must free herself. Yet her mind, only newly opened to the reality of death, shied away from this. It was not just fear, though fear was part of it. It had been more than the prophecy's promise of protection that caused her to leave her poison capsule in its box, instead of carrying it beneath her tongue as she was supposed to. The prophecy, which made it unnecessary that she should ever need it, also made it impossible that she should ever use it—for to kill herself would be to break the prophecy, and she was no more capable of deliberately doing that than she was of raising her hand against Goldwine. Even now, aware that she *had* broken it, knowing that there was no other way to keep her secrets, that inhibition stood huge inside her mind.

She saw Goldwine's face, not prescient now, but harsh with weariness and unspoken knowledge. Why had Goldwine sent her into the Fortress, knowing what would happen? Why had Goldwine not given her a more explicit warning? Anger rose, a brief bright spark against the dark background of Cariad's despair, then died away. Whatever Goldwine's vision had been, it was only a vision of possibility. It was Cariad's own choices that had made it real.

Time passed, measureless in the unchanging brightness of the room. At some point there came a scraping noise, and a small black rectangle materialized on the whiteness across from her. The spyhole, she thought, remembering the cell's door from the outside. Someone was looking in at her. She stared back, though she could see nothing in the dark opening. After a while the spyhole scraped closed again, and the perfection of the bindings was restored.

A little later, she gathered up her will and, lifting the collar, wrapped the chain twice around her neck. If she drew it tight, and then anchored it with her body weight to prevent involuntary release, she might manage to slowly strangle herself. But before she even began to pull, a darkness rose up at the edges of her vision, and she felt herself beginning to lose consciousness. She let go of the chain; at once the darkness receded. She sat for a moment, breathing, and then tried again. This time she held on, savagely, as the darkness bled inward and her senses dimmed. She came back to awareness prone on the floor. The chain was still close about her throat, but not so close that she could not breathe.

She pushed herself upright. The cell was warded against self-injury, then. She unwrapped the chain, pulling the links away from the grooves they had printed in her flesh. She felt a despair so absolute it was like being blind.

After a time there was the sound of a turning lock, and the wall cracked open. A door appeared, swinging outward. Jolyon's bodyservant came softly into the cell. He carried a tray, with a bowl of something steaming, a ragged hunk of bread, and a cup of water. He set the tray on the floor near Cariad, then picked up the slop basin and departed. After a little while he returned and replaced the basin where it had been. His black straw-straight hair was cropped, but not Roundhead-short; it fell across his forehead as he bent down, and as he straightened he tossed it back, a motion that caused his eyes to sweep across Cariad's face. Distantly, so distantly she had to strain to catch it, she perceived his emotion: distaste, reluctance. It was only a flash, gone as he turned away. He left the cell as silently as he had entered.

She sat for a while, considering. Some portion of her Gift still functioned in this place, then—much impaired, but there nonetheless. In what it had shown her, she recognized that Jolyon's bodyservant relished neither the tasks he performed nor the situation that made them necessary. She thought of him—of his power held in servitude, of his Gift kept secret from all but his master. Why should any power consent to such a thing? Perhaps Jolyon held some thrall over his servant, some coercion that kept him bound. Might there be, in that, a possibility of change?

When the servant arrived with another meal, she spoke

to him. "How long have I been here?" she asked. "What's planned for me? When will I be questioned?"

He did not answer. She tried again the next time, with the same result. He was as quiet as a ghost; the cell's bindings swallowed sound, but she suspected he would be just as quiet outside it. Mostly he did not look at her, but when he did she felt him, and knew that his dislike of his tasks had not diminished.

On his fourth visit, she took a different tack.

"The collar is hurting me," she told him. "I think I might be getting an infection."

She lifted up the collar to display her throat, where the bruising of her failed suicide attempt had been exacerbated by the chafing of the heavy metal. He hesitated, then approached her, his flat face expressionless, and bent to inspect her neck. This near, she could feel him, even though he would not meet her eyes: the same distaste she had sensed before, with something else underneath, some kind of deprivation or anguish—though, crippled as she was in this room, she could not tell which.

He straightened and departed. She thought her appeal had been in vain, but after a short time he returned, with a ceramic pot and a roll of bandages. He set them near her and began to turn away.

"Help me?" she said.

Again he hesitated. Then he knelt down beside her. He tapped the collar, indicating that she should lift it. With deft fingers he applied the salve. Almost at once the pain began to ease. He folded the bandages and wrapped them gently around her throat, easing the collar down over them. She stared into his face as he worked, willing him to look at her. He did not, though she could feel his awareness of her gaze.

"Thank you," she said when he was done, genuinely grateful. Silently he rose to his feet. He picked up the tray from her previous meal and moved toward the door.

"Do you think I could have some water for washing?" she said to his back. "Just a little."

He did not pause or otherwise indicate that he had heard. But on his next visit he brought with him, in addition to her food, a bucket and a piece of cloth. The request had been a test of his sympathy, but she was very glad to see the water: she had been dirty even before her capture, and over the past days, with little to distract her, the griminess of her skin and hair had become a torment. A good deal of the water wound up on the floor; it did not pool on the glowing binding-surface, but separated into droplets, like pearls.

"Thank you for the water," she said when the servant returned with her next meal. He did not reply. When he came back with the basin, she tried again: "I made a bit of a mess. I'm sorry."

He shrugged. It was the first time he had directly responded to anything she said.

"You've been kind," she told him. "Kinder than you need to be. Probably a lot kinder than you're supposed to be. I'm grateful."

She was acting a role. And yet there was a part of her that meant it. In her helplessness and isolation, the small things he had done for her seemed larger, somehow, than the game she was attempting to play. This time he met her eyes fully. She saw knowledge in his gaze, and something else. Pity. Even her impaired Gift could not mistake it. It was the opening she had wanted, yet she was not prepared for the sting of it. For just an instant it laid her open as no cruelty could have done. She drew in her breath and turned her face away.

He moved to the bucket.

"Won't you . . ." The shaking of her voice was only partly pretense. "Won't you please tell me what will happen to me?"

He shook his head.

"Please," she said. "What harm will it do?"

Again he shook his head. He picked up the tray from her last meal and set it on the bucket. Lifting both, he moved to the door.

She tried one more time. "What's your name?"

He froze. For a moment he was absolutely still. His back was to her, but even so, suddenly, she could feel him—all the darkness she had sensed before, joined now to a bereavement so profound it caught at her breath. If it came so clearly to her crippled Gift, how wrenching must it truly be? Instinct, unexplained but certain, brought her forward, on her knees.

"Help me," she said. Still he stood motionless. She thought she could see him tremble. "Free me. If I can get out of this cell I can get to a place where no one can find me. You can come with me. You'll be safe, I swear it. You won't ever have to serve anyone again, unless you choose to."

He set down what he carried and turned. His face was utterly blank. He advanced on her; she pulled away, suddenly fearful, pressing herself against the wall. He knelt before her, his face still empty, and reached out to place his index finger against her lips. He held it there a moment, his black eyes fixed on hers. He said nothing. But she knew, as surely as if he had told her, that she had just trespassed in some unforgivable way.

He departed. The next time he came he did not look at her, or acknowledge her when she spoke to him. She understood that somehow she had forfeited his sympathy. She had known there was little likelihood of success. Yet it was surprisingly painful to have the chance removed.

The light in the cell was constant. For lack of any other measure, Cariad had begun to reckon time by the servant's visits, assuming that two visits made a day. By this calculation, four days had crawled past, and still she had not been brought to Jolyon. She did not know why he should delay; if their positions were reversed, she would not wait.

She passed the time between the servant's appearances in a kind of willed blankness, a state that spared her both the tyranny of the empty hours and the futile anguish of her thoughts. She did not have such control over her dreams. When exhaustion overcame her, and even the bright walls and the chafing of the collar were not enough to keep her from sleep, the images she rejected during her waking hours assaulted her without mercy.

Now and then the spyhole set into the cell's door scraped open, and someone watched her for a while. She could not see anything in that black space, but as time went on she became convinced, perhaps irrationally, that the watcher was Jolyon. Was he looking to see how the monotony of imprisonment was wearing her down? Was he gloating over his ownership of her? Was he savoring the prospect of questioning her, like a connoisseur studying an open bottle of wine? She pictured him, in his dusty treasure room, thinking of her, as she had thought of him before she set out to kill him. Imagining her death, as she had imagined his; desiring her suffering, as she had desired his. When she thought of him the tips of her fingers burned, a ghost of power in this powerless place. In spite of everything that had happened, she still willed his ending. She knew that, if she had it to do over again, she might still make the same disastrous choices.

If her measurements were correct, it was on the fifth day that Jolyon finally confronted her. He did not have her brought to him, as she had thought he would. Instead the wall cracked open and he was there, black against the black stone of the prison hallway, his eyes fixed on her face.

His servant slipped around him, carrying a folding chair. He set it up at a point beyond the reach of Cariad's chain, then moved back a few paces and lapsed into immobility, his expression empty, his hands loose at his sides. Jolyon entered, the door falling closed behind him. He seated himself, and locked his eyes to Cariad's.

For a time they watched one another. Jolyon had put off much of his gold to come here: he wore only his Guardian medal, a pair of jeweled ear-pendants, and a large number of rings. His robe, of lustrous black brocade figured with the Arm eye symbol, fell in graceful folds across his knees, hiding all the but the silver-shod points of his red boots. His body was relaxed, his hands clasped loosely in his lap. Above the high collar of his black shirt his face was innocent of either anger or urgency. But the unblinking fixity of his gaze gave the lie to this seeming serenity, a regard as intense as any Cariad had ever experienced. It was an effort to look back without flinching. She saw herself as he must see her: dirty, disheveled, collared like a dog. And yet his confidence was not so great that he risked sitting within her reach. The thought gave her a little strength.

"You've caused me a lot of trouble." Jolyon broke the silence at last. "I've had to replace two companions because of you. It's not hard to find men who are willing to volunteer, but finding the right ones is another matter. I can only be thankful that Baffrid was pursuing his own interests the night you came."

He paused, as if waiting for her to say something. She did not. She did not trust her voice; it was futile, anyway, to reply.

"My servant informs me that your Gift doesn't function as Guardian Gifts do." His voice was high for a man's, reedy and dysphonious, strangely at odds with the graceful composure of his face. "I'm assuming that's why you were able to get through the wards and barriers set on my apartments. Are there others like you where you come from? Or are you an exception? A freak, as my servant is?"

Cariad resisted the impulse to glance at the servant, still as marble at his master's shoulder. She had thought she might sense Jolyon a little with her crippled Gift, but she felt nothing, not a trace. Intuition, however, told her that her silent regard annoyed him. She was aware of the unwisdom of angering a man who held her in his complete control, yet it satisfied some deep adversarial urge in her to do so. Jolyon was as powerless here as she. This was not her death, or even the mindprobe that would precede it. She did not need to be afraid—yet.

"You aren't the first person to occupy this cell, you know. Your father was here for a little while, after his arrest."

Cariad drew in her breath. She had felt his presence in the blooming meadow beyond the Pilgrim's Pass, but she had not sensed it here, not even when she looked in from outside. She thought of him, collared perhaps with this very collar, chained with this very chain, his back set where hers was resting now . . .

"A reaction at last." Across from her, Jolyon smiled. "This is a very special cell. Do you know why?"

She stared at him.

"Actually, this should interest you. These white walls—"

he gestured, his rings flashing "—are really wards, shaped to the currents of your father's Gift, created from the map your mother made of his mind. After he . . . escaped, the assembled Councils decreed that the wards be maintained against his recapture. Of course there's no point to it now, for he's spent so much time in the other world that any cell could hold him. But the Councils never ordered the wards dismantled. It only took a few adjustments to make them work for you. As you've no doubt already realized, your Gift is useless here." He held out his hand, as if inviting her to take it. A blue-white flame shuddered into being upon his palm, trembling as if harassed by some unfelt wind. "Mine, however, is not. Within these wards, I can do exactly as I please."

Cariad stared at the mindfire he had conjured up. It seemed suddenly that all the air had left the room. Terror seized her, the fear she had not thought it was time to feel, the visceral panic that had taken her when she first understood that she was powerless.

Jolyon closed his fist upon the flame. It licked for a moment between his fingers, and was gone. Not wanting to, but unable to stop herself, Cariad raised her eyes to his. He was smiling, fully this time, with the whole of his face. She did not need her Gift to read that smile. In all her life she had never seen an expression so cold, so complex, so replete with triumph and malice and pleasure. She felt as if everything in her had turned to ice.

"Did you think," he said softly, forming each word with care, "that because your Gift was blocked, all power would be useless here? Did you think there might be something you could do to save yourself?"

With an effort, she looked away. She could no longer control her face, and she did not want to watch him watching her.

"You know you're helpless," he told her. "You know you have no defense. There are two alternatives available to you. You may answer my questions willingly. Or I can take your mind by force. Which do you prefer?"

She was silent. Surely he did not expect her to answer such a question.

"You must choose. I require it."

Anger cut cleanly through her fear. She wrenched her head around. "If I choose speech, you'll probe me anyway, and then you'll kill me." She hated the raggedness of her voice. "As you will if I choose the probe. As you will if I refuse to choose. It all ends the same way."

"Actually, I haven't made up my mind about killing you. It could be that you're more valuable living." He leaned forward a little. The sourceless light of the cell rested like a crown upon his russet hair, and drew flashes of red from the stones in his ear-pendants. "But make no mistake. There's no one in this world who threatens me and profits by it. Whether you live or die, be very sure you will be punished. I don't yet know what I'll do. Cause you to witness the process of justice for those whose names you give me, perhaps. Or maybe I'll take your sight, or relieve you of the use of your limbs, or spare your body and kill your Gift instead. But whatever I decide, you will have cause to regret what you tried to do to me, and time in which to regret it."

She could not speak. She had believed, in her anticipation of this moment, that to empty her mind and then kill her was the worst thing he could do to her. But to yield up the secrets of those she had lived and fought with, and then be kept alive to watch their torment . . . perhaps to witness Goldwine's death . . . she would die right now, this instant, rather than experience those things.

Jolyon watched her, his heavy eyes devouring her face. He was reading her, as if she were a written page, as if he himself had a heartsenser's Gift. "Well?" he said. "What will it be?"

"I . . ." It was difficult to form the words. "I can't answer your questions."

He shook his head, his ear-pendants swinging. "I'm disappointed. Truly, I am. I'd much rather hear these things from you. But if that's your choice—" He snapped his fingers over his shoulder. The servant stepped forward.

"Wait!" It sprang from her without conscious intent, more a gasp than a word. Jolyon held up a hand. The servant halted.

"If I agree . . ." She had to pause and breathe before she could continue. "If I answer your questions, will you answer mine?"

He raised his brows. "What in the two worlds," he said, not with anger but as if he were genuinely curious, "makes you think you can set conditions?"

"When I captured you, you asked a favor of me. I allowed it."

"And I'm sure you regret doing so."

"All I'm asking is what you asked. Even though I know nothing can come of it."

He studied her. His eyes, the waxy green of unripe plums, were a weight against her face. It took enormous effort to keep from shifting her gaze away.

"Well," he said at last. "Perhaps it will be amusing. What is it you want to know?"

"I want to know . . . I want to know about your servant."

"My servant?" He seemed surprised.

"About his Gift. I want to understand what brought me down."

Once more she had the sense that he was reading her, staring into her mind and heart as earlier, through the spyhole, he had stared into the cell. Did it divert him to watch her, scurrying like a rat in her horror of the future he held out to her, desperately playing for time she did not have? But she could not help herself. She could no more voluntarily submit to the consequences of refusing his questions than she could agree to answer them. And she did want to know. If she were to lose so much, she wanted at least to understand why she had failed.

"My servant doesn't really have a Gift," Jolyon said. "Or more accurately, he has an anti-Gift. It's like a void, a void in him where a Gift would be in a normal person. His emptiness attracts others' power. He absorbs it into himself, and if he wills, sends it out again."

"Are you saying . . ." For a moment, Cariad forgot everything but her astonishment. "Are you saying that he used *my own Gift* to bind me?"

"Yes. That's exactly what he did."

"But how can that be? I've never heard of an ability like that."

"It's not unknown. Such creatures come into being from time to time—sports of nature, like calves born with two heads or children joined at the heart. Usually they destroy themselves before they reach adulthood. It's a powerful ability, and without control it can do a great deal of damage. With control, of course, it can be extraordinarily useful. But that's the exception rather than the rule."

It was incredible. Yet it explained the feeling she had had, of something spinning out of her into an enormous emptiness. "Your servant has control."

"I gave it to him. When I first found him he had none at all."

"Why would someone with such ability agree to become a servant?"

"It's not a matter of agreeing. He belongs to me."

"He's your slave?"

"I own him more fully than that. When I found him he'd been executed. Among his people, those who are executed aren't actually killed, but made unliving by decree. They're stripped of their possessions, their families, their histories, their personhoods. They truly believe they're dead—they believe it so completely that they forget their lives before they were condemned. Absurd, isn't it? But such are the customs of the unGifted. My servant has only the vaguest memory of who he was before I vacated his sentence and declared him alive again. But no man lives twice, not naturally. He exists only by my will, and at my pleasure. His life isn't his, it's mine, to do with as I wish."

"And he believes this?"

Jolyon smiled. "More fully even than I do."

Cariad glanced at the servant. He might have been made of marble for all the awareness he showed. She thought of the darkness she had sensed in him, of the tide of anguish that had risen up when she asked him his name. Perhaps he did not recall who he had been, but he knew he had lost something, and it seemed clear enough that he mourned it.

"Why was he condemned?"

"When he was twelve, the local Journeyers ordered him

confined outside the village, out of range of their Gifts. He wasn't dangerous that way—where there are no Gifts, his anti-Gift has nothing to absorb. But the unGifted are ignorant and superstitious, and know nothing of power. His people were afraid of him, even confined. They wanted him gone forever. So they took him from his prison and condemned him to death and banished him to wander like a ghost."

"And you arrived in time to save him?"

He shook his head. "The orthodoxers I was traveling with assessed his village about a year later. I saw his sentence in the records and surmised what kind of ability he had. I thought it a shame to waste it. I went looking for him. When I found him, I commuted his sentence and brought him away with me."

"Did you ask him whether he wanted to go?" It had occurred to Cariad that if she could make him angry enough, he might be unable to resist killing her on the spot. "To be alive again? To become a servant?"

But Jolyon only smiled. "Life is life. There are few kinds of life that aren't better than being dead. You agree, don't you, boy?"

Gravely, the servant nodded, his eyes fixed on some indeterminate point of space.

"Why do you call him that? Doesn't he have a name?"

"A person declared unliving loses everything, even that."

"But you commuted his sentence."

"As I said, my servant's life does not belong to him. I didn't want to give him a reason to make the mistake of thinking otherwise. And so I never restored to him the name he had, or gave him a new one to replace it. Besides," he shrugged, "he doesn't need a name, for I never need to call him. We are mindlinked."

Again she saw the coldness in him, bound into his being as the fractured glaciers were locked to the slopes of the Fortress mountains. In spite of herself, she shuddered. He saw it: those intent green eyes missed nothing.

"So you brought him back to the Fortress." She reached for challenge and did not quite find it. "And taught him control."

"Yes. With drugs at first, for safety's sake. But it's been years since I had to do that. He owns his ability now. He can absorb a fraction of a Gift, or the entire sum of it. He can take one Gift, or ten. I've never yet found a limit to his capacity." He smiled. "And believe me, I've tried."

"Yet you keep him in thrall. You keep him secret."

He raised his brows. "You of all people should be able to understand the value of that."

"Why does he never speak?"

He regarded her without replying. His face had smoothed, his mouth relaxed into seriousness. She saw that his attention had shifted. But not from her. It was the thread of conversation he had abandoned. Panic pressed against her heart.

"You're very like him, you know," he said, quietly.

She stared at him. She did not have to ask who he meant.

"It's more than just your face. You speak as he did. You look at me as he did. He and I met in this cell, thirty years ago. I remember it . . ." He paused, as if searching for a word. "Vividly. We faced each other, as you and I are doing now, and we talked, as you and I are doing now. And then . . ."

He paused. She could see the drift of memory across his face. For the first time, she was glad of the muffling of her Gift. She did not wish to know what he felt when he thought about her father.

"What's your name?" he said.

She swallowed. "Cariad."

"Cariad." He said it slowly, testing it. "It's an unusual name."

"It belonged to my mother's grandmother."

"Ah. A family tradition."

She did not reply.

"You're a mercenary of some kind, Cariad, am I right? A professional assassin, perhaps."

She hesitated, and then nodded.

"I've given a good deal of thought to why it was you who was sent. Either it's an incredible coincidence, which I'm not inclined to believe, or your employer has a keen sense of irony, and rather too much knowledge for his own good. That would lead me to believe it was a Guardian. But I've done some research these past days, and I've found nothing to indicate that any of my enemies hired you. Correct?"

She nodded again.

"And yet you used a drug that to my knowledge is available only to Guardians. Do you serve some ambitious politician outside the Fortress—someone allied with the Journeyers, perhaps?"

"No."

"Who, then? I'd like to hear the answer from your own lips, Cariad. But I won't wait forever. Who sent you?"

She looked at him. How could he not understand? How could he lie under the hands of the daughter of the man he had obsessively pursued for thirty years, the man he could not stop trying to destroy, how could he look into her face and see the killing fires there and not recognize the force that had drawn her to him?

"No one sent me," she said. "No one hired me. I came to kill you for myself. For my father's sake. And for my mother's."

Jolyon shook his head. His ear-pendants flashed. "You never knew your father. He left this world before you were born. He was a Violator, and so was your mother, both of them condemned by the Council of Six, of which I was not at that time a part. And yet you would kill me for their sakes?"

"You worked half your life to bring my father down. Not because he was a Violator, but because you hated him. You sent my mother to him, intending that she should open her mind to him and so be judged corrupt. You set out deliberately to destroy them both, because they resisted you in their youth, because they wouldn't yield and bow down to you and give up all their secrets, and you couldn't bear the memory of their defiance. You couldn't destroy my father. But because of you he was driven from this world. You didn't manage to kill my mother, but because of you she became a cripple. That is why I would kill you."

For a long, long moment he watched her. He was very still. Only his ear-pendants moved, trembling slightly with his pulse and with his breathing. His face was set, and oddly empty.

"Where did you grow up, Cariad?" he asked. His voice was as blank, as disconnected as his face. "Who raised you that you heard such things?"

She shook her head, and looked away.

"All these years I believed your mother dead, and you with her. But here you are, a grown woman, your head filled with ideas you should not have. Did your mother's mind survive the destruction of her Gift, so that she could tell you these pointless stories of the past? Was it she who sent you here?"

"I will not tell you," she said. The moment had come, the moment she had sought to delay, the moment in which she must refuse him and in so doing consent to the plundering of her mind. "I'm done answering your questions."

He leaned forward, bracing his jeweled hands upon his knees. For the first time she saw the savage mutilation of his nails, the ragged flesh and the dried blood that ringed them. "If you don't speak, I'll take the answers from you. Why try to hide what can't be hidden?"

"I won't answer you."

Expression was returning to his face. She could see, at last, the anger she had sought to draw from him earlier. "Let me tell you about your father, since you say you came here for his sake. He cared nothing for the principles we Guardians hold sacred, only for his own ambition—though he kept the secret of that so thoroughly even his masters couldn't see it. But I saw it. I recognized the rottenness in him, long before he profaned the medal of Guardianship by wearing it about his neck, long before he dishonored the red sash of the Arm by binding it around his waist. I saw his ambition also, his desire to rise up among us and change us so that we would cease to be ourselves. I made it my life's work to expose him, to bring him down. And when we met again in this cell, and I told him what I knew about him, what I had always known—" His lips had pulled back from his teeth. His face, which for the first time had twisted itself away from its semblance of serenity, was hot with memory. "He showed me, he showed me openly and without shame his contempt for the Arm of the Stone and his hatred of the Limits and his pride in his long deception. I demanded entrance into his mind, as was my right as an Investigator of the Arm of the Stone. He defied me. No one has ever defied me as he did and lived to speak of it. But I wasn't powerful then as I am now, and so I was forced to leave him to others, who botched the taking of his Gift and left him able to break our walls and take the Stone away from us. But his escape has been his destruction. He wanders now through the horrors of that other world, Gift-less and alone, old and undefended. He knows I pursue him, just as I know he flees from me. But he cannot flee forever. Alive or dead, tomorrow or a century from now, I will find him. When I do, I will grind his bones to dust. I will scatter him on the winds of that other world. When I'm done, it will be as if he never drew breath at all."

It seemed to Cariad that he had forgotten her, that his words had carried him backward to that other moment in this cell, when her father, for the last time, withheld the surrender Jolyon so desired. And she saw, in a flash of understanding, that his mind was fixed in that moment, as his body was fixed in an instant of youth: an eternal, arti-ficial pause, from which he could not bear to disengage himself.

The quality of his gaze had altered. He was looking at her now, not beyond her. "You think you know what hatred is," he said, almost gently. "For you say that it's a dream of vengeance that brought you here. But you have no idea. Hatred is a thing that can only be born when two people stand face-to-face and stare into the core of each other's souls. When it's born like that, it endures . . . endures as the stones of the Fortress do. Even after thirty years, even with the distance of a world between us, your father hates me still. He hates me as you never can, because he and I were more than just ideas to one another."

His eyes were hooded again. His face had closed. There was nothing in it now but stillness, a tranquility so entire Cariad could almost believe there was no feeling in him at all, only a vacancy like the core of Goldwine's mountain, cracking with ice and dark as the polar sky.

He rose to his feet. She heard the scrape as his chair moved back, the sigh as the fabric of his robe fell into place.

"There is patterning in the world," he said. "Circles that always, given time enough, find a way to close. This is one of them."

The servant moved forward. Firmly, not ungently but with an absolute strength Cariad would not have expected from a man so small, he seized her from behind, looping his hands through her upper arms and clasping his fists at her back, pulling on her shoulders and biceps so that she was held immobile.

Jolyon sank to his knees before her, his robe billowing out around him like the calyx of a black flower. She could smell his perfume, something sweet and heavy. He raised his glittering, bitten hands. She could not help herself; she began to struggle, heaving forward against the servant's hold, trying to get her legs under her. The servant's grip tightened; he pulled back on her arms so hard she felt her shoulderblades grinding, and pressed his fists brutally into her spine. She cried out in pain.

Jolyon arched forward, leaning over her so that he could look into her eyes. His hands came to rest on either side of her face, almost but not quite touching her skin.

There was a pause, like the endless stretch of time between the beginning of a fall and the moment of impact. Jolyon's face was inches away, so close Cariad could feel the rapid heat of his breath. She closed her eyes so she would not have to look at him. But she could not shut him out. Her Gift, prisoned for so long, was suddenly free. The whole universe of his emotion spun before her, a boiling conflux of desire and eagerness and triumph and need, an arousal that was not truly sexual and yet was not enough like anything else to be named otherwise. She could feel the servant also, a tide of shadow at her back, concentrating himself somehow, as if for enormous effort. And she understood, as surely as she had ever understood anything, that though he hated his master and detested the things he was made to do, he was bound to Jolyon, possessed by him, for he believed that it was only through Jolyon that he was bound to life. And though he loathed his life and mourned his captivity, he still, absolutely, desired to live.

Jolyon breathed in, deeply. Cariad felt something pass from his mind to the servant's: a signal, a command. Instantly, the world fell away into a black abyss. The abyss was emptiness, so profound it could not be comprehended; it was lightlessness, so perfect that it swallowed up even the memory of sight. And yet it was alive somehow, aware; and it was hungry. It cried out for the things it did not have, the things denied it by its very nature: warmth, brilliance, fullness.

Helpless, Cariad felt her Gift answer, drawn by a need so consuming even the wards of the cell could not close it away. It was like an ocean of fire as it streamed from her into the darkness, all the light that she had ever known or ever would know, falling forever into the void Jolyon's servant held inside him. A part of her stood in awe: she had not known she had so much power, or that it was so beautiful. But the rest of her struggled in horror, for she could feel the core of her being leaving her.

The outpouring ceased. For a moment the entire sum of her Gift hung motionless, like a map of a gleaming universe drawn upon the blackest reaches of infinity. She felt the awful void in her where it had been, an echo of the vacancy that had stolen it. And then it rushed toward her, all at once, her own Gift made alien and terrifying by another's use. It struck her mind with a force that seemed enough to tear her apart. It was like self-immolation. The flames lit up everything within her: all her thoughts, all her memories, all her understandings, all her secret darknesses, all the things she knew and all the things she refused to contemplate, every corner and crevice of her soul, exposed and made visible as even she herself had never seen it.

And now she felt Jolyon, sliding eagerly into the light her own Gift had made inside her. He thrust savagely about within her head, snaking up and down the passages of her mind, raking up her thoughts and scattering them again, like leaves. She felt his desire, his eagerness, the awful ascending joy he took in his brutal plundering. He wanted it all—not just her professional knowledge and the truths of her identity, but everything in her. She lived the memories as he devoured them: the exhilaration of a risky mission, a heart slowing to silence beneath her hands, the pain of an arrow in her thigh, Laran's face above her in the darkness, the glitter of ice in the depths of the hollow mountain, the strength of Goldwine's embrace, the silence and cold and flickering light that were the earliest images she owned. It was a violation like nothing she had ever known—she, who in all her life had never allowed another person entrance to her mind, who had never left unguarded even the outermost fringes of her self.

An endless time later, Jolyon withdrew. The light within her faded, and the secret parts of her dropped once more into shadow. The abyss remained, black and desolate. It had feasted on her power, and now was vacant again. Briefly, Cariad felt the anguish of that deprivation, new and old at the same time—like death, like banishment, like exile. For just an instant, it seemed to her that a human voice cried out from within the abyss. There was memory in the cry, and guilt, and pain, and something else, something precious. A phrase. Three words she could not understand.

Then it was gone, the abyss and what it seemed to hold, and there was only the ordinary darkness of Cariad's closed eyes.

She felt her arms released. The servant rose, and went to stand again behind his master. Deprived of support, she slumped against the wall, her tangled hair falling across her eyes. Jolyon had not stirred. He was still bent forward, his hands still poised where her face had been. He was breathing hard, his chest heaving beneath his fine black robe. His face was glossed with sweat, his eyes heavy and unfocused. He looked like a man in the grip of some private transport.

"I can't . . . believe it," he whispered, his words broken by the struggle of his breath. "Can it . . . be true? That the traitor is . . . Bron?"

Cariad stared at him through the veil of her hair. Her mind felt bruised, disordered, like a rifled treasure chest. It was her father's secret name Jolyon spoke, the true name of his ancient heritage. In the lore of the Guardians, it was a curse—for it was also the name of her father's ancestor, the man from whom the first Guardian had taken the Stone. Until this moment, no Guardian had known of the survival of her father's lineage, or of the name, or of the Tale.

"This was what the corruption was . . . all along," he whispered. "I sensed it. I didn't . . . recognize it. But I always . . . sensed it."

He lowered his hands, resting them on his knees, bowing his head in an effort to gain control of his breathing. After a moment he looked up again.

"This prophecy," he said. "This prophecy of return. You believe it."

"Yes," she whispered, though he needed no confirmation.

"It can't happen." He leaned toward her, his bitten hands still braced upon his knees. "He can't return. The other world long ago robbed him of his Gift."

"He can." It was an effort to speak. "He will. Nearly all the prophecy has come to pass. This will too."

"How?" He was frowning. "How can it, if his Gift is gone?"

"His Gift is not gone. He's as strong now as he ever was. He has the Stone."

"The Stone!" Jolyon laughed. "The Stone is a useless lump of rock."

"No." Cariad shook her head. "The Stone survives, as he does. Konstant will find them both. My father will return. And when he does, the Guardians will fall."

She said it like an invocation, like a prayer, though she no longer believed that any Gift could resist the hunger of the abyss inside Jolyon's servant, not even her father's.

"Ah yes. This agent of yours—Konstant, Talesin, whatever his name is. I admit, I'm surprised. Such an excellent Red . . . did you know, at his initiation ceremony, that he emptied the mind of a Soldier in less than five minutes? Many of my colleagues can't match that." He shook his head a little, as if in regret. "But he's been two months alone in the other world. By now the power-sickness has taken him. Soon his Gift will be gone. He won't be able to accomplish anything after that—and before that, what could he have done? More than five hundred Roundheads, and a hundred and fifty of my Reddened, have gone out before him and found nothing. Why should you imagine that he'll succeed?"

"Because I know it," Cariad whispered. She turned her face away. She was weary of these questions. He had already seen the answers inside her mind; why should she be forced to repeat them?

He watched her. She sensed his stillness.

"You have such faith," he said, softly. "I could almost believe you."

She clung to silence, hiding behind her hair.

"But I know better." His voice was hard now. "The evidence of your mind I must accept, though if you had told me of your own free will that these little resistance groups had grown so ambitious, so . . . accomplished, I would have punished you for lying. The Soldier Staff-Holder will have a great deal to answer for, I can promise you." He shook his head. "But your faith I reject. You're Violators, you and all your rebel kind. It fits your Violating defiance to imagine that your agent could find the man hundreds of Guardians have failed to locate. It suits your Violating philosophy to believe that a Gift could live on in a world of unGifted, that the Stone could survive the currents of hand-power, when the evidence of the Split and the testimony of generations of Roundhead travelers confirm it can't be so. You're no better than the unGifted, with their ignorant superstitions and their mindless resistance to ten centuries of Guardian wisdom." He drew in his breath, deeply. "As for the rest, the resistance and the downworld infiltrators and the Violator networks . . . once I am Prior, I will take it all down, piece by piece. And this woman who took you in, this Goldwine, this teller of Tales." She felt the air move; he was leaning toward her. "I will make her my personal business."

The words brought her eyes back to his. He wanted her to weep, to break down, to beg for mercy, to complete his victory over her mind by offering him physical surrender: she could see it in his face. She refused. No matter what it cost her, he would not see her break.

After what seemed a very long time, he moved back, and

pushed himself to his feet. He stood for a moment, looking down at her.

"I've enjoyed our conversation, Cariad. We'll have many more in the months to come. I intend to keep you fully apprised of my progress—you will appreciate it, I think, as few others will." His lips lifted in a smile; she did not need her Gift to read its malice. "And just in case you're hoping for some kind of rescue attempt by your Violator friends, who are so good at getting through Guardian defenses, you might like to know that these bindings have been adjusted to sound an alarm if they're breached."

Hatred burst in her like an exploding star. Everything else—the pain and humiliation, the guilt and anguish—vanished, swallowed by the power of that emotion.

"I know why you keep your servant secret," she said. "I know why you take him everywhere you go. You need him to make you look larger than you are. He steals the power of those around you and gives it back again as you instruct him, and you let everyone think the power is yours. Because you really don't have the power a Second is supposed to, do you? You have only an ordinary Gift."

It was no more than intuition, based on what she had felt of him while he was inside her mind. But in what she saw in his face, she understood that she had stumbled on the truth. He lunged toward her, dropping to one knee, reaching out as if to strike her. She twisted away, slipping as she did so, falling heavily on her side. He came to rest above her, one hand braced against the wall, the other poised over her face. His lips had drawn away from his teeth. She could hear him breathing. She waited for the blow.

It did not come. Instead he lowered his hand and, very slowly, drew it across the air above her forehead, her cheek, her lips, her throat, tracing the contours of her face without touching her. His eyes, like two overheated gems, followed the path of his fingers. Though there was no contact it seemed to her that she could feel him, a dual pressure of hand and eye, moving not on her but in her, an incorporeal caress more crawlingly intimate than any real touch she had ever received.

"I'll keep you here, Cariad," he whispered, his eyes still

moving against her skin. "I'll keep you here forever. You will be my other secret."

For a moment more he hung above her. Then he pushed himself away from the wall, and rose. He moved toward the door. His servant folded the chair and followed. The door cracked open to receive them, and fell closed again at their backs.

Cariad sank full length upon the floor. She was alone now, and could break without being seen. But though anguish filled her, an anguish so huge she did not believe her mind could hold it, her eyes remained dry. It seemed fitting, somehow, that she should be denied the relief of weeping. For what she had done, for all she had betrayed, she deserved no mercy, not even that.

Seventeen

ARIAD LAY prone on the floor of the cell, her face buried in the musty folds of her blanket, her hair spread around her like water weed. Outside her, time flowed on, but within her time had stopped. Her mind was suspended in the instant of Jolyon's probe. Again and again she relived that pillaging, that violation. Again and again she watched, helpless, as the images of her life were stolen from her, a revisiting of her past that seemed to cut her soul open, for it was no longer memory but accusation, a litany of all that would be destroyed.

Minutes passed, or hours: trapped in her private universe of anguish, she did not know. She heard the silence break: heard the turning of the lock, heard the servant's footsteps as he entered, heard the small noise the tray made as he set it down, heard him cross to the slop basin, heard him leave. She did not stir, though she could smell the food, though she was thirsty. She could not live with the horror inside her, or with the knowledge of what waited for her in the weeks or months or years of her subjugation to Jolyon's will. Even the cell, warded against self-injury, could not force her to eat or drink. All the choices that were part of life were lost to her—but this, at least, she could still choose.

The silence broke once more—the sound of the spyhole this time. There was a pause, and then the lock clicked and there were footsteps again, swift ones, and a rush of air as someone stooped down beside her. Hands pulled at her. She did not resist, but allowed herself to be rolled onto her back.

Fingers brushed the hair away from her face, and set themselves against her throat, as if to check her pulse. She felt her shoulders gripped, felt herself pulled upward, into someone's tight embrace.

She opened her eyes, and saw Orrin's face.

She could not comprehend it. His presence was not part of the cycle of reminiscence in which she was snared, nor of the future that waited for her beyond it. Perhaps she had fallen asleep, and he was a dream; perhaps she had gone mad, and he was a vision.

"Thanks be," he said. "You're alive. When I saw you lying there like that . . . are you injured? Are you ill?"

She heard the urgency in his voice. She felt the pressure of his arms, the agitated beating of his heart. Something entered into her, something other than the pain of memory and the despair of betrayal.

"Orrin?" she whispered.

"Sit up." He was pushing her, urging her upright. "Let me look at this collar."

"Orrin . . . oh, Orrin . . . you shouldn't have come . . . it's too dangerous . . . he knows everything . . ."

"Put your chin up." He was not listening to her. "There, like that. Hold still." She felt his fingers, exploring the collar, lifting the chain. "All right. Bend forward now, and brace yourself."

As if in a dream, she obeyed. He moved behind her. She felt a pressure on the collar, heard the sound of metal on metal, felt a twisting and a wrenching. Then he was in front of her again, pushing a tool of some kind up under his tunic.

"You're free now." He held out his hands to her. "Get up. We've got to go."

"How—"

"The collar is solid, but the chain is just an ordinary chain. I bent open a link."

She allowed him to draw her to her feet. Without the weight of the chain, she felt light enough to drift away. She still was not entirely certain she was not dreaming.

"I'll go out first," he said. "When I'm sure no one's there, I'll signal you." He took a deep breath. "This all depends on you being able to make yourself invisible. I would have brought clothes for you, but female prison workers aren't allowed on the cell levels. Are you . . . is your Gift . . ."

"It should be . . . it should be all right once I'm outside," she said, though she was not sure.

"Well, we'll just have to try and see."

He moved to the door, and bent to pick up the bucket and swab he had set down nearby. For the first time she saw that he was dressed as a prison servant, in a gray tunic with the Soldiers' sword symbol on the left shoulder and the sigil of the prison workers on the right, and the leather cap into which workers tucked their long hair during duty hours. He pushed the door open and slipped out into the glittering hallway. Almost at once he turned, beckoning.

Gathering herself, Cariad stepped over the threshold. She felt her Gift unbind, an abrupt release that made her stagger.

"Hurry," Orrin whispered. His pale face was lightly sheened with sweat.

She closed her eyes, reaching inward, coaxing her Gift to do her will. It was difficult. The spark of her power was abused and weak; she was clumsy with it, like a novice.

"Good," Orrin whispered. "That's it."

She opened her eyes again. She was invisible now, she could feel it; and yet, standing in the empty corridor, she felt hideously exposed and naked. Orrin had pushed the door closed as she came out of it; now he knelt before it, doing something with a pair of metal rods. Lockpicks, she thought. The sense of dream rose up in her again.

They set out, traversing the long blind passage that isolated the cell, and then the central corridor. They reached the great spiral stairway that drilled up the middle of the prison annex and began to descend. Orrin, with his worker's tunic and cleaning equipment, did not attract a second glance. Cariad, invisible, pressed herself to one side or the other to avoid servants and Soldiers. Her breath came short with fear: fear that she would slip and make a noise, fear that she would not be able to hold herself to invisibility, fear that the next face she saw would be Jolyon's. By the time they gained the hallways of the prison's downworld, she was trembling.

They reached the warehouse area, where the ungated archway opened directly onto the tunnels, and left the prison behind, following the tunnel for a little distance and then veering off into an adjacent passage. There a transporter cart waited, with four transporters ready at the traces.

Orrin vaulted into the cart. "Get in," he said over his shoulder. "You can drop your invisibility—I've brought transporter leathers for us both."

Cariad released the binding, but she did not take the hand he held out to her. She felt like someone wrenched from nightmare, stunned by the suddenness of the transition, half-expecting each moment to propel her back where she had been. But she was free; and freedom carried a single, overriding imperative.

"I have to get word to my people," she said. "I want you to take me to your recruiter."

"We'll pass by the Speaker downworld. We have a drop point just outside. I'll leave the signal."

"No. We must go in. You must help me find her."

"I can't do that. I don't know her name or where she works, or even what she looks like. She's never let me see."

Cariad could not regret the professional caution that had caused Estrellara to withhold from her the identities of Goldwine's in-Fortress agents, for it was one thing at least that Jolyon had not been able to take. But in her weakened state, she could have wept with the frustration of the delay. "If you leave the signal, how long will it be before we can meet?"

"Tonight. At the twenty-fourth bell. Now get *in*. We have to get moving."

She allowed him to pull her into the cart. At once it began to move, picking up speed as the transporters fell into their smooth, distance-eating lope. She dragged on the leathers Orrin pushed toward her, and then settled herself amid the piles of loose packing-cloth, her back against the cart's high side. She was aware of the collar, heavy around her neck. She wanted it off her, but she did not think she was strong enough yet to split it. She put her hands to it, feeling the hard metal that until a few moments ago had held her prisoner. Belatedly, the astonishment of it swept her; that she should be here, that she should be free. She thought of Jolyon, who had bound the wardings of the cell to sound an alarm at Gifted incursion. But she had to be fed and watered, and so the alarm could not be triggered by a servant's use of a key . . . or a downworlder's use of a set of lockpicks. . . .

She felt something shift inside her. She began to laugh, helplessly. She heard the hysteria in it, the accumulated strain and horror and anguish of her imprisonment, and now the amazement of her freedom, spiraling dangerously toward the edges of control. She buried her face in her hands, her shoulders shaking. Somewhere beyond her, she was aware of Orrin's worried gaze.

"Are you—" he began, hesitantly.

She shook her head. "I'm all right," She breathed deeply, in and out, and then looked up. "I was just thinking. That Jolyon took such care to guard the cell against the Gifted he thought might try to rescue me, but he never thought to guard it against you, even though he saw you in my mind. He has such contempt for the unGifted . . . I suppose it never occurred to him that a downworlder would have the courage to try such a thing, even if he was clever enough to figure out where I was. Oh, he will be angry when he understands." Something rose in her, not laughter this time. She pushed it away, shuddering. "How *did* you know I was there?"

He had settled himself opposite. The hood of the transporter tunic covered his face and hair; she could see only his cheeks now, and his nose, and his gray eyes, fixed intense and unblinking on her face.

"I thought you were dead," he told her. "When you didn't come the second night, I was sure of it. But I looked for you even so. I went through all the downworlds, I talked to the workers in the prisons, I walked the midden from end to end. Then I heard that a Roundhead bodyservant was visiting the power-warded cell twice a day. I took every tool I could hide inside my clothes, and went straight there. I didn't let myself believe it might be you until I saw you, lying on the floor like a corpse. And then I thought

I'd been too late. What happened? How did he capture you?"

"I went to kill him," she said, speaking quickly because she was afraid that if she did not she would not be able to say it. "There was . . . something I didn't know, something I wasn't prepared for. I failed."

"This was the thing you couldn't tell me? The other part of what you were sent to do?"

"Yes." It was easier than the truth.

"You said it was dangerous, but I never imagined . . ." He sounded shocked. "The Second is one of the most powerful men in the Fortress. Certainly he's the best defended. Why would your people take such a risk?"

"The Prior is dying. Jolyon means to take his place. I . . . they . . . planned to stop him."

"But he's not Staff-Holder."

"The Staff-Holder has given him proxy. He'll stand in at the Ceremony. Right now only the Council knows, and Jolyon's secretary. I saw it in his mind when I found out about Konstant."

For a moment Orrin did not speak. He was politically astute; he knew as well as she did what Jolyon's Priorship would mean.

"The Second's Gift is very strong," he said at last. "But the Journeyer Staff-Holder is strong also. And the Speaker."

Cariad shook her head. "Jolyon isn't nearly as powerful as everyone thinks he is. He has a servant . . . who can absorb the Gifts around him and turn them to his own use. Everyone thinks the power is Jolyon's. He's going to order the servant to steal the Gifts of the other Staff-Holders, and then he'll use them to remake the Staff. No one else will have a chance."

Orrin's brows drew together. "Are you sure of this? I've never heard of such a thing."

Cariad looked away. "I ought to be sure. It's how he captured me. I didn't know—no one did. He explained it all to me, in the cell . . ." Her voice shook; she pulled herself to a stop. "And then he mindprobed me," she continued harshly. "He knows about the resistances now, the headquarters and their defenses, the intelligence networks inside the Fortress. Everything."

For a long moment Orrin watched her. She could see the passage of thought behind his face, as his quick mind absorbed what she had just told him and projected the implications of it. "I see," he said at last, quietly. And she sensed—imperfectly, for her Gift was still not fully recovered from her ordeal—that the comprehension he expressed encompassed not just his understanding of what her betrayal meant for the resistance, but of what it meant for her. As if he knew her well enough to understand that cost. As if he cared as much for her suffering as for the price thousands of others would pay. Suddenly she was angry.

"Do you? He knows about you too now. You're a dead man if you go back to the Keep."

"I haven't been back to the Keep since I realized you were gone. I knew you must have been caught. I knew what that meant for me."

As suddenly as it had come, her anger vanished. It was easy for him not to blame her, for he did not know the real folly that lay behind her capture. She felt her shame, running hot and painful beneath her skin, burning in her cheeks: an admission as clear as words.

The transporters turned a corner, into a tunnel that curved like a fingernail paring. The cart rocked, and then steadied.

"Where are we going?"

"To the caverns." He had turned his face away from her, in the direction of their forward passage. "The transporters have agreed to give us refuge."

"Orrin, no!" She sat forward, urgently. "I told you, he took everything out of my mind. That means he knows about your transporter adoption. With me gone and you vanished, he'll be sure to search the caverns. And everywhere else down here as well. We can't stay downworld. It's too dangerous."

"The transporters will protect us."

"But they can't protect us. Even if we manage to hide, the Reds Jolyon sends after me will see us in their minds. What do you think will happen to them then? I can't let anyone else suffer because of me."

"The transporters can protect themselves as well." He turned back to face her. "They are Gifted."

Cariad stared at him. "What?"

"They're Gifted," he repeated. "They have a way of defending themselves that's proof against even the Arm of the Stone. It's the safest place in the world for us to be."

"But—" The sense of dream, which had receded, surged over her again. "But that's not possible."

"I know it's difficult to accept." Orrin's gray eyes held hers. "But you must trust me. You'll be safe among the transporters. A lot safer than you would be on your own."

Everything Cariad knew went against it. But she could feel the truth in him. Her mind returned to that first night in the Fortress, when he had also told her something she could not accept . . . she had made the decision to trust him then, and she had not regretted it. She felt something in her give way. She was too tired to struggle, too tired to run. It would be good to have a place to go to ground.

"Very well," she said. "Orrin . . ." She was not sure yet if she was glad of her survival. But he had done an astonishing thing for her and risked much more than just his life. "Thank you."

He did not reply, but only looked at her—the same intent, unsettling regard he had turned on her at the beginning of their journey. She could sense him suddenly, more clearly than at any time since her release: his desire to close the distance between them, to take her in his arms, even soiled and dirty as she was. She felt the blood rise to her face. She turned away so he would not see. Still he watched her; his gaze was like a hand on her skin. At last, unable to bear it, she lay down amid the drifts of fabric, closing her eyes and pulling the cloth up over her head. Her exhaustion dragged at her, pulling her down into sleep.

Some time later she awoke. They were still traveling, but the floor had acquired a definite downward pitch, and two of the transporters were manipulating the hand-brakes at the front of the cart. The air was warmer than it had been, softer: for a moment Cariad imagined she could smell the earth, and things growing, and was reminded of the meadow her father had made, a miracle of life amid the deadness of a winter world. But to think of any part of her past now was also to think of Jolyon. Anguish, briefly distanced by sleep, returned, heavy as iron within her.

"Where are we?" she asked.

"This is the passage to the caverns," Orrin said. "It leads off the rear perimeter tunnel."

"The caverns aren't under the Fortress itself?"

"No. When you see how large they are you'll understand why."

"Did you leave the signal?"

He nodded. "Go back to sleep. It'll be a while yet before we get there."

When she woke again, the motion of the cart had changed, no longer smooth and swift but rough and uneven. There was warmth against her face where it was not covered by her transporter hood, and she smelled a sweetness, like something blooming. She opened her eyes, blinking at the sudden brightness. Groggily, she pushed herself upright—and froze, struck dumb by what she saw.

They were passing through an orchard. There were trees as far as the eye could follow, rank upon rank of them, planted in ordered rows with grassy alleys in between. The leaves were thick and green; apples, not yet ripe, clustered on the boughs. Light slipped through the latticework of branches, dappling the trunks and the ground beneath.

Feeling as if she had not truly woken, Cariad raised her face, following the sun-warmth she had not felt in weeks. The branches did not quite meet above the center of the alley in which they traveled; high above, she could see wisps and trails of cloud, and the blaze of what truly seemed to be the sun. But there the illusion ended. For the sky was not an infinite bowl of blue, but a rough barrier of gray rock, tremendously distant, but not so far that she could not make out the irregularities and the fissures that marked it, the great stalactites jutting down like rows of jagged teeth. Ice glittered in declivities and along cracklines, as if the warmth of this subterranean sun reached only downward.

She looked at Orrin. "How big is this place?" she breathed.

"Huge. Larger than the entire Fortress." The tension of their journey through the tunnels seemed to have left him. He sat relaxed against the side of the cart, his arm stretched loosely along the rail. He had pulled his hood back from his face; he was smiling a little, as if her wonder pleased him. "In this cavern are the crops, the orchards and the hayfields, the village of the agricultural workers. There's another one beyond, even bigger, for the livestock. A river runs through both of them. Some people think it must be what originally made this place."

"And . . . the sun? What is it? Is it mindfire?"

He shook his head. "No one knows. There are eight suns, actually, four for each cavern, fixed at equal points just below the ceiling. They dim to mark the night and brighten again for morning. Because they never move, it's always noon here, and the season is always summer. Every night just after dark it rains, sometimes for an hour, sometimes for two. Crops grow year-round."

They left the orchard and entered a region of wheat fields, billowing beneath the false sunlight so naturally that, if one did not look up or out, it was possible to imagine oneself in the real world at noon on a day in high summer. Once again, however, the illusion of reality diminished on close observation, for some of the fields were ready for harvesting, while in others the crop was no more than a faint green haze across the soil, and in still others it stood half-mature—a variety of growth impossible in the above-ground world of shifting seasons.

To the right and up ahead, the rock of the cavern's walls was clearly visible, vaulting ceilingward above a fringe of trees. The far left wall showed only vaguely through a shimmer of distance, but its presence was apparent in the way the vast patchwork of fields and orchards came abruptly to a halt, as neat as a piece of cut fabric. In between, the cavern dipped, like the keel of a shallow boat, with the glint of water at its lowest point. A group of white-washed dwellings clustered there: the village of the agricultural workers. In fields and along the narrow lanes that wound between them, workers were visible, hoeing or harvesting, resting in the shade of trees. Six-wheeled carts, drawn by teams of oxen, moved from field to field, ferrying people or produce.

It was beautiful: a captured, artificial beauty, like a painting or a scene enclosed in glass. Again Cariad was reminded of the meadow her father had made—wild and open, not bounded and confined, yet conveying the same dreamlike perfection, the same sense of being all in all to itself. She closed her eyes, overwhelmed. She had had certain images of what the caverns must be like, but she had not imagined anything like this. She had never seen, or heard of, a work of power on this scale. The Guardian Roads, the Gates, even the strange complexities of Goldwine's blending of the powers of mind and hand: all of them paled in comparison to what she saw before her.

Beyond the fields, near the cavern's perimeter, lay forest—not the neat, ordered rows of the orchard, but real forest, haphazard and wild. Tall trunks soared toward the roof, forming a tangled secondary ceiling of branches and leaves that shut away much of the light. From their girth and height, they were very ancient. There was considerable space between them and very little undergrowth, and the cart moved easily across the leaf-litter, jolting occasionally as it ran across an exposed root.

After a little time the forest's end, which was also the end of the cavern, became visible through the trunks. In the rocky wall Cariad could make out several dark openings—caves, some of them flickering with light as if there were fires inside. Nearby clustered a constellation of odd shapes. As they approached, these resolved themselves into tents, no two quite alike: some circular, some pointed, some domed, some square. They were made of a dark material, like tanned hide, and painted round their sides with colorful designs similar to those that marked transporter leathers.

The transporters halted. Orrin leaped out of the cart and held up his hands for Cariad; she avoided them, sliding down on her own. Immediately the transporters turned to go, trotting off in the direction they had come.

A group of women and girls had appeared at the mouth of one of the caves. They were dressed alike in loose garments in pale shadow-colors. Like all transporters Cariad had seen, they wore their hair long, bound with ribbons and beads into braids and tails. There was a likeness to them as they stood against the rock, as if they were all of a single family.

Orrin and Cariad approached. One of the women came forward to meet them, smiling, holding out her hands. Orrin took them; they embraced. The woman held him for a moment, tightly, and then pulled back. Cariad saw, from the way she looked at him, that she had been afraid. Orrin turned toward Cariad.

"My adoptive mother, Jorian," he said. "Leader of the Beechleaf clan. Jorian, this is . . ." His face changed a little. "I don't know your real name."

"Cariad," Cariad said.

Jorian studied her, not smiling now. She appeared to be about Goldwine's age, her braided hair silver, her skin webbed with fine lines. Her eyes were a strange milky gray, like ice above dark water, almost an exact match for the ash-colored garments she wore. She conveyed an impression of strength, and of extraordinary serenity. No . . . not serenity . . . blankness. Closure. With a shock, Cariad realized that she could not read Jorian's feeling at all. Once again the sense of dream swept over her. Only the Gifted were capable of shielding their emotions in this way. Jorian was Gifted.

"For my son's sake," Jorian said, "you're welcome among us." Still she did not smile, though her seriousness seemed watchful rather than unfriendly.

"Thank you."

Jorian turned and beckoned toward the group of waiting women. The authority in the gesture was unmistakable. Instantly one of them came forward.

"This is Beara. She'll see you have what you need."

"Thank you," Cariad hesitated. "I don't know . . . how much Orrin has told you. But it's dangerous for you, sheltering me. I won't stay longer than I need to."

Jorian watched her with icy eyes. "You know very little about us, young woman. You may know your own risk. But don't try to judge ours."

"I . . ." Cariad closed her mouth and nodded. "Yes."

Jorian's expression softened. "Don't worry, child." She reached out, and touched Cariad gently on the arm. "You'll be safe here."

She turned away, holding out her hand to Orrin. He took it, and she drew him with her toward the caves. Cariad watched them go, their heads bent together, talking. She felt, suddenly and utterly, bereft.

"Come," said Beara softly. "I'll get you some clothes, and then you can bathe."

Cariad looked at her. She was perhaps a little older than Cariad, tall and willowy, with gold-touched skin and amber-colored eyes. She was dressed in pale yellow. From a distance, Cariad had thought that she resembled Jorian, was perhaps Jorian's daughter. Close to, the physical likeness seemed much less. But her gaze was as serene and still as Jorian's had been—and she was just as blank. Another Gift, Cariad thought, bemused. Yet there was no feeling of power: no trace of the small, incorporeal vibration that usually marked the presence of Gift.

Beara led Cariad to a tent shaped like the top two-thirds of an egg laid on its side. Stooping, she pulled aside the door-flap and gestured Cariad through. Inside was a richness Cariad would not have expected. Wide carpets, woven in complex designs and jeweled colors, entirely hid the ground. Richly dyed blankets draped the four pallets arranged at the egg's wide end, and tapestry cushions heaped the walls elsewhere. Metal lamps hung from loops in the ceiling; no two were alike, some set with pebbled glass, some with translucent semiprecious stone. Even the curved rods that gave the tent its form were ornamented, carved to look like leafy vines.

Beara moved to a wooden chest and pulled out garments: a high-necked tunic of a shadow-lilac color, painted with purple designs at collar and cuffs and hem, and loose matching trousers. She piled them in Cariad's arms; they were perfumed, a light woodsy scent that made Cariad freshly aware of her own dirtiness. From another chest Beara took several pairs of cloth sandals, and, sitting Cariad down on one of the pallets, held the sandals against the soles of Cariad's bare feet until she found a pair that fit.

All this she accomplished with perfect, self-contained ease, as if fitting strangers with clothing was something she did every day.

She led the way again, back to the largest cave. From a wide mouth it widened still further, pushing back into the rock. Light came from hundreds of small translucent bowl-shaped lamps, wedged into niches and ledges, and from fires smoldering in several pits hollowed into the cave's floor. Evidently this was the transporters' kitchen: following in Beara's wake, Cariad glimpsed containers suspended on tripods, smelled meat and vegetables and bread, saw women and girls preparing food. They glanced up as she and Beara passed, serenely, briefly, barely pausing in their work.

Away from the fires it grew darker, though the lamps still starred the walls, and colder. At its back the cave closed in on itself, becoming a passageway little more than a double armslength wide. Here, water flowed down the rock into a depression in the floor, creating a shallow pool.

"The water's very cold," said Beara. "There's soap in the bucket, and towels over there. When you're done, come find me at the entrance, and I'll braid your hair."

She stooped to place the garments on the floor, and was gone. Eagerly, Cariad pulled off her transporter leathers and her filthy shift. She set her hands against the prison-collar, heavy at her neck, and applied her will. There was a crack. She pulled it off, split neatly into two pieces. Holding it before her, she applied her will again, releasing it from form, breaking it into its smallest elements and dispersing it on the air.

She stepped into the pool. The chill made her gasp. She cleansed herself, scrubbing savagely at the dirtiness of her body—the dirt of the cell where Jolyon had stolen the contents of her mind, the dirt of the downworld where she had worn another's form—as if she could abrade away the sense of these places she still felt upon her skin. She immersed herself in the freezing water until her limbs grew numb, until the cold seemed to reach in and touch her heart.

She pulled herself out at last and, dry and clothed, made her way between the lamp-constellations to the front of the cave, where Beara and three of the other women set to work on her hair, patiently teasing out the tangles and then dressing it in the transporter way: oiling the tresses, braiding and binding them with beads and ribbons. They consulted her as they worked, holding up bits of decoration for her approval; she acquiesced to everything they showed her, uncaring. Their quiet conversation drifted around her, their voices so similar she could barely tell where one left off and another continued. To her Gift they were more distinct—two as unguarded as any downworlder, and the third, like Beara, completely unreadable. How many Gifted were there here? Cariad was aware that she should feel more astonishment. But she was worn out with suffering and change, and she could no longer muster up the energy even for curiosity.

When the women were finished, they brought her a mirror made of beaten metal. The face she saw shocked her: hollow-cheeked, sunken-eyed, slack-skinned, enclosed like some awful jest in the alien complication of her ornamented hair. She put her hands to her mouth, her eyes welling, uncontrollably, with tears. The women, distressed, took the mirror away. Beara stooped and took Cariad's hand, and led her back to the egg-shaped tent. She wrapped Cariad in coverlets as if she were a child, and placed her cool palm on Cariad's forehead.

"Rest now," she said.

That evening, as the suns began to dim, Cariad and Orrin rode out on a transporter cart full of roughweave sacks of wheat. They had pulled on transporter leathers again; Orrin's hood was drawn up to hide his cropped hair and beardless chin, and Cariad had shifted her features to a different shape. Jolyon's servant would have discovered her absence, when he came to bring the second meal of the day. Jolyon might already be searching for her.

The carts ran all hours of the day and night; transporter men and women often rode along, to help load or unload. Cariad and Orrin's presence was not questioned at the warehouse complex just inside the caverns' entrance, where the carts were loaded, or at the inventory checkpoint, where the Journeyer supervisor and his assistants counted sacks, compared the number to the manifest and the manifest to a master order catalogue, validated the manifest with a large wax seal, and waved them out into the passageway.

At the entrance to the Fortress' rear perimeter tunnel, Cariad and Orrin dismounted. The cart moved to the right, headed for the Soldier Wing; they turned left, toward the Speaker Wing. Cariad set a swift pace. Rest and rescue had made her more rational than she had been in the white cell and just afterward; it seemed to her now quite likely that Goldwine, who had seen the possibility of her capture, had also seen the fact of it, and surmised much of what she had to tell. But she knew the elisions of Goldwine's Gift, and so she could not be sure.

She was uncomfortably aware of Orrin, marching silently at her side. He was as intensely focused on her as he had been earlier—a tangled nexus of emotion, of which desire was only the most immediate manifestation. The attraction she had felt during the time they spent together in the Keep had been nothing like this. It was as if some seed had taken root and flowered in her absence. She did not want to examine it too closely, or consider why the thought of reading the deeper convolutions of his feeling frightened her so much. She walked as far from him as the width of the tunnel would allow and wore the strongest guard she could call up.

"Orrin," she said, when she could not bear the tension any longer, "how do there come to be Gifts among the transporters?"

There was a pause. She felt him refocusing his attention. "They believe they're the descendants of a Guardian named Amergin, who designed the caverns and supervised the setting of their bindings. He fell in love with a transporter woman and had a child by her. The child was Gifted. When the Guardians came to take her away, Amergin tried to save her. He was killed, along with the child and the child's mother. But according to the transporters, it wasn't really Amergin's daughter who died. Amergin hid her and put a different child in her place. His child survived, and had children of her own. The Gift has been passed down ever since."

"Do you think that's true?"

"It could be. The Gift had to come from a Guardian originally."

"But even if it did, how could it survive? In other down-worlds, the Gifted children are found and put outside to die. Transporter children are tested for power, aren't they, like other downworlders?"

"Gifted children are withheld from testing. More than half the transporter population has never undergone a Guardian probe, or attended Guardian school."

Cariad looked at him, disbelieving. "How is that possible?"

Again he did not reply at once. This time, she read conflict in the pause. He wanted to answer her; she already knew much of the truth, after all. But it was a very deep secret he was about to reveal, and he had kept it for a long time. It was not easy for him to speak it aloud.

"I told you the transporters have a way of protecting themselves," he said at last. "They're able to maintain a kind of . . . cloud around themselves, something that prevents outsiders from seeing them too clearly. A binding, an illusion . . . I don't really understand it, though Jorian has tried to explain it to me. It's not hiding, exactly—more like deflecting. A constant redirecting of attention. It's something they do both individually and as a group. A transporter by herself clouds only herself, but all of them together do much more—make it so outsiders never see their Gifts or their use of them, so that the Guardians never look too closely at the number of children born in transporter camps, or notice that there are many more transporters than the names actually entered on the master census."

"Where did this cloud come from? How did they learn to make it?"

"The transporters say that Amergin left the secret of it with his little daughter, and she taught it to her children. Does it really matter? The cloud *is*. It exists. That's all."

"And in all these centuries the Guardians have never realized this?" Cariad still found it hard to believe. "They've never noticed that there's illicit power at work around them? The transporters have never made a mistake?"

"You won't notice the cloud either. It's invisible to human senses and the senses of power. It wouldn't be much good otherwise, would it? As for mistakes—I suppose if there were any, the cloud would hide them, or erase the memory of them. But the transporters don't make those kinds of mistakes. They don't oppose the Guardians, or steal from them, or work against them. They don't engage in illegal activities, or plan rebellions. They don't use the cloud to cover anything but the Gift itself. Except for that, they are perfect servants. They obey the Limits, they keep the law, they do their work. The Guardians ask nothing more of their downworlders."

It was a circle: the undetectable power, the unbroken deception. Cariad found it oddly discomforting to think of it, this huge deployment of collective will, unlike any binding or warding she had ever heard of. Yet if Goldwine, in the isolation of the mountains, could find her way to a different kind of power, why not the transporters, in a solitude born not just of the emptiness of the tunnels but of the Guardians' complacency—a certainty of unchallenged rule that ran so deep that they did not look beyond the fact of their unGifted servants' obedience?

"So you and I . . . we're inside the cloud?"

"Inside some part of it, yes. But you're an outsider. They never let outsiders all the way in. You won't see them as they really are, any more than I did when I first came to them."

"But you're not an outsider, surely."

He shook his head. "I'm as close to them as any outsider can be. But I wasn't born among them. That makes all the difference."

There was bitterness behind these words: old, accepted, but still carrying some of its original sharpness.

"How did you find out about the cloud, then?"

"Over time I learned to . . . I don't know, to see through it. It took years—it wasn't until after I'd begun working for your people that I began to notice things like the fact that their lamps never seem to need refilling, or to wonder why, when I'd been visiting Jorian's band since I was nine years old and knew every person in it, I still had no idea how many of them there really were. The cloud didn't just hide these things from me, you understand, it kept me from thinking about them. I'm still not sure why that changed. It does happen, sometimes, with outsiders who are allowed into the camps. That's why they're so careful about who they let cross over. Jorian tells me she always expected I'd see true someday."

He fell silent. She could feel the turning of his thoughts, darker than they had been and shadowed by a weary familiarity, as if these were paths trod too many times.

They reached the meeting point and set themselves to wait. After a time the recruiter shimmered into visibility a little distance away, startling them both. She was dressed in the bodice and skirt of a Speaker servant, with a cloth tied around her mouth and nose to disguise her features. Cariad relayed the information she needed to convey, using voicespeech partly for Orrin's benefit, but also because she did not think she could yet bear another's presence inside her mind. She had known it would be difficult, and it was. Her guilt seemed to compound itself as she spoke, until she could hardly bear to look into the recruiter's face. She held back only the shameful purpose that had led her to Jolyon; the recruiter did not need to know it in order to understand the rest.

"What you've told me is unexpected only in the details," the recruiter said when Cariad was done. "Orrin told me you were missing the day after you disappeared. One of the others here is a farspeaker, and we sent the news to headquarters. We were told to assume the worst."

Cariad breathed deeply; it was, after all, as she had hoped. "What happens now? Will you be pulling out?"

"We've left the downworlds. Our operations have been shut down, and the servant intelligencers have been memory-killed. But we haven't been withdrawn from the Fortress. All of us are solo now, aboveground mostly—the stables in the Great Court, the pilgrim hostels. We've been told to wait."

"Wait? For what?"

"For instructions." Her gaze shifted to Orrin. "You're the last of the intelligencers. I might as well take care of your memory now. Then you can return to your own down-world."

Color ran up all through the translucent paleness of Or-rin's face. Cariad felt his anger, his bitter humiliation. In-stinctively she stepped in front of him, shielding him with her body.

"He'll be killed if he goes back. Jolyon saw him in my mind. He can stay with me. I'll take responsibility for him."

The recruiter's eyes, a startling shade of blue above the cloth that concealed her nose and chin, narrowed. Cariad could feel her considering, drawing conclusions that were not the truth yet still encompassed an uncomfortable mea-sure of accuracy. Though she had kept her voice neutral, she had not, over the course of this interview, troubled to hide her opinion of Cariad and her survival. The white cell's wardings against self-injury were no excuse; she should have had her poison capsule under her tongue when she went to Jolyon, and bitten it even as she was struck down.

"If you like," the recruiter said at last. "But there still has to be a memory-kill."

"I'll deal with that."

The recruiter shrugged. "Very well. I'll relay what you've told me to headquarters. Come back here tomorrow night and I'll tell you what I hear."

Cariad nodded. The recruiter turned, without farewell, and vanished.

Cariad and Orrin began the journey back to the caverns. The agricultural workers would think it odd to see them returning on foot when they had gone out by cart, but in this, as in most other things, transporters enjoyed a greater degree of latitude than other downworlders. They walked in silence. The urgent energy that had buoyed Cariad earlier was gone. She was aware, though she did not want to be, of the tumult of Orrin's feelings—a very different turmoil than that of the journey out.

When they reached the cavern passageway, he spoke.

"Would you really perform a memory-kill on me?"

"No, Orrin," she said, wearily. "I never would."

He gripped her shoulder and pulled her around to face him. They stood an arm's length apart, eye to eye, as they had on the first night they had ever seen each other.

"But you could, couldn't you?" The agitation in him, the anger, seemed to go beyond this moment, beyond the recruiter's harsh order, beyond even her own intentions. "You could empty my mind as easily as pouring water out of a flask."

"I would never turn my Gift on you, Orrin," she repeated. "How could I repay you that way, after all the risks you've taken for me?"

He flushed. "I don't want you to *repay* me. I don't need you to rescue me either. I could have dealt with the recruiter."

"I doubt that."

"I survived my whole life beneath the eye of the Arm of the Stone." His voice was brittle with anger. "I kept secrets as dangerous as any of yours. But still you people think I can't manage to take a breath by myself. Well, I'm not something to be *dealt with.* I'm not someone you need to *take responsibility for.* I'm not your underling, do you understand? I'm not your charge."

"Orrin . . ." She heard the exhaustion in her voice. "That wasn't what I meant. I was trying to help you. That's all."

For a moment he watched her. His anger, suddenly, had gone.

"You were never like the others," he said. "I suppose that's why . . ." He pressed his lips together. "But it doesn't matter. We're too different, you and I. Face-to-face, hand-to-hand, I'd always lose. That's the long and the short of it, isn't it? That's all there is to know between you and me."

Cariad stared at him, transfixed—not by the bitterness of the words, but by the truth that moved beneath them: the whole truth of his feeling for her, revealed in disillusion as it had not been earlier, in hope. For a long moment, deliberately, he matched her gaze. Then he turned and walked on. After a pause, she followed.

They passed the checkpoint without incident. At the transporter camp he left her without a backward glance, heading for the caves, where fires still flickered against the darkness. Cariad made her way to Beara's tent, and fumbled through the dim light of the single lamp to the pallet that had been given her until Beara's husband returned from his current tour of hauling duty. Beara and her children were already asleep, their breathing a small quietness upon the greater quiet of the night. Cariad pulled the covers up, and lay staring at the tent's shadowed ceiling. She was not aware of weeping. But when she turned her cheek on the pillow, she found that it was wet with tears.

Eighteen

HE NEXT night Cariad returned to the tunnels beyond the Speaker Wing, alone this time. The recruiter, still masked, informed her that, rather than wait for the Guardians to come to them, Goldwine and her forces were preparing an assault on the Fortress. Cariad could hardly believe it.

"It's suicide!" Once again she had insisted on using spoken words; her voice, too loud, echoed in the tunnels. "They'll be destroyed!"

"What would you have the Commander do? Be destroyed in place? Break up the resistance and go into hiding? Give up the cause and fade away, after so many lives, so many years of struggle? At least this way we'll take some Guardians with us."

The recruiter's feelings had been clear from the start, but until now she had not allowed them to inform her voice. Cariad felt as if she had been struck. A week ago she would have let anger rule her and replied in kind. But consciousness of her fault deprived her of either rage or response. Anyway, the woman was right.

"Has the time for the assault been set?"

"No. They won't let us know until just before."

"And the plans? The form of it?"

"All we know is that we're to open the outside doors down here. We won't be told more than that till it happens."

"Well, when you find out, I want to be informed."

The recruiter nodded. "I know where you are. I'll come to you." She began to turn away.

"Wait. Don't you have orders for me?"

The recruiter paused. "No."

"A message, then. A message from my mother?"

"There's no message."

"But there must be. She must have sent word."

"Do you believe me to be lying?" Above her concealing mask, the recruiter's eyes were like blue pebbles.

"No. No, of course not."

"Good." Again she turned, fading from sight as she did.

Cariad made her way back to the night-dimmed caverns. She did not go to the transporters' camp, but wandered alone through the ancient forest at the cavern's edge. She had endured a great deal over the past days, suffered in ways she would not, before her capture, have been able to imagine. But she knew now, with the solidity of despair, that none of it was as terrible as Goldwine's silence. She had known Goldwine must be angry at what she had done. Punishments, censures, condemnations—she had expected these, would have welcomed them, for they were contact, and contact offered the hope of reconciliation. But silence . . . silence offered nothing. What could it mean, except that Goldwine—like the recruiter, like any member of the resistance who knew of her act of betrayal—had repudiated her, abandoned her to the changed future her disastrous choice had made?

Throughout Cariad's life, the unconditionality of Goldwine's love had been a fact of existence, as assumed and unchanging as the stars. She had not seriously believed, before this moment, that there was anything Goldwine would not forgive her. Moving now in the nighttime shadow between the trees, she felt she stumbled through a much deeper darkness, an exile from all she knew and had thought she understood.

When the suns began to brighten with the coming day, she returned to camp and took up the work that Beara, her caretaker, had assigned her. Beara had made it clear that Cariad must contribute to the community that had given her refuge. Cariad did not have domestic skills, and so she could not assist with the spinning, or work at the small, collapsible looms the transporters used; she was not artistic, and so she could not paint fabric or decorate leathers; she was an outsider, and so she was not trusted to care for the children. But she could peel vegetables and stir stews and wash plates. And so she was set to work in the kitchen cave.

The women and girls who labored there showed her what to do. They were patient with her; they did not chide her when she cut vegetables too thick, or pressed flatbread too thin. They made attempts, at first, to include her in their talk, but when they saw she would not respond, they were equally willing to leave her alone. She did not care one way or the other. She had little interest in what happened outside her. Her body was free, but her mind was still prisoned, trapped in the grinding cycle of memory and recrimination that had seized her in the white cell after Jolyon left her.

Time had worked some change in the quality of her contemplation. She no longer experienced any shock of disbelief, any hot rush of anger, when she thought of the coming destruction—only a kind of leaden certainty, like a fatal illness lived with for a long time. The condemnation she lavished upon herself had lost its involuntary panicked edge; it was willed and deliberate now, like biting down on an abscessed tooth. And, as the pain of infection will spread beyond the jaw and across the neck and shoulders, so her vision of fault had compounded and expanded, until it encompassed not just what she had done in the Fortress, not just the intent she had formed in the mountains, but the full course of her life.

She saw now that the understanding most central to her being, the thing upon which, from childhood, she had based all her actions, was false. Out of the prophecy of her father's return, she had spun a web of expectation and assumption the prophecy did not support. Because the prophecy decreed that she must live to meet him, she had assumed she must live unaltered. Because it guaranteed her physical survival, she had assumed she must survive unharmed. Because it was immutable, because Goldwine had always told her it could not be altered by the shifts and vagaries of human choice, she had believed that she could do anything, and none of it would change.

Goldwine, who knew her as no one else in the world did, had seen her folly. *No prophecy can protect you in that way,* she had said, in the mountains just after Cariad returned. But Cariad had never more than half-listened to her foster-mother's warnings, and she had not heeded this one at all. In that single fact lay the whole truth of her being. All her life she had looked at the world and seen only the veil of her own understandings. She had listened to the words others spoke and heard only what was inside her own mind. Even when she followed orders, she had not truly obeyed—for she had never understood the necessity of fear, and therefore never grasped the utility of caution. She had gone to Jolyon, bearing like a gift the precious contents of her mind. He had made her helpless and taken them by force. But the truth was that she had given them to him. That was the real measure of her betrayal.

It was new to her, this lacerating pursuit of inner knowledge. She had never been particularly self-reflective. She had been raised in great love and great certainty, and her place in the world and her purpose there had always been clear to her. But her capture had drawn a fault-line across her life. The self she had been, the life that self had shaped, seemed like a bright shore glimpsed from a dark vantage point, hallucinatory in its contrast to the place where she now stood. She grieved for its loss. She mourned the time when she had not been able to imagine defeat, when betrayal had been inconceivable and the world never touched her unless she willed it.

She thought often of Jolyon, and of the white cell. There was a terrible absoluteness to these memories; they claimed her so fully that for instants at a time the world around her vanished and she was a prisoner again, able actually to feel the weight of the collar about her neck, to sense in her bones the vibration of the pearly bindings. Sometimes the images came capriciously, without warning. Sometimes there was a spur—a length of white fabric spread out on the ground to dry, a flash of red from the glass of a tent lantern, a shadow that resembled the fall of black brocade.

The press of an incipient headache or the momentary dizziness of getting up too quickly returned her in an instant to the mindprobe, forcing her to live that invasion over again, the whole horror of it compressed into the space of a few seconds.

When she slept, dreams took her—terrible dreams, in which she struggled and cried out, from which she woke gasping and sweating, her face wet with tears. She dreamed of Jolyon, hovering over her, his green eyes devouring hers, his hands cupping the air beside her face. She dreamed of Fortress servants probed for illicit knowledge, of squads of Reddened dispatched to the cities where the handpower networks hid, of artificial Gates crashing into being inside the hollow mountain and disgorging troops of Soldiers. She dreamed of Goldwine, tormented on the rack or burned with irons or flayed alive. She dreamed of her father, faceless and broken in the Garden of the Stone. Jolyon had seemed to reject the possibility of his return. Yet what chance was there that Jolyon would not be waiting when he arrived?

Sometimes she dreamed images she did not recognize— of a leather leash around her neck, of a tiny room without a window, of wrenching loneliness and a hunger big enough to eat the world. Of savage beatings, meant to kill the hunger; of icy immersions and bitter drinks meant to cure it. Of the times when the hunger could not be contained, and devoured all it could, then vomited back hideous destruction. In these dreams she was not herself but a bewildered child, not quite certain who she was, struggling always to remember. She understood at last that these were not her dreams at all, but the dreams of Jolyon's servant. Somehow, in the taking of her Gift, he had passed them to her.

Often, just before she woke, she heard the voice again— the voice that had cried out, in memory and in pain, from the depths of the abyss. It had given her words: three of them. She could feel that they were precious. But like the child in the dream, she could not remember what they meant.

* * *

In the time following Cariad's disappearance, Jolyon turned the Fortress upside down in search of her. He combed the Keep; he proceeded through the Suborder Wings room by room; he ransacked the downworlds; he hunted the tunnels from one end to the other. According to the story he put out, a dangerous Gifted mercenary brought in for interrogation had been rescued by others of her kind, who slipped into the Fortress disguised as pilgrims. They might or might not still be in the Fortress. They might or might not have a downworld collaborator with them.

The search came to the caverns two days after Cariad's escape, in the form of a hundred Soldiers accompanied by ten Reddened Roundheads. Splitting into ten groups, they spent three days canvassing the caverns, searching huts and dwellings and warehouses and transporter encampments, conducting probes as they went. Cariad, by Beara's order deep inside the kitchen cave, did not see the group that approached her encampment, moving through the trees as far as the tents and halting there, their faces growing blank and strange. After a moment they turned and departed, not looking back. The women who had been working outside the cave described the incident later to those inside, laughing, imitating the stiff, puppetlike movements of the Guardians as they walked away.

The transporters did not say it, but Cariad knew: it was the cloud that had turned the Guardians around and caused them to depart. Since her arrival she had tried to see through it, in spite of Orrin's warning that she would not succeed. But as often as she set her mind to watch for the practice of Gifts, her attention slipped away; and though she counted the children in the morning as they headed off to the Guardian school the cavern's Journeyers maintained in the agricultural village, only moments after they departed she found herself unable to recall how many there had been. Daily, she woke intending to visit the crèche cave, to see how many children stayed behind; but either she forgot what she saw there, or else forgot the intent itself, and each morning the crèche cave seemed as much a mystery as the day before. She was able to identify the Gifted, by the blankness of the shielding they employed, though she could not sense the Gifts behind the barriers. Had it not been for her own rare Gift, she would not have known even this much.

She had not truly believed Orrin when he said it would be so. She was surprised, and a little angry, to find herself so blind. Yet there were things she could perceive, mundane defenses that extended beyond the cloud and ensured a different kind of blindness. The transporter mode of dress, for instance, so limited in style that one often could not tell, from the back or at a distance, whether an individual was young or old, male or female. The braided hair they all wore, and the wild face-concealing beards of the men. The enveloping painted leathers, which evoked an instant recognition that was also a form of dismissal. Gesture, intonation, and stance, so similar from person to person that watching a group of transporters was like watching an endless, interlocking set of echoes. It was this that Cariad, on arrival, had mistaken for family likeness. Yet though each transporter band comprised a single clan, clan marriage was exogamous, and transporter bloodlines were thoroughly mixed. It was will, not breeding, that conferred the likeness, a directed force far more powerful than the random choices of heredity.

A little over a week after Cariad's arrival, a feast of Exchange was held. Transporter bands made a slow circuit of the periphery of the caverns, moving from established campsite to established campsite, where the glittering cave-lamps, the cookfire enclosures, the bathing pools, and the pit latrines stood always ready. Because the caverns were so large, at any given time a band might be eight miles or more from the warehouses at the caverns' entrance, where goods to be transported were gathered and loaded. It was not practical, therefore, for haulers to return home at night and go out again in the morning. A duty camp was set up near the warehouses; haulers lived there for a month, then returned to their home bands while a new shift rotated out. For each cycle of return and departure there was a celebration: the feast of Exchange.

The Exchange was held in the largest of the caves, usually given over to the use of the men in residence. The little bowl-lamps studded the walls from floor to ceiling, forming a mantle of shimmering light. The transporters sat in loose family groupings; the cooks and some of the older children moved between them with serving platters, bending to offer food and then moving on again. The air was murmurous with talk and the soft sound of laughter. The transporters were not a grave people—though, deliberate as they were in speech and manner, it had taken Cariad a little time to realize that. A vein of mockery, a glint of scorn, lay behind much of what they said and did, as well it should, given the thousand-year trick they had played on their masters.

Cariad sat at the edge of the gathering, with a plate of food and a cup of wine. Transporter use-objects were exuberantly individualistic, a constant, practical contradiction to the conformity they imposed on themselves in dress and manner. Her wooden plate was painted with a design of flowering vines, her spoon was shaped to look like an apple bough in blossom, with a concave apple for its bowl, and her stone cup was etched with a design of leaves, carved so thin that the red of the wine glowed through it. The food was beautiful also, in color and taste and texture. But the heat of the kitchen, where she had spent most of the evening, and her constant melancholy, robbed her of appetite. She stared out over the crowd, thinking dark thoughts.

A hand descended on her shoulder. Startled, she looked up, into the face of a woman with dark hair and Jorian's icy eyes: Sosia, Jorian's youngest daughter.

"No one should sit alone at an Exchange." Sosia smiled, with the quiet serenity all the transporters seemed to share. "My mother would like you to join us."

Reluctantly, for she did not much wish to be in company, Cariad rose and followed Sosia over to the raised spur of stone on which Jorian and her extended family were gathered. Her husband was one of the men Exchanging in: she and he sat close together, sharing a plate. Others clustered around these two, siblings and children and grandchildren and those who had married into the family—and Orrin. He had glanced toward her when she entered the cave and not again since then.

They shifted, making room for Cariad, a shuffling of position that deposited her next to Jorian. She nodded at their greetings, silently, because she did not want to misidentify anyone. Even after more than a week among them she had difficulty telling one transporter from another. She was not certain whether it was the effect of the cloud or simply her own unfamiliarity.

Across from her, Orrin was deep in conversation with a young man nearly as fair as himself. He alone had not acknowledged her as she sat down. Feeling flared in her, complicated and painful. On the night they had visited the recruiter, she had wanted to flee from him and the suffocation of his desire. Yet since then it was he who had separated himself from her—leaving places if she entered them, moving away if she approached. Perversely, she was angry at him for this.

Jorian looked toward her from the enclosure of her husband's arms and smiled. Cariad had had little contact with Jorian since her arrival, though she was often aware that the other woman observed her, with the same watchful gravity she had shown at their first meeting. But now she did not seem grave at all, or watchful either. Impulsively, Cariad leaned forward.

"I want you to know how grateful I am for the shelter you've given me."

"It's a small enough thing. One among so many." Jorian gestured outward, toward the gathering.

"Not small at all. Guardian patrols came here because of me."

Jorian shook her head. Behind her, her bearded husband watched—a big man, strong and still, his small dark eyes at rest on Cariad's face. "You owe us no debt, child. Your safety is a gift to my son—" she glanced toward Orrin, a look of great affection "—who asked me for it."

Perhaps, Cariad thought. Yet even so a debt was owed. It occurred to her, suddenly, that there was something she could give these people. Orrin's recruiter would not approve, but she was as certain as she could be of anything that the transporters would guard any confidences they received.

"I have some information," she said. "My people are

planning an attack on the Fortress. I don't know how successful they'll be . . ." She paused, not wanting to lose control of her voice. "But it's certain there will be fighting in the Fortress soon. You should be ready."

Jorian nodded, tranquilly, as if Cariad had told her that the fresh-dyed cloth laid out to dry in the cave next door was ready to be folded and put away. "Thank you," she said.

Perhaps, Cariad thought, she not been clear enough. "There are operatives in the Fortress who will open the outside doors. There'll be fighting in the tunnels. It may very well reach the caverns."

Jorian looked at her and said with calm certainty: "It won't come to us."

"You can't know that for certain." Cariad was aware, suddenly, that the talk had stopped. They were all listening, even Orrin. "There won't be any guarantees, once the fighting starts. I know you can prevent the Guardians from seeing you clearly. But even the cloud—"

There was a sound from the others, a shocked collective indrawn breath. Cariad stopped short. Jorian's face was suddenly set. Above her head, her husband's eyes were hard.

"You know something about us now," Jorian said. Her voice was quiet, but very clear. "We've allowed that, for my son's sake. What you know is very far from the whole. But this one thing I'll tell you. The world above the ground, the Fortress and everything outside it, belongs to the Guardians. But the world below the ground—this world, the caverns and the tunnels—belongs to us. It is ours by right: we are its inheritors. We hold the bindings here. We keep the tunnels open inside the rock that desires, always, to be closed again. We draw the boundaries of our world every day, through our travels and our carts. We make it new with every passing moment, hold it and protect it and keep it real. Outside conflicts have never threatened that. They never will."

Silence. The faces of Jorian's family—not fish-pale like the faces of other downworlders, but touched with color by the false sunlight of their underground world—made a circle around Cariad. They enclosed her in their gaze—unified, identical. And yet they seemed more physically distinct, suddenly, than they ever been, alive with an individuality and a difference she had not seen before—Jorian too, her face sharper, her mouth harder, her eyes like molten silver. There was a heaviness in the air, like the charged feeling of an approaching storm; there was a smell of lightning, and, beneath the voices of the crowd, the roll of distant thunder. Cariad felt a pressure—against her skin, inside her head—as if, somewhere, some vast force were pushing outward, straining the barrier between the seen and the unseen world. The scene before her flattened, grew pale and thin like a painted curtain. For a moment she could see, behind it, the shadow of something larger: a bigger cave, a greater gathering, a brighter light, filling all the spaces of the rock and pouring like a river into the night—

Fear clutched her, like an arrow to the heart. She gasped. That quickly it was gone—all of it, completely.

"I thank you for your warning," Jorian said. Her face was smooth again, her eyes merely gray. "It was kindly meant, and we receive it as it was given."

As if it were a signal, her family turned away and resumed their interrupted conversations. Cariad put her hand to her forehead, disoriented and a little sick. Had she imagined it, that strange instant of clarity? She was seized, abruptly and overwhelmingly, with the desire to escape.

"I'm sorry," she said to Jorian. "I'm not . . . feeling very well. Please excuse me."

Jorian nodded gracefully. Cariad got to her feet and made her way, stumbling a little, through the crowd and out of the cave, where she stood for a little while, taking deep breaths, until the dizziness receded.

Unwilling either to return to the cave or to seek Beara's tent, she began to wander through the trees. The ground was wet with the rain that fell in the hour after sundim. She passed the portable animal pens, where the transporters kept their small herds of swine and goats, and the area where carts brought in for repair or repainting lay upturned. She walked until she came to the forest's edge. There she paused a moment, for the trees marked the limit of the

cloud's ability to conceal her. But it was night, and even
Guardians were abed by now.

She struck off across the fields. The wheat billowed
around her, a sea of heavy stalks higher than her waist,
silvery in the dimness of the suns. The dimlight of the caverns was brighter than true moonlight, but similar enough
so that, if she did not look up, she could imagine herself
in the world above the ground, on a night when the moon
was full.

Halfway across, she became aware, belatedly, of a presence at her back. She turned. Her pursuer was more distant
than she had thought, just emerging from the trees: Orrin.
She recognized him by his walk, and by his blond hair—
but also by her sense of him, a perception that should not
have been possible across the distance that divided them.
She felt an odd constriction of her chest. She could not, for
an instant, decide whether to stand or flee.

He came up to her and halted. He said nothing, but she
could feel him, as clear as words, despite his wish to hold
himself in check, and she knew that things had not changed
since the last time they were together. Her heartbeat quick-
ened. Again she was seized with the impulse to flee. Again
she did not.

"Did I make trouble for you?" she asked, to break the
growing tension of their silence. "Was I not supposed to
know about the cloud?"

He shook his head. "Jorian knew I told you. It's just that
it isn't spoken of. I should have warned you."

"How much of what she said is true? About the bindings,
and the tunnels?"

"This place is a work of power, greater than any that
exists above the ground. Bindings don't last forever, any
more than buildings do. Something must maintain them and
preserve them."

"You believe them, then."

He shrugged, wordless. She shivered, chilly now. The
wheat was heavy with moisture, and her clothing was
soaked through.

"I saw something," she said. "I'm not sure. . . . It
was . . ." But even if she could have found a way to put

that strange sensation into words, he would not understand her. He might have learned to see through the cloud, but he was unGifted and could never feel its power.

Silence fell again, like a living thing between them. After a moment she turned and walked on. He followed, moving in her tracks, treading on the wheat she had pressed down. There was a dreamlike quality to their progress, single file and silent through the silver night, the only moving creatures in a sleeping world. She felt the struggle in him, a mirror of her own. He had not intended to follow her, either out of the cave or across the fields. A large part of him desired to turn and leave her. But he could not tear himself away.

They reached the orchards and passed into one of the wide alleys that ran between the rows of trees. There was room now to walk side by side.

"How have you been?" he asked, after they had gone a little distance.

"Well enough."

"Jorian tells me that Beara says you wake her at night with your dreaming."

She did not look at him. "I'm sorry I've disturbed Beara's sleep."

"That's not the point. Beara says you cry out in your sleep, that you struggle. That you weep. She says she can see the dreams in your face even when you're awake."

"Why should she care?" Cariad was suddenly angry. "And why should you? My dreams are my own business."

"Cariad." He put out his hand as if to catch her arm but did not complete the gesture. Again she felt his conflict: the knowledge that he should leave, his helplessness to go. "What do you dream about that makes you suffer so?"

She shook her head. "It doesn't matter."

"Yes, it does. What really happened to you in that cell? What did he really do to you?"

They were standing still now. Still she did not look at him. "I told you. He mindprobed me."

"Only that?"

"*Only* that?" She whipped her head around. "He opened me up like an oyster. He saw everything inside me, every memory, every secret, every understanding. I couldn't fight, I couldn't escape . . . all I could do was watch as he took it all away, all the things I was trusted to keep safe, all the things I never told another person. . . . Nothing, nothing has ever violated me so. And you say . . . *only* that—"

Her voice broke. She pressed her hands against her mouth; she had not meant to say so much. Tears burned behind her eyes. She had never been a weeper; even when Jolyon took her secrets she had not wept. But in the past week it seemed to her that she had been weeping constantly, more tears than in all her life before.

Orrin reached out to her again, and this time he did touch her, setting his hand lightly on her arm.

"I'm sorry," he said. "I was mindprobed when I was a child, for the branding. But it was nothing like that."

She shook her head. "It doesn't matter what he did to me. It's what he'll do to the resistances, to the networks, to the people I've lived and fought with all my life . . . to . . . to my mother . . ." She stopped; it was too terrible to speak. "Thousands of people, years of work. All gone. Because of me."

"But didn't you tell me that the thief of the Stone will return soon to bring the Guardians down? Perhaps the Second won't get a chance to hunt your people."

"But Orrin, Jolyon saw in my mind that the thief will be returning. He'll be waiting for him when he does, with that servant of his. He'll tell the servant to take the thief's Gift, his *own power*, and turn it back against him. He'll have everything then. The Stone, the Order, the world. He'll have his whole lifetime to hunt us down."

"It may not happen that way. If the thief's Gift is as great as you say, perhaps it'll be more than the servant can hold. And the Stone . . . surely the man who holds the Stone won't be overcome so easily."

"You didn't feel that abyss, Orrin. There wasn't any end to it. The whole of my power was just a spark in its darkness. Being bound by your own power, feeling it twist to someone else's will . . . it's not like being held by another's Gift. It's like . . . like setting yourself on fire. Like tearing off your own limbs. It's the horror of it that holds you, as much as anything else." She shuddered, remembering. "No. The thief will return . . . that I believe. But everything else has changed. Everything."

"Cariad, you can't blame yourself for this. Your people knew the risk when they sent you in. If you'd had the right intelligence, you'd have succeeded."

"That means nothing, Orrin. Jolyon captured me. I should have killed myself before I let him take what was in my mind."

"How could you, alone and chained and almost naked in that cell? It isn't your fault, Cariad. Or at any rate, not yours alone. You were following orders. You were doing what you were told to do."

"But I *wasn't* following orders. I *wasn't* doing what I was told to do. Oh—" She turned from him, moving randomly away between the trees. "You don't understand. You don't know."

"Tell me, then."

She stopped, looked back. The dimlight sifted through the trees to lie in pools and patches on the ground: he stood in one of these, his face fully lit, his blond hair turned to silver.

"Tell me," he repeated.

If anyone had said to Cariad, even half an hour ago, that there would come a point when she would need or want to confess to another person the guilt that followed her by day and tormented her by night, she would have turned away in astonishment and contempt. Pain was for hiding, not for sharing; this was how she had lived her life since she had left the mountains. Yet now she sensed Orrin's feeling, reaching out to her as it had before; this time, instead of spurring her to flight, it drew her, like a light glimpsed at the center of a trackless wood. She sank down where she was, on the damp grass at the base of an apple tree.

"Before I was born," she said, "my father met my foster-mother on the snow . . ."

And she gave him, haltingly at first, but then with growing fluency, what he had asked for: the Tale, her heritage, the childhood genesis of her intent, its reawakening in the mountains. She spared herself nothing, not even her misinterpretation of Goldwine's prophecy. As she spoke, she felt something within her loosen, a release like the physical lightening she had experienced when she removed the collar from her neck. Her guilt was no less, nor her awareness of her fault. Yet she would not have believed, moments ago, how much relief there could be in speaking it aloud.

"So now you see," she said when she was done. "It *is* my blame. Mine alone."

For a moment he was silent. He had sat down beside her as she spoke. His eyes were on the ground; shadow and dimlight lay together there, like a map of another world painted in bright and dark. He had not once interrupted her, though she had felt questions in him, and astonishment.

"I see that you acted out of will," he said at last, slowly. "And perhaps out of arrogance. And recklessly. But not alone."

"What do you mean? It was my desire. It was my intent."

"You didn't make the purpose you followed. It was given to you, when you were a child. How could you grow up, hearing that story over and over, and not want to do what you did?"

"Orrin . . . I don't want you to excuse me. That's not why I told you all of this."

He shook his head. "I'm not excusing you. You acted wrongly. But it was an error of judgment, not a deliberately worked evil."

"What's the difference? The consequences are the same."

"The difference is what you make of it. The difference is how you blame yourself."

"You don't understand, Orrin. I didn't just want a death, Jolyon's death. I wanted . . . I wanted death itself." She stopped, took a breath. "In my last posting, my companions and I captured a Roundhead. We interrogated him. We found out that he was one of Jolyon's aides. Afterward I killed him, because you can't trust a memory-kill to work on a Roundhead. I've killed more than twenty men . . . not because I wanted to, but because I was ordered to, because it was necessary. But this death, Baldric's death . . . I wanted that. I wanted it because he belonged to Jolyon. I gave him pain before he died. And . . . I took pleasure in it." She closed her eyes. This truth, which she had denied to herself for so long, seemed in many ways the worst part of her confession. "I wanted to experience that again, with Jolyon. I wanted to give him the death I gave Baldric. I wanted to feel myself killing him." She put her hands to her cheeks. The tips of her fingers burned. She saw Jolyon in her mind's eye: his pale face, his green gaze. She gasped. "I still want it. After everything that's happened, after everything I've realized. . . . and I'm afraid . . . I'm afraid that's what brought me to do it. Not the Tale or my mother and father, not revenge or retribution, but the desire for death. After all the years I spent teaching myself not to feel it, not to fear it, not to want it . . . after all the years I spent in balance . . . I never thought this could happen. I'm afraid of what I've become."

Orrin watched her. His eyes glinted in his shadowed face. "If you can fear it, then you haven't become it yet."

She turned away. The brief relief of speaking was entirely gone. Pain drew tight within her again, a feeling that in the past days had become as familiar as her own skin. "I'm so tired, Orrin. I think about him all the time. *All the time.* Wherever I turn inside my mind, he's there. It's as if he never left. How long can it go on like this? When will it stop?"

"Cariad . . ." Orrin hesitated. "Cariad, has it occurred to you that maybe all of this—your capture, your interrogation—is the way it was meant to be?"

"No." She shook her head. "The way it was meant to be was what it was before I betrayed my people."

"But it's your mother who told you that story. It's your mother who taught you to hate the Second, from the time you were a child. How could she send you to the Fortress and not know what you'd do there? If she didn't want you to do it, why didn't she forbid you? Or warn you?"

"It doesn't work that way, Orrin. The future isn't fixed. There are many outcomes. Which one becomes real depends on people's choices. This—to do what I did—was my choice. My mother must have seen it. She sees all the possibilities. And she did warn me, in a way—but she couldn't tell me what to do. She can't interfere. Who knows what that might change?"

"I don't know," he said. "It seems to me that just knowing is a kind of interference. Because then it's her choice also, isn't it? To act or not to act? Anyway, if it's true that your . . ." He had to pause before he could say it. ". . . your father's return can't be altered, no matter what the choices are, isn't it also possible that all choices are subordinate to that? That anything you do, any choice you made or will make, will find a way to lead to the same moment? And if the moment is the same, how can the consequences not be the same also?"

Cariad said nothing. She had tried to tell herself this, or something like it, in the white cell after she failed to kill herself. Now, as then, she could not bring herself to believe it.

Her eyes were bent upon the ground, on the shadowy patterns of the grass. But she could feel him watching her. She sensed his emotion, subordinated for a time to what she had told him, rising up again to fill the silence. Something in it had changed. The resistance was gone, the holding back.

"You're further beyond me even than I knew," he said, softly. "Not just Gifted, not just highly placed within the resistance, but the foster-daughter of the resistance's commander. The daughter . . . the daughter of a legend."

She felt her heartbeat at her throat, in her temples. She knew what was coming, but was powerless to move away from it. She did not even know if she still wanted to.

"I don't care anymore," he said. "If what you've said is true and it's all about to end, what difference does it make who and what we are?" He was edging toward her now, slowly, like a man approaching a cornered animal. "You know what I feel for you, Cariad. There's nothing I can hide from you. Let me be with you. Let me be with you for a little while."

He reached out and touched her shoulder. She felt the heat of that contact in every part of her body. Unresisting, she let him turn her, let him encircle her with his arms and set his lips on hers, a touch so gentle it might have been a

dream. She felt his warmth, his breath, the accelerating
rhythm of his pulse. Desire rose in her, powerful and terrifying. She gasped and pulled away.

"Orrin—"

He placed a finger on her lips. "Ssssh."

He drew her back against him and kissed her again. Cariad felt something give way inside her. Perhaps it was the
need for comfort. Perhaps it was the wish for oblivion.
Perhaps she was simply tired of resisting. She did not
know; she no longer cared. She slid her arms around him
and opened her mouth to his.

They sank to the damp ground, pulling at each other's
clothing. He smelled of smoke and sweat and leather; he
trembled as he touched her, his heart beating like a run-
ner's. She felt the urgency of his desire, his need to lose
himself in her. Yet he held back, as if he were afraid of
what might happen if he let go—a gentleness on the outer
edge of discipline, a tenderness with violence behind it. It
was she, at last, who pulled his body down on hers. He
groaned, a sound like a man in torment, and gripped her so
convulsively she cried out. Her heartsenser's barriers, the
defense of long practice, rocked under the assault of his
feeling, pulling inward toward her core. The rush of physical sensation was like nothing she had ever known. She
could no longer find the boundaries of her body. His flesh
in hers, hers enclosing his; the wet grass beneath her back,
the chilly air on his; the spinning pattern of leaves and
dimlight overhead, the reeling mosaic of brightness and
shadow below. They were the same. A single rhythm. A
single flow.

At some point during the night he pulled away from her.
Feeling and sensation spun out between them, a chord that
could not fall silent, a thread that could not break. His face
was pale in the shadow beneath the trees, his eyes so dilated
they were almost black.

"I love you," he whispered.

She drew him down again and stopped his mouth with
hers. But the words were still there. His body spoke them,

and his mind. They sounded in the harshness of his breath, the drumming of his blood. She tasted them in his mouth, in the sweat that slicked his face and neck and back. And though she tried, she could not close them out.

Nineteen

HEY LAY in the shadow of the apple trees, on a pile of blankets they had brought with them. Cariad reclined on her back, her arm behind her head; Orrin leaned over her, resting on his elbow. Gently he caressed her, tracing the contours of cheek and jaw and throat, the curves of shoulder and breast and belly. She lay like a cat under his hands, her eyes closed, half-dozing. They had made love not long before, but she could feel his unslaked desire for her; she could feel his love for her also, like perfume in the dimlit night.

They had returned here on each of the eight nights that had passed since they first lay down together. There was an urgency to these dark hours: both of them knew their sojourn in the caverns was time out of time, that the reality of the outside world must eventually reclaim them. In Orrin this produced a kind of desperation. He drew her to him again and again, compulsively, as if each time might be the last. In Cariad it produced a sense of freedom. Other lovers had suffocated her with their need, with the threat of the commitments they might one day demand of her. Yet Orrin's feeling, more unguarded than any of the others', much deeper and more encompassing, did not oppress her in this way, precisely because she knew that the time they spent together was finite, as bounded and artificial as a bubble blown in glass.

The assault upon her barriers, that first night, had caught her by surprise, but in the past nights she had deliberately courted the experience, pulling her defenses inward, exposing more of herself than ever before. She had never allowed herself to know so much of her own unfiltered passion, or opened herself so fully to what her Gift made uniquely possible—the intoxication, the delirium, of feeling everything twice. She knew the risk she ran. Her guard had drawn very close to her vulnerable core; she could feel how small the margin that protected her had become. Yet it was rapturous to fly this way, on the outer edges of control. For the first time in her life she did not wish to step back. She turned to Orrin as ardently as he to her, a collision of opposing needs whose differences, in the meeting, ceased to matter.

"What are you thinking?" he asked her softly.

She opened her eyes and looked up at him. Milky light slipped through the leaves, resting pale on his cheek, leaving half his face in shadow. His blond hair was colorless in the monochrome illumination; his tilted eyes, below their winged brows, seemed very dark.

"Nothing in particular." She reached up and brushed back the hair on his forehead. "Your hair is growing."

"Yes. I think I'll let it get long. I always wanted to be able to braid it."

"I hate these braids." She shook her head a little, feeling the weight of them. "It's like carrying an entire tinker's stall on my head."

He laughed softly. "I hadn't thought of it like that."

She reached up to him again. "I like you with short hair. It suits you."

"No. Cropped hair is a badge of servitude. A mark of what I was in the Keep. I don't want to look that way to you."

He bent to kiss her. There was desire in it—there always was—but for this moment, love was uppermost. Perhaps it was his mention of the Keep, or perhaps the undiluted quality of his emotion, but Cariad felt suddenly that she could not breathe. She pulled away from him and sat up, drawing her knees to her chest and wrapping her arms around them.

"What is it, Cariad? What's wrong?"

She felt his fingers on her back, sliding along the curve of her spine. He was reluctant, when they were together, to allow any distance between them; he touched her constantly, even when they were not alone. In her other lovers, such behavior had seemed proprietary or possessive, but Orrin's touching was not like that, and she felt no urge to pull away when he sat against her as they took meals, or slipped his arm about her waist and laced his fingers in hers as they walked.

"Nothing's wrong," she said, not turning.

His hand withdrew. She felt him watching her.

"You don't need to lie to me, Cariad," he said. "I wish it didn't matter so much to you, the differences between us."

She shook her head. "It isn't that, Orrin."

"What is it, then?"

She hesitated. "When I'm with you . . . it's as if the rest of the world goes away. I don't dream when I'm with you. The things I think about during the day . . . I don't think of them when we're together." She turned toward him. "But the world is still there. And Jolyon. And what he did to me, and what I did. Sometimes I can't help remembering. That's all."

He had pulled himself to a sitting position, on the other side of the blankets—for once not bridging the space between them, but making it wider. She looked at the lean shape of him, pale in the shadow of the trees. His body was corded with muscle in the transporter way, a strength born of the hundreds of miles he had traveled underground. But his skin, which had never known true sun or wind, was like a child's, smooth as a fall of silk and, except for the two small brands on his right arm, entirely unblemished. A moment ago she had pulled away from him, unable to breathe; now she felt breathless with the desire to touch him. But something in the way he had separated himself from her held her back. She felt determination in him, and a sudden darkness.

"I know you care for me, Cariad," he said. "But you don't love me. Do you?"

She had sensed this before, turning in his thoughts, but until now he had not uttered it aloud. She looked down at her bare legs, unwilling to answer.

"Is it because I'm unGifted?"

"No!" Her head came up. "No, Orrin. I don't care about that."

"You don't?"

"No. I don't." It was true. At some point over the past nights, this fact, which once had mattered so greatly, had ceased to be important to her. "What you are . . . what you've done . . . those are things that go beyond Giftedness. You're an extraordinary man, Orrin. I've never known anyone like you."

"*Why*, then?" The words were explosive with frustration. "If it's not because of Gift, then why?"

She sighed. She had been a fool to think this moment would not come. The outside world seemed suddenly very close, the cold reality of its danger and obligation piercing this false idyll beneath the apple trees. The boundary of their time together was clear now. He himself had drawn it, with his question.

"It's not you," she said, heavily. "I can't love anyone. Not that way."

"Why not?"

"Because I'm a heartsenser. Heartsensers can't . . . it's very difficult for us to endure that kind of feeling. We're more vulnerable than other Gifted to begin with—you saw the heartsensers in the prison annex when we were there, the mad ones, the ones who couldn't bear the weight of their Gifts. That doesn't happen to all of us, or even to most of us. We're taught to protect ourselves, and in the ordinary run of things most of us are successful. But if we let ourselves love as men and women do—if we open ourselves up like that—we lose our ability to guard ourselves against the person we love. We experience that person wholly, all the time we're with them."

"Would that be so terrible, Cariad? Would it be so awful not to guard yourself against me?"

"You don't understand, Orrin. You don't know what it's like, to spend your whole life sensing others' pain, their joy, their anger. Even guarded, it's a burden. But to feel those things without filtering, as fully as your own emotions—the feelings of a person you love, a person you have no defense against . . ." She had to stop and breathe. Just to speak these things was to dread them. "It's too much. You drown in it. It overwhelms you. You lose all sense of where your boundaries are, where you end and the other person begins. That's what happened to my mother. She allowed herself to love my father, and she lost herself to him utterly, body and spirit. She suffered terribly because of it. She suffered until the day she died."

"Perhaps it wasn't the love that made her suffer, but the loss of it."

"That's just the other side of the coin. If a heartsenser loves, it's forever. There's no turning away, no drawing back. Even if we survive the love, how can we survive its ending? And it always ends. Other people can't make that kind of commitment."

"I could." His eyes held hers. "You know I mean it."

"Orrin . . ." She looked at him with something like fear. He did mean it; she could feel his certainty. But she also felt the love that drove it, drunk on its own newness, fueled by sexual intoxication and the strange artificiality of their situation as much as by genuine care. She had spent a good portion of her life fleeing from such emotion, but that did not mean she did not understand it. She knew such intensity could not endure. "Orrin, don't say that. I don't want you to say it. You can't know what you'll feel in ten years, in twenty. It's not possible."

"It's a risk for me too, Cariad. What do you think it would be like to live the rest of your life with a person you could never lie to? To understand that no matter how many years you spend together, you'll never know that person as they know you? To know all the time that the one you love could best you with a thought or kill you with a glance? I have as much to lose as you do. And yet I'm willing to try."

Cariad felt breathless again. The others with whom she had had this conversation had been Gifted; they had understood the limitations she described, even against their own wishes. But Orrin, with his outlaw grasp of power, did not possess a Gifted man's acceptance of the inevitabilities a Gift imposed upon its owner. She felt the pressure of his will, of his belief that it was not necessity, but intent, that shaped such things—a belief so strong that she found herself wondering, for a moment, whether he might be right.

"I love you, Cariad. I always will. If you let me stay with you, I'll stay forever. I swear it."

He moved through the light and shadow that divided them. He reached out and set his fingers lightly against her collarbones, drawing them downward, between her breasts.

"Do you feel what I feel now?" he whispered.

"Yes," she breathed.

He pressed his lips to the hollow of her throat. "And now?"

She went into his arms. They joined their bodies slowly, as if their limbs were weighted. The divisions between them blurred. She felt her barriers tremble. And again, for just an instant, it seemed possible to give him what he asked for, to drop her guard and turn to him fully, without defense. In terror she gripped him, digging her nails into his shoulders, changing the rhythm of their motion so that, in the surge of sensation, both thought and the fear of thought were left behind.

Seven days later the Prior died at last, in the deep hours of the night. One of the men from the duty camp brought the news. For the next three days, the body would lie in state in the Great Amphitheater. On the fourth it would be taken to the Garden of the Stone where, by the combined will of the Staff-Holders, both it and the Staff of Order would be rendered into dust. The dust would then be scattered across the lawns and pathways of the Garden, joining the dust of all the Priors that had gone before, an unbroken line of leadership united with the soil.

The Ceremony of Recreation would take place at noon on the fifth day. For all the centuries past, the Recreation had been a struggle to prove which Staff-Holder was capable of summoning the power of the Stone and using it to create, out of the individual Suborders' staffs of office, a new Staff of Order. This time, it would be a struggle of individual Gifts—or so it was generally believed. Only Cariad, and Jolyon, and his servant, and a few others, knew it would actually be much more.

"Do you want to attend the Ceremony?" Orrin asked Cariad.

"Of course I do. But how can we?"

"There are behindwall passages in the Great Amphitheater. Whenever there's a ceremony, downworlders attend."

They did not speak of it again, passing their time as they had before. But the consciousness of ending, of something drawing to a close, was strong in both of them. When they lay together at night, Cariad could feel Orrin's fear—not for the Order and the world, but for herself and him. He did not accept what she had told him. And yet, with the acute perception that was the equal of any Gift-enhanced understanding she had ever encountered, he recognized the line she had drawn in speaking of it. She could feel him struggling against that boundary, setting himself, and everything in him, against it.

It was time to disengage, she knew, to begin the severing process. But she could not find it in herself to turn away from him at night, or to treat him coldly during the day. When she tried to push her barriers outward, to close off the expanses of herself that she had opened to him, she found she could not do it. She had given up too much; the ground relinquished could not be regained. She did not love him, she told herself—at her core she was still separate, still defended, inviolate behind the monolith of her remaining guard. Even so, a large part of her was bound to him. If she remained with him, she might not be able to prevent him from reaching in and taking the rest.

Had it been this way for her mother? Cariad had always, in her heart, believed her mother's surrender stemmed from weakness, from a lack of will. Perhaps it was not that her mother had allowed herself to fall, but that, prisoned by her mission and by Jolyon's orders, she had lacked the freedom Cariad possessed, to draw away before it was too late. For the first time, Cariad found in herself a thread of compassion for her mother, a heartsenser trapped into love and loss against her will.

It would be difficult to leave. She did not want to think

about how difficult it would be. But leave she must. She would wait until the Recreation. After it, she would go.

It had occurred to her that Goldwine, who must surely have seen the Prior's death through her Gift, planned to attack during the Recreation, disrupting it and delaying Jolyon's accession for at least a little while. But the days slipped by, and Orrin's recruiter did not arrive with news. It had seemed impossible, before the Prior's death, that Jolyon could accede without interference or opposition; now it seemed more and more unlikely that anything would intervene to keep him from it. Cariad found her mind turning, irresistibly, to a fantasy of stealing into the Keep in search of him. Yet even as she thought of it, she knew she would not act. Jolyon, knowing she was loose within the Fortress, would surely be on guard against just such an attempt, and she no longer had the drug to give her an advantage. Before her capture, she would probably have tried even so, trusting her skill and experience to provide her with an opening, but she understood risk now, as she had not then, and the costs of failure. For the first time in her life, fear of consequence held her motionless.

On the day of the Recreation, Cariad and Orrin rose well before the caverns' artificial dawn. Descriptions and likenesses of them had been handed out among the downworlds, and so Cariad created semblances for them both. She dressed them in gray: gray leggings and tunic for him, gray skirt and bodice for her, with a stylized representation of a sheaf of wheat at their left shoulders to identify them as agricultural workers, and a broken circle at their right to mark them as members of the planting clan. They could not be transporters: transporters did not attend Guardian ceremonies, even this one. Cariad was not certain whether it was caution for their secret that prevented them, or simply indifference to the affairs of their masters.

When she was finished, Orrin looked down at himself. "I can see through it," he said. "I can see myself underneath."

"That's because you're inside it. To others it'll seem solid. As mine does to you."

He reached out and touched her hidden cheek. "I still

know you. As I did when you were Margit."

And she knew him. Her eyes showed her a stranger's face and body, but in his motions, his expressions, his steady gaze, he was still Orrin, the indefinable and utterly familiar light of his own selfhood shining even through the cover of his disguise. She turned away from this understanding as she would from a knife thrust, closing her mind to what it might mean.

They set out through the orchards, emerging onto the main highway that cut down the center of the caverns. It was surfaced with firm-packed gravel, laid wide to accommodate the agricultural drays and wagons that trundled constantly along it, bound for the warehouses at the caverns' mouth. So long before dawn, the road was free of traffic, but there would be none even later on. The business of supply had continued as always while the Prior rested in state, and on the day he was rendered into dust. But the Recreation drew the entire Fortress to a standstill, a vast collective suspension at the edge of change.

At the inventory checkpoint, the agricultural supervisor on duty leaned in the lamplit doorway, waiting for the last of the transporter carts to wheel in. He waved to Cariad and Orrin as they passed, the first of many workers who would seek the tunnels this day. The warmth of the caverns quickly dropped behind; the biting cold of underground enfolded them. They walked in silence. Cariad could feel Orrin's tension, with her Gift and also through the viselike grip he kept upon her hand. Her mood echoed his. She was aware of her pulse, fluttering at her throat like the beat of insect wings.

Ordinarily, few downworlders besides transporters used the ways below the ground. But Guardian ceremonies were an exception, for the behindwall passages of the Amphitheater could be accessed only from this level. As Cariad and Orrin gained the tunnels beneath the Suborder Wings, they began to encounter other travelers, workers in the uniforms of their various downworlds, with the marks of clan and service on their shoulders. There were even workers from the Keep: for this one occasion, the Roundheads allowed their downworld gates to stand unlocked. The downworlders proceeded quickly, in silence but not without sound. The underground ways, whose quiet was as essential to their being as their piercing cold, were sussurant with the rustle of fabric, the slap of shoes on stone, the sigh of breath.

The entrance to the behindwall passages was located just before the Amphitheater's downworld, a narrow turnoff that created a bottleneck, and transformed the separate groups into a crowd. Still there was no talk, and the sounds of motion had dwindled, but to Cariad it was as if the air were filled with shouting. Not since the pilgrim camp had she encountered so powerful a mass emotion: awe and reverence, breathless expectation. This ceremony, which over the whole span of the Guardians' rule had been conducted perhaps fifteen times, was the rarest and most sacred of all the Order's rituals. Those here would recount their experience until the end of their days and receive honor for their witness.

Cariad and Orrin gained the turnoff at last. It opened onto a short passageway, with stairs leading upward at its end. The stairs mounted in short flights around a square central stairwell, each flight finishing on a blind landing. Not until ten landings up did the arched entrances of the behindwall passages appear.

On the fourteenth landing Orrin and Cariad stepped off. The behindwall passages were unlit, but they were not dark: the spy stations, which did not pierce the stone like pinpricks here, but made a continuous narrow opening all along the passages' outer length, allowed the illumination of the Amphitheater to spill through, a pale radiance that spoke of mindlight. Early as it was, the passage was nearly filled. The downworlders mixed freely, without regard for the distinctions that usually divided them—Journeyer workers and Speaker workers, men and women, those in training and those too old to serve. Many had brought children with them, holding them up to the spy slot so they could see.

Cariad and Orrin moved at the watchers' backs until they came to an empty space and pushed into it, side by side.

The spy slot was just slightly too low for comfort; Cariad had to stoop a little to set her eyes to it.

The Amphitheater was a circular building of vast proportions. A palace could have been set within its walls, a forest grown beneath its roof. It was built of pale mica-strewn granite, great blocks and slabs joined together apparently without mortar. Tiers of backless benches girdled its circumference, rising like stairsteps to a third of its height; the behindwall passages began just above the final tier. A series of narrow stained-glass windows, depicting scenes from Guardian history, ran like a circlet of dark jewels below the point where wall and ceiling met. At the ceiling's apex, six enormous globes of mindlight clustered like glowing pearls. Their cold radiance shimmered across the reflective granite, as if the Amphitheater were built not of stone but of moonstruck ice.

At the foot of the circling benches lay a round arena, bounded by a shin-high iron rail and paved in a glittering black material that reminded Cariad of the stone of the prison annex. In the middle of this space five chairs had been arranged in a circle: the chairs of Recreation, used for this Ceremony and for no other purpose. They were identical in shape and decoration, differing only in their inlaid gems: malachite and emerald and tourmaline for the Journeyers, tigereye and citrine and topaz for the Soldiers, lapis and sapphire and beryl for the Searchers, ivory and moonstone and rock crystal for the Speakers, and for the Arm of the Stone, jet and hematite and garnet.

The chairs of the four original Suborders were centuries old, dating from the first days of the Order, but the Arm's was freshly made. At all the Recreations before this one, the inclusion of the Arm had been purely a formality: the Arm Staff-Holder had no chair of his own, but stood beside the chair of the Journeyers, a position symbolic of the Arm's subjugation to the Journeyer Suborder. But now it was a Suborder in its own right, entitled to full participation. Its chair, pristine in its newness, stood apart among the time-smoothed others, a break in an otherwise perfect continuum.

The Amphitheater was empty. Dawn had only just broken, a rising luster against the eastern windows, and the

Guardians would not begin to arrive until just before noon. Over the course of the morning, as the sun made its slow circuit around the chain of glass, the Guardians' servants continued to gather, filling up the length of the behindwall passage, massing two and three and four deep as latecomers pressed in. The passage, initially chilly, heated with the crowding; beneath her heavy clothes, Cariad was soon drenched in sweat.

She had found it difficult, earlier, to endure the collective emotion around her, but as the hours passed she grew less conscious of it—her Gift adjusting to the overload, like the ear to too much sound. She was aware of Orrin beside her, his eyes glued to the spy slot, his body jammed hard against hers by the pressure of the crowd. It was all of him she could feel, for the clamor of mass emotion shut individual detail away from her Gift. Her legs ached from standing, and she was tired. But her mind was clear, and the clutching dread she had felt as she and Orrin walked the tunnels was gone. It was a relief. She had dreaded, in the past days, how it might be to wait above the Amphitheater for the moment of Jolyon's accession.

The Guardians began to arrive at last, a sudden eruption of gray robes through the wide entrance passage that lay on the right side of Cariad's viewpoint. They filled the benches like a rising tide of ash. The other Suborders mixed freely, but the Arm of the Stone held itself separate—a solid block of black, accented with red and flashing with gold.

At last the influx ended. The Guardians waited, silent. The downworlders had fallen silent also, though their feeling still pressed against Cariad's Gift, an intangible echo of the taut scene below: masters and servants, physically separate as always, joined now in anticipation and in faith. She was aware, suddenly, of how many people were present in this place, visible beneath the mindlight and invisible between the walls—all of them waiting, on the same indrawn breath, for the same moment of affirmation. For just an instant she—the outsider, the rebel, the assassin—saw what they must see, in the ecstatic glory of their belief: the great continuum of Guardianship, all the centuries of authority that had gone before and all those that would come after, united and affirmed in this single moment of ceremony. A chain of being as eternal as the world itself. A cycle as unassailable as time.

A reeling dizziness overtook her. Her composure vanished, as if a bandage had been ripped away. She had known what she would witness, in the black arena—for weeks she had known it. Yet only now, viewed through the prism of others' faith, did it truly seem real.

A blast of sound broke the air, recalling trumpets in its resonance, but in its echoes suggesting no instrument made by man. One by one, the Councils of Six marched into the arena: the Speakers, heavily bearded, belted in white, with ivory-colored diagonal sashes across their breasts; the Journeyers, with long braids and green belts, their diagonals the color of spring leaves; the Searchers, with blue belts and skullcaps of the same color, their sashes the hue of a twilit sky; the Soldiers, shaven-headed and gold-belted, with broadswords at their waists and saffron sashes; and the Arm of the Stone, black robes swinging, red belts like bloodstains against the dark fabric, sashless—and, for once, unaccompanied by companions.

Jolyon walked at the left of this group. From so far away he was like a toy man, his features as small as a doll's. But in the instant of glimpsing him Cariad saw him full-size, his face inches from hers—a flash of remembered vision that took her like a blow and released her just as quickly, leaving her cold and short of breath.

The Councils ranged themselves around the chairs of Recreation, each Council behind the chair of its Suborder, the Seconds standing a little in advance of the rest. Another discordant blast shook the air. The Speaker Staff-Holder entered the arena, a tall man with a white beard that reached nearly to his waist. He wore a magnificent embroidered surplice and bore his staff of office, a thick shaft of moonstone topped by a globe of crystal, glowing faintly with the power that had been bound into it at its making. With measured ceremony he passed between the chairs, halting at the center of the circle they made. Raising the staff to the full length of his arm, he drove it downward like a spear. There was a sound, like the shattering of stone or the cracking of lightning; and the staff stood upright, its end buried in the black material of the arena. The Staff-Holder withdrew and seated himself in the chair of his Suborder.

One by one the other Staff-Holders entered and set their staffs as the Speaker had, forming a circle that echoed the placement of the chairs: moonstone, malachite, lapis, tigereye. The Staff-Holder of the Arm of the Stone came last, leaning heavily on two of his companions. At the circle, the companions stepped back. The Staff-Holder, unsteadily but with unmistakable power, raised his onyx staff and set it, completing the pattern. Then, painfully, he turned to face the Roundhead Council.

"It is my right as Staff-Holder of the Arm of the Stone to pass proxy for this Ceremony." His voice, untouched by his physical weakness, echoed in the silence. "In accordance with that right, I call my Second to come forward."

There was no one here—not the servants, avidly watching through the spy slots, or the Guardians, packed upon the benches—who had not known this statement would be made. The proxy had been announced, officially, just after the Prior's death. Yet with the words a ripple passed across the crowds—one within the walls, one outside them—not a sound, exactly, or a motion, but something in between, an acknowledgment of the import of this moment.

Jolyon approached. The Staff-Holder reached toward him. Joined, the two men moved toward the chair. The Staff-Holder lowered Jolyon into the seat and bent to lay his hands upon the armrests. He straightened and stepped back; his companions moved smoothly forward and supported him out of the circle, assisting him to his carry-chair, which his remaining companions had brought in and placed at the edge of the arena.

Now the Seconds—for the Arm of the Stone it was the Investigation-Master—began to bind the Staff-Holders in place, using lengths of white silk to tie them at ankle, wrist, and chest. Last they set a blindfold around each man's eyes. Finished, they stepped away from the chairs, their Councils behind them, out of range of the huge forces that would be invoked and contained within the circle.

Even as the Councils settled to stillness, a third blast of sound tore the air—longer this time, a cacophony that split into a hundred different timbres and recombined as one, dying away at last into echoing silence. There was a moment of utter suspension, like the pause between an indrawn breath and its release. Mindlight slid along the standing staffs, pooling in the hearts of the precious stones that topped them. The Staff-Holders, bound and blind, sat like men carved from stone; the assembled Guardians were just as still. The servants, invisible between the walls, echoed their masters' immobility. Cariad's heart, beating frantically in her throat, seemed the only thing that moved.

In the arena, the staffs had altered—not quite solid now, nor quite confined by qualities of length and width. More and more indefinite they grew, losing form but gaining color, journeying from the deep, occluded hues of semiprecious stone toward the purer tones of light. The staffs were spirit as much as matter, imbued with the power and the essence of the Gifted men who had created them; they naturally resisted joining, just as Gifts and essences did, and must be broken down into their most basic components and freed of the power that saturated them before they could be remade into something new.

This, the breaking-down, the Staff-Holders did as one. It was the next step, the combining, that was the battle.

When the staffs seemed less corporeal things than cascades of elemental force, the battle began. Distant as she was, Cariad could only dimly feel the vast forces being summoned, but she could clearly see the turmoil that seized the center of the circle. The colors, which till now had retained their separation, began to seethe and struggle, splitting and fragmenting, twisting and interpolating into a hundred different forms and combinations. The Staff-Holders strained against their bindings, hands clawing at carved armrests, lips drawing back from teeth.

There was an enormous grinding sound—Cariad thought the material of the arena must be dragging itself out by the roots—and the violent play of light and matter began to shift, inching unmistakably toward the Journeyer Staff-Holder. As it moved, it coalesced—coils of blue twisting into coils of blue, bolts of gold flashing into other bolts, streaks of green melting together, bands of white falling into unity—with at the center, a blackness like the night sky, steadily gathering mass.

Cariad felt a moment of wild hope. Could it be that Jolyon's servant—who must, like herself, be concealed within the walls—was too distant from the arena to work his sleight of power? Could it be that the forces here were too powerful even for the void in him to catch and hold? Could it be that the Ceremony would play out as it would have if Jolyon had not possessed the means to subvert it?

But even as she thought it, she perceived the change, and knew, with a sense her imprisonment had made infallible, that the void was here, yawning into being within the arena. The core of black began to grow—not incrementally, as before, but like a leaping beast. It overtook the colors, darkening their prismatic purity, stealing their intensity. Even from so far away Cariad could feel the power of that draining, the irresistible flow of Gift into the hungry maw of the abyss, like a whirlpool opening all the way down to the ocean's floor.

The blackness was larger than the play of color now, a margin of midnight steadily eating up the air. The colors lost the cohesion the Journeyer Staff-Holder had imposed on them—coils breaking, bands splitting, bolts fragmenting—until at last what seemed to be a multihued dust storm boiled upon the air, disorganized and incredibly violent. Slowly, it began to draw together, gradually forming itself into something the approximate size and shape of a staff.

There was a cry—Jolyon? One of the Staff-Holders? With a soundless concussion, the abyss folded in on itself and vanished. The colors, left behind, collapsed into solidity. The new-made staff hung upon the air a moment, and then, with an enormous crash, fell at Jolyon's feet.

Utter silence followed. Cariad felt the emotion of the servants, wrapping her as closely as the air: not reverence now, but fear. The downworlders did not understand what had just occurred; they had not perceived more than a fraction of the play of forces that had been joined here. But they knew the proper form of the Staff of Order—a graceful, measured braiding of moonstone and malachite, lapis and tigereye, joined for the first time by a ribbon of onyx— and they saw as clearly as any Guardian that what Jolyon had created was nothing like this. The staff that lay before him was misshapen and irregular, a confusion of colored chips and shards of stone, all pressed together like a child's attempt at baking.

"Release me." Jolyon's voice broke the silence, reedy in the great hush that weighted the air. And then, when no answer came: "Release me!"

The Investigation-Master sprang forward. The Seconds moved forward also, bending to their Staff-Holders' bonds. With his freed hands, Jolyon reached up and ripped his blindfold off. He vaulted to his feet almost before the Investigation-Master had finished removing the cloth from his ankles. Pushing the other man aside, he looked for the first time on what he had wrought.

For an instant he froze, his face like white marble beneath the mindlight. Almost at once he recovered himself. He stepped forward and bent to the staff. It was so thick he could barely close his hands around it; he had to visibly struggle to raise it. It towered over him, more than two heads taller than he. He stood, braced, and looked out over the assembly.

"The Staff of Order is remade." It was the beginning of the ritual formula of accession. "I claim Priorship, in the name of the Order of Guardians, in the name of the power it serves, in the name of the world." Once, he would also have invoked the Stone; but that could not be done now. "I am Percival, now and until the day of my death."

This time there was a sound, a kind of sighing, racing across the crowd like wind over water. Behind the walls the downworlders stirred in sympathy. The Staff-Holders, free, stood before their chairs, staring with clear horror at the abomination Jolyon held before him. The Journeyer Second and another member of the Journeyer Council gripped their Staff-Holder's arms, as if to prevent him from charging forward.

"Accept me!" Jolyon shouted. This was not part of the formula. The words he had spoken were meant to be followed by phrases of confirmation, spoken by every Guardian present. "I am Prior! Accept me!"

Still the crowd did not reply.

The close group of the Roundhead Council parted. Marhalt, the gaunt Apprentice-Master, stepped forward between the chairs.

"I made you a promise once," he said to Jolyon. He did not shout, or even perceptibly raise his voice, but each syllable sounded clearly, like a bell. "Do you remember it?"

Cariad saw a sudden commotion in the area where the Arm of the Stone sat packed upon the benches: three men, pushing violently past their fellows, struggling toward the arena. Jolyon's companions. Two of them she did not recognize, but the third, Baffrid, she knew by his coal-black hair and by the thick bar of his eyebrows, meeting above his nose. They halted at the iron rail that bounded the arena's edge, like hounds paused in flight.

"Think well before you challenge me, old man." Jolyon's reedy voice was steady, but his hands, around the hideous thing he had created, were white. "Before the assembled Order of Guardians I have remade the Staff of Order. I am Prior now."

"I do not know what you have made. But it is not the Staff. And you shall not be Prior." Marhalt reached out his hand, and pointed. "I fulfill my promise now."

The Staff shattered, a silent explosion that transformed it for an instant into the dust it had been. The air swallowed it, and it was gone.

Jolyon's companions sprang forward at a dead run. They knocked the chairs of Recreation aside, scattering the Staff-Holders like so much timber. Baffrid seized Jolyon—who stood stunned, his hands closed on empty air—and heaved him backward. The other two came together before him, like a pair of slamming doors, their arms outspread, their faces deadly with rage.

"Release me!" Jolyon struggled against Baffrid's grip. His voice cracked with fury. "Release me!"

Baffrid let him go. Jolyon lunged forward, pushing the other two companions aside. He was transfigured with passion—his face as white as chalk, his lips drawn back from his teeth, his hands curved into claws. Between himself and Marhalt the air distorted. Marhalt was flung up and backward. His body crashed against the Speaker's chair, knocking it to the side. He fell to the ground and lay motionless.

Cariad heard the downworlders' cries and felt their horror, a blow against her Gift. Below, in the Amphitheater, the crowd sat frozen, locked in a stasis of appalled disbelief. For a moment Jolyon did not move. He was bent over, his hands braced upon his knees. Even from this distance Cariad could see that he was panting, as he had in the white cell after he probed her. It had not been power harvested by his servant that he had used to strike Marhalt, she realized, but his own unaided Gift.

At last he straightened. He raised his face to the Amphitheater's ceiling, to the cold radiance of the mindlight.

"I am Prior!" he shouted. His mouth was stretched, his eyes wide, his hands fisted at his sides. Even in the white cell he had not worn a face as terrible as this. "I will remake the Staff!"

Cariad felt the shift of pressure as, somewhere behind the walls, the servant again released his hold on the void of his anti-Gift and began to eat the power of those around him. It was a larger opening this time, much larger, as if master and servant were equally unhinged by the destruction Marhalt had wrought. Cariad felt the terrible pull of it against her own Gift, and knew it was not just the Staff-Holders who were being drained, but every source of power here. A blackness began to grow, not a defined form now, but a general darkening, as if the air were filling up with soot. High above the arena, the globes of mindlight flickered, dimming. Jolyon stood beneath them, his mouth still open, every muscle rigid as he strained to grasp the power his servant harvested for his use. Even as the umbra around him deepened his own light endured, white across his face and hands, flashing like a beacon from the gold he wore.

Pandemonium had broken out across the Amphitheater. Guardians fought to get free, trampling one another in their desperation to escape. The downworlders too were struggling; Cariad was crushed against the wall as those behind her threw themselves against those ahead, though they were too tightly packed in the narrow corridor to do much more than shove and shout. Their fear battered at her guard, like a physical assault. Orrin was clutching her, his fingers digging into her arm. In the dimming glow of mindlight, his semblanced face was stretched with fright.

There was a huge concussion. The mindlight vanished. A choir of screams rose up, a sound so violent it was almost beyond hearing. The downworlders tore at each other, trampling and clawing and kicking in their panic, climbing one another like stairsteps. A blow caught Cariad in the spine, another in the back of her head, cracking her cheekbone against the edge of the spy slot. She saw, in an instant of complete clarity, that she and Orrin would die if they remained here.

She opened herself to the whole strength of her making Gift, reaching past the solidity of matter to the vacant spaces in between. She saw the way back underground and moved herself and Orrin into it, flying *through* into the vacuum where all cohesion had its source. But she had never before gone so deep; the tides of emptiness confused her, so that she lost her hold upon that centered vacancy, and they flashed back into the material world not at the mouth of the caverns, as she had intended, but somewhere else within the tunnels.

They landed in a painful tangle on the floor. The silence was like a blow. For a moment they lay, too stunned to move.

At last Orrin stirred, pushing himself upright. They had lost their semblances in the process of transition; his face, blank with shock, was his own again.

"What . . . did you do?" he said.

Cariad shook her head. She was a maker, capable of passing through solid substances, but she had no Gift of transportation and had never before attempted bodily translation. She thought of her loss of control and felt cold: they might just as easily have materialized not in the tunnels but inside the rock that lay between them.

"I meant to bring us to the caverns," she said. "I don't know where we are."

He looked around. "Under the Library, I think." Painfully, he got to his feet. His lip was cut: blood marked his chin and neck. "If we walk for a while, we'll find a landmark."

Cariad pushed herself to her knees, swaying there a moment before she could rise. She was so drained that even the air seemed heavy. Her face throbbed where she had hit it; she suspected her cheekbone was broken. Orrin drew her arm over his shoulder and hooked his own arm around her waist. He was trembling, long convulsive shudders that shook him from head to foot. They began to walk.

As they gained the more central passages, they began to encounter servants, returning stunned and bloody to their downworlds. Some limped purposefully along; others shambled as if in a trance, holding to the walls for balance. Some wept as they walked. Men and women supported each other; parents carried injured children in their arms.

"What happened?" Orrin said after a time.

"Jolyon used his servant's power to steal the Staff-Holders' Gifts and remake the Staff." Even speaking was a strain. If Orrin were to let go of her, she was not certain she would be able to stand up on her own. "Either the servant didn't steal enough . . . or Jolyon didn't have the skill to do what needed to be done."

"And after? When the Apprentice-Master destroyed the Staff?"

"The servant opened up his Gift again. It wasn't just the Staff-Holders he stole from this time, but everyone. I think that must be why the mindlight went out."

"Oh." A pause. "What happens now?"

"I don't know, Orrin."

It was not true. The words of the prophecy, in Goldwine's voice, spoke themselves inside her mind: *When the Staff breaks. When the Garden falls again to winter. . . .* Stumbling through the tunnels she felt that understanding expand within her, crowding out the pain of her injured face, the shock of what she had just witnessed, even the burden of her own guilt. The first of the prophecy's signs had come to pass today. It would not be long, now, before her father returned.

The
Place
Between
The
Worlds

Twenty

ONSTANT TRAVELED through the world of handpower. Somehow, during his time with Bron, his Gift had adjusted to this place, so that he found himself able to farwalk as he always had, without the dizzy disorientation that had slowed him before. Three days after setting out, he halted briefly to eat and realized, from the pall on the horizon and the smell of the air, that he was not far from the poisoned region that had driven him back on his outward journey—how long ago? A month? Two? More? He could no longer remember.

In a way, it was as if no time had passed at all, for he was alone and empty-handed as he had been then, traveling through a world apparently devoid of any power but his own. But then, he had had a purpose, and the hope of fulfilling it. Now, he had only this journey back and the knowledge that he had failed.

As Bron had promised, the loss of memory was gradual, even gentle, entirely unlike the catastrophic amputation produced by Guardian memory confiscations. Konstant tried, at first, to track the process, striving to inventory the images he still owned and hold onto at least the shape of those he was losing. But he could not feel them as they died, neither did they leave any sense of emptiness to mark the places where they had been. It was so painless, this dispossession, so incremental and yet so absolute, that had he not known it was happening he might not have noticed it at all. Yet he did know; and so he was aware that each time he looked inside his mind there was less to see.

Location was the first to go. The route Bron had provided to get Konstant to the Gate was detailed and precise, yet each mile vanished as he traversed it, so that though he understood at all times exactly how to move forward, he could not at any point have turned around and retraced his path. Details were next to disappear. Hourly, he recalled less about the house and its setting, until he could not call up even the image of the bed in which he had slept. Incidents were last. By halfway through the second day he could not remember how he had arrived in Bron's house, or what he had done to pass so much time there. Now, on the third day, he retained only flashes: the water-clear depths of a slab of crystal, the swirl of amber liquor inside a belled goblet, starry light upon a face whose shape he could no longer see clearly, the touch of a vast Gift. And a voice—Bron's voice, speaking with chilly precision the tenets of his beliefs and the phrases of his refusal; and a spark—the final touch through which Bron had both given and rescinded knowledge; and an understanding—that he, who had been Goldwine's messenger, was now Bron's.

There was anger in this dispossession—for Konstant, who had never truly been Red, nevertheless had a Red's horror of mental incursion, and would have preferred physical torture to what Bron had done to him. There was anger in the fragmentary images as well; and a sense of bitter purpose, as if he had planned or undertaken some action in response to Bron's refusal. But what the action might have been, and whether he had accomplished it, he no longer knew. Deprived of the anchor of specific memory, the anger shifted, turning inward. It would have been more just, perhaps, to focus the heat of his recrimination on Bron. But Bron had not been charged with a purpose he had been too weak or too clumsy or too incompetent to carry out. Bron had not been given the hope of a world and let it slip out of his hands. Bron had not been charged with the weight and promise of ensuring prophecy's fulfillment, and proved himself unequal to the task. Konstant could not recall the precise details of his failure, or the exact nature of the mistakes he had made: the process that had erased the shape of Bron's face had erased these things as well. And yet the fact of error was clear—for if he had not erred, he would not be alone.

Konstant spent the third night of his journey beneath a bridge, an arch of rusted metal that spanned a waterless area between two sets of hills. There was a town not far off, but the area around the bridge had been relinquished to the wild, and trees and ragged underbrush, stripped and brown with winter, gave sparse cover for a campsite. He swept an area clear of snow; in the quilted sleeping sack that was part of his travel equipment, with his travel pack for a pillow, he was far more comfortable than he ever had been traveling in his own world. But he did not sleep. All night he lay staring up at the bridge above him, a dark fretwork against a sky sharp with stars. Bron's voice spoke in his crippled memory, uttering over and over the phrases of his refusal. Goldwine's face hung before his inner eye, by turns dark with grief and hard with anger. Despair turned in him, and a self-loathing more poisonous than any he had ever felt.

In the morning, when the light returned, he found himself unable to muster the will to rise and resume his journey.

He was aware that he should force himself to go on. Goldwine should have the news of Bron's refusal. And yet how could he go to her, emptyhanded? How could he bear to see how she would look at him when he told her that the prophecy was broken? Better, perhaps, not to return at all, but to remain in this alien world, wandering purposeless and placeless until he found a natural death. Time would bring Goldwine to understanding as surely, if not as quickly, as his own words. As for Bron's message, what difference did it make whether or not it was passed on? It was the refusal that mattered, not the why of it.

And yet . . . there was a third option.

Konstant had not planned, when he hurled Jolyon's talisman into the darkness, to make a link or mark a trail. He had been sure that distance would eradicate the voice of its connection to him. Distracted by his fading memory, it was not until the second day of traveling that he realized that the voice was still there, a tiny presence at the very bottom of his consciousness. Now, more than three days distant, he could still hear it, only a little less clearly than he had in the woods where he first farsought Bron. And he knew that, if he drew quiet within himself, if he focused his Gift upon the call, it would be possible to close his eyes and follow it as he had then, and so return where he had been.

What, he asked himself, would be the point? Bron, surely, would not tolerate it. If, by some miracle or oversight, he did, what could Konstant do that he had not already tried and failed to achieve? And yet, knowing it was possible to return, how could he not? As long as he was breathing, how could he do otherwise than to throw himself against the walls of Bron's indifference, again and again, until his life was gone or things had been made right?

He remained beneath the bridge, as day drew past and cycled into night. He knew he must choose, either to return to his world, or to remain in this one, or to follow the talisman to Bron. But choice seemed beyond him. It seemed more possible simply to stay where he was, until time and the processes of nature removed the necessity of decision.

But he did not get the chance, either to choose or to let choice go. As first light crept grayly across the world, five Roundheads emerged out of the waning night and captured him.

He had not been watching for other powers—as, he told himself bitterly later on, he ought to have been. Yet why should he have thought he needed to? He did not know how much time he had passed in this world, but it was certainly more than the two weeks Jolyon had given him; surely the Second believed him dead. The legitimate Roundhead parties that walked this world, in search of Bron and for the sake of study, had no reason to look for him. Yet a group of Roundheads did come looking for him, and he did not sense their presence until the net of their power fell upon him, as if the bridge had collapsed above his head, locking him body and Gift against the boulder where he sat.

They shimmered out of invisibility, their black robes like a small return of night. One stood a little in front of the rest. Even in the dimness of the not-quite-dawn, Konstant recognized him: Baffrid, Jolyon's chief companion. In that instant, as if time had stopped, he knew the whole of what would come.

"Bind him," Baffrid said.

One of the Roundheads moved forward. He carried a leather bag, from which he pulled a set of chains. By the bluish glow that hung on them, Konstant recognized the warded manacles the Soldiers used to confine Gifted prisoners. Immobilized by the others' power, he could not struggle as the Roundhead fitted the collar to his neck and the cuffs to his wrists, and snapped the beltpiece around his waist beneath his bulky outergarment. He felt the wards set upon the iron, a baffle against his Gift.

The Roundhead dipped into his beltpouch and removed a ceramic vial. He grasped Konstant's hair, pulling his head back, and struck a sharp blow to Konstant's chin, so that his mouth fell open. He poured something down Konstant's throat. Konstant choked, unable for a terrifying moment to draw breath. It was a power-drug: he felt the acid burn of it inside him, felt his Gift sinking down into darkness, like a flame deprived of air.

"All right," Baffrid said.

The Roundhead stepped back among the others. With his Gift in suspension, Konstant could not feel the unbinding of the collective power that held him, but he recognized it by the fact that he could move again.

Baffrid came forward and crouched down a little distance away. He was a swarthy man, heavyset, with black hair that grew low on his forehead and thick eyebrows that met above his nose. A scar from a duel ran vertically down the right side of his face, disfiguring features that had not been pleasing even when unmarked. He had beautiful eyes, however, large and clear and amber-brown. In the rising light of dawn, Konstant could clearly read the mixture of triumph and contempt that filled them.

"How did you find me?" His voice was hoarse with the passage of the drug. He was aware of the pounding of his pulse, as if he were afraid, and yet he was not conscious of any sense of fear.

"We tracked your Gift. You didn't even bother to barrier it."

"I didn't expect to be followed."

"That's clear enough." The words were rich with scorn. "Why are you here? It must be important, if the Second's willing to let you off the leash."

Baffrid grinned—a peculiar, mirthless expression, which did not curve his mouth, but only stretched it sideways into a wider shape. "Jolyon—who by the way is no longer Second—seems to think you might have succeeded in your quest. On your own account, that is, not on his. He'd like to know what you found."

"Wait." Konstant's lips felt stiff. "No longer Second?"

The grin widened. "Jolyon is Prior now."

Konstant closed his eyes. The manacles, the drug, the questions—these he had known he must endure. But this he had not anticipated. "When?"

"Eight days ago. But that's not your concern. Answer my question."

"Nothing." Konstant opened his eyes again. "I found nothing. There's nothing here to find."

"And that's why you never came back through the Gate?"

"Yes. I couldn't fulfill my charge, and I was ashamed to return a failure."

Baffrid lunged forward. Konstant had known it in the other world, this shocking quickness of motion, so apparently at odds with the heavy, musclebound body. Baffrid's thumb and middle finger closed behind the points of Konstant's jaw. The other man, an experienced interrogator, knew exactly where the pain centers were. Konstant sucked in his breath.

"No more games," Baffrid said. "We know who you are. We know why you became Red. We caught a compatriot of yours—an assassin, sent into the Fortress to kill Jolyon. The daughter of your rebel leader, as it turns out. Jolyon probed her himself."

"Cariad? You captured her?"

"Didn't I just say so?" With a final, agonizing compression, Baffrid released Konstant's jaw and moved back to his former distance. "So stop the pretense and tell me the truth."

"I've already told you the truth. I've been searching since I got here, but I haven't found a trace. Either he's dead, or too well-hidden for any Gifted to find."

Baffrid watched him, unblinking, like a confident reptile.

"In that case," he said, "how do you explain your health?"

"My health?"

"You've been here two months. By now you should be nearly dead from power-sickness. But you're not. Why is that?"

Two months. Of all his time in this world, Konstant could clearly recall only the last four days, and the three weeks of solo travel at the beginning. That meant he had been nearly five weeks beneath Bron's roof, waiting to deliver his summons or waiting while Bron considered it, while in the other world the things he had sought to prevent came to pass. . . .

"I did get sick," he said. "I recovered."

"Power-sickness isn't something you recover from."

"Power-sickness is a myth. There's nothing in this world to threaten Gifts."

Baffrid leaned forward, casually this time, and clouted Konstant across the cheek. "Watch your tongue, Violator. I won't hear such blasphemous filth."

Konstant pulled himself straight. The left side of his face was numb. He had bitten his tongue: there was blood inside his mouth, a metallic overlay upon the lingering acidity of the drug.

"Let me tell you how I think it happened," Baffrid said. "Your rebel cohorts sent you here to find the thief of That Which Was Most Precious to Us. They gave you some special tool, or some special technique, that made it possible for you to be successful. You took shelter under his roof. And the power of That Which Was Most Precious to Us preserved your Gift, as it has preserved his all these years."

"That power is dead. It didn't survive this world. Isn't that what the Reddened believe?"

"The assassin said otherwise. And Jolyon thought she might be right. Or rather, he wasn't willing to conclude she was wrong without sending us here to make sure. For my-self, I didn't credit it at all. But when we reached this world three days ago and sensed your Gift, I began to wonder. . . . And now I see you here before me, fit and healthy, and I think it must, after all, be so. Now. Will you speak the truth? Or will I have to probe you? I'd hoped to save that for the Fortress." He smiled his mirthless smile. "But I'd be glad to do it now."

This, of course, was the crux of the matter—the inevi-table climax to which this verbal interrogation was merely foreplay. It was mainly reflex that had led Konstant, earlier, to deny Baffrid's questions. From the moment the Round-heads' power fell on him, he had known he would have to speak.

"If you probed me," he said, "I couldn't help you. And you need my help."

"Oh?" Baffrid's thick eyebrows arched. "And why is that?"

"I did find him. But we had a falling out, and he took away my memory. If you probe me you'll find nothing, because I remember nothing—not where he is, not even what he looks like. But I left a marker behind, at his house. I can follow it back to him. I need my Gift to do it, though. If you want me to guide you, you'll have to take away these manacles and let the drug wear off."

"Ha." This time Baffrid's grin held what looked like gen-uine amusement. "Manacles off. No drugs. Very neat, Tal-esin. Of course it's completely absurd."

"It's the truth."

"An awfully convenient truth, from your point of view. Try again. And make it a bit more plausible this time."

Konstant felt something turn over inside him. He began to laugh, helplessly, a kind of unhinged mirth that was not so very far from weeping. Baffrid's hand flashed out, half-closed; this time his knuckles caught Konstant in the soft flesh below his left eye. A galaxy of light burst across his vision. For a moment he thought he had been blinded.

"I do not see," Baffrid said, his voice flat, "that you have anything to laugh about."

Konstant turned, with difficulty, to look at the other man.

A veil lay across the world, the color of blood. The pain of the blow vibrated in the altered bones of his face. Still the laughter bubbled up within him; but he did not want to be struck again, and so he pressed it back.

"It's just," he said, his voice uneven, "that I actually am telling you the truth. The whole truth, all of it. What are the odds I'd ever do that? In the Keep you believed every lie I spoke. But now I'm not lying, and you don't believe me. Don't you think that's funny?"

For a long moment Baffrid was silent. His heavy brows were drawn together. At last he said: "This falling out you say you had. What was it?"

"I asked him to return with me. He refused. When I tried to persuade him, he took my memory and threw me out of his house."

"And that's why you're willing to lead us to him? Because he wouldn't join your Violating rebel cause?"

"Yes. And because he tampered with my mind."

Baffrid blinked. Red that he was, this was a motivation he could understand. "The marker you left. What is it?"

"The talisman Jolyon gave me. You know he binds them to his agents. I can sense it. Or I could if I had my Gift."

For a moment longer Baffrid was still. Then, abruptly, he rose to his feet. "Very well. I'll have one of the others search you, to make sure the talisman isn't on you. If it isn't, we'll wait until the drug wears off, and then see what you can do for us. But you must wear the manacles. And if I sense you're leading us astray, if by so much as an eyeblink you give me the impression that you're lying . . . well. Let's just say that I won't be so lenient if I have to question you a second time."

"I understand."

One of the Roundheads came after a little while to conduct a body-search. He wore the violet teardrop of Jolyon's service, but Konstant did not recognize him: another executor, most likely, culled from Jolyon's force outside the Keep. He touched Konstant only with the tips of his fingers, as if he were handling something pulled out of a sewer. As a final gesture, he slit Konstant's quilted sleeping sack and padded outergarment to ribbons, in case the little glass globe might be hidden in their stuffing.

For the rest of the day Konstant sat against his boulder, shivering with the bitter cold that leaked through the rents in his coat, as the drug slowly released its hold upon his Gift. The cuffs of the manacles were too tight; his eye had swollen nearly closed from Baffrid's blow, and his bitten tongue was thick and throbbing in his mouth. He had nothing to do but think: about his capture, about Jolyon's accession to Priorship, about Cariad and her failed mission. The open wound of their association had long since scarred over, but still he found it difficult to think of her, dead or mindless as she must surely be by now. It was over, he told himself, truly over: all he had fought for, all he had learned so painfully to believe in. And now he was preparing to give up the final secret and take Baffrid and his men to Bron. If he were wrong in his memory of Bron's power, then Jolyon would truly have everything, even the Stone.

He did not think he was wrong. Dim as his recollection of that vast Gift was, he was certain that even five Roundheads would not challenge it. And yet, with the bleak self-understanding that had dogged him throughout his life, he was aware that it was not his confidence in Bron's Gift that had driven him to offer to lead Baffrid and the others, but only his abject, bone-deep horror of the Reddened mindprobe. He would do anything, say anything, betray anything to escape it. And though he knew that it would be pointless to give up the structures of his mind for a man who did not need such a sacrifice—a man, moreover, who did not deserve it—he could not help but despise himself for not being strong enough to do so.

Beyond the skeletal screen of trees, the Roundheads waited, amusing themselves with conversation and with dice. Konstant could hear the murmur of their voices, though he could not make out what they said. Periodically, Baffrid came to set blunt fingers upon his forehead, tracking the awakening of his Gift. The Roundhead did not employ the lancelike delving of a probe, only the small spark of mindtouch, which dipped deep enough to sense the fires of power, but was not strong enough to harvest thought or memory. Even so, as his Gift rose to strength, it took all the will Konstant had to endure this intrusion without defending himself. He could feel the corruption of Baffrid's Gift, in character and quality not unlike his own; he could read, in the tension of Baffrid's fingers and the tight control of his face, how much the Roundhead wanted to drain his mind. Each of Baffrid's departures left him shaking.

At last, well after night had fallen, Baffrid pronounced Konstant's Gift unbound. Two of the Roundheads grasped him beneath the arms and hauled him to his feet. Baffrid stood before him in the pallid glow of the mindlight he had summoned, his black robe fading into the darkness. It had begun to snow, tiny flakes that glittered on the Roundheads' shoulders and cropped hair.

"I will link my mind to yours," Baffrid said. "You will follow your sense of this marker, and I will follow you, and the others will follow me."

Konstant jerked against the hands that held him. "No." His swollen tongue made it difficult to speak. "The manacles already make it hard for me to reach out. With a mindlink—"

"It's either this," Baffrid said gently, "or the probe."

Konstant felt despair settle within him, colder than the falling snow. He had hoped, vaguely, for some chance of escape; but Baffrid, hooked into his mind, would never let go. He longed to turn his face away, to refuse the false choice Baffrid offered him. But as long as he had will, he could not give himself to the probe.

"The mindlink," he said.

Baffrid's mouth stretched. He reached out and set cold fingertips on Konstant's temples. Konstant closed his eyes and waited for the touch of Gift.

Nothing happened.

Cautiously, Konstant opened his eyes. The world around him had not changed. Snow still fell; the night still pressed round. The Roundheads stood immobile, like pieces of dark sculpture. Baffrid's eyes still rested on Konstant's face. But

Konstant could tell, by their flatness, that they no longer saw him.

Light began to rise—not the chilly glow of mindlight, but a larger, warmer radiance, golden as a summer noontime. Power rose also, expanding hugely into the emptiness of this world. The Roundheads' mindlight flickered and paled, faltering beneath the weight of a Gift vastly greater than their own. From behind their frozen forms, a man emerged. He was tall and slender, dressed all in black. The light moved with him, springing out around him like the corona of the sun.

The instant Konstant saw him, the binding of forgetfulness that had been set upon his mind collapsed. In that moment he recalled everything, a flood of memory so powerful that his legs buckled and he fell, slipping out of Baffrid's unmoving grip, landing on his knees on the cold ground.

Bron halted in front of him and stood a moment, looking down. He wore a long coat with a sable collar; in his hand he held a cloth bag with leather handles and, tucked under his arm, the scarred wooden box Konstant had seen among his clothes. Konstant could not read that marble face, those still dark eyes. It occurred to him—distantly, as if he were thinking about someone else—that he should be afraid.

Bron stooped to set down what he carried. Then he turned to Baffrid. He placed the tips of his fingers on Baffrid's temples, bowing his head, as if listening. After a moment he removed his fingers and placed his palm flat against Baffrid's forehead. Something passed—a spark, a flash of light. Baffrid's body rocked a little. Bron lowered his hand and moved on.

He touched each of the Roundheads in turn, palm to forehead. Each time there was a passage of power. When he had marked them all, he stepped back. Konstant felt no change, no sense of loosening, but all at once the Roundheads' stasis was gone. They stepped forward, Baffrid in the lead. Their eyes were open, but their faces had the closed, blind look of sleepers. Silently, in single file, they moved off into the night. Bron stood motionless, gazing after them.

"You let them go." The words fell away into the darkness and the blowing snow. For a moment Konstant was not certain whether he had really spoken them aloud. But then, slowly, Bron turned.

"Yes."

"Why?"

"I have a use for them. They carry a message for me."

Painfully, with the help of his manacled hands, Konstant pushed himself to his feet. He stood, swaying a little. Still he felt nothing—no shock, no fear, not even surprise. Bron, with his golden aura, seemed distant, like someone viewed through an imperfect pane of glass.

"You saw them take me?"

Bron nodded. "I was watching."

"So you heard—"

"The offer you made them. Yes." Bron dipped a hand into the pocket of his coat and drew something out. He held it before him on his palm: the talisman. "I found it, after you left. Could you really have followed it back to me?"

"I think so." Konstant's lips felt stiff.

"What's inside it?"

"Shavings of your Guardian medal."

"Ah."

"It's feeble—it could never have located you. But the binding is strong. I could still hear it, even here."

"Is that why you left it behind? So you could return?"

"No. I only wanted to be rid of it. I never thought it would still speak to me, so far away."

Bron stepped toward Konstant, his footsteps soundless in the deepening snow. At last Konstant felt, slipping through his numbness, the cold touch of dread. Bron halted before him. He held the talisman up to his own light, turning it in his long fingers so that the flakes of gold fluttered and fell within it.

"Did you think they could destroy me?" he asked, his eyes still on the talisman. "Is that why you were willing to bring them to me?"

"No. I forgot nearly everything. But your power I remembered."

"Why, then?"

"They threatened me with a mindprobe, done the Reddened way." Bitterly, Konstant gave him the truth. "I'd hand over my own mother to avoid that. Believe me, it was much easier to give them you."

"Ah. Well, you're honest, at least."

Bron turned the talisman once more. Then he tossed it upward. It spun high, glass and metal flashing, and exploded into a glittering haze. For a moment it hung upon the air, then the air swallowed it, and it was gone.

Bron returned his gaze to Konstant's face.

"You're free now."

"Free?"

"Free of binding." Bron blinked, and the cuffs and collar and waistpiece of Konstant's manacles split into pieces and slid from his body. They made hardly a sound as they fell upon the snow. "Free to go."

Konstant stood a moment, blank. He felt the pain as the circulation returned to his blood-starved hands; he felt the lightness of his unchained arms and neck, and of his unencumbered Gift. He felt these things, but he did not quite believe them.

"Why?" he said.

"Why what?"

"Why are you letting me go?"

"Because there's no reason not to." Bron raised his brows. "Would you rather be a prisoner?"

"You aren't going to . . . take my memory again?"

"No."

"But I remember everything now. I remembered the moment I saw you."

Bron shook his head. "Your memory no longer matters."

"Why not?" Beneath Konstant's disbelief, below the accumulated shocks of the past hours, a thread of anger had begun to grow. "If it doesn't matter now, why did it matter in your house? If you can leave me intact this time, why couldn't you before?"

There was a long, long pause. "Because before, I hadn't decided to go back."

Konstant felt as if the world had spun out from beneath his feet. "*What?*" he whispered.

"You heard me."

"But—" For a moment Konstant could not shape the words. "But why? Why now?"

"What's the difference? I'm going. Isn't that enough?"

Out of nowhere, rage vaulted into being. "No." Konstant felt his body shaking. His face was on fire, his skin alight. "It's not enough. I nearly died trying to get to you. I spent weeks trying to persuade you after you refused me, while in my world Jolyon became Prior and a member of my resistance gave up all our secrets. And then after that wasted time you refused again, and crippled my memory, and threw me out of your house to wander this world believing I had failed. And now you tell me that you've changed your mind, just like that? No. It's not good enough. I want to know why. I have the *right* to know why."

Bron's brows rose again. "You, the man who was ready to bring five Roundheads into my house?"

"Five Roundheads whom you dealt with like someone crushing cockroaches. Who never would have found me if you'd made the decision when I first asked you to. Whose hands you gave me into when you cast me out into this world without my memory."

Bron watched him, a narrow scrutiny that seemed to go on forever.

"My reasons for returning are my own business," he said at last. "But you're right. There is something owed to you. If you like, you can come back with me. I don't know what will meet us there. I can't guarantee you'll live through it. But I suppose you think you have the right to that too."

"Yes." Konstant stepped forward, over the ground that separated them, his feet sinking into the snow. So transported was he that he hardly felt he moved. "At least that."

They stood, eye to eye. It was Bron, at last, who broke the gaze. Turning, he moved toward the bag he had set down.

"Are you strong enough to farwalk?" he said, over his shoulder.

"I think so."

"Good." He picked up the bag, and the box beside it. "Then follow me."

He vanished into the night.

Twenty-one

T WAS still night when Bron led them out of travelspace, at a place where miles of land had been paved over into great thoroughfares, and a warren of enormous curve-roofed buildings stood under lights that seemed only a little less powerful than the sun. From here, he planned to summon the flying machine he owned, housed at a similar facility further north. They would be traveling not by power but by technology.

"We have a lot of distance to cover," he said, imperturbably, when Konstant protested. "We must go to the mountains you know as the Fortress mountains, to the place between the worlds. It'd be tiring even for me to travel all that way by power, and you're so exhausted you can barely stand." He smiled a little. "I learned few habits of value while I was a Guardian, but one of them was not to expend Gift on something the hands can do just as well."

"But the delay . . ." Konstant felt the whole force of his old impatience, welling unbearably up within him.

"If we got there faster, we'd still have to wait. The Roundheads need time to get back to the Fortress. I put a compulsion on them, but that won't increase their speed, just their motivation."

Konstant shook his head. "Why should we wait for that?"

"I told you—they are my messengers." Bron smiled again, without humor this time. "The message is for Jolyon. I've invited him to meet me in the Garden of the Stone."

"Ah." Konstant understood now.

"You were right about him." Bron's tone was somber.

"The Roundhead leader was at the Recreation—I saw the whole thing in his mind. Jolyon did remake the Staff of Order. But not as it should be . . . and so he tried a second time, and nearly brought the roof of the Amphitheater down in the process. I don't understand it. He never showed such strength when I knew him. Why should he conceal such a Gift?"

"As an advantage to be used later, perhaps."

Bron shook his head. "He was never one to hide his assets. He tried to probe me once. I was power-bound, but even so he couldn't manage it. If he could have broken my mind that time, he surely would have done it." Bron turned away. "He killed Marhalt. Marhalt challenged him when he remade the Staff the first time. Jolyon struck him down."

There was anger in his voice. There were bad Roundheads and Roundheads less bad, but there was not one whose death Konstant could imagine regretting, even Marhalt, who had been, perhaps, the best of them. But then, Marhalt had been Bron's Mentor; there was history between them. Konstant's mind flew back across the weeks, to that last Council meeting. *You shall not have what you seek,* Marhalt had promised Jolyon then. But Jolyon did have what he had sought. And Marhalt was dead.

It would be several hours before the flying machine arrived, and so they took breakfast in the dining room of a nearby tavern. At this early hour they were the only customers. The girl who served them cast covert glances at Konstant, whose face, despite the application of self-healing disciplines, was still marked by Baffrid's bruises. At least he no longer wore the outergarment the Roundheads had slashed. Bron had created him a coat, black wool like his own, soon after they emerged from travelspace.

"Tell me," Konstant said when they were finished, and the girl had removed their plates and brought a fresh pot of the bitter black drink Bron was so fond of, and for which Konstant himself had acquired a taste during his time in this world, "when we reach the place between the worlds, what will you do?"

It would not have surprised him if Bron had refused to answer. Over the past hours, he had had time to adjust to his incredible shift of fortune—to grasp, at first falteringly, but then with growing conviction, that he had not failed after all, that the goal he had pursued for so long stood, amazingly, on the edge of fulfillment. The understanding placed him as close to joy as he had been at any point in this long, weary quest. Yet he was acutely aware of the narrowness of the chance that found him here, in this ugly dining room, taking yet another meal in Bron's company, rather than adrift somewhere, with his injured memory and his bitter message. It would have been easier, surely, for Bron make this journey unencumbered. Why he had made a different choice was as much a mystery as anything else.

Bron looked up from his cup, into which he was stirring cream, and replied without reticence.

"I'll pass through, of course. And you with me."

"Why there? Why not use the Gate?"

"Because the place between the worlds opens directly into the Garden of the Stone."

"The place between the worlds is in the Fortress?" Konstant said in some surprise.

"Yes. The Fortress was built around it. I don't know if the Guardians ever really understood its nature, but they recognized it as a place of power. They sealed it off with bindings, and built the Room of the Stone above it. They harnessed some part of its power to create a baffle-field within the Room so that the ordinary Gifts of Speakers could touch the Stone and survive. When I took the Stone, the Room was destroyed, and all the bindings and baffles as well. That's how I first discovered it."

He fell silent, as if remembering. Around them the dining room lay empty, a sea of small square tables with shiny yellow tops and metal legs. Light glared harshly from the ceiling, casting everything into too-sharp relief. There was a smell of old cooking and, from the kitchen beyond, the sound of voices.

"And when we're in the Garden," Konstant said. "What will you do then?"

"Then I'll deal with Jolyon, if he's waiting, which I assume he will be. And then I'll destroy the Fortress. And then I'll break the Guardians' bindings—all of them, all across the world, from Road to Gate to Orderhouse."

A litany of incredible acts, recited as matter-of-factly as a list of household items. "And then?"

"And then? And then I'll have done what you called me back to do."

"But the Guardians. If they survive, they'll fight to get back what they've lost."

"And the resistances will be there to oppose them. For years you've waged your battle in secret. Now you'll be able to wage it openly."

"But that will plunge the world into war! Decades of it, perhaps. And who's to say the Guardians won't win in the end?"

"That is the chance your world must take."

"Then the task will be only half done." Konstant felt something terrible rising in him, swallowing all his fragile joy. "Then you will have returned not to end the conflict, but just to shift it into a different shape."

Bron fixed Konstant with hard dark eyes. "Do you think there wouldn't be war, even if the Guardians were gone? That if your world woke up tomorrow and found the whole of its centralized system of authority vanished into thin air, it would just settle down and peacefully divide the spoils?"

"Of course I don't think that! But it would be *our* fight. It would be *our* war. A beginning, not a . . . a continuance, the same conflict fought on different ground. It's change we need, change! Not more of the same!"

"I understand your need." Bron's voice was quiet. "Truly. But I can't do what you want. I cannot—will not— deliberately take the lives of a hundred thousand men and women. I have never killed, not once in all my life, even when it meant my own survival to do so. I know that will change, when the stones of the Fortress fall and people are crushed beneath them." He paused. "But I won't defile my power by the intentional pursuit of death. Especially, I won't defile the Stone's."

Deep within himself, unwillingly, Konstant was aware of a certain understanding, drawn from his own detested past. Yet his horror at Bron's rejection of one of the most crucial aspects of the task he had been called back to perform did not allow him to acknowledge that. He saw what would come, as clearly as if he shared Goldwine's Gift: the savage conflict that would eat away the decades, laying waste to the earth and blasting its people back into a primitivism beyond even the strictures of the Limits. But he was aware that to release his feeling would accomplish neither good nor change—and, worse, might strain whatever tenuous chance that kept him at Bron's side. And so he breathed deeply, and said something other than what he wanted to say.

"You'll use the Stone's power, then?"

"Yes. And my own."

Bron glanced down at the floor beside his chair, where he had placed the cloth bag, his tense face relaxing into the complex, possessive expression he had worn in his work-room, when he spoke for the first time about the Stone. Konstant had known from the moment he saw it that the bag must hold the Stone, as much from the care Bron took with it as from the fact that there was nowhere else the Stone could be. Even so close, Konstant could not sense it—though as they walked through the cold predawn dark-ness to get to this place, it had seemed to him for a moment that he saw light leaking a little through the seams of the cloth.

"Tell me." Bron was looking at him again. "What does Goldwine think should become of the Stone, after I return?"

"She believes its power should be harnessed for human use."

"Ah. And she, I presume, wants to do the harnessing."

"She would work to learn the uses of its power, yes. And then it would be given to the world."

"You really believe she'd give it up?"

"Of course. That's the whole point. That it should never again belong to any one group. That it should never again be hidden."

Bron shook his head. "I can see you believe that. But even the best intentions run afoul of human nature. If she did take custody of the Stone, she'd never be able to rest for fighting off those who wanted it for themselves, or thought they were more fit to guard it. If she didn't lose it, she'd eventually be forced to hide it, just to make sure it didn't fall into hands less responsible than her own. And how long would it be then, do you think, before she and her followers became like the Guardians in other ways, and began to use that hidden power as a justification for social engineering and temporal oppression?"

"You don't know us, and you don't know Goldwine." Konstant did not try to hide his offense. "The resistance serves the world. It has no wish to rule it. We don't fight to perpetuate ourselves, but to establish the conditions under which we can cease to exist."

"Perhaps. Perhaps not. I intend to make sure the question never arises."

Konstant stared at him. "What do you mean?"

"When I'm finished with the Guardians, I will remove the Stone from the knowledge and understanding of your world. In time it'll be forgotten, or transformed into myth—remembered, but not believed. No one will covet it. No one will use it as a pawn, a tool, a mirror to give back their own delusions and desires. No one will make it a justification for a corrupt ambition, or a worthy one. If I accomplish nothing else of value, at least I will accomplish that."

There was absolute finality in his voice. He could do as he promised; Konstant had no doubt of it.

"What you do in the Garden of the Stone is yours to decide," he said, quietly. "I understand that it has to be that way. But after that it will be different. There will be other voices, other wills. And they won't consent to this."

"Of course." Bron nodded, acknowledging. "I expect that. And I imagine they'll believe, as you do, that I'm acting out of caprice or avarice." Again he glanced down at the bag, his face softening. "Perhaps it's true, a little. I won't deny that it would be difficult for me, very difficult, to be apart from the Stone now. I've had it to myself for thirty years. I've learned to understand its vision. I've joined my Gift to it, spread my consciousness out across the whole of the world, like light, like air . . ." For a moment he was silent. Then he looked up, his expression set again. "You don't understand what it is you want. The Stone was hidden in its Room for so many centuries that people came to believe that ordinary Gifts could merge with it and survive. But without the kind of baffle-field the Guardians used, it will tear apart all but the strongest minds that touch it. Even if Goldwine had it, she couldn't use it as she wants."

Konstant felt no anger now, only a kind of bleak understanding. In his own world, he had known prophecy's power—in its invocation of the future, in its shaping of his own destiny. In this world, he had perceived its fragility, in the weaknesses and failings of the vessels of its fulfillment. Now he recognized its irony. Bron would return, as prophesied. He would break the Guardians' rule, as had been foretold. But his will was, intractably, his own—and so the form in which he would cast these acts would be nothing like the deliverance Konstant, and Goldwine, and the other members of the resistance, waited for. It came to him, with a feeling like sickness, that in this sense his quest could still be said to be a failure.

He looked at Bron, who had receded into reverie, his eyes lowered on the glossy surface of the table, his fingers laced around his cup.

"Will you come back when you're done? To this world?"

Bron glanced up, then down again. He shook his head. "If I must seek exile, I'd rather do it in a world of Gifts. There's nothing here for me. There never really was."

"What about your house?"

"It belongs to Emme and Kari now."

At noon they returned to the place of flying machines, where Bron's machine now waited, sleek and shining as a new-forged sword. They entered it and left the earth behind. It was less difficult than Konstant might have expected to cope with this mode of travel, soaring so high that the world, below, seemed like a wrinkled cloth tossed across a vast flat tabletop. They barely appeared to move, but Bron assured him it was only distance that made it so, and in reality they were proceeding with almost the swiftness of farwalking.

They came to ground again in the Fortress mountains, dropping between the peaks toward a city that glittered like a jewel in the twilight. They spent the night at an inn, and in the morning transferred to a ground vehicle. In his travels Konstant had grown used to the sight and sound and smell of these swift-rolling conveyances, but an outside familiarity was something quite apart from being inside one. For much of the first day of travel he kept his eyes closed, so that he would not perceive the awful speed at which they hurtled forward along the twisting alpine roads.

In the final stage of the journey, which led to places where even in this world no roads ran, they returned to the ways of power. Bron, who could have covered the distance in a fraction of the time, accommodated his pace without apparent impatience to Konstant's lesser ability. They spent three days farwalking, with stops for food and sleep under the protection of weather-wards wrought out of Bron's Gift.

Toward the end of the third day they drifted out of travelspace, not into the cold and wind of a mountain night, but into the balmy warmth of a spring twilight. Around them spread a great expanse of verdant meadow, rich with tall grasses and ablaze with flowers. High above, the first stars pricked the dimming bowl of the sky.

Konstant, who had not expected anything other than the rock and snow through which the past days of traveling had taken them, stumbled in astonishment.

"This is—" He turned toward Bron. "This is like—"

"Exactly like." With calm practicality, Bron was removing his heavy coat. He glanced about, orienting himself, and then pointed. "In your world, the Fortress would be over there."

He began to move through the chest-high vegetation. The grasses bowed before him, forming a passage a little wider than his shoulders. Konstant followed, bemused, through a landscape as unlikely as a dream. At last the passage expanded into a clear area, where the grasses grew only ankle high. At the clearing's center stood a slat-built house, with a stone chimney, a plank door, and wood-shuttered windows.

"I came here not long after I arrived in this world." Bron, occupied with the lock, spoke without turning. "I had a fancy to stand in the Fortress mountains and see no Fortress there. I hadn't yet tested myself with a great work of power, and this seemed an appropriate parallelism. It's warded—it can't be seen from above, and any human being who comes here will be turned away. The house I made later, after I decided to study the place between the worlds." The lock yielded; he pushed the door open onto darkness. "We'll wait the night."

Frustration rose up within Konstant, and his muscles jumped, as if he had been standing still for hours. "Why?"

"Because I'm tired," Bron said. "Because I'm not yet ready to go."

Inside the house, Bron unlatched the shutters and threw them back, and set about calling flame upon the candles and oil lamps set about the room. It was seven years at least since he had been here, for Konstant knew from Emme that since retiring to his barren shore he had not left it, and yet there was no sign of neglect or decay. The floor was made of wood planks, and the plaster walls and ceiling were whitewashed. A wide fieldstone fireplace took up much of the left-hand side, equipped with an iron spit and pot-arms; to the right, a curtained opening led to a small bedroom. It looked much like a neat and prosperous peasant dwelling in Konstant's world. There could not have been a greater contrast to the hard, bare aesthetic of the house where he had first met Bron.

Bron woke a fire on the hearth, casting a welcome warmth into the room. He sat down on a bench nearby, setting the bag down beside him, and the wooden box, which had not been beyond the reach of his hand since they set out. Konstant seated himself in an armchair opposite, his legs stretched out before him. Already he felt the tyranny of this enforced stillness. He was aware of the closeness of what lay ahead—not a distant goal now, not divided from him by a gulf of travel and struggle, but present, imminent. The understanding was a vibration in his bones, an agitation in his blood. His soul yearned toward it, as eagerly as a lover. The whole of him protested the need to wait.

Outside, full night had fallen. The air of the meadow breathed in through the open windows, sweet and chilly, textured with the rasping song of crickets. Bron sat silent, one leg crossed beneath him, his arm on the bench's back and his eyes turned toward the fire. The weariness he had mentioned showed clearly in his face. By his expression, his thoughts were dark, as over the course of the journey they had seemed increasingly to be. During the past days he had treated Konstant with surprising consideration, as if Konstant were not an interloper but a chosen companion. It was not at all what Konstant might have expected, given the roughness of his dismissal from Bron's house and the way he had planned to return. But then much in Bron's demeanor had altered since they set out. The cool, slightly sardonic manner was rarely in evidence now. There was still the sense of inwardness, of formidable self-containment, but the serenity was no longer there, and something of the hardness had also gone.

"Tell me . . ." Bron stirred out of his glassy stillness. His words, barely rising above the insect-song, trailed away into silence; he was silent for so long that Konstant did not think he would speak again. "Tell me about my daughter."

Konstant stared at him, astonished.

"You said once that you knew her." Bron's eyes were fixed upon the fire. His voice was almost supernaturally remote. "Tell me what you remember."

And so Konstant spoke of Cariad. He spoke of her clear honesty, her swift intelligence, her reckless bravery. He spoke of her physical strength, her odd angular beauty, so like in feature to her father's. He spoke of Goldwine's care of her, of her own desire to escape that care and launch herself headlong into the outside world. He spoke of her career, which he and Goldwine had discussed a little when he returned to the hollow mountain for retraining, and of her Gift.

"She's a heartsenser, then," Bron said. "As her mother was."

Konstant held back only their liaison, the desperation with which he had loved her and the agony he had suffered when she rejected him. There had been a core of isolation in her, a distance deliberately maintained, very much like her father's; he felt it especially when they made love. She explained to him the dangers strong emotion posed for her, but he was able to read her mind, and so he knew it was more than that. He battered at the walls of her withdrawal, certain he could change her, certain she was meant for him—for was she not more like him than any woman he had ever met, in her constant stealing of the deepest secrets of others' hearts? In the end, he had succeeded only in driving her away sooner than she might otherwise have gone. It was a long time since this had had the power to hurt him. But he still, sometimes, wondered what his life might have been like if she had been willing to love him as he loved her.

Bron listened as Konstant spoke, the firelight moving on his pale skin and laying blacker shadows in the folds of his black clothes.

"And her mother," he said when Konstant was finished. "Do you know what became of her?"

"Only that she died when Cariad was three or four."

Bron nodded. His face was as set as porcelain. In anyone else Konstant would have read such rigidity as concealment of some difficult emotion, but in Bron he could not be sure. Had Bron cared for this woman? Cariad had been transcendently certain that he had, just as she had been sure he cared for her.

"There's one more thing." Konstant did not want to say it, but he could not, in conscience, keep it back. "Cariad was sent into the Fortress to assassinate Jolyon. They captured her before she could do it. She may be dead by now."

Bron shook his head. "Not dead. She was imprisoned, but she escaped somehow. They searched, but they never found her. I saw it in that Roundhead's mind."

"She was interrogated, though. Probed, by Jolyon himself. Even if she is alive, she's as good as mindless."

"Her mother . . ." Bron paused. "Her mother had a way of defending herself. A place inside her mind where she could take refuge. Cariad . . ." He hesitated, very slightly, over the name. ". . . inherited her heartsensing. It's possible she inherited that defense as well."

Konstant doubted it. Cariad had never spoken of such a thing, and he had never gleaned it from her thoughts. But he said nothing.

"I've thought about her, over the years," Bron said softly.

"About how she might grow, what she might become. She's the last of my line. The final holder of a tradition that goes back more than a thousand years. I wonder what that means to her." He paused. Light and shadow moved on his averted, weary face. "Was it really she who told you about the prophecy? This prophecy Goldwine made of my return?"

"Yes."

"It's true what I said to you, that Goldwine never spoke it to me when we met that one time." His lips lifted, fractionally. "Perhaps she understood that if I knew, I'd never let a messenger of hers get near me."

Konstant shook his head. "Why do you hate the prophecy so?"

"I hate all prophecy. I labored half my life under prophecy's burden. That's enough for anyone."

"Cariad told me about that. About the Tale, and the One Who Comes."

"I rejected it, you know. When I first came into my power, and my mother told me that was who I was, I turned away from her. Not just because I couldn't believe it—because I couldn't bear to submit to a purpose that wasn't all mine. When I was an adult I rejected it again, in a different way, for I'd learned to understand the stories of my heritage as myth. And yet there came a moment when I found myself undertaking—no, *choosing*—exactly the actions that had been foretold for me. As if will and choice and chance were meaningless. As if all the passages of my life were nothing more than devices to bring me to that point. I vowed, when I left your world, that I'd never be coerced that way again."

"Why did you change your mind, then?" Bron had refused this question once before. But it seemed to Konstant, now, that he might answer. "Why did you decide to go back?"

Bron did not reply at once, so that Konstant began to believe that he had made, by silence, the same refusal that he had spoken aloud a week ago. But at last he stirred, and sighed.

"When I decided to let you talk to me," he said, "I never

thought that you could tell me anything that would compel me. I was done with your world. I'd renounced both prophecy and ambition. But I was curious about the things you'd told me at our first meeting. And so I thought, as long as you were in my house, that I could indulge myself a little. I knew you'd be willing, for I could see you still believed you could persuade me.

"But . . ." He paused. "The first evening we spoke together I heard from you a thing that seized my imagination. You told me of Goldwine's machines, of her mixing of the powers of hand and mind. I said to you, before I sent you away, that mindskills die out in a world that's free to choose technology. And I do believe that's so. But I wonder if perhaps Goldwine has found a third path. If the choice never had to be made . . . if the powers weren't left separate, but were fused, joined . . . if an entirely new power were created at the meeting point . . . then, perhaps, Gift might survive the lifting of the Limits."

"Yes." Konstant was surprised. It had never seemed to him that his words had more impact than grains of sand. Each night he tossed them outward into darkness; each night Bron shook them from his clothes and left them to lie upon the floor. "That's exactly what Goldwine is working to achieve. A third power, created from the joining of mind and hand."

"You made that clear. You also made it clear that the promise of this third way would most likely die before it was truly born. Your stories of Reddened atrocity shocked me, I admit. I think I had forgotten a little, in this world where so many people live in relative freedom, the truth of the kind of tyranny the Guardians practice."

He shifted on the bench, turning to face Konstant directly. "And then there was you yourself. It's been . . . a long time . . . since I was in the company of the Gifted." He shook his head. "It's a hollow place, this world. Gifts are irrelevant to the forces here. To possess one is meaningless, and to use one . . . to use one is to venture into nothingness, and return with messages of the void. I've gotten used to it, over the years—I've had to, in self-defense. And I had the Stone, of course. But the Stone isn't human. One longs, after a time, to stand face-to-face with someone like oneself. I wasn't prepared for . . . the power of that, when it came. I knew that I should make you leave, or at least stop listening to you. But I was . . . reluctant to be alone again in this Giftless world."

Konstant felt a stab of anger. This, from the man who had set a blind across his memory, and cast him out into the night. "Not too reluctant," he said, before he could stop himself.

Bron glanced away. "I was angry, I admit it. Angry that the world I'd renounced still had the power to command my sympathy. Angry that it wasn't you I questioned, or what you told me, but myself. Before you came, I had a kind of peace. I'd taught myself to set aside purpose and ambition. I'd found a way to live without passion or compulsion. But you told me to take up all those things again. To believe again, to step back into the way of pain and failure. And to compel me, to make me think that I should do this, you invoked prophecy. I saw it coming toward me yet again, the willing embrace of a destiny spoken for me by others. I couldn't accept that, and so I gathered up my will and turned you out." He was silent for a moment. "I thought, once you were gone, that I could forget you and your words. Instead I found myself thinking about what you said to me before you left."

If his altered skin had allowed it, Konstant would have flushed.

"I was . . . not myself. I didn't know what I was saying."

"Oh, I think you did." Again Bron shifted his position, leaning forward, his hands clasped between his knees. His eyes were fixed on the floor at his feet. "You saw me very truly. I thought about that, about why I had refused you. About the peace I thought I'd found, which was also the peace of a prison or a coffin. And I saw the truth: that I could live for centuries, or die tomorrow, and either would be equally meaningless." He smiled, a bitter stretching of his lips. "Once I believed with all my heart that the withdrawal from suffering by those with the power to address it was among the greatest of all evils. And yet that was what I myself had done. What I had become. When I saw that, I understood I could not remain in this world. Not just because it was right to do this thing you asked of me, not just because I was the only one who could do it, but because no matter how much I detested the thought of acting, refusing to act would be worse.

"So now it'd as you wanted." He looked up, into Konstant's face. "Yet again, of my own free will, I've chosen the path of prophecy. And still I don't want to do this thing. I fear the damage that may follow. I fear that your third way of power will fail, and Gift will die out after all, as it has in other worlds. Your prophecy takes no account of that, does it? It doesn't address the consequences of fulfillment. Do you ever think about that, you resistance people? Do you ever think that getting what you want may not bring you what you wish for?"

"I already know we won't get either one," Konstant had thought about this, a great deal, over the past days, "because of the way you plan to answer the prophecy. What you'll give us is much, much less than we want or need. But it's something. And whatever comes of it, it'll be better than what we have now. Because it will be ours. Ours to build, ours to shape. Ours to fail, if it comes to that."

"I might have answered the same way, when I was in your world. If I'd known, on the night I took the Stone, how to join my mind to it as I do now, I have no doubt I'd have done all you want and more out of my own desire. The Fortress would be a pit. Every Orderhouse and Residence would lie in ruins. There would be adults in your world who could not remember the years when Guardians walked the earth."

For the first time Konstant seemed to glimpse the sort of passion he had, long ago, imagined he must find in this man. "Do you truly no longer feel those things?" he asked, curiously.

Bron glanced away, back toward the fire. "I must feel them. Or at least some part of them. Why else would I be unable to talk myself out of going back? But it's hard to tell, after so long."

Silence fell between them. The insect-song rose up to fill it, and the small sound of the flames. Konstant fixed his gaze on the patterns they made. He was aware that Bron had turned again and was watching him.

"I've used you badly," Bron said.

Konstant looked at him, startled.

"Perhaps you think I'm not aware of that, but I am. I didn't need to take your memory. I have nothing to fear from the Arm of the Stone, from any Guardian. But I was angry, and I took it out on you. It was unfair. It's been on my mind for some time that I should apologize."

"There's no need." Because Bron had chosen—for whatever reasons—to answer the prophecy, because he allowed Konstant at his side, because there was no purpose in anger, Konstant had made an effort to bury his consciousness of this injury. Yet he still felt it, and this tardy admission only increased the sharpness of that. "It's past and done with."

"Still. It should be acknowledged."

"There's no honor in being sorry for something once it's done." Konstant could not stop himself from saying it. "Honor lies in not doing it in the first place."

"Perhaps you're right." Bron did not seem to take offense. "It's a rare thing, honor. I haven't encountered it very often in my life. Certainly I haven't always shown it myself. But you—you are a man of honor. A brave man. From the start I recognized that."

"No," Konstant said, not certain what he was denying.

"You journeyed through a world you didn't understand, a world that nearly killed you, to bring me a summons I refused. And then you sat across from me night after night, patiently speaking the truth as you understood it, though I gave you nothing in return, not a shred of hope that I would ever do what you wanted. You didn't yield; you didn't give up. You spoke, and spoke, and your words were like the drops of water that over time wear great stones down to nothing. The truth has been revealed to you, hasn't it? The dross, the doubt, the pointless desires and distractions that muddy intent and will—it's all been burned out of you. You are a true believer. I could almost envy you. Things were never so clear me, even when I was in your world."

Konstant was amazed, at last, into laughter. But it was not amusement he felt, though he could not quantify the insult that churned within him, or define what it was in Bron's tone, Bron's profound misreading of his character, that produced in him such a feeling of indignity and disgust.

"You know nothing about me," he said, harshly. "Nothing about my beliefs or the way I've lived my life. You have no right to tell me about myself."

"I'm sorry," Bron said mildly. "I meant to pay you a compliment."

"A compliment!" Konstant felt anger burst within him, flying up out of nothing—or perhaps out of everything, out of the whole course of his time in this world, out of all the nights he had spent in Bron's company, speaking not patiently as Bron had said, but on the barest knife-edge of control, his doubt heaving in him like a secret sickness. And his corruption, which could abide in silence, but could not, suddenly, bear to hear itself so misnamed. "Why should you compliment me? I have none of those qualities you admire. I'm the opposite of those things."

"Why is it," Bron said, his dark eyes acute, "that you dislike yourself so much?"

"Do you really want to know?" Konstant leaned forward, speaking directly into Bron's face. "You said once that you'd never killed. Well, I have, or as good as, and done much other damage besides, and none of it in battle or self-defense. Fifty-four minds I've destroyed, in the Reddened way, and all before I was twenty years old. Fifty-four. How honorable is that? How admirable? Do you still envy me, now you know the truth?"

He forced himself to stop. It seemed that he could still hear the words, echoing on the silence. He could not quite believe he had said them. Across from him, Bron's face had grown still.

"I take it, then, that the baiting group you were part of during your Arm Apprenticeship was connected with the Reddened."

Konstant had never confessed to a living soul what he had just told Bron. Before this moment, he would not have thought that there was anything in the world that could induce him to speak it aloud. He certainly would not have believed, if by some disastrous error he did let something slip, that he would feel a need to say even more. But he had unlocked a door, a door he rarely opened even to himself; and now he found himself possessed by the desire to let it all fall out of him, this poisonous truth of his inmost being: the whole of it, just once.

"Yes. It was."

"Baiting is a filthy practice. It doesn't surprise me the Reddened would encourage it. Yet it's hard to imagine that even they would allow Apprentices to probe that way."

"Not just allow. Train. The group was run by Reddened Masters. They skimmed the incoming classes for the Apprentices with the strongest mindspeaking Gifts. I was recruited before the end of my first year."

"And they taught you to do this kind of probing?"

"Yes. I spent eight months learning theory. Then I was given a subject to practice on. They didn't expect me to succeed. New recruits never do. But I did. I got it right the first time." He paused, remembering. His victim had been a servant boy from the Apprentice College downworld, a thin youth a little younger than Konstant himself. A weird mix of terror and resignation had filled the boy's face; when Konstant was done he had no expression at all, and his eyes, which had been blue, were dilated nearly black. At the sight of this, at the understanding of what his Gift was capable of, he had been overcome by icy nausea and had nearly disgraced himself, after his great triumph, by vomiting on the floor. "They told me no one had ever done that before. I became the group's star. I gave demonstrations. I instructed others. I was rewarded. They were all in awe of me, even the Masters."

Bron's regard held uncomfortable understanding. "But you took no pleasure in it."

"I can't . . . honestly say that I didn't feel the power of it." Konstant swallowed. "Of my Gift's . . . mastery. But I knew it was abominable, what I did, what I could do so well. I always knew that."

"And yet you did it."

"I was ambitious. I wanted the things they promised me." The words, often thought, never spoken, seemed to lacerate his throat. "Later . . . I thought this must be the path I was meant to walk. Why else would I have this horrible skill, this understanding no one else possessed? I thought it was my own deficiency that made me hate it. That I didn't believe strongly enough in the corruption of the world, or the mission of the Arm, or the cleansing mandate of the Reddened. I thought that if I did it often enough, and violently enough, I would come to want it, as my companions did."

"And did you?"

"No. No, I never did."

Bron watched him. His ivory face was smooth. There was no judgment in it, no disgust. "Is that why you defected?"

"No. Well, yes, but . . . it wasn't the cause. I was to give a demonstration. One of the Masters was present. The victim was a Soldier. I told you it was my habit to skim the thoughts of the people around me, and so I knew the Masters had chosen this Soldier because the Soldier had insulted him—some stupid matter of etiquette. This Master was . . . especially fond of torture. And he hated this Soldier. When I finished the probe I turned to him—skimming, as I always did. His guard was down, and mine was too. He was careless, and I reached too deep. And I saw it: the truth about the Stone. And I knew I'd done it all for nothing. Fifty-four dead minds . . . the torture . . . the sickness after . . . the dreams . . ." For a moment he could not continue. "All for a lie. For a hoax. I wanted to die. The Master would have killed me anyway, for invading his mind. But I was afraid of the pain. So I went out onto the snow."

"And Goldwine's people found you. And you, who were almost a Roundhead, who were actually a Red, gave yourself to the cause of Guardian overthrow."

"Yes," Konstant said harshly. "I thought I could atone."

"And have you?"

Konstant looked away. "No."

"Why not?"

"Because . . ." Konstant paused, struggling. "Because this thing exists in me. This skill, this corruption of my Gift. Actions can't change it. Belief can't change it. No matter what I do, it will always be there."

"But you renounced it. You repudiated your past."

"But I probed for two years. Two years! I didn't have the strength to refuse it. I didn't have the courage to believe in the rightness of my own disgust. It wasn't until I found out about the Stone and knew I would die anyway that I found the will to leave. But for that, I'd probably be Red today. Still killing minds. Still trying to love it. And maybe I would have learned by now."

"Have you used this part of your Gift since you defected?"

"I had to probe Talesin . . . the man whose face I wear . . . in order to take his place. And then . . . when I became Red . . ." He shuddered. "And there's the thought-skimming, which comes from the same place, I think—I've never been able to make myself give that up . . ." He took a breath. "But other than those things, no. I swore an oath. I've kept it."

"Do you miss the probing?" Bron's eyes were steady. "Do you desire it?"

"No!" said Konstant violently. "Never!"

"Then it seems to me you that judge yourself too harshly." Bron's tone was surprisingly gentle. "For—how many years? Ten? Twelve?—you've served the cause you chose. That's longer than you served the Guardians. Whatever stain remains in you, you've put a great distance between that and where you stand today. And I think . . ." He paused. "I think that whatever punishment you might have deserved, you inflicted it on yourself long ago."

Konstant shook his head. The feeling that had urged him to confess had entirely left him. Depression lay across his soul, flat and gray as ash. It was not often that he allowed himself to look so deeply into his memory, though the sense of it was always with him—not just because of the images that were so painful, but because of the layers of distraction it peeled away. He saw his life naked now, stripped of either hope or deception: the attempts to remake himself through conversion, through risk, through work; the efforts to redeem with present actions the atrocities of the past. All of them pointless, fruitless. For no matter what cause he wrapped around himself, no matter what deeds he did in hope of transformation, the self beneath endured, unchanging and inexpiable. And to this fact he must, always and inevitably, return.

The fire leaped upon the hearth. Outside, the moon had set, and the insect song was quiet. Bron stirred and got to his feet. He moved to the hearth and stood looking down, his hands thrust into the deep pockets of his black woolen trousers.

"What will you do?" he said, gazing into the flames. "Once all of this is over?"

"Fight in the war that follows." The words seemed inexpressibly hollow. "Though perhaps I'll go to Malinides first and ask for my face back."

"Could that be done?"

"Probably not. Oh, the makers could remold me, if I were willing to endure it. But I doubt any of them remembers what I looked like. And I wouldn't go through that again just for another stranger's face."

He had not meant to inject such loathing into the words. Bron turned. For a moment the dark eyes rested on him.

"I could give you back your face," Bron said. "Painlessly, I believe."

"How? You never knew my face at all."

"You carry an image of yourself within your mind, don't you? And your bones hold the memory of how they used to be. I can do this for you," he repeated. "If you want it."

"But—" Konstant stopped, afraid to acknowledge the hope that struggled in him. "I don't—"

"Do you want it?"

Their gazes held. "Yes," Konstant whispered.

"Stand up." As if in a dream, Konstant stood. "Close your eyes."

Konstant did so. He felt the motion of the air, and then Bron's hands, the palms against his cheeks, the long fingers splayed across his forehead and temples and eyelids, the thumbs upon his lips. Bron's touch was warm, and as dry as sand. Konstant could feel the heat of his body, radiating even through his heavy garments. He could smell their scent, something faint and aromatic, with an arid undertone, like dust.

"Think of your face," Bron said softly. "Imagine your features. Hold them in your mind."

Konstant obeyed. The shape of his lost face bloomed behind his eyes, like the face of a lover. Bron's heat was within him now, reaching through his skin, through his blood, down to his bones. He felt a presence in his mind, sliding through his thoughts; then it vanished, and there was only the heat, leaping violently up inside his body as if everything in him had turned to fire. It was fierce, this blaze of transformation, and wrenching, but it was not painful. And though the fires were Bron's, they burned not to Bron's will but to Konstant's, to his own sense and body memories, to his own desire for change. And in that instant it seemed to him that if he reached a little more, stretched a little further, the power of that heat might remake not just his face, but the whole of him, inside and out—

And then the fire was gone. Bron's hands withdrew. Konstant cried out in loss, reaching out his own hands, closing them on empty air.

"It's done," Bron said. "Open your eyes."

Konstant did. The room bulked around him: the white-washed walls, the rough furnishings, the leaping flames. He was deeply cold, as if the generative fire had hollowed out his bones and left them empty.

"There's no mirror," Bron said. "I'm sorry." Then: "You're younger than I thought."

Slowly, fearfully, Konstant raised his hands to his cheeks. Beneath his fingers, his skin was no longer stiff and coarse, but smooth, supple. He felt the planes of cheek-bones and nose and forehead, the long clean lines of jaw and lips. He had not been certain he would recognize the feel of himself, if he ever became himself again. But he did. This was, unmistakably, his own face, the face he had believed he would never wear again.

Bron was watching him, his dark gaze unreadable. He seemed to be waiting—for gratitude? Phrases of thanks? Konstant's lips were soft and flexible again, and yet his mouth was frozen. Words struggled within him, but he could not utter even one of them.

He turned and stumbled through the open door. The

grasses closed around him, sharp and spring-scented. The sky arched above him, cold with stars. He moved aimlessly, not knowing where he went, on legs that seemed too weak to hold him. The new skin of his cheeks was wet with tears. He wept for what he had been given, for the return of a thing he had thought was lost forever. He wept for what had been taken from him, for the fire that had filled him and left him too soon. He wept because, this time, he really had been remade. And still he was himself.

When the sky grayed with dawn, Konstant returned to the house. He felt wrung out, transparent, drained of feeling. Bron was waiting, arrayed upon the bench, his eyes fixed on the still-burning fire. There was no sign that he had moved the whole night long. He glanced up when Konstant entered and rose to his feet, bending to take up his coat. Konstant did the same.

They left the house. Bron pulled the door carefully closed behind him. On the edge of the clearing, he paused and turned; Konstant, ahead of him, could not see his face, but he could have sworn there was sadness in the way he stood there, looking back.

They pushed through the meadow, Bron in the lead now. The grasses thinned as they reached the edges. A margin of frost and sere vegetation marked the transition between spring and winter. They passed back into the realm of cold, into a monochrome world: white snow, gray sky, and themselves, black-clad, printing a dark trail of footsteps behind them. The air was frigid, the wind a knife. Konstant lifted his face to its painful caress. The cold spoke to him, enfolding the planes and angles of his restored features, telling him that his skin was his own again.

Some distance from the meadow's edge, Bron halted and turned. Konstant felt the swell of power, so huge that for an instant he could neither breathe nor see. And then the meadow was gone. There was no explosion, no cloud of dust, nothing at all to mark the destruction. The grass, the flowers, simply vanished, like a mirage dispelled by a blink of the eye. All that remained was a great blankness of barren, snowless ground.

Konstant stood, shocked. "Why?" It was the first word that had passed between them since he had returned. "Why destroy it?"

Bron's gaze did not shift from the place where the meadow had been. "Nothing is ever truly destroyed," he said. "I simply released the matter that composed it."

"But why not let it stay?"

Bron shook his head. "Such things have no place in this world."

They turned, and moved on.

Deep within the snowfield, they came upon the place between the worlds. It was a circle of utter blackness, perhaps six manlengths in diameter, an onyx interruption in the perfection of the snow. It seemed flat and solid as a plaque of stone. But now and then there was motion, a stygian shuddering deep within it, and it could be seen that its darkness was not the darkness of solidity but of void.

Bron knelt by the circle's edge, the skirts of his long coat falling around him like a pool of ink. He set the wooden box upon the snow and turned to the bag. Sliding back the tag of its metal closure, he reached inside, parting layers of cloth. Light sprang up, a golden radiance so intense Konstant gasped and flinched away. Slowly, with great care, Bron drew out the Stone.

It seemed to Konstant that he held the sun between his hands. It did not appear to be a corporeal object at all, but a gathering of golden fire, coruscating furiously at its heart with every color of the rainbow. The brilliance it cast off burnished all the world around it, gilding the white snow and banishing the arctic grayness of the sky. Only the place between the worlds resisted its illumination, for its emptiness was greater than any source of brightness, capable not of being lit but only of swallowing light.

"It's beautiful, isn't it?" Bron's face, bent upon the Stone, seemed to be burning. His eyes were half-closed, his mouth soft. "Listen. Listen to its song."

Konstant, nearly blinded, closed his eyes. He stretched out his Gift, strained with all his senses. But he could hear nothing.

He opened his eyes. Bron had set the Stone upon the

snow. He placed the wooden box inside the bag.

"Will you carry this for me?"

Konstant nodded.

"Take care with it. What's inside has meaning for me."

Konstant stooped, and took up the bag. Bron lifted the Stone again. Rising, he turned to face the black circle.

"Are you afraid?" Across the splendor in his arms, he met Konstant's eyes.

"No." It was the truth. Konstant had never feared this. It was not the things outside him he feared, in any case.

"We must be linked," Bron said, and held out his left hand. Konstant looked at it, at the face above it, the ivory skin and black hair and clear black eyes, which he had come to know so well over the past weeks, better certainly than his own. He could not feel the Stone, but he could feel Bron's Gift, the great continuum of his power, an invisible counterpart to the Stone's raging golden light. It came to him that though he had been angry at this man, had mistrusted him, had even hated him, he had not once, not ever, doubted his ability to accomplish the thing they went to do. His faith in that Gift was absolute.

He reached out. Bron's fingers closed around his own. Even in this cold, his skin was hot. They stepped forward, toward the empty blackness of the place between the worlds.

The Winter Garden

Twenty-two

ARIAD CROUCHED against the coping that bounded the roof of the Searcher Wing, gazing down on the field of snow that had been the Garden of the Stone. It was deeply cold, and the sky was veiled in cloud. From the Journeyer Wing came the sounds of fighting, rising up on the still air: the crash of collapsing stone, the splintering of wood, the barking phrases of the Soldiers' battle-language.

Two weeks earlier, when she first mounted here, the Garden had rested safe within its bindings—wintry, for it was winter outside the Fortress, but gently so, untouched by snow, the grass still green in sheltered spots. The Garden once had been a place of constant spring, an ever-blooming paradise covering the full expanse of the hollow square described by the windowless back walls of the four Suborder Wings. But when Cariad's father destroyed the Room of the Stone and the bindings that held the Stone in place, the Garden's weather-bindings were also broken. The bindings the Guardians created to replace them lacked the scope and power of the originals; the remade Garden was not a place of unchanging spring, but of seasons that mimicked those of the natural world—milder seasons to be sure, but seasons still. All around the perimeter lay a margin of deep cold, where snow piled up in drifts and ice hung from the branched skeletons that had been living trees.

But three days ago, the binding-failures that had wracked the Fortress for the past week reached out to touch this place as well. On the second of her daily visits to the roof,

Cariad looked down to find the Garden fully claimed by winter, the dome of the Room rising at its center like a frozen pearl. It was the second of Goldwine's signs. Since then, Cariad had not left the roof. Day and night she waited here, watching for her father's return.

With the shattering of the Staff of Order, the doubt and torment she had suffered since her mindprobe had shattered also. It was not that her shame at her betrayal had lessened, or that she had forgiven herself for the heedless hubris that had led her into captivity, but if those actions had changed the world, they had not changed the necessity of living in it. Better to accept that altered shape than to expend her energy in recrimination or allow remorse and self-blame to paralyze her. There was no honor in having done harm, but there was even less in failing to redress it, where the possibility of redress existed. She was alive, and she was free. If Jolyon was waiting for her father when he arrived, then she must be waiting also.

She had already made up her mind, before the Recreation, to quit the caverns. Her new goal only added force to that determination, for she could not watch the Garden from underground. But in the stunned aftermath of Jolyon's accession, she did not have the heart to tell Orrin she was leaving, and each day that passed seemed to make it more difficult to speak. She did not want to hurt him. She did not want to see his face change as she spoke the words he dreaded so, or to hear him plead or rage at her. Most of all, she did not want to have to use her Gift on him, should he be foolish enough to try and stop her. It had not been this way with the other lovers she had fled. She had tried, always, to be kind, but their wounded feelings had never made her pause, neither had she flinched from the thought of their pain. In her reluctance she saw yet again the extent to which she had become bound to this man, and this made her even more certain she must leave.

Orrin, no doubt suspecting what she planned, refused to quit her side, shadowing her like a ghost during the day, lying wakeful beside her at night. She could feel his fear, constant as a heartbeat. His split lip pained him, bleeding afresh whenever he spoke or ate, but he would not allow her speed his healing through her Gift, as she did for her own broken cheekbone. He turned instead to the transporters' herbalist, who stitched up the torn flesh and gave him compresses to hold off infection.

In the end she stole away in secret, three nights after the Recreation, when at last Orrin lost his struggle against sleep. So that there would be no mistake about the finality of her departure, she left behind the bracelet he had given her, a graceful design of braided wheat stalks worked in the translucent rosy stone the transporter carvers favored. She had worn it only to please him, for she was not fond of jewelry. She had not thought it would cost her anything to part with it. Yet she felt a pang as she slipped it off her wrist, and was seized by a sudden desire to keep it, as a token of him.

She had told herself she would not look back. But she could not help herself. As she stood watching him, his skin white in the shadow of the apple trees, his fair hair patched with silver by the drifting dimlight, she felt a pain she scarcely comprehended, as if something in her were being ripped away. And she understood that it was this that had really held her here these past days: not her reluctance to speak of her intent, not the fear of hurting him, but the dread of what she was feeling now.

With an effort of will, she forced herself to turn away. With another, she moved on.

There had been signs, in the caverns, of the disaster in the Amphitheater. Hundreds of servants had perished in the panic between the walls; in the days after the Recreation there was hardly an agricultural worker who did not display the white headband and ash-marked cheeks that signified the loss of a blood relative of three degrees or less of removal. Yet the business of supply, going on as usual, cast a misleading semblance of normalcy over cavern life, and in the closed and secret world of the transporters it was possible to imagine nothing had changed at all. It was not that the transporters lacked knowledge of what had happened: pan-Fortress travelers that they were, they owned all the details within a day. But none of them had been there, and none had died. Beyond that, Jolyon's accession meant no more to them than any other Guardian's, for they cared nothing for the world above the ground.

It was something of a shock, therefore, to find how deeply change had printed itself elsewhere. In the downworlds, as in the caverns, work went on, for the Guardians must still be tended and supplied. But here too were headbands and ash marks—and, beyond the mourning, a kind of stunned bewilderment, as if it were not just the mindlight of the Amphitheater that had been extinguished, but the sun or the moon. The Amphitheater itself lay devastated, the formerly flawless material of its arena a expanse of fractured rubble, its stairstep benches tumbled and fissured and streaked with the colored dust that had once been the glass of the high windows.

The Fortress's great entrance court, usually a teeming bustle of Guardians and workers and arrivals and departures, now stretched all but deserted. The vast Library, ordinarily crowded with Searchers composing treatises or pursuing research, now was a domain of ghosts. In the Novice Wing the training went on, the teachers shepherding their charges through the misery of cold and discipline that was the Novitiate, while in the Apprentice Wing the Apprentices were confined to quarters, all classes suspended. Pilgrims and guests were locked up inside their barracks and hostels, against the possibility that they might flee back to the world with rumors of the Recreation and the changes that had followed it. Desertions and new alliances had entirely altered the population of the Suborder Wings, emptying some, crowding others to bursting.

And everywhere were Soldiers: patrolling the entrance court, policing the pilgrim compounds, stationed around the Prior's Palace, drilling on the vast parade ground beyond the Suborder Wings. Jolyon had not yet brought his fellow Guardians under his control, but he had lost no time setting the seal of his command upon the Fortress itself, which now resembled a city under hostile occupation.

His second attempt to create the Staff of Order had wrenched all the stones and jewels from the Chairs of Recreation, and produced out of that raw material something closer to the proper form. But the Guardians, fleeing for their lives from the destruction of that remaking, had never given him the formal acknowledgment the ritual of accession required, and so, officially, he was not Prior. When he went out to claim the Prior's Palace, with his servant and his companions and a retinue of Reds, he found a group of Speakers waiting for him, the Staff-Holder and his Second among them. They had summoned up a strong collective warding of obstruction; standing behind it, they denied him entrance. Jolyon did not bother with diplomacy. Using his servant's skill to steal the power he needed, he broke the warding and struck the Speaker Staff-Holder and his Second dead, as he had Marhalt. It was said, by those who told this story, that he and his Reds walked upon the bodies as they made their way into the Palace.

When he received this news Siringar, the Journeyer Staff-Holder, withdrew inside the Journeyer Wing, where he declared himself true Prior and set Journeyer farspeakers to disseminate the news of his accession to the Guardians outside the Fortress. The Journeyers, largest of the five Suborders by reason of their charge of teaching and administration within the world, possessed a huge core of makers, a power-resource even the Speakers could not claim. Within an hour of Siringar's retreat, the Journeyer Wing was closed and barred by impenetrable mindmade defenses.

These were opened, the following day, to admit the Treasurer and Limit-Master of the Roundhead Council together with those moderate Roundheads who had been loyal to Marhalt, and, a little later, the Searcher Staff-Holder, who before the Ceremony had strongly backed Jolyon's proxy. Less than a quarter of his Ordermen followed him, and only two members of his Council. The Searchers were deeply conservative; the majority of them, though profoundly shaken by what Jolyon had done, were unwilling to support the liberal Siringar. They remained unaligned, as did the Speakers, outraged by Jolyon's murder of their Staff-Holder, but like the Searchers adamantly opposed to Siringar's claim.

All this information Cariad gleaned in the first days of her freedom, ghosting about the Fortress, clad now in a semblance, now in invisibility. With her skills of subterfuge and disguise, she had no difficulty surviving undetected. It might not have been so easy if the Fortress had been less in turmoil, or if Jolyon had still been looking for her. But, presumably preoccupied by his efforts to consolidate his new position, he seemed to have given up the search. The likenesses of herself and Orrin posted on the walls of the downworlds had been torn down. Soldiers, fully occupied above the ground, no longer patrolled the tunnels or guarded the entrances to what lay below.

She ate food pilfered from the downworlds and slept warmly amid the hay of the stables of the entrance court. From the grooms she stole a shirt and tunic and leggings and boots, sturdier and more practical than her filmy transporter garments. She picked the ribbons and beads from her hair, and braided it into a single plait; it was a great relief not to have that noisy decoration dragging at her scalp. She slipped past the defenses of the Soldier Wing, into the armory that took up the whole of the second floor, and chose a dagger to carry in her belt and another for her boot.

Twice a day she mounted to the roof of the Searcher Wing, to see whether Goldwine's second sign had yet come to pass. The rest of the time she ranged the Fortress, spying on the Guardians and their servants. She avoided the Keep, where the Reddened now held exclusive sway, and the Prior's Palace, where Jolyon and the Soldier Staff-Holder plotted strategy, but no other part of the Fortress was closed to her, not even the mind-defended sanctums of the Journeyer Wing. There was nothing she could do with this intelligence; she gathered it from habit, and to sharpen her physical skills, which her time in the Fortress had depleted, and also in hope that the resistance—whose plan of attack, in the context of the Fortress's conflict, no longer seemed quite so suicidal—would find it useful when it came. Mostly, though, she gathered it to distract herself, so that she would not have to think the thoughts that came to her whenever she stopped moving.

It had taken all her will to turn away from Orrin forever. She had told herself, then, that this was the greatest effort she would have to make, the worst pain she would have to feel. But the days passed, and the wound of their separation did not close. His absence was a void in her, as deep as the abyss at the core of Goldwine's mountain. She strove to purge herself of him, to close her mind to the memory of his face and voice and hands. But the whole world spoke to her of him. She saw his eyes in the gray of Guardian robes, and the color of his hair in the straw of the stables where she slept, uncontrollable associations that stopped her in her tracks sometimes with the force of longing they carried. Now and then, in the tunnels or the downworlds, a flash at the corner of her eye or a figure half-seen through an archway caused her to whirl about, her heart pounding, certain he had come searching for her, as he had done when she was captured. But it was never him. She had left him, and he had let her go.

Time, she told herself when she could not fight the memories, when she woke from dreams with tears on her cheeks. Time would release her—quickly, if she did not survive her father's return, or through attrition, if she lived beyond it. One way or another, she would be free.

Five days after the Ceremony, Jolyon sent a party of Reds to Siringar, with an ultimatum: bow to Jolyon's rule, or suffer the consequences. Siringar, who for all his liberal politics was as ruthless as any Roundhead, reduced the Reds to a pile of disarticulated body parts which he set outside the doors of the Journeyer Wing in seven blood-stained baskets. Within an hour, the Journeyer Wing and all the unaligned Guardians of the Fortress were under siege.

The Journeyers' defenses held—but the Soldiers were assisted by the powerful Gifts of the Reddened, who fought at their side. In order to keep their barriers whole, the defenders were forced to pull them inward, giving the Soldiers access to the Journeyer Wing inch by inch. In the Searcher Wing, the battle went more quickly: the Searchers, unworldly teachers and scholars with little experience of conflict, put up almost no defense, and within a day they had all surrendered to Jolyon's demands. The Speakers mounted a stiffer resistance. They were the smallest of the Suborders, but they had once been the keepers of the Stone, and except for the Arm of the Stone, they were the most

Gifted of all Guardians. The battle for the Speaker Wing proceeded slowly, room by room. To a man, the captured Speakers refused to capitulate. The midden-pit outside the walls was soon littered with their bodies.

"It hardly matters if we kill them all," Cariad overheard a cynical Soldier say. "Why do we need an entire Suborder just to stand in the Garden and give false answers to pilgrims? Any of us could do it just as well."

That such a thing could be said aloud was a sign, as clear as the fighting itself, of how fractured the once-impermeable structure of Guardian unity had become.

Three days into the conflict, Cariad was wrenched awake in her hayloft bed by an enormous thundering roar. It seemed the mountains themselves must be falling. Emerging, shaken, she found the air almost solid with dust and sharp with an odor that made her think of lightning strikes. Slowly, as the dust cleared, it became apparent that a portion of the walls had fallen in: the whole of the rebuilt section that her father had destroyed. The warehouses at its base lay crushed beneath tumbled blocks. The snow outside was black with chunks and shards of stone.

In the great stillness that succeeded the collapse, even the battle for the Journeyer Wing came to a halt. Roundheads and Soldiers gathered, awed. Downworlders and Searchers stole out to join them. Jolyon himself came to inspect the damage, wearing the Prior's robe of many colors and carrying the Staff of Order—which looked much as it should but not quite, like an inexpert reproduction of a famous piece of jewelry. A retinue of Reds followed him; his servant walked directly at his back and, behind him, two companions. Neither was Baffrid. Cariad, watching invisibly from the roof of the stables, wondered where Jolyon's favorite henchman might be.

It was the first time since the Ceremony that she had seen him. But the fear that had gripped her in the Amphitheater, the plunge into memory, did not take her this time. Instead she felt the killing fires, burning hotly in her palms. Her hands curved around the memory of his bony shoulders as she had felt them when she hauled him out from behind his desk. For the first time, consciously, she understood that he no longer filled her dreams, or tyrannized her waking thoughts. She wondered, surprised, what had worked the change. The return to the freedom of her operative ways? Passing time? Or perhaps it was simply that she had a plan again and was no longer adrift.

When he had looked his fill, Jolyon turned, drawing his train of followers behind him like the tail of a snake, and made his way back to the Prior's Palace. The crowd remained for some time after he had gone, murmuring uneasily.

Cariad had thought, briefly, that Goldwine and her people might have caused the walls to fall, making a way in for themselves in preparation for the promised attack. But in the days that followed there was no sign of the resistance, or of any other outside force. The gap was never without watchers: sometimes just a Soldier or two, sometimes larger groupings, now and then a huddled crowd of downworlders. Speculation ran rampant. It was Siringar and his makers who had caused the destruction. It was the Journeyers outside the Fortress, come to add their numbers to the battle. It was the Speakers, prepared to destroy the Fortress rather than let it fall to Jolyon. It was Jolyon himself, demonstrating once again, for the benefit of those who opposed him, the ruinous power of his Gift, which was now universally acknowledged to be the strongest, and the strangest, in living memory.

It had not been masonry that held the repair in place, but a binding: Cariad discovered this two days after the collapse, passing through the Searcher Wing on the second of her daily journeys to the roof. A little group of Searchers stood clustered on a landing of the Wing's great central stairway; she paused below them, listening.

"No," one of them was saying, a bent man at least twice the age of the oldest of his companions. "It isn't commonly known now. But I remember it. They even brought in masons from the outside world, and still they couldn't get more than a dozen courses high before the stones fell in again. After a year the Prior decreed that the Journeyers should gather together all their makers and create a binding to do what mortar could not. It took them some time, but eventually they did get it to stand."

"It just goes to prove what I said before," said a second Searcher—the youngest of them, by his looks no more than a couple of years beyond his Investment. "It was Siringar and his makers, opening a way for the outside Journeyers they've summoned as reinforcement."

"And as *I* said, the Fortress Passage is surely blocked, and no one can get through," said a third Searcher, a woman somewhere in her middle years. "If Siringar did it for that, he wasted his strength."

"Perhaps he meant it as a sign of defiance," said the fourth Searcher, a stout man who wore the protective cuffs of a copyist over the sleeves of his robe. "Or as an insult to the Prior. Why collapse that particular section of wall, after all?"

Cariad was too far from them to glean emotions, but the tone of this Searcher's voice as he uttered Jolyon's new title told her all she needed to know. She had not realized that Jolyon's enmity with her father was such open knowledge.

"Because whoever did this found a binding easier to undo than stone and mortar, maybe," said the female Searcher.

"In the days of the seventh Prior," said the oldest Searcher, "there was a dispute over Prioral succession. It was said that the Journeyer Staff-Holder arranged to drug the Speaker Staff-Holder before the Ceremony. The rumor was eventually proved false, and it was established that the Journeyer had won Priorship on his own merits. But for a time there was considerable division between the Suborders. Some of the chronicles indicate that during that time there was difficulty with the bindings inside the Fortress, of a kind that had never been seen before, and has not been recorded since."

The other three looked at him. "What are you saying?" the female Searcher finally asked.

"We all know that bindings don't last forever, that they must be cared for, like children. But is it only skill that maintains them? Or is it also will? Mark my words—we'll see more of this."

"If we're so divided that even our works of power cannot hold," said the stout Searcher in a hushed tone, "what hope is there that we will ever unite again?"

"We have been that divided since That Which Was Most Precious to Us was stolen," the oldest Searcher said. "Since the Reddened unleashed their orthodoxy upon the world. This is not the beginning of the undoing. It is the end of it."

True to the Searcher's prediction, more bindings faltered in the days that followed. Cariad, slipping about the down-worlds, heard stories of dimming mindlight, of automated doors that ceased to open, of courtyards that disappeared, leaving bare ground where flagstones and benches and fountains had been. On the fifth day of the conflict, the Great Cess rebelled, spewing sewage up through the drains of all the Suborders' downworlds and forcing the servants to take refuge in their masters' space. On the sixth, the wards and barriers of the prison annex vanished simultaneously, freeing some prisoners and killing others, and rendering most of the prison's restraints, the power-bound cuffs and collars and anklepieces, useless. There was no discernible logic behind the failures—the wall was a new binding, the Cess a very ancient one, the rest somewhere in between—or to the exemptions, for though many bindings failed, many others remained intact.

In the growing chaos, Cariad read the imminence of what she waited for. But it was not until the seventh day of the conflict, twelve days after she had come up from underground, that the Garden's bindings finally gave way, signaling that her time of wandering was over.

She waited now upon the roof, wrapped in wardings to keep the cold away, eating food she created for herself out of the raw materials of the world around her. It was not the kind of waiting that had preceded other forays into danger, the hazardous special missions she had loved so much: an impatient urgency focused only on the moment, a drive to fulfillment without care for risk or thought of consequence. She knew, this time, what the coming confrontation might bring. The possible futures stretched before her, as if she shared Goldwine's Gift, and in many of them, she did not survive.

And yet she felt no fear. The consciousness of what lay ahead filled her too fully—a pricking in her flesh, a vibration in her bones, a gathering of light at the edges of her vision. After her time in the white cell, her father's return had become a source of dread, a goad to guilt, a symbol of all she had betrayed. After her emergence from the caverns, it had become the focus of purpose, a thing she must put right. Now, as the stillness of her waiting settled ever more deeply within her, it was again the thing it had been until Jolyon seized her: the pinnacle of prophecy, the crux of desire, the defining moment of her existence.

Twenty-three

IDWAY THROUGH the afternoon on the fourth day of Cariad's vigil, her waiting ended at last. On the wall of the Speaker Wing, a door blinked into being. Three men stepped out onto the jeweled snow: Jolyon, wearing not the Prior's robe but Roundhead black, his servant, and Baffrid. They struck off in the direction of the Room of the Stone, leaving a trail of dark prints behind them.

This was what Cariad had hoped for: that Jolyon would arrive before her father did. She leaped to her feet. Time, which had barely seemed to pass while she waited, leaped with her, a sudden headlong flow. She let go of the wardings with which she had surrounded herself, shifting to invisibility as she did so. No other preparation was necessary: she was already armed and had been ready from the moment she had begun to wait.

Lightly, she vaulted atop the coping. With her making power she reached out before her, grasping the particles of the air, drawing them together into a transparent thickness that would carry her to the ground. She tensed, ready to leap.

In the eyeblink instant between thought and action, something fell on her, like the collapsing masonry of the Fortress wall. Her breath constricted; her muscles clenched. The drop before her yawned like a chasm to the center of the world. The men beyond it, nearing the center of the Garden now, seemed so close she could feel their power on her skin.

Fear. This, at last, was fear.

Not once in her life had it struck her thus, in the shift from stillness into motion. It was the exhilaration of the chase that came to her at these times, the sureness of her Gift, the certainty of control. But what she felt now, with the whole of her body and all her senses, was the truth of her own vulnerability. And she understood, in her blood and bones as well as in her mind, that the leap she was about to make might carry her not just into empty air, but into a much greater nothingness.

She breathed deeply. She called upon her will, upon her purpose, upon the discipline of her profession. She closed her eyes and leaped.

She descended, a long controlled glide to the ground. She reached out across the snow, gathering it as she had the air, so that her feet would not print a trail. She began to run. The fear slipped from her as she did, leaving behind it not quite the joy she craved, not quite the certainty she knew, but something harder and more even, a determination that measured risk even as it understood skill, and out of the two created balance.

Jolyon and his minions stood before the Room of the Stone. A shimmering had sprung into being on the air above them. Dodging between the frozen trees, Cariad saw a barrier begin to take shape, curving out and down, composing itself with astonishing quickness. By the time she reached it, it was complete: an insubstantial, opal-shaded dome enclosing the Room and a wide space around it.

She halted. Like all Goldwine's operatives, she was expert in the crossing of Guardian barriers: barriers set against physical objects, which she could open as easily as she might pick a hole in a piece of loose fabric, and barriers set against Gifts, to which her resistance-trained power was invisible. But already she could tell that this barrier was different. Physical barriers were similar to walls: one did not sense them until one touched them. And barriers to power had no more effect on her than they did on the unGifted. But she could feel this one, even from a distance: a heaviness of the air, a pressure on her breathing.

She extended her Gift, probing at what lay before her. It

was at least partly physical, with the blank, hard heft of something made to stop solid objects. Yet she could not truly read its structure. It resisted her power, or rather repelled it, a rejection that increased in proportion to the force she brought to bear. It was as if there were some sort of armor here, and her Gift, knocking up against it, simply bounced off and away.

She felt the first cold touch of misgiving. Ignoring it, she began to advance. The air seemed to thicken, impeding both her progress and her breathing. A clutching pain blossomed inside her head. It was not physical, this pain, but Gift-sourced, as if a hand had closed itself around her mind, tightening with each successive step—

She backed off, panting. This barrier was effective not just against her body but against her power. How could it be? The Guardians knew no power but their own. And yet . . . Jolyon's servant had devoured her Gift, not once but twice. He and Jolyon had altered the white cell to hold her.

She should have thought of this. Jolyon knew she was loose, knew what it meant to her to be here. Yet it had not once occurred to her that he might protect himself in this way.

Horror rose in her, and panic. She pushed forward again, probing for a gap, trying by strength to make one. She forced herself onward even as her vision faded and her lungs clutched for air. Only when it became clear that if she continued she would not be able to draw away at all did she retreat, staggering backward on the snow, falling to her knees, clawing silently for breath, her heart hammering as if it would burst.

"I knew you'd come."

Cariad's head whipped up. Jolyon was standing close to the barrier's edge.

"You are out there, aren't you? It is you, isn't it?"

The snow beneath her was still hard. Her binding of invisibility was intact. Had her struggle triggered some kind of contact warning? Or was he just guessing?

"What do you think?" He gestured, indicating the barrier. "It's the first of its kind. A prototype. I expect it will be very useful, once all this is over."

His face and body were a little distorted by the barrier's opalescent shimmering. But she could see his smile, and his green eyes, and his bitten hands, twitching restlessly at his sides. Beyond his rings, he wore no jewelry at all, not even his Guardian medal. He had not yet started to grow the Prior's beard, but his russet hair had begun to straggle out of its severe Roundhead crop. He seemed weary beneath his expression of satisfaction, and thinner than when she had seen him last.

"If you've already set yourself against it," he said, "you're aware of its effects. If you haven't, know that you can't get through it. If you push too far, it will kill you."

He could not see her. Surely he could not. Surely it was illusion, this sense that he was speaking directly to her.

"And I would like you to survive, to see what I do when he arrives. You won't have long to wait. Or so Baffrid tells me."

Hopelessness and hatred flooded her. She felt the killing fires, licking in her fingertips, up her palms, along her arms. They meant nothing, nothing more than the hatred did, for she would never use them now.

"When I'm finished here, I'll come for you, Cariad. You may run again, you may hide, but I will find you, I promise it. And when I do, we'll talk, you and I. You'll tell me how you got free. And I'll tell you what the rest of your life will be like."

He smiled. Lifting his hand, he set it against the opal scrim of the barrier. It stirred like oil, mimicking the shape of his palm and fingers. Still smiling, he turned and moved back toward the Room, while behind him, the image of his imprint smoothed away.

As the afternoon dwindled Cariad prowled the barrier, outside the reach of its influence, surveying it inch by inch. She did not expect to find anything, but her operative's thoroughness, and the need to know that she had exhausted every possibility, insisted she search. As she had suspected, it repelled physical objects as thoroughly as it did her Gift: the spears of ice she hurled at it, hidden behind the Room from Jolyon's view, lost momentum and dropped to the ground before ever touching that shimmering surface.

At last she circled round again and settled down to wait. The three men had positioned themselves in front of the Room of the Stone. Jolyon sat on a folding chair the servant had brought; Baffrid crouched at his side, and the servant stood at his back. They neither moved, nor did a word pass between them. Cariad knelt on the snow, adjusting her heartbeat and circulation so that her knees and extremities would not freeze. Despair was a weight within her, and self-blame, as powerful as it had been in the time just after her capture. If she had anticipated the barrier . . . if she had waited in the Garden instead of on the roof . . . if she had not allowed herself to be paralyzed by her treacherous fear . . . but she had done none of these things, and so had sacrificed all chance to accomplish the purpose that had brought her here. If her father could not best the servant, all was lost; and she did not believe he could. She remembered the Amphitheater, and knew that Jolyon had not been boasting when he described his servant's capacity.

With a large part of herself, she desired to steal away. She did not want to watch Jolyon's victory, or see her father die. But she had made this disaster, first by betrayal and then by error, and she owed it witness. And, deep within her, a stubborn voice insisted that as long as she was alive and free, all was not lost. That she could not allow herself to surrender until it was proved beyond question that there was no chance.

Night fell, and passed, and yielded to dawn. As the first edge of the sun crept above the roof of the east-facing Speaker Wing, the surface of the Room began to ripple, like the skin of some pearl-colored beast. Jolyon leaped up, his chair tipping backward. Baffrid also stood. Outside the barrier, Cariad was on her feet, her dagger unsheathed in her hand.

The white dome of the Room shuddered violently and vanished. Where it had been a circle of blackness spread, like a hole punched in the snow. And on it, two men, one of whom seemed to hold the sun cradled in his arms.

The void vaulted into being, chasm-wide in the first instant of its manifestation. Cariad's Gift twisted toward it, irresistibly, dragging her body after. She fell to the ground, plunging her dagger into the hardened snow to hold herself. Inside the barrier, Baffrid staggered, his hands clapped to his head. And the two men, in the act of stepping from the black circle onto the snow outside it, froze, as if they had turned to ice.

Cariad, on her knees, gasping with her proximity to the barrier, saw what she had waited all the years of her life to see: her father's face, lit to unearthly clarity by the blazing thing he held. But so still was he, so rigid in the thrall of the servant's hold, that he seemed not like a living man at all, and she was seized by the conviction that he was already dead, that Jolyon had taken vengeance in the very instant of his arrival—

But then he blinked, with underwater slowness, and she saw that he was still alive.

The void had eaten all it needed: its pull was gone. Jolyon began to move toward his prisoners, his servant following. Baffrid, his black-browed face taut and strangely fearful, remained where he was. Cariad, on her feet again at a safer distance, saw that the man at her father's shoulder was Konstant: not the altered, overfleshed Konstant whose image Malinides' assistant had shown her, but the Konstant she remembered from twelve years ago, sharp-featured and slender and beautiful. His frozen features were stretched in an expression of horror, as if he had comprehended what was happening to him even as the void locked him to immobility.

An arm's length away from Cariad's father, Jolyon halted. He was more than a head shorter than the other man: he had to tilt his face up in order to meet those dark eyes.

"For thirty years I've been searching for you," he said, in his reedy voice. "And now it's you who comes to me. Ironic, don't you think?"

Cariad's father blinked again, painfully.

"You've kept yourself young, I see. You, who scorned the customs of the Arm so much while you were in this world. Like your dead master, Marhalt. But even he came to our methods in the end."

Cariad's heart pounded with dread. She felt the void, pulsing like a living thing, the fulcrum of the balance that held this dreadful tableau. Could her father feel it also? Did he understand the power that held him?

Jolyon's gaze dropped, coming to rest on the gathering of light Cariad's father held. "So this is the Stone. I wondered what it might be like." He tilted his head, first to one side and then the other, as if he were testing his vision. "For a thousand years only Speakers saw it thus. And then you. And now me. But you will soon be dead, and in a few days the Speakers will also be gone." Another tilt. "Perhaps I won't rebuild the Room. Perhaps I'll keep it with me. I am Prior, after all. It's my right."

Another Guardian might have said such a thing with reverence. But then, another Guardian would have gazed at the Stone with awe, not with the greed Cariad saw in Jolyon's face, glazing his features like the mark of some private perversion. She shuddered, colder now than even the winter air of the Garden could make her.

"This isn't what you intended when you sent your message, is it?" Jolyon was smiling into her father's eyes—fully now, possessively, as he had smiled at her in the white cell. "You remembered me as less than this, didn't you? As I was before I came into my true Gift. How does it feel to be bound utterly to my will?"

Struggle appeared in her father's face, like a sudden current beneath a weight of ice. His lips parted, just a little. "Not . . . quite . . . utterly," he whispered, the words as slow as glaciers.

A beat. Jolyon's smile faded. Clearly he had not expected an answer.

"Utterly enough." For a moment he stared at his enemy, flatly, all pretense gone. Then he turned to Konstant, to Konstant's rigid face and wide fixed gaze. "And you. My former companion, I presume, restored to his proper shape. Baffrid tells me you and this one had a falling out. But you seem to have patched things up." His eyes shifted. "What's this? Baffrid. Do me the favor of taking this thing away from him."

Baffrid came forward, averting his face from Cariad's father and the Stone. He pulled free the cloth bag that hung from Konstant's left hand. It required some effort—as if, even paralyzed, Konstant contrived to resist.

Baffrid placed the bag at Jolyon's feet. Jolyon stooped; Cariad saw Konstant's eyes move, and her father's also, following him. He fumbled with the bag, but could not open it. With a grimace of annoyance, he snapped his fingers toward his companion, who slid a knife from his sleeve and handed it to him. Jolyon slit the bag along its top. Reaching into it, he pulled out a wooden box, which he set upon the snow. He flipped back its lid and surveyed the contents, frowning now, as if what he saw puzzled him. At last, shrugging a little, he closed the box and rose.

"As far as I'm concerned, it's not worth the effort to probe you." He addressed Konstant again. "I have all the intelligence I need about you and your band of rebels. But Baffrid seems to feel it will be of use. And so I've granted his request to spare your life, so that he can work on you when this is over."

Locked in stasis, Konstant was as still as if he were already dead. Even so, at these words, his eyes stretched, so that the whites showed all around the dark irises. For a moment Jolyon looked into his face, smiling; then he moved to stand once more before Cariad's father.

"Did you know," he said, "that you have a grown child? A daughter. Fostered by the leader of the heretic group this one—" he cocked his head toward Konstant "—is a part of. Trained as a mercenary and an assassin. She came here, in fact, to assassinate me. But she was foolish, and I captured her. I probed her myself. Everything that was in her— everything she knew, everything she was—is mine now." The smile widened. "She's here. Outside the barrier. She's hidden, but she is here. She will see me destroy you. And when I'm done, I'll take her too."

Again Cariad saw the struggle in her father's face as he fought against the force that held him. His lips parted. "Take . . . it," he whispered.

Jolyon blinked. "What?"

"Take . . . the . . . Stone."

"The Stone is already mine. As you are. As the Order is. As the world will be."

"If . . . it's truly . . . yours . . . then hold it . . . in your hands." In the huge illumination of the Stone, his eyes were like openings onto night. "As . . . I . . . hold it . . . in mine."

Silence. Nothing moved now except the barrier, rippling with rainbow currents.

"Yes," Jolyon said. And again: "Yes."

He moved forward, into the nimbus of the Stone's light. The darkness of his black robe intensified; his face shone white as bone. His eyes, bent upon the Stone, seemed transparent. His ringed hands rose.

He paused. For a moment he stood motionless.

"Baffrid." He spoke without turning. "Come forward and take the Stone out of this Violator's hands."

Baffrid, who had fallen back to his former distance after giving Jolyon the knife, shook his head. "I will not."

Jolyon pivoted. "What did you say to me?"

"I can't do it. Don't ask it of me."

"I am not asking." Jolyon's expression was deadly.

"No." Baffrid backed up a step, and then another. There was dread in his dark face. "I won't do it. It's blasphemy. Only a Speaker can touch it."

Jolyon's lips drew back from his teeth. Baffrid snapped rigid, as if he were a puppet and all the strings that controlled his limbs had been twitched taut. Stiffly, he began to advance. He was resisting—Cariad could see it in his face, locked in a rictus of fear or rage—but he could not break the force that held him. Closer to the Stone he moved, and closer. His arms rose, reached out. His hands vanished into the coruscating light.

His body jerked. His eyes stretched. His mouth fell open. Blankness spread across his face, as if something in him were being erased. For a moment he stood. Then, slowly, his knees buckled and he fell, with the full force of his heavy body. He carried the Stone with him, dragging it out of Cariad's father's paralyzed grip. It flew from his hands as he struck the ground, arcing through the air in a cloud of radiance, coming to rest upon the snow as gently as if it had no mass at all.

Jolyon, who had leaped back as Baffrid fell, stared down at his fallen companion. For a moment he seemed frozen.

Then, stiffly, he glanced toward his servant, who stepped forward and knelt, setting his fingers against Baffrid's throat. He looked up at his master, and shook his head.

Jolyon turned, with a slowness that seemed to echo his prisoners' stasis. "What trickery is this?" His voice was hushed. "The Stone doesn't kill. What have you done to it?"

This time Cariad's father did not try to speak. His face, in ordinary light, seemed a good deal older, and much wearier, marked by harsh lines the Stone's unearthly luminance had wiped away. Behind him, Konstant watched, his eyes still stretched and wild, as they had become when Jolyon described his fate. But Cariad had the impression that it was no longer fear but struggle that made them so, as if Konstant were fighting his bondage with all the strength he had.

"You thought to trap me." Jolyon's voice was rising. "You thought to kill me." He began to move, stepping over Baffrid's twisted body. "But there's nothing you can do to match me now. You see that, don't you?"

He halted. Less than an arm's reach divided him from Cariad's father.

"I've waited a long time for this. If I could, I'd take your mind in spoonfuls, so you'd know what you were losing even as you lost it, so you'd spend each day in fear of what the next day would steal from you. But too many things can happen, and I won't lose this chance the way I did the first. And so I will do it now, all of it. I will take your mind, your memories, your Gift, all the things that make you what you are. And it won't be as it was thirty years ago, when you defied me. I recognized you then, but I didn't know you. I know you now. I know you fully. That's your daughter's gift to me." His voice had dropped to a whisper. "And when I'm done, when your mind is gone, I will erase you from the history of the Order and from the history of the world, as entirely as if you had never been. I will destroy every living soul who remembers even your false name. But I will remember you. Over the centuries of my life, as I bring this world to orthodoxy, as I bind it to the rule of law, I'll think of you. And I will know, each time I act, how it would have tormented you to see it."

Jolyon was a man who wore cruelty like a garment, who layered avarice and ambition about himself like armor. But he was naked now, stripped bare by the force of his desire. He was defenseless, Cariad knew it; if she had been able to reach him, she could have killed him with a touch.

He moved forward, closing the last distance between them. The thunder of Cariad's heartbeat filled the world. She saw what was before her—the sunstruck snow, the blazing Stone, Konstant and her father, Jolyon and his servant—but she could not grasp it. She could not connect this moment, in which her father's mind and body and the promise of his power were still intact, with the destruction that would come after.

Jolyon raised his bitten hands, cupping them upon the air to either side of his enemy's face. The gesture plunged Cariad into memory, utterly and without warning. She was in the white cell again, Jolyon's green eyes staring into her own. The void opened, ate her power, sent it back against her. Jolyon's mind plundered hers and withdrew. The void remained, bereft, despairing, calling grief out of its black depths. Calling memory. Calling selfhood. Calling—

A name.

She understood then, in a moment of blinding insight.

"Geshe Gudun Gyatso!" she shouted.

The servant cried out, the first sound she had ever heard him make. He staggered, turning toward her. The void slammed closed, expelling what it held. The force of Gift's return flung Cariad's father and Konstant violently to the snow. Jolyon alone did not move, swaying a little, facing nothing now, his fingers closed on empty air.

For an instant all was still.

Then Konstant began to struggle, trying to free himself from where he lay, half-pinned beneath Cariad's father. Cariad's father rolled aside, pushing himself to his knees; his face was blank with shock. And Jolyon, with a shout of rage or perhaps terror, stumbled back, his hands thrust before him as if in self-defense. The air in front of him distorted, a force leaping outward to bridge the gap between himself and Cariad's father—except that it did not strike

Cariad's father but Konstant, who had moved as Jolyon did, flinging himself forward and to the side, his arms outstretched, shielding Cariad's father with his own body. Jolyon's blow caught him full in the chest. Konstant flew backward, as Marhalt had, taking Cariad's father with him.

Jolyon's act of power had knocked him to his hands and knees. With dreamlike slowness, Cariad saw his head come up. She saw his eyes fix on his frozen servant. She saw them narrow in command—

And then he collapsed onto his face, and lay still.

Cariad's father was on his feet now, beside Konstant's crumpled body. His face was bloodless. His eyes were fixed on Jolyon, prone in the snow.

Through all of this the servant had not moved, immobilized by the syllables of his forbidden name. He was an instrument, a tool; without his master to direct him, he was surely powerless to do harm. Yet there was no way to be certain.

"The barrier!" Cariad called. "Break the barrier!"

Her father turned. He seemed not merely shocked but bewildered, and she remembered that she could not be seen. She relaxed the disciplines that held her. He drew in his breath, his eyes moving over her face.

"Break the barrier," she said to him. "I can't get through it on my own."

He blinked. The barrier flared and vanished. Cariad's dagger was ready in her hand; she launched it, with practiced force, at the servant's chest. He fell to his knees, then toppled on his side. Blood made a spreading pattern on his gray garments and on the snow beneath him. His eyes were still open.

Cariad's father stared at her, as if she were not quite human. "He was the one who held you," she explained.

"What?"

"He has . . . had . . . a not-Gift, a void in him capable of absorbing other Gifts. Jolyon kept him secret and used his ability as if it were his own. It was your own Gift he used to capture you."

"Ah." She saw a dawning comprehension in his face.

"Is he dead? Jolyon. Did you kill him?"

"No. But his Gift is bound."

He knelt and set his hand on Konstant's throat. She moved toward them, across the snow.

"He's dead." He looked up at her. The shock seemed to have left him, but his mouth was taut, and there was tension around his eyes.

"He saved your life," she said.

"I didn't understand," he said. "I saw Jolyon's power in his companion's mind. But I thought it was a Gift—a great Gift, an inexplicable Gift, but a Gift all the same. I was prepared for that, when we came through into the Garden. But not for . . . what happened. To feel my power leaving me . . . And then, when it returned . . . It nearly took my consciousness. I couldn't have barriered myself in time." He looked down, into Konstant's face. "I never would have asked such a thing of him. Even though, in a way, I think it was what he wanted."

Death had smoothed Konstant's restored features. There was no trace of the terrible determination Cariad had seen as he flung himself in the way of Jolyon's killing blow. He looked vulnerable and very young—as if not twelve years, but only twelve days, had passed since she had seen him last. She was visited, suddenly, with a memory of how his sleep had sometimes frightened her, taking him so profoundly that she felt compelled to wake him, to reassure herself that he was still alive. Now, dead, he appeared to be merely sleeping, his limbs relaxed, his mouth a little open, his face turned slightly to the side.

Her throat tightened. She felt emotion rise in her, tearing up through the layers of her self-control: grief, shock, wonder. She pressed it back. They were not finished here.

"Jolyon must be dealt with," she said. "He can't be left alive."

Her father looked toward the place where Jolyon lay. For the first time she realized that she could not feel him. He was as guarded as the transporters.

"I never understood why he hated me so," he said, softly. "He thought he saw something in me when we were boys, something no one else perceived . . . he wanted me to give it to him, and I would not. But even so . . ."

"He was too small for his own ambition," she said, seeing it as she spoke. "Even as Prior, he was a sham. But you, who took the Stone and turned your back upon a world . . ."

"I was never his rival, if he'd only known. I never wanted the things he did." He was silent for a moment, and then turned toward her. "I know he must be dealt with. It's one of the things I came to do. Bind him to powerlessness, cripple his Gift. But I cannot kill him."

"Then I will."

She moved away from him. At Jolyon's side, she knelt. She grasped his shoulders, with fingers that were already burning, and rolled him on his back. His face was patched red and pale from the snow into which it had been pressed. He was conscious: his green eyes blazed up at her. She felt his hatred, and his rage.

"It should not be you," he hissed at her.

"What difference does it make?"

"You are not my enemy." His lips were wet with the force of his feeling. "You are nothing."

"No." Fire rose in her. "I'm the plant grown from the seed of your own hatred. I'm your own act of spite turned back upon you."

"You weren't meant to be. You're a mistake."

"No. I am a consequence."

She straddled him, sitting hard upon his chest so that the breath went out of him and he could not speak. She placed her hands above his heart, spreading her fingers across the cold silk of his robe. She closed her eyes, focusing her Gift. She summoned up a phantom blade of force and drove it through his flesh, past bone, deep into the warmth of blood. She found his heart and set her will against it. He fought her with all his strength, with all his rage, sending the pure force of his hatred out against her, as his henchman once had done. But she was armored against him, with purpose and with memory: the memory of her father, driven from this world; the memory of her mother, pining for her lost power. It would not be only the fires of her Gift that brought his heart to stillness, but the spirits of those who owed him vengeance. She felt his agony; it seemed the greatest joy she had ever known.

As his pulse slowed, she opened her eyes and leaned over

him, for she wanted to see death in his face in the instant that it came. He gazed up at her, gasping through his open mouth, his features twisted with the force of her killing will. His green eyes were wide and filled with tears; they trickled down his temples to lose themselves in his russet hair. The rage, the hatred, were all gone; there was only pain now, and fear, and a desperate struggle against what could not be resisted. He looked, not like the ancient evildoer he was, but like a suffering boy.

Cariad felt something shift in her, as if she had crossed some threshold of perception she had not known was there. It vaulted her beyond herself. For a clear brief moment she saw herself from the outside: a greedy killer crouched spiderlike above her victim, drinking in his pain like blood. And she understood, beyond any possibility of doubt, that the thing she had feared in the time after her capture was true. She had let the killing fires burn too high, and they had turned her balance into ash.

Horror rose in her, and revulsion, as powerful as the killing fires themselves, but cold, as cold as winter. Out of the melding of the two, something new was born. It swelled, as the fire had, borne outward on the tide of her killing will. But this time it was not heat, or pain, but a force as soft and cool as water. Jolyon's face smoothed. His lips relaxed. His eyes fell closed. He took one deep, tranquil breath, and died.

For a moment she sat motionless, her hands still resting on his chest. Then she rose, a little unsteadily, and went back to her father, who stood by Konstant's body, watching her as he had after she killed the servant, as if she were not quite human.

"He's dead," she said.

She felt it again, the shifting of desire that had brought Jolyon not agony, but peace. And it all rose up in her, the feeling to which she had not allowed herself to surrender during her time in the embattled Fortress, during the days of her vigil, during the night she spent outside the barrier, certain she had failed and that her father would die. She bowed her face into her hands, shaking with silent sobs. There was a long, long moment; and then she felt a motion of the air, and arms went gently round her. She clutched the thick fabric of her father's coat and wept into its soft fur lining, helplessly, as if there had been no victory, as if something had been lost.

At last, calmer, she pulled away, wiping her face with her sleeves. She felt drained and ashamed. In the awkward silence between them the sounds of battle, which here at the center of the Garden were barely perceptible, rose suddenly—a crescendo of crashing and shouting, and a great grinding, as if plates of stone were being pushed past one another.

"What is that?" her father asked, glancing toward the edges of the Garden.

"The Guardians are at war with one another. There's fighting in the Journeyer and Speaker Wings. The Journeyer Staff-Holder—"

"No." He shook his head. "Don't tell me. I don't need to know. It won't matter soon, anyway."

His dark gaze moved across her face, as it had when she first emerged from invisibility. She was aware, suddenly, of the astonishment of it, that this moment she had awaited so long should be here at last, that she should be gazing in reality at the face she had tried so often to conjure out of imagination. And it came to her, opening her mind like a blow, that this was her father. Not the thief of the Stone or the destroyer of the Guardians, not the hero of the Tale or the promise of prophecy, but the flesh-and-blood man who had made her.

"Tell me," he said. "What was it you shouted, when you broke the servant's hold?"

"His name."

"His *name*?"

"He was meant to have forgotten it. It was a punishment . . . But he remembered. He told it to me, in a way, when Jolyon used him to probe me. He gave me his dreams . . . I don't know if he meant to." She thought of the void, and the grieving spirit within it. "I killed him. But he was dead long before."

He did not question it. "Konstant thought the probe must

have made you mindless. But I thought you must have defended yourself."

She shook her head. "I couldn't have defended myself. Jolyon wanted me intact. He could inflict more suffering on me that way." She took a breath. She was alive, her father was alive. Jolyon was dead, and his threat with him. But Konstant was also dead, and the difference between defeat and victory was as small as a name. She could not stand here and look her father in the face, and not confess her fault. "It's because of me that he was waiting for you. I'm the reason he nearly killed you."

Her father shook his head. "He was here because I sent him a message, by way of Baffrid and his Roundheads, when they came after Konstant in the other world."

"But it was because of me that they were sent. Because of what Jolyon took out of my mind. The only reason he was able to do that was because I went out to kill him, without authority or permission. He'd never have captured me otherwise."

"It wasn't an ordered assassination?"

"No." Cariad dropped her eyes. "It was my intent. Only mine."

"Why?"

"For you. For my mother." She took a breath. "I've wanted his death since I first heard the Tale. I thought it was right that it should be done, and right that I should do it. I never thought I could be harmed. I never thought the future could be changed. I was wrong, wrong. I set all my people in jeopardy. You almost died. And Konstant . . . Konstant . . ."

Her voice caught. She closed her eyes a moment, struggling for control.

"The fault is mine as well," he told her. "Because Konstant warned me, and I didn't heed him, or understand what I saw in Baffrid's mind. Because I was arrogant in my power and believed nothing could touch a Gift like mine. Besides." He gave her the ghost of a smile. "Whatever else you did, you also freed me."

"Yes." She brushed tears from her cheeks. "Though it shouldn't have been necessary."

"Come." He turned, and moved away from her. "There's something I want to show you."

He led her past Konstant's body, to the place where the wooden box sat on the snow, next to the ruin of the bag Konstant had carried it in. He crouched before it. She knelt beside him. He slid his hands caressingly across the box's scarred wooden lid, and then, gently, raised it on its hinges.

"This is your heritage," he said.

The box held earth, drier than dust, scattered with bits of rusted metal.

"What is it?"

"It's all that's left of my family and yours. When I was captured in this world, the Arm of the Stone also captured my brother and his wife and children. They were condemned as Violators and executed, and their land was razed. Before I left this world I went back to where they had lived. I knew the Arm had destroyed everything for half a mile around the house. Still, I thought I might find something, some token. . . . But this was all there was. Earth and iron." He glanced at her. "My brother was a blacksmith."

"I know," Cariad whispered. For the first time, faintly, she could feel him: old loss, old love, stirring like shadows behind his powerful guard.

"I never loved anyone in all my life, except my family." He returned his gaze to the box. "I left the Tale for you because I wanted you to understand what you came from. Not because I believed in the myth of the Tale, or in my family's divine right to the Stone, but because . . . because you were the last of us. The endpoint of a line stretching back a thousand years. That meant something to me, even when I left the Tale behind. I couldn't bring myself to let it vanish." He looked at her again. "But I think now that I was wrong. You're the last of my line, yes. But you were born after the ending of the Tale, into a world without the Stone. I shouldn't have tried to preserve my heritage through you. I should have let you live free of that burden."

"No." Cariad shook her head.

"I left this world before you were born. You never knew me, except through words spoken by another. Why should you make my enemy yours? Why should you suffer for my history?"

"But it's my history too." Her voice shook. "And it was your gift to me, the only one I had. Because of it, I knew . . . I knew . . ." Knew you loved me, she meant to say. But, looking into that hard pale face, which after all did not seem much like her own, she found she did not know. He had embraced her as she wept. Love lived in him, she could feel it. But she could also feel that it was given only to the dead and to the lost. And she was neither.

He was watching her. "I often wondered which of us you'd favor," he said, softly. "Myself or your mother. But it's my own mother you remind me of. You have her eyes. Her hair." He reached out, and placed his hand against her cheek. "You, the last of all of us."

Her eyes filled with tears. She could not speak.

He took back his hand and his gaze. He picked up the box and closed its lid. "These remains are yours now. Guard and keep them, in memory of what you come from. But make me a promise. Promise me that the memory will die with you. Promise me that you will not pass on the Tale, or my story. Promise me that you will be not the last of my line but the first of yours. A new heritage for a new world." His dark eyes held hers. "Promise me."

She felt him strongly now: memory, regret, a complex twining of loss and renunciation, the shadows of disillusion and a deep reluctance—and, clearest of all, the force of his will. She had never imagined the world beyond this moment. She had never thought of the life it might bring her. And yet, in the struggle she felt, she understood that she had always, somewhere in her heart, believed she would pass the Tale on to her child, as he had passed it on to her. She wanted to refuse him. But she knew he would not let her.

"I promise," she whispered.

He set the box in her hands. Her fingers closed around it. It was cold from the snow it had rested on; there seemed more weight to it than its wood and metal, the earth and iron inside it, warranted.

He rose to his feet and moved away from her, toward

where the Stone sat blazing on the snow. She set the box down and followed him. The Stone burned, a restless storm of light, almost too bright to look upon. So close to it, she could sense it—not directly, but rather as someone standing in the belly of a ship might sense the power of the ocean.

She sank to her knees. Like the box, this was her heritage. She was descended from those who had held it before the Guardians claimed it; she was the last possessor of its true story; she was the daughter of the man who had taken it and brought it back. Soon it would belong to the world, to no one. But right now it lay as close as her hand. She reached out—

"No!" Something struck her away, hard. She looked up into her father's face. "No Gift can touch it, unshielded. It would be deadly to you too."

"Are you shielded?" she asked, remembering how he had cradled it in his arms.

He shook his head. "I have never needed to be."

She turned again to the blinding rainbow light. "What is it?" she whispered. "What is it really?"

"I don't know. It's the one question I've never been able to answer."

He leaned forward and lifted it up. The blaze of it swallowed his hands, so that he seemed to be sunk to the wrists in light. Its brilliance lit his face, as it had when he first stepped out of the black circle, erasing the weariness, smoothing the lines, so that he seemed scarcely older than Cariad herself. His eyes fell closed. His mouth relaxed. He became still, as still as the frozen trees.

Cariad did not know where he had gone. She knew only that he had left her, and that she was not ready to let him go. Following an impulse she scarcely understood, she moved close to him and set her hand on his shoulder, reaching out with the whole of her heartsensing Gift.

The world around her vanished. She seemed to be falling into light. She thought at first it was the Stone, but it was a human Gift that enclosed her, huge and turmoiled, shot with golden currents and pulsing like the beat of blood. Darkness enclosed it, and a galaxy of smaller, dimmer luminances: the other Gifts of mindspace, tangled like stars within the shimmering, phantom matrix of the world's bindings and works of power. And beyond it all, rising from some figurative horizon, a huge white brilliance, an infinite diamond light.

Her father's Gift arrowed forward, streaking through mindspace like a traveling sun, and plunged over that blinding boundary. Distanced as she was, linked only to her father's perceptions, the shock of it nearly overwhelmed Cariad's senses. This was the Stone. The Stone was the world, the whole vast body of its consciousness, a burning crystal network of perception linked to everything that existed. There was blood and bone, rock and dust, desert and forest, city and wilderness, permanency and change, all that was opposite and all that was the same. There was the whole of the past: footprints frozen in rock, strata entombed in hillsides. There was the entirety of the future: fire stirring beneath the ocean floor, the slowly changing tilt of the earth. There was the constancy of the present: the sum of all that had been and all that might be, joined in an eternal instant of balance. And across it all, within it all, the bright thread of Gift, flashing like lightning or like fire, braided into the essence of everything that *was*—not merely an element of the world perceived, but the very heart of what was real.

For a timeless instant, the power to which Cariad was bound retained its coherence within the heaving multiplicity of the Stone. Then, as if a tether had been cut, it rushed outward, expanding across the jeweled weave of the Stone's awareness. Further it spread and still further, like smoke taken by the wind, until it seemed it must disintegrate entirely—and yet it did not. A human will, her father's will, bound it to wholeness. She felt the strain of it, the almost inconceivable effort of that control; felt, also, the power he drew from the alien currents of the Stone, as if his Gift did not merely lie over, but in some sense partook of the world-consciousness it touched.

At last there came a halt. For a moment the forces held in balance: the prismatic immensity of the Stone, the leap and play of the world's Gifts, the golden mist of her father's power. There was a gathering, like a long indrawn breath;

then, sharp and sudden, a *twisting*, like the turn of the wrist that breaks an animal's neck. And all across the world, the light of Gift went dark.

Cariad's father drew his power toward coherence. As he did, the spark of Gift returned. But not as before. The mindspace he crossed on his journey back to himself was a darker place than it had been when he set out. The weave of force-lines, the gossamer web of binding, was gone. There were only the pinpoints of individual Gifts—static now, fixed and separate, like signal fires on an endless plain.

On the dividing line between mindspace and his own bounded self, Cariad's father gathered his strength again and *twisted* another great undoing. The Stone was not part of this destruction: the power was all his own. In the material world, there was an echoing thunder of collapse. In the realms of mindspace, ten thousand Gifts winked out forever.

He fell back into himself, like a man falling from a mortal wound. He had used up all his power. There were no barriers now, no guards upon his inner self. Cariad felt him fully: his hope for the new world and his fear for it, his guilt for what he had destroyed and his understanding of the rightness of destruction. She felt the restlessness in him, too long confined, and the conflict, and the bitterness of a destiny he both fought and embraced. She felt his longing and his love—or perhaps only his memory of it—and his grief as well, not only for the living beings who had passed out of his life, but for the many things he had believed in and left behind. And, at the center of it all, a deep essential solitude: a chosen loneliness so profound it made her want to weep.

But only for an instant. The world seized her awareness like a fist, dragging her back into present time. Her lungs were burning; her skin was raw. She opened her eyes. Dust hung about her like a curtain, so thick she could barely see the snow she knelt on. The air was rank with the smell of fire and blood and riven rock. Through the obscurity she saw her father, to whom she was still joined by touch: his eyes closed, his mouth slack, his faced hollowed by his terrible effort. The Stone rolled from his hands, settling again upon the snow. He swayed and fell toward her. She caught him in her arms.

He had used too much of himself. The emptiness at his center was taking him. Cariad could feel his Gift—which was also the spark of his life—dropping into that darkness, like a torch down a well. Instinctively, she reached within herself, focusing her will as she did before an assassination. But it was not the killing will she called on this time, but its reverse, the generative power she had always recognized within herself, but never tapped for anything except her own healing. With all her strength, through Gift and love and touch, she wrapped her father in the forces of creation, battling away the darkness, coaxing him back toward life.

When, hours later, Goldwine led her band of fighters across the rubble that had been the Speaker Wing, she found Cariad seated crosslegged, a wooden box cradled in her arms. Her father slept beside her. Beyond them, four bodies lay dark upon the snow. And before them, clad in a corona of dust and brilliance, the Stone pulsed glory across the snow.

Twenty-four

CARIAD ROSE as Goldwine and her fighters approached—apprehensively, for she was not certain how Goldwine would greet her. But in her foster-mother's face she saw only joy. Goldwine held out her arms; Cariad went into them. In what she felt, she knew that things were right between them.

After a time Goldwine pulled back. There were tears on her cheeks. "Can you forgive me, Cariad?" she said, gravely.

"Forgive you? For what?"

"For not giving you more warning. For allowing you to come to harm."

And Cariad saw that in the days after her capture Goldwine, Gift-driven, must have suffered just as Cariad had: the guilt of betrayal, the fear that by her actions she had forfeited the love of the person who meant most to her in all the world. Cariad shook her head, and took her foster-mother in her arms again.

"There's nothing to forgive," she murmured. "You did what was necessary. The choices were all mine."

At last Goldwine set Cariad away from her and turned to Cariad's father, who had risen from his resting place to stand silently, watching. His face was harsh with exhaustion, but he stood straight and steady on the snow; one would not have known, to look at him, how close he had come to dying a few hours before.

They greeted each other warily, like adversaries rather than allies. They spoke of what had occurred: of the great destruction Cariad's father had accomplished, of Gold-wine's march upon the Fortress—not in full force, but with a band of less than two hundred fighters. They had waited outside the Fortress until the collapse was complete, enter-ing only then to kill surviving Guardians, gather up down-worlders, and free the pilgrims and traders and visiting dignitaries from their long house arrests. Simultaneous at-tacks were being mounted in the world outside.

It was not only the Guardians' bindings that were gone. When Cariad's father stretched his Gift out across the world, he had undone every work of power in existence. The hollow mountain was dark now, its machines silent. In the Zosterian headquarters all the mindlight had gone out. In the wild places of the earth, where groups of Gifted gathered beyond the scope of either Guardian law or resis-tance to it, other secret works of power lay in ruins. Gold-wine had not seen these things with her own eyes. But she knew them, through her Gift.

The talk turned to the future. Cariad's father told Gold-wine, with clear respect but absolute authority, what he planned for himself and for the Stone. It did not surprise Cariad to hear it; the sense of it had been there, in her brief glimpse into his soul. But Goldwine, whose Gift had never shown her much of what lay beyond the moment of the Guardians' overthrow, had not expected it. Cariad felt her shock, then her disbelief, then her rising rage. The discus-sion became heated, and foundered at last upon a glacial silence.

Stiffly, Goldwine turned away. She crossed to where Konstant's body lay on the snow. Stooping, she gazed into his face. Her own was hard and controlled, but Cariad knew her foster-mother, and she could read Goldwine's feelings even from a distance. Her suffering was not Goldwine's only guilt.

Rising, Goldwine gestured to two of her fighters, who came to take up Konstant's body. Without another glance at Cariad's father, she led the little group away. Cariad, holding the box, followed. She looked back once as she went. Her father stood like a statue on the snow, the Stone blazing at his feet. She thought, but was not certain, that his eyes rested on her face. He had spoken no word of good-bye. Nor had she.

Beyond the Garden, she turned to Goldwine. "There's something I have to do."

Goldwine nodded: she already knew. "Take an escort with you."

"No. I'll go alone."

The Fortress lay in ruins. The level of destruction seemed to correlate with the distribution of Gift: the Great Court, the warehouses, and the guest quarters—domains mainly of unGifted—were virtually untouched, while the Speaker Wing, the Prior's Palace, and the Keep had been turned into gravel. The Journeyer Wing was also gone, but at least it was possible to tell, from the tumbled columns and pediments, that it had been a building. Parts of the Searcher Wing still stood, and bits and pieces of the Library and the Apprentice College and the Amphitheater. Still more of the Novice and Soldier Wings remained intact, as did a large portion of the prison annex.

Entering here, Cariad found the central staircase undamaged. At its foot, the prison's downworld was intact; the only sign of disaster was its desertion, and the lingering stench of sewage. Even so, Cariad did not allow herself to hope that anything else had survived, until she emerged into the tunnels and saw with her own eyes that they were whole, even to the mindlight on the ceiling.

The journey seemed the longest she had ever made. At first she feared for the caverns' survival also, but then she met a transporter cart, laden with goods, trundling along as if, down here, time had stopped and everything was as it had been. Of all the strange sights she had seen over the past night and day, this seemed, somehow, the strangest.

The caverns, when she reached them, produced the same surreal impression, spreading out before her in all the verdancy of their growth, all the brilliance of their false sunlight. It was almost possible to believe that there had been no cataclysm, that the Fortress still stood and the Guardians still ruled. And yet there were signs of alteration. The inventory checkpoint at the caverns' mouth was deserted. A tangle of tent encampments had sprung up around the neat white dwellings of the agricultural workers' village: servants from other downworlds, probably, migrating here to escape either the fighting or the ravages of the Great Cess. As she entered the transporters' campsite, Cariad saw children at play—not in the crèche cave, but among the trees. As powerfully as the ruined Suborder Wings, this spoke of change: that these children, once secret, were now free to live in the open.

Cariad found Jorian in the women's cave. She sat at her loom, her daughters and daughters-in-law around her. In their pale garments, they were like a gathering of flowers. They looked up as Cariad entered, their hands falling to stillness. Their eyes followed her as she approached them.

"Orrin," Cariad said as soon as she was in earshot, too consumed by need to bother with courtesy. "Is he here?"

Is he safe? was what she meant. Is he alive? Jorian seemed to understand.

"He's well. But he's out traveling. I don't know when he'll return." She regarded Cariad with her icy eyes, watchful as she always was, but not hostile. "Have you come back for him?"

Cariad had to breathe deeply before she could speak. "Yes."

"I don't know how he'll greet you. You wounded him when you left."

"I know."

"But I think he'll go with you, if you ask him." Jorian's tone was sad. "He always wanted the world above the ground."

"You can go also," Cariad told her. "My people are gathering up survivors. We'll lead them out of the mountains by way of the Fortress Passage."

Jorian shook her head. "Why should we leave?"

"The Fortress has been destroyed. The Guardians have been overthrown. There's nothing left—no buildings, no bindings. It's a wasteland up there."

"But down here, it's a garden. A living world."

"There's a bigger world outside, Jorian. And it's free now. You can go anywhere in it. You no longer need to live your lives in hiding."

"We are not in hiding. This *is* our life." Jorian looked at her—gently, with forbearance, as one might look at a person too misguided for anything but compassion. "We thank you for your offer. But it doesn't interest us."

Cariad nodded. She had not really expected a different response. "Will you tell Orrin I'm waiting in the apple orchard?"

Jorian smiled, the glinting, secret smile behind which stirred the whole strangeness of these people's lives. "I will."

In the orchard, Cariad seated herself in the shade of the trees, her back against a trunk. The air was warm and moist; light slipped through the leaves to cast a golden net across the grass. Somewhere, a gang of pickers was working: she heard their singing, punctuated now and then by bursts of calling and laughter. Weariness reached up to claim her; she fought it back. In this push and pull of consciousness she drifted, neither fully wakeful nor completely asleep, until she opened her eyes and saw Orrin watching her from the other side of the alley between the trees.

"What are you doing here?" he said, when he saw she was awake.

He looked thinner than when she had left, and haggard. His cut lip still bore a scab. As she looked at him, utterly familiar, completely known, she felt something release within her. Until this moment, she had not been completely certain he would come.

"I've come back," she said, simply.

"Back?" He had placed himself too far away for her to properly feel him, but she saw the anger that struggled in his face. "Why?"

"I should never have left you, Orrin. I should have recognized . . . the truth of what I felt for you. What I feel for you. But my life . . . my upbringing . . . the things my mother taught me . . . I wasn't able to understand. Or to . . . accept. But I do now."

"Oh? And what brought you to this revelation?"

"Many things." She glanced away. "I've seen more of myself in these last weeks than I ever wanted to see. Including this. What I told you . . . before . . . about heartsensers . . . it's true. I still fear it, Orrin, I won't lie to you. But I can't deny it anymore."

He watched her. His eyes were narrow, his lips a tight line. "So what do you want me to do about it?"

"I want . . ." Alone in the Garden of the Stone with her sleeping father, she had faced the truth of what she felt for Orrin and consciously surrendered to it. Yet, except for her love for Goldwine, she had been all in all to herself for the whole of her life. It was profoundly difficult to make herself a supplicant to another's feeling. "I want to be with you again."

"Just like that. As if nothing had happened. As if you'd never run away."

"It was wrong of me to leave the way I did." She breathed deeply. It was his right to speak to her this way: he was the wounded one. "It was cowardly. I'm sorry."

"Do you know what I've been through, Cariad? Do you know what I've suffered, not knowing if you were alive or dead? Wondering what I did to make you go, what I might have done differently to make you stay? Wondering if you ever cared for me at all, or if you were only with me to pass the time? You made me feel like garbage, Cariad. Like something you used up and threw away."

"I'm sorry, Orrin," she said again, helplessly.

"How can I trust you, Cariad? If I take you back, how can I know you'll stay?"

"I'm a heartsenser, Orrin. I can never leave you now."

"Oh, and is that supposed to comfort me? That you're not with me out of choice, but because of some . . . coercion of your Gift?"

She met his angry gaze squarely. "I could have lived with the pain of being without you, Orrin. I'd made up my mind to do it, in fact. I'm not here because I have to be. I'm here because I want to be."

There was a long, long silence. She could not read his face, or feel him. At last he began to move toward her, slowly.

"I can't lie to you, Cariad," he said. "I can't pretend this isn't what I want, more than anything in the world. Not even to punish you. And I would like to punish you. I'm angry. Very angry. I don't know how long it'll take me to come to terms with that."

He halted, looking down at her where she sat against the tree. She could sense him now, fully—the anger he spoke of and the pain that was woven into it, dark and wrenching, reaching down into her soul and turning there like a knife.

"I understand," she half-whispered.

"I saw a body today," he told her. "A woman with black hair. I thought she might be you."

And in that, at last, she felt what she was waiting for. She closed her eyes, afraid to speak.

There was a motion of the air as he sat down beside her—at a distance, out of reach.

"Tell me what happened," he said, not looking at her. "Above the ground. I've only been able to glean bits and pieces."

And so she told him—of her long vigil, of her father's capture and Jolyon's death, of the leveling of the Fortress and the breaking of the world's bindings.

"There's only the caverns now," she said, "and the tunnels with their mindlight. Of all the works of power on this earth, only those things remain. They shouldn't have survived either. I don't understand why they did."

"They aren't on the earth, but below it. And the transporters' power isn't like the Guardians', or like yours. Or perhaps your father did destroy the bindings here, and the transporters recreated them."

"Or perhaps he meant to leave them whole." For it was her father's intent to remain in the ruined Fortress, with the Stone, which he had decreed the world must forget.

"What will happen now?" Orrin asked, quietly.

"I suppose there will be war. There are still many Guardians outside the Fortress, and they won't give up easily." She paused. "It's a new world, Orrin. From this moment, everything begins again. I saw it happen. I felt it when it did. And yet I can hardly believe it."

He nodded, silent. The light had dimmed as they talked: it was now nearly full night. He had not looked at her as she spoke, keeping his eyes fixed on the trees opposite. She had felt him, in his disciplined way, subordinating the turbulence within him so that he could give her his full attention. But now, in the quiet between them, the discipline slipped away. The darkness of his emotion, the lingering anger and hurt, was painful to her, for she was wholly open to him, undefended. This, she thought, was how it would be from now on. Even now it frightened her. But the alternative frightened her more.

"What is that?" he asked. "That box?"

She glanced down at her father's box, sitting on the grass between them. The promise she had made pressed behind her lips. But Orrin already knew the Tale, and so she answered him. She felt them as she did, her unknown ancestors, marching backward across the centuries—secret now, a memory that would die with her and him. She felt the sadness of it, of those who would be forgotten, of future generations that would not know their past.

Orrin listened without comment. When she was done he turned to her. She turned also and met his eyes.

"Come here," he said, and held out his arms.

She went into them, gripping him tightly, turning her face into the hollow of his neck. The feel of him was like rescue, like coming home. This was what she had dreamed of during the time of their separation, what she had longed for with a need that would not let her rest: his body, hard and lean against her own, the texture of his skin, his smell of woodsmoke and transporter leather. Something rose in her, too huge to name. In him it was the same. There was no darkness now, no pain, but only love. She could no longer tell where he ended and she began. For just an instant she recalled the isolation she had seen inside her father, the frozen emptiness of a man who had followed solitude for so long that what had once been choice was now the very shape of his being. A profound and bitter loneliness that, she understood, might well have been her own.

Orrin tangled his fingers in her hair and drew her face away from his shoulder. It had begun to rain, lightly; she felt the moisture on her skin.

"I love you, Cariad." He kissed her forehead, her eyelids, her mouth. "Say it back. I want to hear you say it."

She met his eyes, black now in the fully-fallen night. "I love you."

It was what was in her heart. Yet she thought she felt something leave her as she spoke it, as if she had just surrendered the last of herself to the new world.

Cariad returned to the Garden of the Stone two days later. Clouds were piled thick across the sky, and an icy wind cut across the wastes of the Garden, its force no longer blunted by walls or bindings. It caught at the falling snow, sweeping it into dancing patterns, driving it like sand against her cheeks.

The black circle through which her father had reentered the world was no longer visible. It was not snow that covered it, but a semblance, seamlessly blended with the surrounding world so that all that could be seen was a field of unbroken white. There was a barrier here, as well: she could sense it as she approached, a deadness in the air. She could touch it also, as hard and slick as glass.

Beneath the semblance, behind the barrier, was the Stone. This was to be its permanent abode, at the center of the ruined Garden, where the Guardians had also kept it hidden for all the centuries of their rule. Cariad's father had built the barrier to repel anything that might come against it; like the Speakers when the Stone lay inside its Room, only he knew the secret of entry. But Cariad was aware that Goldwine had been here, taking the barrier's measure. Someday, perhaps, its impregnability would be tested.

She did not know whether her father was behind the barrier also, though she thought perhaps he was. She had not seen him since Goldwine drew her away. She did not expect to, ever again. They had been meant to meet only once, in the realm of prophecy, in the moments that divided the old world from the new. Until now he had touched her life as a promise; from now on he would touch it as a memory, but never again as a presence, as a living man.

She set her hand upon the barrier. It was smooth beneath her palm, as cold as ice. She thought of him, lone watcher among the ruins, true guardian of the Stone. How long would his vigil endure? Very long, perhaps, for his Gift was vast enough to preserve his body for centuries. Would he think of her, across the years, the decades of his life? She thought he would. Those years, after all, were her gift to him.

She turned away. She felt wind on her skin, sharp and frigid. She saw the rubble that had been the Suborder Wings—a tumble of shapes and textures, blurred now by the snow. She smelled the lingering odor of smoke and the faint taint of decay; she heard, distantly, the sound of shouting. These sensations seemed extraordinarily vivid, immediate, important, as did her awareness of herself, sensing them. For years she had walked armored through her life, cocooned in the promise of her own invulnerability. But like the Guardians' bindings, that promise was now gone. There was no longer anything to divide her from the world, from its delights or from its dangers.

She was mortal now.

AVON
EOS

AVON EOS PRESENTS
MASTERS OF FANTASY AND ADVENTURE

A SECRET HISTORY
The Book of Ash #1
by Mary Gentle   78869-1/$6.99 US

THE GILDED CHAIN:
A Tale of the King's Blades
by Dave Duncan   79126-9/$6.99 US/$8.99 CAN

THE DAUGHTERS OF BAST: THE HIDDEN LAND
by Sarah Isidore   80318-6/$6.50 US/$8.50 CAN

SCENT OF MAGIC
by Andre Norton   78416-5/$6.50 US/$8.50 CAN

THE DEATH OF THE NECROMANCER
by Martha Wells   78814-4/$6.99 US/$8.99 CAN